nocturnes

JOHN CONNOLLY

HODDER

First published in Great Britain in 2004 by Hodder and Stoughton
A division of Hodder Headline

This paperback edition published in 2007

A Hodder paperback

8

All characters in this publication are fictitious and any resemblance
to real persons, living or dead, is purely coincidental.

A CIP catalogue record for this title is
available from the British Library

ISBN 978 0 340 93399 2

Typeset in Monotype Sabon by Hewer Text UK Ltd, Edinburgh
Printed and bound by Clays Ltd, St Ives plc

Hodder Headline's policy is to use papers that are natural, renewable
and recyclable products and made from wood grown in sustainable forests.
The logging and manufacturing processes are expected to conform to the
environmental regulations of the country of origin.

Hodder and Stoughton Ltd
A division of Hodder Headline
338 Euston Road
London NW1 3BH

Contents

For Adèle, who will always be missed

The Cancer Cowboy Rides

I

The rutted track was playing hell with Jerry Schneider's shocks. He could feel every cleft and furrow ramming hard into the base of his spine and shooting up to the top of his skull, so that by the time the farmhouse came into view he already had the beginnings of a raging headache. Migraines were his affliction, and he hoped this wasn't about to be the start of one of them. He had work to do, and those damn things left him near puking on his bed, just wishing to die.

Jerry didn't much care for the detour to the Benson farm at the best of times. They were religious nutcases, the whole bunch of 'em: a family of seven, living pretty much apart from the rest of the world, keeping themselves mostly to themselves except when they headed into town to buy supplies, or when Jerry made his twice-weekly call to pick up a load of free range eggs and a selection of their home-made cheeses. Jerry thought the cheeses stank to high heaven, and he only ever ate his eggs scrambled and with enough salt to empty the Dead Sea, but the new wealthy who flocked to the state during both summer and winter swore by the taste of the Bensons' cheese and eggs, and were prepared to pay top dollar for them at Vern Smolley's place. Vern was a smart one, Jerry would give him that: he'd spotted the gap in the market straight off, and transformed the rear of his general store into a kind of gourmet's paradise. Jerry sometimes had trouble even finding a space in which to park, Vern's lot being filled to the brim with

Lexuses, salesroom-polished Mercedes convertibles and, in winter, the kind of snazzy 4WDs that only rich people drove, with a smattering of designer mud on them for that authentic country look.

The Bensons would have no truck with folks like that. Their old Ford was held together with string and faith, and their clothes were thrift store when they weren't hand made by Ma Benson or one of the girls. In fact, Jerry sometimes wondered how they squared selling their produce to the kind of people they regarded as being on a one-way express ride to hell. He wasn't about to ask Bruce Benson himself, though. Jerry tried to avoid having much conversation of any kind with Bruce, seeing as how the old man used any kind of opening as an opportunity to peddle his own particular brand of God-hugging. For some reason, Bruce seemed to believe that Jerry Schneider could still be saved. Jerry didn't share Bruce's faith. He liked drinking, smoking and screwing around, and last he heard those pursuits didn't much enter into the Bensons' scheme for salvation. So twice weekly Jerry would drive his truck up that migraine minefield of a track, pick up the eggs and cheese with the minimum of fuss or talk, then head back down the track at a slightly slower pace, since Vern would take breakages of more than ten per cent out of Jerry's fee.

Jerry Schneider never felt as if he had quite settled back into life in Colorado, not since he'd come back from the east coast to look after his mother. That was the curse of being an only child: there was no one to share the burden, nobody to take some of the strain. The old woman was becoming forgetful, and she had taken some bad falls, so Jerry did what he had to do and returned to his childhood home. Now it seemed like every week some new misfortune befell her: twisted ankles, bruised ribs, torn muscles. Those kinds of injuries would take some of the steam out of Jerry, and he was near thirty years younger than his momma. Inflict them on a woman of seventy-five, with osteoporosis in her legs and arthritis in her elbows, and it was a miracle that she was still standing.

Truth to tell, things had slackened back east since 9/11, and Jerry was working short time before he made the decision to move home. If he hadn't moved, then pretty soon he would have been working a second job in a bar to make ends meet, and he was just too beat to consider putting in seventy-hour weeks simply to live. Anyway, he had no real attachments in the city. There was a girl, but they were coasting. He didn't figure she'd be too cut up when he told her he was leaving, and he was right. In fact, she looked kind of relieved.

But returning here had reminded him of a lot of the reasons why he'd left to begin with. Ascension was a small town, dependent for its prosperity on outsiders, and it resented that dependence even while it concealed its true feelings with smiles and handshakes. And it wasn't like Boulder, which Jerry liked because it was a little enclave of liberalism. Most of the time, folks in Boulder seemed just one step away from raising their own flag and declaring independence. People in Ascension, by contrast, were proud to live in a state with enough radioactive material under the ground to make it glow in the night. Jerry figured that, like the Great Wall of China, parts of Colorado could be seen from outer space, the Rockies gently luminescing in the darkness. He suspected that folks in Ascension would be proud to think that their state acted as a kind of radioactive beacon for God or aliens or L. Ron Hubbard. It was worse further south in places like Colorado Springs, down by the USAF academy, but Ascension still remained a bastion of blind patriotism.

Jerry wondered too if people grew stranger as they got

closer to Utah, like the Mormons were putting something into the water or the air. That might explain the Bensons, and the other religious types like them that seemed to have gravitated toward the area. Maybe they just got lost on the way to Salt Lake City, or ran out of gas, or it could be they thought they were already in Utah, and that the state was just joshing with them by making them pay taxes to Colorado.

Jerry couldn't figure the Bensons out, but he wished they'd devote a little of that time spent praying to fixing up the road to their farm. The track seemed tougher to negotiate this week, a consequence of the cold weather which had already begun to settle on the state. Pretty soon the first snows would come, and then Bruce Benson would have to plow the route to his house himself if he were planning to continue making money out of cheese and eggs. Vern's other suppliers all made their own deliveries, but not Bruce Benson. He seemed to equate his hatred of sin with a hatred of the town of Ascension, and preferred to keep his contact with the population at large to the absolute minimum. His wife was the same way: Jerry Schneider couldn't recall ever meeting a more hatchet-faced bitch, and he'd been around some. Still, Bruce must have plucked up the courage to fill her purse at least four times (although Jerry would lay even money he'd kept the lights off and the windows blacked out while he did it) because they had four kids, three girls and a boy. Then again, the kids were all good looking, maybe with a little of Bruce to them but not so much that it would bother anyone, so maybe Bruce had seeded up someone better looking than his wife. The old hag probably sent him off with her blessing, grateful not to have to do something she might enjoy.

The boy, Zeke, was the youngest. He had three sisters, the eldest of whom, Ronnie, was beautiful enough to make

Jerry listen to Benson's ravings for a time if she happened to be out in the yard doing chores. Sometimes, the sun would catch her just right and Jerry would see the shape of her through her long skirt, her legs slightly apart like a pitched tent inviting him inside, and the rays gilding the muscles on her calves and thighs. Jerry suspected that Bruce knew what he was doing, but chose to ignore it in the hope that Jerry might see the light. Jerry was hoping to see something else entirely, and wondered if Ronnie might be prepared to show it if he got her alone and away from her daddy's influence for a time. She occasionally smiled at him in a way that suggested she was suffering the frustrations that a good-looking young woman like her would surely feel, cut off as she was from any outlet for her appetites. The children were educated at home by their parents, and Jerry figured that the sexual component of that education could pretty much be summed up as 'Don't do it, and especially not with Jerry Schneider.' Educated at home, their ailments kind of treated at home – Jerry just hoped that nothing serious ever happened to any of the family, because the Bensons didn't hold with doctors or medical intervention – and their lives revolving only around one another and a miserable, distant God; it would be some time before the networks got around to basing a comedy on the Benson family.

One of Bruce Benson's brothers also lived with them. His name was Royston, and Jerry figured him for mildly retarded. He didn't say much, and his head was always nodding like one of those little dogs that some people kept on the dashboard of their car, but he seemed fairly harmless. There was talk around town that he'd once tried to feel up Vern's mother in the store a couple of years back, although Jerry had never worked up the courage to ask Vern – or his mother – if this was true. Maybe that was another reason why Bruce Benson never came down to the store. Nothing sours relations between folk like the dimwit brother of one party coming over all Italian on the upright Baptist mother of the second party.

Jerry passed through the main gates to the Benson farm, instinctively turning down the volume on the truck radio, since Bruce didn't appreciate music much, and certainly not the stuff that was pouring out of Jerry's speakers just now: Gloria Scott's sultry vocals, backed up by the late, great Barry White's production skills. Jerry liked the old Walrus's touch. He might not have been quite as out there as Isaac, and he could legitimately be blamed for setting the tone for the limp, insipid stuff that passed for modern R&B, but there was something about those massed strings that made Jerry want to find some willing young thing and mess up the sheets with baby oil and cheap champagne. He wondered if Ronnie Benson had ever heard of Barry White. As far as Jerry knew, the Bensons didn't even listen to the crazy preachers at the end of the dial, the ones who testified to the love of God yet seemed to hate just about everyone, or at least the kind of people that Jerry knew and liked. Introducing the Benson kids to Barry White would probably kill the old man stone dead, and drive the daughters into some kind of frenzy.

Discreetly, Jerry turned the volume back up a notch.

The Bensons always moved their chickens into a big barn as soon as winter came. In fact, Bruce had told Jerry last week that they'd be inside next time he came, but as he approached the chicken runs on the right, Jerry could see small bundles of white scattered upon the ground. They lay still. The wind ruffled their feathers some, so that they seemed to be trembling on the ground, but it was only a false impression of life.

The sight made Jerry stop short. Leaving the engine

idling, he stepped from the truck and walked to the wire. Close by lay the body of one of the Bensons' chickens. Jerry leaned in to touch it, pressing gently into its flesh with the tips of his fingers. Black fluid instantly oozed from its beak and its eyes, and Jerry withdrew his fingers hurriedly, rubbing them on the seam of his pants in an effort to cleanse them of any potential contagion.

All of the chickens were dead, but no animal had done this. There was no blood upon the feathers, and no damage that Jerry could see. In the far corner of the run, Jerry spotted the Bensons' rooster strutting among his dead concubines, his red coxcomb clearly visible as he pecked at the ground, hunting for the last grains to stave off his hunger. Somehow, he had survived the slaughter.

Jerry leaned in and turned off the engine of the truck. Everything here was wrong. There was desolation on the wind. He walked across the yard. The door to the Benson house was wide open, held that way by a triangle of wood at its base. He stood at the base of the steps leading up to the porch, and called out Bruce Benson's name.

'Hello?' he said. 'Anybody home?'

There was no reply. The door led directly into the Bensons' kitchen. There was food on the table, but even from outside Jerry could tell it was rotting.

I should just call the cops. I should call them now, then wait for them to come.

But Jerry knew that he couldn't do that. Instead, he went back to his truck, tipped open the glove compartment, and took the cloth-wrapped Ruger from under the accumulation of maps, restaurant menus, and unpaid parking fines. The gun wouldn't change anything, not now, but he felt better for having it in his hand.

The kitchen smelled bad. The dinner of chicken and biscuits looked as if it had been there for a couple of days.

Jerry recalled the dead fowl in the run, and the black substance that had oozed from the mouth of the bird he'd touched. Christ, if the chickens had somehow become contaminated, and that contamination had spread to the family . . . His thoughts went to the eggs that he had been collecting and delivering to town for the past six months, and to the chicken that Benson had given to him as a Thanksgiving present less than a week before. Jerry almost threw up there and then, but he regained his composure. In all his life, he'd never heard of anyone dying from a poultry disease, except maybe that flu they had over in Asia, and what killed the Bensons' chickens didn't look like any flu Jerry had ever seen.

He checked the living room – no TV, just a couple of easy chairs, an overstuffed couch, and some religious pictures on the walls – and the downstairs bathroom. They were both empty. Standing at the bottom of the stairs, Jerry gave one more holler before making his way up to the bedrooms. The smell was stronger here. Jerry took his handkerchief from his pocket and jammed it against his nose and mouth. He already knew what to expect. He'd worked for a time in a slaughterhouse in Chicago when he was younger, one that wasn't too fussy about the quality of its meat. Jerry had never eaten a hamburger since.

Bruce Benson and his wife were in the first bedroom, lying beneath a big, white quilt. He was wearing his pajamas, and his wife was dressed in a blue cotton nightgown. There was black fluid on their clothing and on the bed, and more of it caked around the lower half of their faces. Bruce Benson's eyes were half open, and his cheeks were streaked with black tears. From their expressions, Jerry figured they'd gone out hard. Even in death the pain remained fixed upon them, as though they were models carefully sculpted by a disturbed artist.

The three daughters were in the next bedroom. Although there were bunks in one corner, the girls had congregated on the big bed in the center of the room. Jerry guessed that this was Ronnie's bed. She held her younger sisters cradled in her arms, one on each side. There was more black blood here, and Ronnie was no longer beautiful.

Jerry looked away.

The youngest child, Zeke, was in a little box room at the far end of the hallway. He had been covered up with a sheet. First to go, Jerry thought, when someone still had enough strength to shroud him after he died. But if there was strength to do that, why not call for help? The Bensons had a telephone, and even with their peculiar beliefs they must have realised that something was very wrong. Whole families didn't die this way, not in Colorado, not anywhere civilized. This was like the plague.

Jerry turned to leave the boy's room, and a hand touched his shoulder. He spun around, the gun raised, and let out a kind of tortured shriek. Later, he would describe it as a woman's scream, a sound such as he never thought he would make, but he wasn't ashamed. Like he told the cops, anyone would have done the same, if they'd seen what he'd seen.

Royston Benson stood before him: poor dumb Roy, who loved God because his brother told him that God was merciful, that God would look out for him if he prayed hard and lived a good life and didn't go around feeling up other people's mothers in grocery stores.

Except God hadn't looked out for Roy Benson, didn't matter how much he prayed or kept his hands to himself. His fingers were swollen and blackened, and his face was covered in dark tumors, red at the edges and dark at the center. One masked the entire left half of his face, closing the eye to a slit and disfiguring his lips so that they turned up at one side in the semblance of a grin. Jerry could make out what was left of his teeth, barely held in place by his rotting gums, and his distorted tongue flicking in the cavern of his mouth. Black fluid flowed like oil from his nostrils and his ears and the corners of his mouth, pooling on his chin before dripping onto the floor. He said something, but Jerry couldn't understand what it was. All he knew was that Roy Benson was rotting away before him, and crying because he couldn't understand why this was happening to him. He reached out for Jerry, but Jerry backed away. He didn't want Roy touching him again, no matter what.

'Take it easy, Roy,' he said. 'Be cool. I'm going to call for help. It's going to be okay.'

But Roy shook his head, the movement causing snot and tears and black blood to spray Jerry's face and shirt. Again, he tried to form words, but they wouldn't come, and then he was jerking and spasming, like something was trying to burst out from inside of him. He fell to the floor, his head banging against the boards with enough force to dislodge his dead nephew's toys from their shelves. His hands scraped at the wood, wrenching the nails from the tips of his fingers. Then, as Jerry watched, the tumors on his face began to spread, colonising the last fragments of untainted skin, rushing to meet one another before their host died.

And as the last trace of white disappeared from his face, Roy Benson stopped struggling and lay still.

Jerry staggered away from the dead man. He stumbled to the door, found the bathroom, and vomited into the sink. He continued retching until only spittle and bad air came up, then looked at himself in the mirror, half expecting to see that terrible blackness erasing his own features, just as it had consumed Roy Benson.

But that was not what he saw. Instead, he turned and looked at the cigarette in the ashtray by the toilet. The ashtray was filled with butts, but this one was still smoking, the last tendril of nicotine dissipating as Jerry watched.

Nobody in this house smoked. Nobody smoked, or drank, or swore. Nobody did anything except work and pray and, over the last few days, rot away like old meat.

And he knew then why the Bensons had not called for help.

Someone was here, he realized.

Someone was here to watch them die.

II

Ten days later, and two thousand miles to the east, Lloyd Hopkins said the words that nobody wanted to say.

'We're going to have to replace that plow.'

Hopkins was wearing his new uniform trousers, which seemed to him to be fitting a little more snugly than they should have. He was wearing new pants because one change of clothes was in the wash, while the second had been ripped to shreds during a recent search for a pair of hikers. The hikers were reported missing by Jed Wheaton, the owner of Easton's sole motel, after they failed to return from a scoot around Broad Mountain two days earlier. As it turned out, the couple – from New York, wouldn't you know it – were apparently overcome by lust for each other while on the trail, and had checked into a lodge under assumed names, because they thought it would spice up the occasion. They didn't bother to tell Jed Wheaton, and so when they didn't come back to their room that night he called the station house, and Chief Lopez rounded up the rescue team, which included Lloyd Hopkins, his only full-time patrol officer, to begin searching first thing next morning. They were still out on the mountain when the couple, their appetites under control again, turned up at the motel to settle their bill and collect the rest of their stuff. Under instructions from the chief, Jed had refused to let them leave until Lopez got back to town and gave them the kind of dressing-down that stopped just short of beating them to a pulp and hanging them from the town's 'Welcome' sign as an example to others.

Now, Hopkins, Lopez, and Errol Crisp, Easton's new mayor, were all standing in the garage of the municipal building, looking at the town's sole, ancient snowplow.

'Maybe we could get someone to patch it up,' said Errol. 'That worked before.'

Lopez snorted. 'Yesterday, it bled oil like someone had just stabbed it with a spear. Today we can't even get it started. If it was a horse, you'd shoot it.'

Errol gave one of his long sighs, the ones he used whenever the idea of spending money was raised. He was the first black mayor Easton had ever elected, and he was trying to step lightly in his first month on the job. The last thing he wanted was people complaining that he was spending money like a freed slave. At sixty, Errol was the oldest of the three men in the garage. Lopez, who didn't look even the one-sixteenth Spanish that he claimed to be, was twelve years younger again. Lloyd Hopkins, meanwhile, looked like a teenager. A chubby teenager, maybe, but a teenager none the less. Errol wasn't even sure if the kid was legally allowed to drink.

'The council's not going to like it,' said Errol.

'The council's going to like it a whole lot less when its members can't see the town for snow,' said Lopez. 'The council's not going to like it when businesses start complaining that nobody can park on the street, or that folks are falling off the curb and breaking their legs because they can't tell where the sidewalk ends and the road begins. For crying out loud, Errol, this thing doesn't owe us anything. It's older than Lloyd here.'

Lloyd shifted his thighs, trying to work some space between the fabric of his pants and his skin. When that didn't work, he tried to discreetly extract the material from the crevices into which it had lodged itself.

'The hell is wrong with you, son?' asked Errol. He took a couple of steps back from the young policeman, just in case whatever was ailing him could jump.

'Sorry,' said Lloyd. 'These trousers don't fit right.'

'Why are you wearing them, they don't fit right?'

Lopez answered.

'He's wearing them because he was too vain to admit that he'd put on a little weight since the last time he had to buy new pants. Thirty-four inches, my ass. I told you when you were ordering them that you ought to get measured up. Errol here will see thirty-four again before your waist does.'

Lloyd reddened, but didn't reply.

'Don't worry,' said Lopez. 'We'll get you another pair. Put it down to experience.'

'You better put it down to "miscellaneous expenses,"' said Errol. 'I don't want people asking how come we buying pants like they's a shortage on the way. Shit, son, I got a two-year-old grandson don't need two pairs of pants in a month, and he's growing like grass in summertime. Two years old, even *he* knows when a pair of pants ain't going to fit him.'

Lopez grinned and let the mayor ride on Lloyd for a while. He knew what was going on, even if Lloyd didn't. Errol would get himself worked up in a lather over a forty-dollar pair of blues so he could feel better about spending one hundred times that amount on a new plow. Once he'd finished, Lopez would walk with him back to his office and they'd work out the details of the purchase. There would be a new plow in the garage in a week. Lloyd might even have trousers that fitted him by then. Still, the young patrolman could be forgiven his little idiosyncrasies. He was honest, diligent, smarter than he looked, except when it came to his weight, and he didn't claim overtime. Lopez would have a talk with him about his diet. Lloyd tended to listen to his superior on most things. Who knew, maybe those trousers could end up fitting him after all. It might take a while, but Lopez viewed Lloyd as a work in progress in any number of ways.

Easton was a typical New Hampshire town: not quite pretty, but not ugly either; a little too far away from the big winter playgrounds to enjoy much of a tourist trade from them, but close enough for the locals to hop in a car and spend a day on the slopes, if they chose. It had a couple of bars, a main street on which more than half of the businesses made a reasonable income year round, and one motel which was as much a hobby as a business for its owner. Its school had an adequate football team, and a basketball team that most people preferred not to mention. It also had a sense of civic pride out of all proportion to its apparently modest aspect; a conscientious, if frugal, town council; a police department which consisted of just two full-time cops and a handful of part-timers; and a crime rate just slightly below the average for a town of its size. All told, the chief sometimes reflected, there were better places to live, but there were also far, far worse.

Frank Lopez, the chief's father, worked as an accountant in Easton from 1955 until 1994, when he retired and moved to Santa Barbara with his wife. His son Jim had by that time been a policeman in Manchester for almost twenty years. In 2001, the chief's job in Easton became vacant and Jim Lopez applied for it, and got it. He had his quarter century under his belt, and while he didn't want to leave law enforcement he fancied a quieter life for himself. His marriage had broken up ten years previously, childless but also without bitterness, and Easton, his home town, offered him familiarity, comfort, and a place in which to settle comfortably into middle age. The job didn't tax him unduly, he was liked and respected, and he had met a woman whom he suspected he loved.

All told, Jim Lopez was happier than he had ever been.

The Easton Motel was quiet that week. After the fuss about the hikers, Jed Wheaton was kind of grateful not to have too many guests to worry about. Things would pick up again once the snows came, when Easton usually enjoyed a small trickle-down from the winter tourist trade. It would still be a bad year, but something might be salvaged from it.

Of the twelve rooms, only a couple were currently occupied. There were two young Japanese tourists in one, who giggled a lot and took too many photographs but kept their room so tidy that Maria, the maid, said she felt like she was making more of a mess than they were. They folded their towels, didn't leave hairs in the shower or the sink, and even made their own beds.

'Wouldn't it be great if everybody who stayed here was like them?' Maria asked Jed that morning, after she came back from checking the rooms.

'Yeah, wonderful,' he replied. 'I could fire you and spend the money I saved on making my old age more comfortable.'

'Tcah!' Maria dismissed him with a flick of her wrist. 'You'd miss me if I wasn't here. You like having a pretty young girl around.'

Maria was Puerto Rican, big and ribald, and happily married to the town's best mechanic. She might have been a pretty girl once, but now she looked like she'd just eaten one. Maria worked hard, was never late or bad-tempered, took care of the desk and the reservations, and generally had more to do with keeping the motel running from day to day than Jed did. In turn, he paid her well and didn't complain when she used her knowledge of the inner workings of the vending machines to feed herself the occasional free candy bar.

As if to test her skills, and Jed's tolerance, Maria walked over to the big red candy machine in the corner of the office, put her ear to its side, listening to it like a safecracker would to a safe, then gave it a sharp slap with the palm of her hand.

A Snickers bar fell from its perch into the tray.

'How do you do that?' asked Jed, not for the first time. 'I try, but I just end up hurting my hand.'

Then, as if realizing that he was effectively condoning theft against himself, he continued: 'And if you're going to do that, at least don't do it in front of me. It's like robbing a bank and asking for a receipt.'

Maria sat down and unwrapped the candy bar.

'You want some?'

'No. Thank you. Why am I even saying "thank you"? I paid for the damn thing.'

'What'd it cost you, a whole seventy-five cents?'

'It's the principle.'

'Yah, yah, yah: the principle. Some principle, costs seventy-five cents. Even with what you pay me, I could buy me a lot of principles.'

'Yeah, well maybe you should consider investing in some, like not stealing, for one.'

'It's not stealing, you see me doing it and you don't say nothing. That's *giving*, not stealing.'

Jed left her to it. He reviewed the guest register. They had nobody else checking in that day, then two confirmeds for Thursday and five for Friday. Combined with those who might follow the signs from the highway when they tired of driving, it didn't look so bad for the rest of the week.

'Guy in twelve,' Maria said.

'What about him?'

Maria stood, walked to the door to check that there was nobody around, then leaned in toward Jed.

'I don't like him.'

The guest in room twelve had arrived in darkness two nights before. Jed's son Phil, who was home for a couple of days from college and didn't mind earning a few extra bucks on the desk, had checked him in.

'Why? He won't let you steal his candy?'

Maria didn't reply immediately. Usually, she was quick to make her feelings known. Jed put his pen down and looked serious.

'He do something to you?' he asked.

Maria shook her head.

'So what is it?'

'He's got a bad feeling about him,' she said. 'I tell you, I went to clean his room. The drapes were closed, but there was no sign on the door. I knocked, heard nothing, so I opened the door.'

'And?'

'He was just . . . *sitting* there, on the bed. It didn't look slept in. He was just there, his hands on his knees, facing the door like he'd been waiting for me to come in. I said I was sorry and he said, no, it was all right, I could come in. I said, no, I'll come back, but he insisted. He said he didn't sleep so good at night, and that he might try to have a nap later in the morning, so he'd prefer if I cleaned the room now. But it didn't look like there was nothing to clean, so I said to him, what do you want me to do? He told me he'd used some towels in the bathroom, that was all.

'So I got some clean towels and went to the bathroom. He was still sitting on the bed, but I could see him watching me. He was smiling, and I felt like there was something wrong.'

For the first time, Jed noticed that Maria had not eaten the candy bar. It remained untouched in her hand. She saw him looking at it, then carefully wrapped it and put it on the counter.

'I don't want it now,' she said.

Jed thought that she was about to cry.

'That's okay,' he said. 'I'll put it in the refrigerator. You can eat it whenever you want.'

He picked it up and placed it carefully on a shelf in the little unit behind the counter.

'Go on,' he said. 'You were telling me about twelve.'

She nodded.

'I went into the bathroom, and all of the towels were on the floor. When I picked them up, I think there was blood on them.'

'Blood?'

'I think so, yes, but it was black, like oil.'

'Maybe it was oil.'

Jed wasn't sure which was worse: blood, or some jackass using his towels to mop up an oil leak from his car.

'Maybe. I don't know. I got them in a bag in the laundry. I can show you.'

'Well, we'll see. So that's it: dirty towels?'

Maria raised her hand. She was not finished yet.

'I put on my gloves and picked up the towels. I was going to take them outside when I looked at the toilet. The seat was up. I always check anyway, just in case, you know, it needs to be cleaned. There was more black in there, like he'd puked it up from inside him, or worse. It was all over the bowl.

'I turned around, and he was standing beside me. I think I cried out, because he frightened me. I almost fell, but he reached out so that I didn't slip. He told me he was sorry, that he should have warned me about the bathroom.

' "I been ill," he said. "Real sick."

'His breath smelled bad. "You need a doctor?" I said.

'"No, no doctor. No cure for what ails me, ma'am, but I feel like I'm on the mend. I just needed to get some stuff out of my system."

'Then he let me go. I picked up the towels, replaced them with clean ones, and flushed the bowl. I was going to scrub it, but he told me I didn't have to do that. When I left, he was just sitting on the bed, like he was when I arrived. I asked him did he want me to pull the drapes and he said, no, he was sensitive to the light. I closed the door and left him there.'

Jed thought for a time.

'So, he's been sick,' he said at last. 'Nothing to stop a sick man renting a room, I guess, though I figure we'd better be careful with those towels. You said you wore your gloves, right?'

'I always wear my gloves. The HIV, the AIDS, I'm always real careful.'

'Good,' said Jed. 'That's good.'

He nodded to himself.

'I'll go down and check on him myself, once I'm done here, maybe convince him to let Doc Bradley take a look at him. Doesn't sound to me like he's on the mend, he leaves black blood in the bowl. Doesn't sound like he's getting better at all, if he's doing that.'

He told Maria to head home early, spend some time with her grandchild. He would roust Phil if there was anything that needed to be done. Sure, Phil might whine some, but he was a good kid. Jed would miss him when he headed back to school at the end of the week. He wouldn't be seeing him again until after Christmas, since Phil was spending the holidays with his mom over in Seattle. Jed consoled himself with the thought that the boy would be back before New Year's and, if the choice were his own, he would probably have preferred Easton to Seattle anyway. Most of his buddies would be back for the holiday season in the hopes of getting a little skiing in, and Phil was as good as any of them on the slopes.

In the meantime, he'd talk to the guy in twelve and try to figure out if there was anything that needed to be done. He might even send him on his way, since there would be nothing worse for business than a stranger dying in one of his rooms. Maria thanked him before she left. He could see that she was badly shaken, although he wasn't certain why. Sure, finding bloodied towels and a bloodied bowl in a room occupied by a sick man wasn't nice for anyone, but they'd had to mop up a lot worse in the past. Hell, there was a bachelor party that stopped off a couple of years back and left Jed thinking it might be easier just to burn down the motel and rebuild it instead of cleaning it.

Jed drew the register toward him and ran his finger down the page until he came to the name of the man in twelve.

'Carson,' he read aloud. 'Buddy Carson. Well, Buddy, looks like you may be checking out sooner than you think.'

In more ways than one, he thought.

Although the man who gave his name as Buddy Carson had arrived at the motel only two nights before, he had been drifting around Easton and its environs for more than a week, ever since he left Colorado. Two thousand miles, and he'd covered it in less than two days. Buddy didn't need to sleep more than an hour or two at most, and didn't eat much other than candy bars and sweet things. Sometimes, he wondered about his eating habits, but it didn't occupy him for long. Buddy had more important things to worry about, like easing his pain and feeding the appetite of the thing that dwelt within him.

On Monday, shortly after crossing the Vermont/ New

Hampshire state line, he came across Link Frazier changing the wheel on his truck, and knew it was time to begin again.

Link was seventy, moved like he was fifty, and came on to young women like he was seventeen, but changing a tyre was still a damn chore. Link used to own Reed's bar in Easton, but back then it was called The Missing Link, on account of the fact that his wife used to joke that whenever there was hard work to be done, Lincoln Frazier was always unaccountably absent. When Myra died ten years ago, some of the spark had gone out of Link and he sold the bar to Eddy Reed, on condition that Eddy changed the name of the bar to something else. The joke seemed less funny, now that Myra was gone.

Link's knees weren't what they were, so he was kind of pleased when the red Dodge Charger pulled up in front of him and the driver climbed out. He was younger than Link, decades younger, and wore faded blue jeans and an antique black leather vest over his equally faded denim shirt. From beneath the frayed ends of his jeans peeked the pointed toes of a pair of snakeskin cowboy boots. His hair was black and long, slicked back against his head, with the parallel tracks of a wide-tooth comb visible among the strands. The hair was thin, though, and the white of his skull gleamed between the rows like rainwater shining on a rutted mud track.

The driver reached into his car and removed a battered straw cowboy hat from the passenger seat, then placed it carefully on his head. An oval of white material was stuck to the front of the hat. It looked as if it had been torn from a pair of coveralls, the kind worn by auto shop mechanics, and written on it was the word 'Buddy' in red cursive script.

As the Dodge's owner drew closer, Link got his first good look at the man's face, slightly shadowed though it was by his hat. His cheeks were very gaunt, so that Link could see the tendons move as his jaws worked, chewing at something in the corner of his mouth. His lips were deep red, almost black, and his eyeballs bulged slightly in their sockets, as though he were slowly being choked by a pair of unseen hands. He was almost ugly, yet he carried himself with a kind of grace. There was a purposefulness about him, despite the laid-back air his clothing and manner seemed calculated to communicate.

'You having some trouble?' he asked.

His voice had a distinct southern twang to it, although Link had the feeling he was exaggerating it a little, the way some men will do when they believe that a certain quality adds to their charm.

'Took a nail back a ways,' said Link.

'Flatter than a pancake, that's for sure,' said the man.

He knelt down beside Link.

'Let me do that,' he said. 'No offense. I know you can do it yourself. I know you could probably lift the whole damn truck without a jack, but just because you *can* do a thing doesn't mean you should have to do it.'

Link decided to accept the compliment, excessive though it was, and the help that came with it. He rose, and watched as the man in the cowboy hat swiftly loosened the wheel nuts and hoisted the tire off. He was stronger than he looked, thought Link. The older man had been planning to beat on the tire iron with the heel of his boot to loosen the nuts, but this guy just flipped them free with barely a stretch of his back. Pretty soon the tire was changed with the minimum of fuss or conversation, which suited Link just fine. Link wasn't much for polite conversation, least of all with strangers, didn't matter how many tires they changed. When he owned The Missing Link, it was Myra who did the charming, and Link who dealt with the beer and liquor people.

The cowboy stood, took a bright blue rag from his pocket, and wiped his hands clean.

'I appreciate your help,' said Link.

He stretched out his hand in thanks. 'The name's Link Frazier.'

The cowboy looked at Link's outstretched palm the way a child molester might respond to an unexpected flash of young thigh in a playground. He finished cleaning his hands, put the rag back in his pocket, then shook Link's hand in return. Link felt an unpleasant sensation, as if there were bugs crawling on his skin. He tried to hide it, but he felt sure that the cowboy had seen the change in his expression.

'Buddy Carson,' said the cowboy.

He had noticed Link's response. Buddy was finely attuned to the rhythms of other people's bodies. It made him good at what he did.

'It was my pleasure,' said Buddy, as the cells in Link's body started to metastasize, and his liver began to rot.

He tipped the fingers of his right hand to his hat, gave Link a little salute, and headed back to his car.

Later that day, Buddy picked up a waitress in a bar over by Danbury. She was fortyish, and overweight. Nobody would have called her good looking, but Buddy worked her pretty well and by the end of a night's drinking he had convinced her that they were kindred spirits: two lonely but decent people who'd taken some knocks in life, but who had somehow managed to pull through. They went back to her place, a neat little two-bedroom duplex that smelled faintly of musty clothing, and Buddy rattled her bed and her bones. She told Buddy that it had been a long time, that it was just what she needed. She moaned beneath him, and he closed his eyes as he moved upon her.

It was easier when he could get inside people, when he could touch the interior of their mouths with his finger, maybe cut them slightly with a nail. Open wounds were good too, and even a kiss, if he could force the lips apart and get a bite in, but sex was best of all. With sex, it worked faster, so that he could stay and watch with little risk to himself.

The second time, the tone of her sounds changed. She asked him to stop. She said there was something wrong. Buddy didn't stop. Once it started, it couldn't be held back. That was the way of it. When he finished, she was already breathing more shallowly, and some of the flesh had receded from her face. Her fingers were like talons gripping the sheets, and her back arched with pain. She couldn't speak.

There was some blood now. That was good. It was red, but soon it would turn to black.

Buddy sat back on the sheets and lit himself a cigarette.

It was slowly getting worse.

There was a time when once a week would have been enough to ease the pain, but no longer. Now, once daily permitted him to rest for a time, but only for a couple of blessed hours. If he managed to corrupt more than one, the hours without agony increased exponentially, but the risk was that folk would notice, so multiple victims were rarely an option for him.

That morning's troubles were a sign that the thing inside him was becoming harder to control, and to sate. The black blood began to appear while he was making water. Pretty soon he was coughing it up, soaking the towels. He was only just recovering when the fat maid entered the room. He wondered if she would tell anyone about it, and felt certain that she would. He got a sense of her as he held her, his skin working against hers, the rottenness within him seeking purchase in the new host.

He would have to move on soon, but he was so weak.

There was another option, of course, but it represented an enormous gamble. He had been turning it over in his mind for some time, calculating the odds, assessing the risks. Now with his own pain increasing, and the presence of the black fluid in his urine, the prospect was growing more and more enticing. If one offered temporary ease, he reasoned, and two doubled the time he could sleep, what would happen if he took on more, many more? He thought about the family in Colorado: after them, the pain was gone for days, and even when it returned it was diminished considerably, so that he had taken the waitress more out of desire than out of necessity. What might happen if he corrupted a town, a city? Weeks, perhaps months of respite might ensue. Maybe he could even rid himself of it entirely. The possibility of an extended peace dangled invitingly within his grasp.

This was a small community. Under ordinary circumstances, it would be hard to reach out to enough people, but when he was taking a walk the day before he saw something that had caused him to reconsider his options. He spent the rest of the day thinking about it, weighing up the pros and cons and trying to work out how best it might be done.

That morning, with the black blood pooling in the bowl, he reached a decision. He would make a stand here, in Easton, then head north and find somewhere quiet to rest for the winter, maybe forever. His eyes were closing: touching the maid had clouded the pain enough to enable him to sleep. He put the chain on the motel room door, then stretched out on the bed and began to dream.

The cowboy's name was not Buddy Carson.

The cowboy didn't have a name, not now. There might

have been one a long time ago, but if there was then it had been lost to him for many years. His new life began on the day he awoke in the middle of the Nevada desert wearing ragged clothes, and with tumors on his skin. He had no memory of any existence before that. His insides felt as though they were being slowly roasted, and when he squeezed his hands to his stomach to try to ease the pain, black blood shot from beneath his nails.

At last, he found the strength to rise. He made his way to the highway and thumbed a ride from a garage mechanic who was hauling a red Dodge Charger over to a dealer in Reno. The mechanic had spent months restoring the Dodge in his spare time, and now figured that he was about to make a good profit by selling it on.

The cowboy felt the growing pain in his insides ease the moment his hand accidentally brushed the mechanic's hand. Most of the tumors were hidden beneath his clothes, but after he touched the mechanic he could see the one that peeped out from under the cuff of his shirt sleeve begin to fade. Within seconds, it was entirely gone.

The cowboy touched the driver again.

'Hey, the fuck are you doing, man?' said the mechanic. 'Keep your hands away from me, you fucking faggot.'

He started to pull over. There were no other cars visible on the highway.

'Get out,' he said. 'Get the fuck out of my—'

The cowboy grasped the mechanic's right arm, then clasped his left hand around the man's throat. He squeezed. A trickle of blood appeared in the mechanic's nostril, then dripped down over his lips and chin. The force of the flow began to increase, and the color of the blood began to darken until it turned a deep black. As the cowboy watched, the skin around the mechanic's eyes began to tighten. His skin grew waxy, and his cheekbones grew sharp in his face.

And for the first time, the cowboy had an image of something inside of himself, like a great black worm that had found purchase within him. It lay in his bowels, feeding off him, slowly turning his cells to black, simultaneously destroying all that was human about him while keeping him alive, pumping its unknown poisons into his system. If it had a consciousness, then it was beyond the cowboy's capacity to understand. All he knew was that it had chosen him as its host, and if he did not do what it wanted then it would destroy him.

The cowboy howled, and his fingers broke through the mechanic's neck and into his flesh. He felt a pressure building in his arm, and then his fingers straightened convulsively as the poison erupted through the pores of his skin. The sockets of the mechanic's eyes flooded with darkness. He stopped struggling, even as the cowboy's own pain faded, and then was gone.

The cowboy buried the mechanic's body in the desert. He kept his wallet, and when night fell he found the mechanic's apartment and spent the night there. As he rested up, he thought of the image of the worm in his body. He didn't know if it was really there, or was simply his mind's way of trying to explain to itself what was happening to him. He decided to talk to a doctor as soon as possible, although in his dreams that night the worm inside him spoke to him, its blind head splitting to reveal a barbed mouth, and it told him that no doctor could ever help him, and that his purpose in life was not to be cured, but to spread the Black Worm.

Despite his dream, he visited a doctor's surgery the next day. He told the old man who examined him of his pain, and of the dark blood that he had coughed up in the desert. The doctor listened to him, then opened a syringe and prepared to take a sample.

The agony as the needle entered was impossible for the cowboy to bear. As soon as it penetrated his skin, he felt the worm in his being convulse, as though the needle were entering through his stomach wall and puncturing his internal organs, scraping and tearing as it went. His screams brought the doctor's receptionist, and he took them both, just as he had taken the mechanic.

But the pain did not go away that night, and he felt that he was being punished for his temerity in trying to cure himself.

The mechanic lived alone, and received no calls that were not related to his business. The cowboy kept the Charger as a souvenir, as well as a pair of the mechanic's overalls. When they began to fall apart, he held onto the mechanic's name badge, which he attached to a straw hat he took from a drifter outside of Boise, Idaho. He already had the boots. They had been on his feet when he came to in the desert, and they felt as if he had been wearing them for years.

The mechanic's name was Buddy, so that was what the cowboy decided to call himself. As for Carson, well, that was his private joke. He had found the word in a medical book for folks suffering from cancer, and Buddy figured that it pretty much summed up what he was, or what he had become. He was Buddy Carcinogenic, Buddy Carson for short.

By the time folks might have come to understand the humor, they were already dying.

III

Lopez drove around the streets, letting folks see that he was on the job. Like most small towns, Easton was a peaceful place with little real crime beyond petty theft, the occasional bar fight, and the omnipresent shadow of domestic violence. Lopez dealt with all of it as best he could. In a way, he suited the town: there were probably better cops than him, he figured, but there couldn't have been too many who tried as hard.

After a couple of hours, during which he did nothing more than hand out a speeding ticket to a salesman doing sixty in a forty-mile zone, and warn off a couple of kids who were skateboarding in the bank's parking lot, he slipped into Steve DiVentura's diner for coffee and a sandwich. He was about to take a seat at the counter when he saw Doc Bradley alone in a deuce by the window, so he asked Steve to send his order over.

'Mind if I join you?' he asked.

Greg Bradley looked as if he'd been jolted out of a reverie, although Lopez didn't think it was one that he was particularly sorry to leave. Bradley was about Lopez's age, but pure whitebread: tanned, blond hair, good teeth, and money to his name. Lopez guessed that he could have earned a whole lot more for his services someplace other than Easton, but his family were from the county and he had a genuine attachment to the area and its people. Lopez could understand that. He shared Bradley's view.

He also suspected that Bradley was gay, although he had

never broached the subject with him. He could see why the doctor might want to keep that quiet. Most people in Easton were pretty tolerant – after all, they had a black mayor and a police chief with a Hispanic name in a town that was ninety-percent white – but patients were funny about their doctors, and there were some who would drive to Boston for a consultation before they would allow an openly gay man to touch them, and that went for women as well as men. So Greg Bradley remained single, and mostly the folks in Easton chose not to comment on the fact. It was the way things were done in small towns.

'Sure, take a seat.'

Bradley's tuna on rye had barely been touched, and his coffee looked cold.

'Glad I didn't order the tuna,' said Lopez.

'Tuna's fine,' said Bradley. 'It's me that's not so good.'

A waitress brought Lopez his coffee and told him his sandwich was on the way. He thanked her.

'Anything I can do to help?' asked Lopez.

'Not unless you can work miracles. I guess you'll find out soon enough, but you may as well hear it from me first. Link Frazier has cancer.'

Lopez leaned back in his seat. He genuinely didn't know what to say. Link seemed to have been a fixture around the town for as long as he could remember. Lopez had even dated one of his daughters, many years before. Link had been good about the whole thing, not even holding it against Lopez that he'd dumped her one week before senior prom.

Well, not holding it against him for more than a couple of years, anyway.

'How bad?'

'He's riddled with it, as bad as I've ever seen. He approached me a couple of days back, first time he ever came near me. He'd passed blood that morning, a lot of it. He may have hated the idea of seeing a doctor about anything, but he knew there was something seriously wrong. I sent him for tests that afternoon, and they called me later that night with the results. Hell, I don't think they even had to wait for the biopsies. The x-ray was enough. Looks like the liver's where it's worst, but it's spread to his spine and most of his other major organs. I spoke to his son this morning, and he gave me the all clear to start telling people close to his father.'

'Jesus. How long has he got?'

Bradley shook his head. 'Not long. The thing of it is, he swears he had no pain before a couple of days ago, and no symptoms until the blood appeared. It's almost impossible to believe.'

'Link's strong. He could lose an arm and he wouldn't notice until he tried to wind his watch.'

'Nobody is that strong. Believe me, he should have been in agony for months.'

Lopez's sandwich arrived, but, like Bradley, he no longer had much of an appetite.

'Where is he?'

'Manchester. I think they'll keep him there until . . . well, until the end.'

The two men sat in silence, watching the life of the town pass by the window. People waved, and they waved back, but their smiles were automatic and without warmth.

'You know, my father died of cancer,' said Bradley.

'I didn't know that.'

'He smoked a lot. Drank some, too. Ate red meat, fried food, didn't believe he was eating a real dessert unless his arteries began cracking halfway through. If cancer hadn't taken him, there were about a dozen other candidates lined up for the job.'

'I had a friend who died of cancer,' said Lopez. 'Andy Stone. He was a detective with the state police. He didn't drink, didn't smoke, and ran fifty or sixty miles every week. They diagnosed him, and he was dead within a year.'

'What was it?'

'Pancreatic cancer.'

Bradley winced. 'Bad. It's all bad, but some are worse than others.'

'I hear a lot of stories like that. Some of them are people that I knew, or friends of friends, people contracting that shit without any apparent cause, people who ate like they were supposed to, didn't work in risky jobs, didn't even seem to have much stress in life. Next thing, they're just shadows. I don't think I can go that way. I don't know how good I am with pain, to tell the truth. I've never been shot, never broken a limb, never even been in hospital since I had my tonsils taken out as a boy. I saw the way Andy went, and I don't think I could take that kind of suffering.'

'Folks are strong,' said Bradley. 'Like Link, I suppose. Our instinct is to fight, and to survive. It never ceases to amaze me, the reserves of strength that lie inside the most ordinary men and women. Even in the worst of suffering, there's cause for hope, or admiration, anyway.'

Lopez pushed his sandwich away. 'This is a conversation I didn't need to have,' he said.

'Let's hope it's the last time. You should feel sorry for Stevie over there. He's going to think his food sucks.'

Lopez glanced over his shoulder to where Steve DiVentura stood at the register, a pencil behind his ear as he totaled his customers' checks.

'Maybe he'll give us a discount if we complain.'

'Steve? If we complain he'll charge us extra for his time.'

The subject of food brought Lopez's mind back to Link Frazier, and the bar that he had once owned and that he still used to frequent, driving the new owner crazy by commenting on what he described as the 'fancy' food that it now served.

'You talk to Eddy Reed yet?' he asked.

'No, you're pretty much the first person I've told.'

'I'll tell Eddy. If I see anyone I think should know, I'll spare you the trouble of telling them too. I can give you a call later, maybe let you know how things have gone.'

Bradley looked grateful. 'I guess it's a job we share sometimes, giving people bad news about their friends and relatives.'

'I guess. The difference is, I usually don't have to tell people that they're dying.'

Bradley smiled blackly. 'Yeah, I suppose most of yours already knew they were dead.'

'Is that what they call "laughing in the face of death?" '

'Whistling by the churchyard.'

'Whatever works.'

It was Bradley who stood first. 'I'd better be getting back. It's hard enough to get people to come to see a doctor in the first place. If I keep them waiting, they just go home and treat themselves with aspirin.'

Lopez wished him luck. It was terrible about Link Frazier, just terrible. Lopez sipped at his coffee. He'd read somewhere that too much coffee was carcinogenic. It seemed like so many things these days were. He wondered what had caused Link Frazier's, or if the connection was even that simple. Maybe Link Frazier had done nothing at all, except live his life as best he could. He supposed that there was only so much you could do to protect yourself from things you couldn't see.

Lopez abandoned his coffee, and instead bought an apple on the way out.

* * *

Greg Bradley walked back to his surgery, his head down and his mind filled with thoughts of Link Frazier. He wondered what might have happened had Link come to him earlier. The doctor tried to encourage the town's senior citizens in particular to see him for routine check-ups, even if they weren't feeling ill, but the good folk of Easton weren't great believers in spending money unnecessarily on doctors, or on much else. It was almost funny: dentists had more or less convinced the population at large that it was important to have their teeth looked at on a regular basis, but it was near impossible to persuade those same people that they should extend that care to the rest of their bodies. Sometimes, it was enough to make Greg Bradley roar with frustration.

There were already six patients waiting for him when he reached the surgery, a couple of them flicking listlessly through the stock of out-of-date magazines, others probably indulging in that age-old waiting-room pastime of wondering just what was bothering their fellow sufferers, and whether or not they should try to keep their distance from them. Lana, his receptionist, gave him a mildly disapproving look as he walked by, discreetly tapping her wristwatch to let him know that he was already running late. He asked her to give him another five minutes, then closed the door to his office behind him and made a telephone call. Lopez, had he been there to witness it, would not have been surprised at the conversation that followed between the doctor and a man named Jason Coll who worked as a tax lawyer in Rochester, although others in the town might have been. The more open-minded among them might even have envied the fondness in Greg Bradley's voice, and could not have failed to note the obvious consolation he derived from talking with the other man. When he at last hung up the phone, the doctor took a moment to consider, as he often did, if their relationship, and his practise, would survive if Jason moved to Easton. Perhaps it was more realistic to think about moving to Boston, but Greg didn't want to leave the town. He belonged here, it was as simple as that. For the present, telephone calls and snatched weekends would have to suffice.

He tapped the intercom on his desk, and told Lana to send in the first patient.

The rest of Lopez's day was quiet, apart from a phone call from Errol wondering if the plow had to be brand-new, or if they could settle for one with a reconditioned engine.

'False economy,' Lopez told him.

He wasn't sure if it was a false economy. He just liked the idea of a new snowplow, even if it would be someone else's job to drive it. But on a practical level, he knew that winter took its toll on the older folks, and the last thing he needed was an ambulance stuck in drifts because a used plow had broken down.

Lopez touched base with Lloyd when he returned to the station house. Ellie Harrison, one of the part-time cops assigned to each shift, had just arrived and was doing paperwork at the desk in the back office. She gave him a wave. He left her to it.

Lloyd came around the counter and leaned in quietly to Lopez.

'You hear about Link Frazier?' he asked.

'Yeah. How did you know?'

'I heard it from my mom. She was with Doc Bradley this afternoon.'

Lloyd looked genuinely upset. He still lived with his mom and dad, occupying two rooms over the garage at the side of the house. He was dating Penny Clay, who worked at the drugstore and, as local gossip had it, was less than the silent type in the sack. Lopez wondered what Mr and Mrs Hopkins did when their son took Penny back to his place, assuming that they let him bring girls back. Could be that they were lucky enough to be going deaf, but if they weren't already then exposure to Penny Clay in the throes of ecstasy could well be the thing to do it. Penny was an unlikely partner for Lloyd. She was kind of full-on, and sometimes seemed to be missing a filter between her brain and her mouth, but she seemed to adore Lloyd, in her way, and Lopez hoped that she might instill a little more steel into the young man.

If Lopez had a criticism of Lloyd Hopkins, it was that he sometimes seemed just too sensitive for his own good, but it meant that he had a way about him that Lopez lacked. When Renee Bertucci was attacked by her ex-husband a year or so back, and arrived at the station house all black and blue with her blouse torn and that glazed look in her eyes that told you something real bad had happened back at her place, it was Lloyd who took care of her. True, Ellie was there for the tests and the swabs, but it was Lloyd upon whom Renee seemed to lean the most. He sat on a chair outside her room at the medical center for the rest of the night, until word came that Aldo Bertucci had been picked up by the smokies outside of Nashua, and then drove her to her mother's the next day. In a situation as delicate as that, there weren't many male cops who could be relied upon to do the right thing. Lloyd Hopkins didn't even have to think about it. It just came naturally to him.

'I think I might drive down to see him, if I get a chance,' said Lloyd.

'You give him my best.'

'I will. You heading home?'

'No, I'm meeting Elaine for dinner over at Reed's. You need me for anything, the cell will be on.'

'Big night tomorrow,' said Lloyd. 'You think it will go ahead, once folks hear about Link?'

Reed's was hosting its annual pre-Christmas fundraiser the following night. Each year, Eddy Reed handed over one night's takings from Reed's Bar And Grill to local charities. It was a tradition that he had inherited without complaint from Link Frazier. Pretty much everyone in town tried to make it along for part of the evening at least, and most added a couple of bucks extra to the cost of their meals and drinks to boost the pot.

'I don't know, but suppose we assume it will unless we hear otherwise,' said Lopez. 'Everyone is still on duty. We don't want anyone taking it into his head that this might be a good night to rip off the bar.'

Lloyd's comment reminded Lopez that he had not yet spoken to Eddy Reed about Link. He also wondered how Link stood regarding medical insurance. He didn't know how well off the old man was, and if the cost of proper care was going to be a problem then maybe some, or all, of the proceeds from the charity night at Reed's could be used for Link's benefit. He made a mental note to ask Greg Bradley about it when next they spoke.

Lopez showered and changed, then left Lloyd and Ellie and drove the five blocks to Reed's in his own Bronco. There were other bars in town, but Reed's was the only one with food that went beyond burgers and fries. The bar was about a quarter full when Lopez arrived, most folks clearly electing to wait for the following night's festivities before spending their money. Lopez ordered a beer and took a seat at the bar. Somebody had left a newspaper, so he flicked idly through it, exchanging small talk with the patrons and Eddy himself until Elaine appeared.

Elaine Olssen was the kind of magazine-quality Scandinavian blonde over whom Lopez used to weep tears of frustration when he was a teenager. She was easily the most beautiful woman he had ever dated: five-eleven; her face always a little sallow, even in winter; her hair hanging just below shoulder length. Her eyes were a very pale blue, and her lips parted in repose, creating a tiny diamond at the center of her mouth. He could see other men glance at her as she approached him, following her progress. Men always did. Most of the ones in Reed's stopped as soon as they saw Lopez clocking them in the mirror above the bar.

Only one man did not seem troubled by the policeman's presence. He continued to stare at Elaine as she took her seat, then turned casually away. He was drinking soda, the remains of a piece of apple pie on the table before him. His hair was slicked back on his skull, and he wore snakeskin cowboy boots and blue denims. A straw hat lay on the table beside the plate of pie. There was something written on the front, but Lopez couldn't read what it said. He considered rousting the stranger, partly out of annoyance at the way his gaze had lingered on Elaine, but also because of the feeling of unease he got when the man briefly caught his eye.

'What's wrong?' said Elaine, after they had kissed.

In the mirror, she followed the direction of Lopez's gaze.

'Yeah, I saw him checking me out,' she said. 'Creep.'

'He does it again, I may have words with him.'

Elaine touched her fingers to his lips. He kissed them lightly.

'Isn't that abusing your position?'

'Only if I beat him up after.'

'Oh. I never realized the law was so subtle.'

She sat down beside him and shrugged off her coat. She was wearing a red polo neck that followed her curves in a way that made Lopez catch his breath. Almost instinctively, he shot a look at the man in the window booth. He seemed to be staring through the glass at the street beyond, but

Lopez was pretty certain that Elaine was reflected in that same glass.

She ordered a white wine while they browsed the menus.

'How was your day?' he asked her.

Elaine was an assistant D.A. with responsibility for communications over at the New Hampshire A.G.'s office, which made her the first point of contact between the media and the attorney general. It meant that she appeared on TV whenever the A.G.'s office was handling a big case, or when something controversial occurred that needed to be defused. Elaine Olssen was an expert at dealing with potentially explosive situations. Even the tougher male reporters tended to go a little weak when she turned the full wattage of her smile upon them, while female reporters simply tried to stay out of her way in case she made them look bad.

'Pretty quiet for me. The rest of the office is looking to clear up as much stuff as possible before the holidays kick in. Nothing focuses the mind better than the prospect of putting someone in jail for Christmas. Gets you right in the spirit of the season. And you?'

He finished his beer and called for another.

'Same. Pretty dull. Errol whined about paying up for a new plow, Lloyd needs new trousers—'

'What are you, his father?'

'That boy just keeps growing and growing.'

His beer came. He picked at the label.

'And Link Frazier is real sick. Cancer. I'm sorry.'

Elaine closed her eyes. Her house was only a mile up the road from Link's, and he'd been kind to her when she first moved to Easton three years before.

'Are you sure?' asked Elaine, once she had recovered herself. 'I saw him just a few days ago. He didn't look sick, and he wasn't complaining about any pain.'

'I met Greg Bradley this afternoon. He said it was bad. He doesn't think Link's going to last too long.'

Lopez reached out for her and stroked her back. This was what Lloyd Hopkins was good at. Lopez knew that he just wasn't in his league.

The news cast a shadow over the rest of the evening, but still they ate, and drank and talked. Eddy now knew about Link, and he offered to approach the family about the state of Link's insurance and the possibility of the townsfolk making a contribution to his care if it was needed. Lopez thanked him, then walked out with Elaine to the parking lot.

'You want to come back with me?' asked Elaine. 'I'd like you to.'

'I'd like it too.'

She smiled and hugged him to her. Over her shoulder, he saw the man at the window watching them. He was licking his lips.

Lopez pulled back from her.

'Can you give me a minute?' he asked.

'Sure. Is there something wrong?'

He took his badge from his back pocket, his hand brushing the gun on his belt.

'If there isn't, there soon will be,' he said.

Buddy Carson watched the big cop approach. He'd seen him in town, cruising the streets giving the nod to just about everyone he encountered. Buddy had found out his name, and his position. Lopez was a danger, and Buddy knew it. Over the years, he had developed a predator's instinct for spotting those equal to or above him on the food chain who might prove dangerous. Where possible, he avoided them. When there was no other option, he got rid of them. He'd never taken a cop, though. Cops were different. You killed one, and others came after you. There was a pecking order in the amount of heat a killing drew: young men, particularly ethnics, drew the least; women and children brought down much more; but killing a cop was like putting yourself in front of a flamethrower. Still, if Buddy was to achieve what he hoped to accomplish in Easton, then something would have to be done about this one.

The cop was heavily bundled up: only his hands and face were bare, and Buddy wasn't sure that he would be able to find an excuse to touch him for long enough. If he pushed the cop too far he might end up in a cell, and Buddy didn't like to think of what would happen if he were incarcerated. There was an additional risk factor involved in trying to corrupt him in the bar, when he wouldn't have long enough to really get to work on him. Buddy had learned from experience that some people were more aware than others when they were touched by him. It was as though they actually felt themselves changing, as if they sensed the sudden distortion of themselves at the most basic of levels. They were the most dangerous, and Buddy's practise was to destroy them utterly, to remain in contact with them until they were completely subdued. He was like a spider poisoning a wasp, pumping it with venom even as it tried to sting, because to back away before its prey was completely subdued would leave it vulnerable to a lethal counterattack.

Buddy had become adept at spotting the alert ones. The nature of their work meant that cops were particularly sensitive, and for that additional reason he tried to avoid even casual encounters with them whenever possible. Something about the way Lopez carried himself told Buddy that he was good at his job, which meant that Buddy had to be especially careful.

Other customers were watching as Lopez approached the end table. He flashed Buddy his badge.

'You got some ID?' he asked.

'Why, did I do something wrong, Officer?' said Buddy.

'Sir, just show me some ID, please.'

Buddy reached for his jacket. The cop's hand was resting on the butt of his gun. The gun withdrew an inch from its holster, exposing the Glock's dull frame.

'Slowly,' said Lopez.

'This is a tough town,' said Buddy, as he felt in his jacket pocket. 'Got laws against minding your own business, laws against looking at a pretty woman. That's what this is about, isn't it? I looked at your woman, and you don't like it. I'm sorry, but she's a good-looking lady. I didn't mean nothing by it.'

He found his wallet and removed his Nevada state driver's license. It was the genuine article. The man who had acquired it for Buddy assured him that it would stand up to scrutiny, and he had told nothing less than the truth. It was worth every penny that Buddy had briefly paid for it before the man's death made redundant his need for Buddy's money. He handed it to the cop, and was almost tempted to brush his knuckles against the policeman's hand. The barest of contacts would enable him to gauge the cop's sensitivity, as well as delivering a little added dose of mortality, but the policeman was too quick for him.

'And what is your business, Mr Carson?'

'I'm between jobs. I'm just traveling around, trying to take in some of this great country.'

'We don't get many people coming all this way just to visit Easton. You know anybody here?'

'Not yet. If this is anything to go by, doesn't look like I'll be making too many friends here in the future.'

'I guess that depends,' said Lopez.

'On what?'

'On how friendly you really are.'

'I'm the real deal,' said Buddy. 'I just want to reach out to people.'

Lopez told Buddy to stay where he was, then used his cell to call the station house. Ellie answered, and he asked her to do a check on Buddy Carson. He gave her the license number, then waited. He watched Buddy Carson sitting quietly in his booth. He wasn't looking at Elaine any longer. Instead, he was just staring at the blank wall before him.

The check came back clean. Lopez was disappointed, but he still had his suspicions about the man in the booth.

'Where are you staying?' he asked Buddy, when he returned.

Buddy was slightly disappointed that the cop didn't hand him back his license. Instead Lopez placed it flat on the table, picture-side up, his finger holding down one corner.

'The Easton Motel,' said Buddy. 'It's real nice. I might extend my stay, it's so nice.'

'Let me tell you something, Mr Carson,' said Lopez. 'There's not a whole lot for a man to do in Easton at this time of year. I reckon that, by tomorrow, you should have exhausted all of the possibilities, and then it will be time for you to be on your way. You have a safe journey.'

He flicked the license back across the table.

'That sounds like I'm being run out of town,' said Buddy.

'No, you'll be leaving under your own steam. But if you want me to help you along, that can be arranged. You have a good night.'

Buddy watched him leave. He had hoped that by goading the cop he might get the opportunity to touch him if he lost his temper and made a move, but the cop had kept his cool. In the end, it was probably for the best. Buddy was storing up his venom now, getting ready for the big play. Making a try for the cop might have dulled his edge, or alerted the policeman to the threat Buddy posed. Better to let him go now, and hope for another chance at him later. Buddy did not consider himself to be a vindictive man, but he would take pleasure in giving the cop a little something if the opportunity presented itself. He envisaged himself squatting on the cop's chest, his fingers in his mouth and the cop's tongue slowly turning black in his grip. Buddy allowed himself a small smile. Dealing with the spic cop would be a real pleasure.

As for the woman, well, in her case the pleasure would be doubled.

'So?'

Elaine was driving. Lopez would pick up his car when she dropped him back to town the following morning. Elaine owned a black Mercedes CLK430 convertible, and Lopez reckoned it was a good thing that she had a job with the A.G.'s office because Elaine Olssen had never met a speed limit that she liked. There were times, driving with her on the stretch of 95 between Montpelier and White River Junction, that Lopez doubted even their combined influence would be enough to keep her out of jail, or from being recruited for some form of secret NASA rocket-testing program.

'So what?'

'You've hardly said a word since the bar. Did that guy do something to you?'

'He got under my skin, that's all. I've never met a guy called Buddy that I liked. It's one of those names that's trying too hard. Men named "Buddy" are right up there with guys who call you "pal" or "friend." '

'Are you going to give him the bum's rush?'

'I already did. I told him I wanted him gone.'

'Rough justice. Bet every girl who gets eyed up by a creep in a bar wishes her boyfriend could just have him thrown out of town.'

Lopez wasn't sure if she was being sarcastic or not. He glanced at her. She made sultry eyes at him.

'I like it,' she purred. 'It's kind of sexy.'

For the first time since his encounter with Buddy Carson, Lopez grinned back.

'Next time I'll beat him up for you.'

'Ooooh,' she said. 'I can hardly wait. "Hit him harder, officer. Hit him *harder* . . ." '

IV

Buddy Carson left the bar and drove his Dodge back to the motel. He hadn't planned on checking out the next day. He wanted a place to rest up before the night's exertions, but Buddy had no doubt that the cop would check up on him, and he needed to avoid another confrontation until he was ready. Now that he had scouted out the bar, he was convinced that he could take a couple of dozen people easily without arousing any suspicion at first, maybe more if they were all packed together tight. If his plan of action worked like he hoped, he would gain respite for weeks, maybe months. He liked the idea of moving on to New York, but it would be hard to find skin to touch casually in winter. With his pain alleviated for a time, he could afford to hibernate until the Spring. Maybe Florida, he thought, or California. San Francisco, with its hobos and tourists, appealed to him.

Buddy had been sick again in the men's room of Reed's bar. It was almost as if the black worm knew what he was planning and wanted to make sure that he didn't back out by reminding Buddy of its dominion over him. Buddy sometimes wondered what would happen if he tried to resist the impulse, if he took the pain and tried to see it out to the end. Would he die? In the beginning, on that second night after the deaths of the doctor and his receptionist, he had found a gun in the mechanic's nightstand. He drank a couple of shots of bourbon to give him a little Dutch courage, then placed the gun in his mouth. He closed his eyes and thought about pulling the trigger, but in the end he did not. It wasn't that he couldn't pull the trigger if he actually wanted to. That was the thing of it: what he thought of as the black worm couldn't make him do anything against his will. Sure, it could use pain to force him into a certain course of action, but it didn't control him. He still had his own freedom of choice.

No, the reason why Buddy didn't pull the trigger that night was at once simpler, and infinitely more complex, than mind control. Buddy didn't pull the trigger because Buddy *liked* what he was doing. Passing on to others some small aspect of the disease that had colonized his own body gave him not only release, but pleasure. He enjoyed it. He relished the sense of power it gave him, the ability to decide who lived and who died. It was godlike.

Buddy still did not know for sure if the black worm really existed in the form that he imagined, sleek and black in its plated carapace, vestigial eyes buried at either side of its pointed head, its mouth little more than a ridged wound; or if it was merely his mind's way of picturing the corrosion within himself, the foulness that had always been intrinsic to him. If the worm was present within him then it was evil, and some part of the pleasure that he felt was shared, or even generated, by that alien presence. But even if it did not exist, there was still evil inside Buddy, evil beyond the worst atrocities he had witnessed on his TV screen, and Buddy knew it. He wondered sometimes if there were more like him, if there were others scattered around the country, even the world, passing on their contagion with a single touch, alleviating their own pain by gifting it to others. Buddy didn't know, and he suspected that he never would. He still had no understanding of how he had come to be this way. It might have been the work of some outside agency, but equally it could just have been a consequence of Buddy's own moral decay. Maybe, he thought, I'm the next step in human evolution: a being whose physical form has become a reflection of his moral state, a man whose soul has corrupted and rotted within him, poisoning and transforming his insides.

Whatever he was, Buddy was certain of one thing: he was stronger and more lethal than anyone in this shithole town, and pretty soon a lot of people were going to learn that lesson the hard way.

Buddy was still smiling when he pulled into the parking lot of the Easton Motel and saw someone leaving his motel room.

Buddy stopped smiling.

Jed Wheaton had asked Phil to check up on the guy in twelve. Phil was about to take over the night shift, but he didn't have his study books with him like he usually did. Phil wasn't even carrying a paperback to read. There was a TV behind the desk, but Phil, like his father, usually only turned it on when he was desperate. Perhaps he was hoping to catch up on some sleep: there was a couch in the office, and after two A.M. a sign on the door told people to ring the bell in order to wake the night clerk. Phil certainly looked tired and distracted enough to want to curl up for the night.

'You okay, son?' Jed asked.

Phil reacted as if he'd just been woken from a trance.

'Huh? Yeah, I'm fine, just fine.'

Jed wasn't sure that he believed him, but Phil tended to keep himself to himself most of the time. If there was a problem, his son would get around to telling him when he felt like it.

Phil didn't have much to add to what Jed already knew when he asked him about the night Buddy Carson checked in. Phil said that he had seemed okay. He'd even insisted on introducing himself, his hand outstretched as soon as his bag hit the floor.

Buddy, Buddy Carson. How you doing tonight?

His teeth were bad, and his breath smelled some, but that was about the sum total of Phil's recollection.

Jed had called Greg Bradley that evening to discuss the health of his new guest, but Bradley, still troubled by Link Frazier's diagnosis, was already on his way to talk with the oncology people at Manchester Medical. A recording on his machine advised anyone needing a doctor in a hurry to call the surgery over in Brewster, five miles west of Easton. Jed left a message, asking Greg to call him because he was worried about one of his guests, but there was nothing more that he could do than that. He wasn't even sure that there was anything Greg Bradley could do. After all, it wasn't as if he could force Carson to consult with him.

Still, when Phil arrived Jed told him to take a quick look-see at twelve. Carson's Dodge wasn't in the lot, so Jed figured it was a chance to check the room and make sure that his guest hadn't bled a gut over the bed.

'Just stick your head in, take a look at the bathroom, then come back to me,' he said.

Phil, after what seemed like a couple of seconds while his addled brain tried to make sense of his father's simple request, grabbed the master key and headed out.

Phil had found the lump while showering that afternoon.

Like most men, he wasn't as careful about checking his privates as he should be. Secretly, and also in common with most men, he had a 'don't ask, don't tell' attitude toward his own health. The last time he had consulted a doctor was two years before, when he broke his wrist snowboarding. Since then, Phil had suffered nothing worse than headcolds and hangovers.

But this lump couldn't be ignored. Hell, Phil could *see* it when he looked in the mirror, like someone had slipped a grape in there. It was tender, but not unduly painful, and Phil was certain that it hadn't been there the night before. There was no way that he could have missed something like that. But it couldn't be anything serious, right? I mean, these things took time. They didn't just happen overnight. He'd give it a day. Maybe it was just one of those oddities, and by morning it would be gone. He couldn't get rid of the image of it from his mind, though. Worse, he couldn't shake off the sensation that he had, like there were worms beneath his skin, burrowing into flesh and marrow, transforming everything within to black.

Now, as he walked past the motel's small, clean rooms, he felt the throbbing in his groin, and knew that he would have to talk to someone about it. He had almost told his father what was troubling him, but he was simultaneously concerned about worrying the old man, and mortified at the prospect of Jed Wheaton asking his son to show him his privates. He decided that once the night shift was done, he would head over to Doc Bradley's first thing and get himself looked at.

Phil opened the door to twelve. There was a smell in there, the kind he always associated with his grandma dying. She'd been in one of those old people's wards where nobody was ever going to see home again, and the whole ward stank faintly of vomit and piss and mortality, all unsuccessfully masked by cleaning products and industrial-strength deodorant. There was the same smell in twelve, except there was nothing strong enough to really hide it. Phil thought he could detect the residue of Maria's spray, but she might just as well have hung one of those pine tree air deodorisers on a corpse for all the effect it was having.

The smell was worst in the bathroom, but at least it was

clean. The towels were folded and unused. The shower was dry, and even the soaps remained wrapped. The toilet had been flushed, but there was some blood on the floor nearby.

Phil stepped back into the bedroom. There was a bag in one corner, an expensive-looking leather holdall, but it was locked. It was the only sign that the room was occupied. Everything else was just as Maria always left it for arriving guests, even down to the remote for the TV lying perfectly centered on the cover of the latest HBO schedule.

Phil hit the lights, locked the door, and turned to find himself face-to-face with Buddy Carson.

'Can I ask what you're doing?' said Carson.

In the moonlight, his face looked gaunt and cadaverous, and up close his breath smelled like a distilled version of the stink in his room. Instinctively, Phil backed away from the stench.

'Just checking to make sure you don't need more towels. We do it for everyone,' Phil lied.

Buddy made a big play of looking at his watch.

'Kind of late to be doing that, isn't it? You'll wake folks up.'

'We got tied up with other stuff this evening, and you're the only guest tonight. I knew you were out, because your car wasn't in the lot. Seemed like the best chance I'd have without disturbing you.'

Buddy didn't say anything in reply. He just eyeballed Phil, nodding to let the kid know that what he was saying might sound like the most reasonable thing he'd ever heard, and yet he still didn't believe one damn word of it.

'Well, I appreciate it,' he said at last. 'You have a good night.'

Phil made as if to walk around him, but Buddy gripped his wrist and, once again, Phil had an image of black creatures moving under his skin.

'Hey, you feeling okay?' asked Buddy, and although there was concern in his voice the moonlight made his face appear to be leering. 'You look kind of sick.'

'Tired,' said Phil, then winced as something stabbed into his groin. He looked down, half anticipating the sight of a needle sticking into his pants, but there was nothing.

'I got to go,' he said.

'Sure,' said Buddy. 'You be careful now.'

He watched the kid stumble away. He'd make for the bathroom. That's what Buddy would do if he was the kid. He'd go to the bathroom, unbutton his pants, and take a look at what was going on downstairs, because it surely felt now as if that thing were growing and spreading.

It was, of course, but not in any way that the kid would be able to see. Buddy figured the true pain would start in a couple of hours' time, as the cancer really started to eat away at him, making steady progress toward the major organs and eroding his spine.

But in the bathroom, the lump would appear unchanged.

Just a lump, folks. Nothing to see here. Move along, move along.

Buddy closed the door and glanced around his room. His bag had not been touched. That was good. Buddy had things in there that he didn't want other people looking at. Time was pressing. Buddy figured that the kid would go to the doctor the next day. By then, the bitch maid would probably have discovered the lump in her breast. On top of the old man, that would make three in less than two days, more if some of the other folks he'd touched that day proved weaker than suspected. A cluster like that would not go unremarked. Buddy had done some asking around that day. There wasn't but one doctor in the town, and he ran his clinic out of a peachy little one storey house on the eastern outskirts of town. It made things easier for Buddy. He would have only one call to make.

He knelt down and used a small silver key to open the lock on his bag. Inside were a couple of changes of clothes, identical to those he was already wearing; a passport and a driver's license in the name of Russ Cercan (another of Buddy's little jokes); and a glass jelly jar. It was this that Buddy now reached for, holding it up to the light the way an entomologist might examine a particularly interesting bug.

Inside the jar was a black tumor. It had come from inside Buddy's own body, coughed up that morning as the pain began to tell upon him. He had crawled to the bathroom but didn't make it to the bowl. Instead, he lay retching on the tiles, coughing up blood and black matter, including the tumor now contained in the jar. It was a reminder of what dwelt within him, a gift from the disease to help him in the work to come.

Dead cells, thought Buddy. That's all you are, just dead cells.

He tapped the glass gently with his fingernail.

And the tumor moved.

Across town, in Elaine Olssen's untidy bedroom, Lopez sat at the window and looked out on the fields. Elaine's place was right at the edge of Easton, where town met country. There was a stream close by, and distant mountains silvered by the moon. He heard an owl hooting. He wondered if it had already fed itself that night, or if it had not yet found its prey.

Lopez could not stop thinking about Buddy Carson. Earlier that evening, as he stood over him in Reed's, he had been conscious of a ringing in his ears, a kind of high-pitched whine. Lopez knew what the sound was: it was his senses kicking up a gear, like they did when, distantly, he thought he heard his garden gate open and knew that someone was approaching his door, even if he could not hear their feet on the path; or when a person came too close behind him and he felt his personal space being encroached upon, even though he could not see the individual in question without turning around.

Faced with Buddy Carson, Lopez's senses appeared to go on high alert. Even though he had no reason to think it, Lopez believed that Buddy Carson was trying to touch him in the bar, as though some game were being played between them, the rules of which were clear only to Carson. It was in the awkward way that he turned his hand in order to pass his license over, or in the way his fingers leaped forward to take it back when Lopez returned, aiming at once at and beyond the license itself.

Lopez didn't want to be touched by Buddy Carson. Something told him that to have any physical contact with the cowboy would be a very bad idea indeed. Knowing that Carson had left town would help, but it would not alleviate his concerns entirely. He was bad news for somebody, and moving him along would only transfer to another man the burden of eventually dealing with him.

There were times, when he was a trooper, that Lopez encountered individuals who brought nothing of worth to the world, who in fact seemed to enjoy making it worse for anyone who had the misfortune to cross their path. Lopez would often try to imagine what they had been like as children, in an effort to modify his feelings of hatred for them. Sometimes it worked, and sometimes it did not. When it didn't, Lopez would find himself agreeing with those of his peers who felt that the best thing for everyone involved would be if those people were dead. They were like bacteria in a petri dish, spreading out and colonizing their surroundings, tainting everything that they touched.

Lopez tried to picture Buddy Carson as a child, and found that he could not. Nothing came to him. Maybe it was tiredness, but in his head Carson seemed both old and young, both newly formed yet ancient, like old metal that had been smelted and reused again and again, becoming more and more corrupt in the process.

Lopez looked to the bed, where Elaine lay sleeping. She always slept the same way: curled up on her right side, with her right arm pressed against her breasts and her left hand close to her mouth. She rarely moved in the night, and uttered no sounds in her sleep.

He slipped back into the bed, and made as if to reach for her. Instead, his hand remained hovering inches above her skin, unwilling to make contact. He drew it back to himself and moved away from her, finding his own space at the very edge of the mattress, where at last he drifted into sleep.

V

Buddy Carson checked out of the Easton Motel shortly after eleven the following morning. The pain was growing in his right side. He could take a small hit from someone, but just a little in case he might be tempted to rest, for he usually felt sleepy after release, and there was work to be done. He would accept some discomfort now in return for more lasting relief later.

Jed was too distracted by his family problems to care much about being polite to his sole guest. Phil Wheaton was already sitting in the waiting room of Greg Bradley's surgery, his face white and stretched taut with pain. He told his father that he wasn't feeling so good, that he had pains in his lower body, but Jed didn't need to be told that his son was sick. His physical appearance had changed drastically overnight. He seemed to have lost pounds in a matter of hours. Jed wanted to go see the doctor with him, but Phil said he would prefer to go alone, and that he'd give his father a call if there was a problem. Despite that, Jed was considering heading over to the surgery anyway when Maria called to say that *she* wasn't feeling great, and that she'd be late. When Buddy Carson came in, Jed was already calling around his relief staff, trying to find someone who might be prepared to cover at short notice.

Buddy had paid up front for his stay. Now that he had decided to check out early, he wanted his money back. Jed didn't argue. He just wanted Buddy gone so that he could set about seeing to his son's needs.

'Bad morning?' asked Buddy.

'Not so good,' said Jed.

He reached out to count the cash and Buddy Carson tapped him softly on the back of the hand with a yellowed index finger.

'You need to take a deep breath, try to relax,' said Buddy solemnly. 'You'll make yourself sick. Believe me, I know.'

Jed remembered the description of the blackened, bloodied towels, and registered the way Buddy Carson's teeth were streaked brown with nicotine, his gums a vivid purple. I'll bet you know all about sickness, he thought. I'm glad that you're leaving, but if I find out that you brought something into this town, if I discover that it was you that made my boy sick, I'll hunt you down, you fuck. I'll hunt you down and I'll take a knife to you, and then you won't have to worry about bloody towels, or your teeth falling out of your head, or your ragged fucking nails cracking and disintegrating, because I'll tear you apart, I swear to God I will.

'Sure,' said Jed. 'You have a good day, now.'

Lopez woke with Elaine. They made love quickly, then Elaine showered while he toasted some bagels. He listened to the news on the radio in the kitchen, then took his shower while Elaine dressed. She dropped him outside Reed's, kissed him goodbye, and told him that she'd see him later that evening. He watched her drive away, waving to her as she turned the corner and left his view, then strolled over to talk to Eddy Reed, who was sweeping the steps outside the bar.

'Economy drive?' he asked. 'I thought you had employees to clean steps while you counted your millions in a back room.'

'Two called in sick,' said Eddy. 'Today of all days they have to get sick.'

'You'll have no problem getting folks to help out, if you're in trouble.'

Eddie stopped sweeping and leaned on the handle of the brush.

'I guess you're right.'

He sucked on his lip, as though trying to reach a decision with himself, then said to Lopez: 'You got a minute to look at something?'

Lopez shrugged, and followed him into the bar. Reed led him to the men's room, then opened the door.

'Last one,' he said.

Lopez walked past the urinals. The door to the end stall was half closed. He pushed it open with the toe of his boot.

There was black fluid on the wall, and more liquid pooled on the floor. An inexpert attempt had been made to prevent it from spreading by dumping toilet paper on top of it. The paper was almost entirely soaked through.

'Found it when I was locking up. It was quiet last night, so I guess nobody used the stall after it happened. I was going to call Lloyd, but it was after two in the morning and I figured that maybe it wasn't worth troubling him about.'

Lopez squatted down and took a closer look at the blood.

'Give me that brush for a second,' he said.

Reed handed over the brush, and Lopez used the handle to explore the accumulation of paper and fluid. At the center of the mass, he found pieces of black matter.

'What are they?' asked Reed.

'I don't know. Looks like someone might have coughed them up.'

'Whoever it is, he's real sick.'

Lopez stood, then washed the tip of the broom in the sink before handing it back to Reed.

'You remember who was in the bar last night after I left?'

Reed considered the question.

'Locals, mostly. I can name them. Two couples from out of town. Don't think they were staying here. And the guy in the corner booth, the one you were talking to. Creepy sonofabitch. Kept brushing up against the wait staff.'

Lopez swore softly. 'I think I know where to find him,' he said. 'I want you to make a list of the people who were here, just in case. Put some Scotch tape over the door to this stall, maybe an "Out of Order" sign too. I'll get Greg Bradley to stop by and take a look at it. And Ed, don't tell anyone about this, okay?'

Ed looked at him as if he'd just advised him not to stir cocktails with his wiener.

'You mean you don't want me to tell my brunch customers about what looks like black blood in the men's room, which might make them think twice about ordering the beef? I don't know, Chief, but if you insist . . .'

Lopez called by the Easton Motel. Jed was no longer behind the desk. A young girl, one of Pat Capoore's kids, was looking after things while Jed was gone. A teen magazine was open in front of her, and she was sipping a can of soda through a straw.

'You know where he is?' he asked.

'His son Phil isn't feeling so good. He told me he'd be over at Greg Bradley's if there was a problem.'

Lopez asked for the motel's registration cards. He flicked through them until he came to Buddy Carson's.

'Did this man check out?'

'The motel's empty. I guess he must have done.'

'Have you made up the room?'

'I don't think it's been done yet. I guess I'll have to do it when Jed gets back.'

She made a barfing gesture by sticking her finger in her

mouth, then gave Lopez the key to twelve before returning to her magazine.

'Hey,' she called, as he was about to leave. 'Should I ask you for a warrant or something?'

'Why?' he asked. 'You got something to hide?'

'Maybe,' she said, coquettishly. Her lips closed around the straw. She sucked deeply, never taking her eyes from him the whole time.

Lopez left her to it, wondering if maybe he shouldn't have a talk with Pat Capoore about his little girl.

The room was neat and empty. The toilet roll was folded into a little triangle at the end, and none of the towels had been used. The bed had been slept on rather than in. Lopez could see the depression Buddy Carson's body had made on the quilt. The quilt was yellow and green. Where it covered the pillows, Lopez saw a dark stain.

Black blood: not much, though. Lopez thought he could see traces of it in the toilet bowl too, although nothing like the men's room at Reed's. It looked like Buddy Carson wouldn't be creeping people out for much longer. Lopez tried to find an ounce of sympathy for the man, but failed. He closed the door, returned the key, and headed home to change into his uniform.

Greg Bradley was having a bad morning. First, there was Maria Dominguez, with a lump in her breast the size of a walnut. He'd warned her again and again about screening, but she was a big, buxom woman in the fullest bloom of health. People like her believed that they just couldn't get sick. He'd given her a referral for Manchester, and made the appointment for her for that afternoon. She'd called her husband from the surgery and he had collected her. As soon as they were gone, Greg called Amy Weiss, the counsellor he used, and told her the details. She assured him that she'd call the house and offer to accompany Maria to Manchester.

Now there was Phil Wheaton. He began to cry almost as soon as Greg examined him, big silent tears that rolled down his cheeks and exploded on his bare thighs.

Greg tried to keep his voice calm as he examined him.

'How long have you had this, Phil?' he asked.

'Just since yesterday.'

Greg looked up at him.

'Seriously, Phil. I need you to tell me the truth.'

'That is the truth. Honest, I wouldn't lie about something like this. I mean, *look* at me.'

It flew in the face of all medical knowledge, but Greg was inclined to believe him. The expression on Phil Wheaton's face was one of absolute fear and panic, and Greg had become adept at spotting the liars in his surgery. But this made no sense: he was looking at what he very much suspected was an advanced stage of testicular cancer. He tested him for discomfort, and found pain centers as high as his abdomen.

'Okay, Phil, we need to get you looked at by a specialist. You got someone you can call?'

'My dad,' said Phil. 'Can I call my dad?'

Greg told him to pull his pants up, then went out to ask his secretary to call Jed Wheaton, but the older man was already in the waiting room, staring at the noticeboard on the wall without taking any of it in. Greg walked over to him, touched his shoulder, and gestured toward the second consulting room at the opposite end of the hallway from where his son was dressing.

'Jed,' he said. 'You want to come inside with me for a moment?'

Lopez relieved Lloyd and Ellie, then left Chris Barker, another part-time cop, in charge of the station house while he did his rounds. It would be a long day today, culminating in the event at Reed's which would require him to be present and in uniform for the occasion. He called Greg Bradley's surgery, but Lana told him that the doctor was pretty much tied up for the morning, and asked him to call back later. Lopez decided that the blood in Reed's could wait until the afternoon. Once Greg had taken a look at it, Reed could get the stall cleaned up before the crowds started to arrive.

Buddy Carson: the guy certainly managed to leave his mark on a place.

It was Lloyd who spotted the red Dodge Charger. He was halfway home, and thinking only about his bed, when he saw it parked under a bank of trees beside Easton's old bowling alley, long since boarded up and slowly falling into disrepair.

Lopez sometimes commented that Lloyd had a mind like a sorting office: everything in its right place, the smallest of facts correctly filed away. A seemingly innocuous detail could set Lloyd off, leading him to flip diligently through the storehouse of his mind until he came up with the relevant case.

Among the heads-ups in the 'In' tray that morning was a bulletin concerning the deaths of a family in Colorado. While medical experts were still examining the bodies, state police – and, for reasons that weren't made clear in the bulletin, the Feds and the health authorities – were anxious to talk to a man who might have visited the scene. Apparently, the owner of a neighboring ranch had noticed a red Dodge Charger entering the property a day before the bodies were discovered. He couldn't make out the plate, but the driver was male, and the witness thought he might have been carrying a white hat in his hand.

Now here was a red Dodge Charger. It was a long way

from Colorado, but there was no mistaking it. Standing beside the car was a thin man wearing a white cowboy hat, and eating a candy bar. There was something stuck on the front of the hat, just above the brim. Lloyd didn't know that this was Buddy Carson, the same man upon whom Lopez had asked Ellie to run a check the night before, because Lopez hadn't mentioned a car.

Lloyd pulled into the lot. He didn't have a radio in his truck, but he did have a cell phone. He could call Lopez, he supposed, but he decided to see what the guy had to say for himself first of all. He pulled up about ten feet from the man in the hat and opened his door. Lloyd was still wearing his uniform, but the man didn't appear troubled by the sight of him. Either he was very cool, or he didn't have a lot to hide. The trouble was that those who had the least to hide tended to worry the most when confronted by a cop in uniform. It was the quiet ones that needed to be watched.

'Morning,' said Lloyd. 'Everything okay here?'

Buddy Carson finished the candy bar, rolled the wrapper into a ball, then placed it carefully in his shirt pocket, just behind his wallet. He was wearing black leather gloves.

'Everything's just fine,' he said.

'You got some identification?'

'Sure,' said Buddy.

He took his wallet from his pocket, found his driver's license, and handed it to Lloyd, but Lloyd jerked his hand away at the last moment and the license fell on the ground between them. Lloyd felt as though he had come close to an electrical field, bristling and humming with dangerous energy, contained only by the thin leather of the man's gloves.

'What the hell was that?' he asked.

Buddy Carson didn't answer. Instead his mouth opened wide, and a steady stream of black fluid struck Lloyd

Hopkins in the face. He stumbled backward, his eyes burning. He tried to reach for his gun, but Buddy moved in on him, wrenching his arm away from the weapon and hitting him on the bridge of the nose with the heel of his right hand. Lloyd went down, and Buddy took his gun.

Buddy listened for a second, but could detect no cars coming. He considered shooting the cop, but was afraid that someone as yet unseen might hear, and he couldn't risk dissipating his energies by taking him in the usual way. Instead, he slipped the gun into his belt, then raised his foot and brought the heel of his boot down hard on Lloyd's head.

By the third strike, Lloyd Hopkins was dead.

Greg Bradley cleared his surgery by twelve-thirty, then told Lana to go home. Fridays were always half-days, but Lana was in even more of a hurry to leave than usual since she was due to help Eddy Reed with the preparations for the charity evening. Once she had left, turning the sign on the door to 'Closed' on her way out, he sat down at his desk and put his head in his hands. It was as bad a morning as he could ever remember: Maria and her husband driving out of the lot, she with her head lowered, too stunned even to cry; Jed Wheaton trying to console his weeping son; and a call from Manchester to say that Link Frazier had passed away during the night. Three cancer cases in as many days, at least two of them massively advanced and two of them connected with the Easton Motel. He replayed the message Jed had left on his machine the night before. He had wanted to question him more closely about his sick guest, the one who had bled all over the towels, but Jed's attention was now fixed entirely on his son. Anyway, the guy had checked out that morning. The towels were still there, Jed told him. Maria had placed them in a bag in the laundry room, just in case.

But this was cancer, and different forms of cancer. How could they be linked to one man?

There was something terribly wrong. He had to talk to Lopez. He was about to get his coat when he heard someone enter reception and close the door. There was the sound of the lock being engaged. He walked out to the receptionist's desk.

'Sorry,' he began. 'I'm—'

Buddy Carson had wiped most of Lloyd Hopkins's blood from his face, but it still streaked his nose and forehead. His lips were drawn back from his mouth, and Bradley could see what looked like oil caked at the corners.

Buddy's right hand swept across from left to right, knocking Greg Bradley back into his surgery. The pointed toe of a cowboy boot struck the doctor in the left kidney, and then Buddy Carson was sitting on his chest, his knees pinning his quarry's arms to the floor.

'I'm sorry, Doc,' he said, 'but Buddy ain't got time for your shit.'

He held a glass jar in his left hand. Using his thumb and forefinger, he unscrewed the lid. Something black inside the jar twisted in response to the action.

Buddy shifted his position, now using his shins on the doctor's arms while his knees gripped his head. He leaned over, then slammed the open end of the jar against Bradley's left ear.

Like a slug, the black tumor began to slide across the glass toward its host.

The day crawled by. Lopez got tied up with a domestic dispute, eventually hauling in the husband to give him time to cool off in a cell. There were couples in the town who seemed to spend most of their married lives first beating up on each other, then breaking up with each other, before finally getting back together in time to start the whole cycle once more. Charges were often threatened but rarely pressed, and Lopez had forced himself not to become clinically depressed by the number of women who stayed in, or returned to, abusive relationships despite every effort to help them. He knew it wasn't that simple, and he had heard all the complex psychological arguments about the nature of such relationships, but that still didn't stop him from wanting to take a length of rubber hose to some of the men, and to shake some sense into the women.

The guy currently languishing in a cell had not come to his attention before. According to his wife, he had lost his job a couple of months earlier and begun drinking more than usual. Money was tight, and bills were going unpaid. What began as an attempt to have a reasoned discussion had escalated into shouting and then, briefly, violence. A neighbor called the police, and now the husband was in a cell and Lopez had left another message on Amy Weiss's phone asking her to try to schedule an appointment with the wife.

Lopez called Greg Bradley's surgery, but got the machine. He tried the doctor's cell, but got a 'powered-off' message. Finally, he made a call to Greg's house and, when there was no reply, got Lana over at Reed's and asked her if she knew where he was. She told him that she'd left him at the surgery, and filled him in some on the morning's events without mentioning the names of those involved, but she couldn't talk for long. Already there were people starting to arrive, and Lopez could hear Eddy Reed shouting in the background. Lopez let her go.

He checked his watch. Lloyd Hopkins was late. He'd promised to return early to help out with the parking at Reed's. Again, Lopez was forced to call both his cell and his home, but got no reply from either.

'Don't anybody answer the damn phone anymore?' he

asked nobody in particular. The only people within earshot were Barker and Ellie. They just exchanged looks and returned to their business with renewed vigor. Lopez asked Ellie to head over to Reed's until Lloyd made an appearance, then left Barker at the station while he took a ride over to Greg Bradley's surgery.

The door was unlocked.

He stepped inside and saw the papers on the floor, and the cracked glass in the surgery door where Greg's body had struck it. He drew his gun and advanced toward the room. It was empty, but there was a dark stain on the carpet. He checked the other rooms and found them empty. He had just picked up his handset to call Barker back at the station when he heard a sound from the closet at the end of the hallway. Its doors were chained and locked.

Lopez ran to it. Someone was trying to speak, but the words were indistinct.

'Greg?'

The voice spoke again.

'I'll have you out of there in a second,' he said.

He took his baton, twisted it against the chain, then pulled. The handle on the closet popped out of the wood, releasing the door. It shot open and what was left of Greg Bradley tumbled out onto the floor. His face was entirely black, and his eyes were hidden beneath his swollen flesh. Most of his hair had fallen out, and what remained were gray strands, stuck to the lesions that had opened in his scalp. Lopez turned away, feeling himself start to retch at the smell coming from the doctor's insides.

'Uh-ee', said Bradley.

'I can't—'

Bradley's hand tried to grip at Lopez's shirt, but it had no strength.

'Uh-ee,' repeated Bradley. 'Uh-ee *sick*.'

His consciousness was failing, the black things eating away at him, consuming him by turning his own body against him. He could not remember his own name, or where he was. He was lost in the growing darkness, and he would never be found again. All that was left was pain, and the memory of the man who had brought it.

And then even that was gone.

Lopez eased Bradley's body slowly to the floor.

Uh-ee.

Buddy.

At that moment, Buddy Carson was standing in the shadows at the back of Eddy Reed's bar. The place was filling up nicely, with more cars arriving every minute. A small, lithe female cop was helping to direct the new arrivals into the parking lot. Buddy waited patiently. He knew his chance would come, and it did.

A fat woman in a Nissan, three of her howling brood crammed into the back seat, tried to buck the one-way system in the lot in order to grab a parking space close to the bar's back door. Unfortunately, she reckoned without a big Explorer, which was next in line for the space and which pipped the Nissan. There was some shouting, which confirmed Buddy's view that the neighborliness in this town was only skin deep, before the Nissan backed away, glancing against someone's Lexus and setting off the alarm. The couple who owned the Lexus had not yet made it to the bar, and the sound of the alarm brought them scurrying back. It also brought the cop, who had to skirt the Dumpsters behind which Buddy lay.

He grabbed her quickly and without fuss, then left her bleeding amidst the trash.

Five minutes later, he was heading for the bar.

* * *

The call about Lloyd Hopkins came just seconds after Lopez finished up with Barker. He had given the young part-timer a description of Buddy Carson and told him to alert the state police. He was trying to raise Ellie when Barker came back to him on the radio. He sounded on the verge on tears.

'Chief, it's Lloyd,' he said. 'A couple of kids think they've found his body behind the old Metzger's Bowl. His car's there too. They say he's been beat on pretty bad. What do you want me to do?'

Jesus, not Lloyd. Lopez felt a wrenching in his gut.

'Who are the kids?'

'Ben Ryder, and the Capoore girl.'

Pat Capoore's daughter, the girl from the motel: she knew Lloyd Hopkins by sight.

'I'm heading out there,' he told Barker. 'Get back on to the troopers again. Tell them we have one officer dead, and the suspect is Carson, Buddy Carson.'

Lopez didn't know for sure that Carson was responsible for Lloyd Hopkins's death, but he was the best suspect. Nobody local would ever even raise a voice to Lloyd Hopkins.

'And Chris,' he added, 'you tell them to use extreme caution. Tell them not to even touch this guy. I think there's something wrong with him. He may be contagious, you understand?'

He was about to hit the lights and speed to Metzger's, but paused before activating the siren. First Link Frazier was diagnosed with cancer, then Greg Bradley's receptionist had alerted him to two further possible cases. Now Greg was dead, his face a mess of tumors, and Lloyd Hopkins's body was lying in the deserted lot of a disused bowling alley, beaten and maybe diseased. But cancer wasn't contagious. It didn't work that way.

He tried raising Ellie again, but with no success. Instead, he took out his cell and called Reed's. Eddy picked up on the third ring.

'Reed's. How can I help you?'

'Eddy, it's Jim Lopez. Do me a favor. Look out into the lot, see if you can't spot Ellie Winters.'

He could hear voices in the background, and laughter. Music was playing.

'Hang on, Chief,' said Reed.

The phone was put down, and in that instant Lopez made his decision. Minutes went by before the phone was picked up again, but by the time Eddy came back on the line Lopez was in sight of the bar.

'No, I don't see her anywhere. Her car's outside, but—'

Eddy Reed paused.

'Hold on, there's something happening,' he said.

Then the music died, and Lopez heard somebody start to scream.

Buddy had been preparing himself all day, working on the poison within him until it was distilled to its purest essence. He could feel it responding to his thoughts, readying itself for what lay ahead. The fluid with which he had blinded Lloyd Hopkins was waste matter, and nothing more. He had kept back the real stuff, so that when he touched the first woman over by the ladies' room, the release of energy rocked him on his heels. He could almost see the black fluid seeping through his pores and entering the base of her skull. He felt light-headed, and giddy with power, even as the woman's skin puckered and blackened before him. She spun toward him, her fingers reaching back to try to find the source of the pain, but Buddy was already moving. He touched a fat man on the hand, and a waitress on the shoulder blade. Her tray fell to the floor, the glasses upon it shattering.

Then a woman screamed. Buddy thought it might be the bitch at the toilets, but in fact it was one of her companions, responding to the sight of the creeping tumor colonizing her friend's face. Buddy felt somebody reach for him, the man's hand closing firmly on his shoulder. Without looking, Buddy slapped back at his face, and felt the surge again as the transfer occurred. He was making for the far corner of the bar, where a familiar blond-haired woman was talking to a man in a grey suit. He had spotted the cop's girlfriend as soon as he entered the bar. He liked the idea of taking her while the venom was still so strong in him. He stretched out his arms in a crucifixion pose, his fingers trailing behind him, brushing against skin, cloth, hair, as he began moving like a dark messiah through the crowd, quickly losing count of those whom he touched. For a moment, he found himself in a clear space. He drew a deep breath, his eyes briefly closing, and felt the worm uncoiling deep within his bowels. He released the breath, and opened his eyes.

The bullet hit him in the right shoulder, spinning him into the bar. He saw the female cop in the side entrance hallway, cold air entering through the open door behind her. Her hair was matted with blood and rivulets of red ran down the side of her face. She was almost slumped against the doorjamb, weakened by her injuries and exhausted by the effort it had taken her to get to the bar. Buddy reached under his shirt for the gun he had taken from Lloyd Hopkins as Ellie tried to clear her vision for a second shot. There was no pain from the wound, but the arm of his shirt was soaked in a black, viscous fluid. People were shouting and screaming, trying to put as much space between him and them as possible. Most of them were already on the ground, or seeking cover behind tables and flimsy chairs.

Buddy felt his body changing. It was as though he were

being stretched to bursting by some unseen force. He looked at his hands and saw his pores widening, expanding in size until his skin appeared to be pocked with half-inch-wide holes. They spat black fluid, like miniature volcanoes erupting. He felt more of them appear on his face, and liquid pressure building behind his eyes, increasing the bulge in his sockets and distorting his eyesight. The great worm writhed in his belly, and he felt it shoot tendrils through his system, causing him to spasm in agony. His clothing started to tear as dark nodes pressed upward, bursting through the denim and twisting in the air like newborn eels in clear water.

Buddy's hand found the gun and drew it from his belt. The muzzle of the cop's pistol wavered, then fell as Ellie lost consciousness, her body sliding down the jamb. Buddy aimed, following her progress down. He saw her as a vague blue blur, almost lost amid the blackness encroaching upon his vision. He could kill her now, or use her to relieve some of the great force that threatened to overwhelm him. Buddy dropped the gun, and advanced on the prone cop.

Something tore a hole in the center of his being. A black spray erupted from his chest, dousing the tables and the floor. Buddy was propelled forward, tripping over Ellie's body as his hands scrabbled at the walls to prevent himself from falling. He opened his mouth to scream, aware of the massive shock that his system had endured. There was a great wound in his chest. He touched his fingers to it and thought that he saw at last the black worm, twisting and biting in the corrupted remains of his flesh. Its movements appeared frenzied and tormented, as though it sensed Buddy's end was near and was now intent upon chewing its way out of its host's system before it collapsed entirely.

He turned to see Lopez standing at the bar, the stock of the big shotgun firm against his shoulder. Buddy's mouth was filled with fluid. It coursed down from the corners of his mouth as he spoke, turning his chin dark and losing itself in the hole in his chest. His vision left him, and he felt a great absence within as the link between the worm and himself was abruptly severed.

'No cure,' said Buddy.

He was smiling in his final agonies, his mouth a mass of yellow and black like the half-chewed remains of wasps.

'No cure for cancer.'

Buddy raised his gun blindly, and Lopez blew the top of his head off.

VI

By the time the state police arrived, Buddy Carson's remains had turned to a dark, clotted mass on the floor of Reed's bar, with only his clothes, his boots, and his white straw hat to indicate that this had once been the form of a man.

The snows came the next day, and piles of earth later marred the whiteness of the town cemetery as the bodies were buried. More would follow, as Buddy Carson's victims succumbed to the disease with which he had infected them. Some died quickly, others dragged on for weeks. Nobody lasted longer than one month.

Reed's bar closed. So did the Easton Motel, as Jed followed his son Phil into the ground. People left for new places and the town began to decay, as surely as if Buddy had found a way to taint its buildings and corrode its streets. It was the beginning of the end for Easton. Even Lopez left: he followed the trail of pain and death back to Colorado, and drank a beer with Jerry Schneider, who told him of what he had seen at the Benson farm. He traveled through Wyoming and Idaho, and ended up in Nebraska before the trail ran dry. He returned to New Hampshire and settled down near Nashua with Elaine Olssen, but he never forgot Buddy Carson.

He never forgot the cancer cowboy.

In a desert in western Nevada, a man dressed in cheap denim opens his eyes. He is lying on the sand, and though the sun beats down upon him, his skin has not burned. He cannot remember his name, or how he came to be here. He knows only that he is in pain, and he needs to reach out to someone.

The man rises to his feet, the lizard skin cowboy boots strangely familiar upon his feet, and heads for the highway.

Mr Pettinger's Dæmon

The bishop was a skeletal man, with long, unwrinkled fingers and raised dark veins that ran across his pale skin like tree roots over snowy ground. His head was very bald, tapering to a point at the top of his skull, and his face was either scrupulously clean-shaven, or quite without natural hair of any kind, an outward manifestation of the bishop's apparent subjugation of his sexual appetites. He was dressed entirely in purples and crimsons, apart from the white collar that rested at his neck like a displaced halo. When he stood to greet me, deep reds flowing from the pale sharpness of his head, I was struck by his resemblance to a bloody dagger.

I watched as the fingers of his left hand curled slowly and carefully around the bowl of his pipe, while his right hand gently tamped tobacco into the hollow. There was something almost spiderlike about the way those fingers moved. I didn't like the bishop's fingers, but then, I didn't like the bishop.

We sat at opposite sides of the marble fireplace in his library, the flames in its grate the only source of illumination in the great room until the bishop struck the match in his hand and applied it to his pipe. The action seemed to deepen the sockets of his eyes and gave a yellow aspect to his pupils. I watched him draw upon the stem until I could abide the sucking of his lips no longer, then turned my attention to the volumes upon his shelves. I wondered how many of them the bishop had read. He seemed to me to be the kind of man who distrusted books, wary of the seeds of sedition and independent thought that they might sow in minds less disciplined than his own.

'How have you been, Mr Pettinger?' the bishop asked, when his pipe was lighted to his satisfaction.

I thanked him for his concern and assured him that I was feeling much better. I still had some trouble with my nerves, and at night I twisted in my sleep to the sounds of shelling and the scurrying of rats in the trenches, but there was little point in telling that to the man before me. There were others who had returned in a far worse state of disintegration than I, their bodies ruined, their minds shattered like dropped crystal. Somehow, I had managed to retain all my limbs, and a little of my sanity. I liked to think that it was God that protected me through it all, even when it appeared that He had turned His back upon us and left us to our fate, although sometimes, in my darkest moments, I believed that He had deserted me long ago, if He ever existed at all.

Strange the things that one recalls. There were so many horrors experienced amid the flesh and dirt that to choose one above another seemed almost absurd, as if an ascending graph might somehow be created in which offences against humanity were graded according to their impact on the individual psyche. Yet again and again I came back to a group of soldiers standing against a flat, muddy landscape broken only by the trunk of a single, blasted tree. Some still had blood around their mouths, although so mired in filth were they that it was hard to tell where men ended and mud began. They were found in a shell crater by advancing troops, after a furious battle led to a minute shift in our lines: four British soldiers crouched over the body of a fifth man, their hands working upon him, tearing strips of warm meat from his bones and feeding them greedily into their mouths. The dead soldier was a German, but that hardly mattered. Somehow, this quartet of deserters had contrived to survive for weeks in the no man's land between the two lines by feeding upon the bodies of slain soldiers.

There was no trial, and no record was kept of their execution. Their papers were long gone, and they declined to offer their names before the sentence was carried out. Their leader, or at least the one to whose authority the others most clearly deferred, was in his thirties, the youngest still in his teens. I was permitted to say a few words on their behalf, to beg forgiveness for what they had done. I was standing to one side of them, praying as they were blindfolded, when the eldest one spoke to me.

'I have tasted it,' he said. 'I have eaten the Word made flesh. Now God is in me, and I am God. He tasted good. He tasted of blood.'

Then he turned to face the guns, and they spoke his name.

I am God. I taste of blood.

This, too, I decided not to share with the bishop. I was uncertain of the bishop's views on God. Sometimes, I suspected that he considered the concept of the Lord merely a convenient way of keeping the masses in check while securing his own authority. I doubted if his beliefs had ever been tested beyond the occasional intellectual joust over sherry. How he would have fared in the mud of the trenches, I do not know. I think, perhaps, that he would have survived, but only at the expense of others.

'And how are you finding your time at the hospital?'

As with all of the bishop's utterances, it was important to understand the subtext before one answered. Thus, in reply to the bishop's earlier question, I was tolerably well, even though I was not. Now he was enquiring about the army hospital at Brayton, to which I had been assigned upon my return from the war. I ministered to those who had been deprived of limbs or senses, attempting to ease their pain and to make them understand that God was still with them. And while I was, nominally, a member of the hospital staff, I felt that I was as much a patient there as they were, for I too required pills to help me sleep, and had occasional recourse to the more enlightened of the 'head doctors' in an effort to shore up my fractured sanity.

I had been back in England for six months. All I wanted was some quiet place where I could minister to the needs of my flock, preferably a flock that was not intent upon blowing out the brains of someone else's flock. The bishop had the power to grant me my wish, if he chose to do so. I had no doubt that he was astute enough to sense my dislike of him, although I imagined that my feelings were of little concern to him. If nothing else could be said for the bishop, at least he was not in the habit of allowing his emotions, or the emotions of others, to influence his decisions.

His question still dangled in the air between us. If I told him that I was happy at the hospital, he would transfer me to a more arduous posting. If I told him that I was unhappy at the hospital, I would be there until my dying day.

'I was hoping that you might have found a living for me,' I replied, opting to answer a different question entirely. 'I am anxious to resume parochial work.'

The bishop waved those arachnoid fingers in response. 'In time, Mr Pettinger, in time. We must walk before we can run. First, I require you to comfort an afflicted member of our own flock. You know Chetwyn-Dark, I assume?'

I knew it. Chetwyn-Dark was a small parish, perhaps a mile or two from the southwest coast. One minister, hardly any parishioners, and not the most rewarding of livings, but there had been a church there for a long time.

A very long time.

'Mr Fell currently has responsibility for the parish,' said the bishop. 'Despite possessing many admirable qualities, he has endured his difficulties in the past. Chetwyn-Dark was adjudged to be a suitable place for him to . . . *recuperate*.'

I had heard stories of Mr Fell. His disintegration was rumoured to have been quite spectacular, involving alcoholism, unexplained absences from services, and obscure rantings from the pulpit during those services that he remembered to attend. It was the last that proved to be his undoing, for in making public his difficulties he embarrassed the bishop, and the bishop was a man who prized dignity and decorum above all else. Mr Fell's punishment was to be banished to a living where few would be present to listen to his ravings, although I did not doubt that the bishop retained agents in Chetwyn-Dark who would keep him apprised of the minister's activities.

'I was told that he suffered a crisis of faith,' I said.

The bishop paused before answering. 'He sought proof of that which must be understood through faith alone, and when that proof was not forthcoming he began to doubt everything. In Chetwyn-Dark, it was believed that he might find a place in which to heal his doubts, and to rediscover his love of God.'

The words, I thought, emerged hollowly from the shell of the bishop.

'But it appears that we were wrong to assume that Mr Fell was capable of restoring himself in comparative solitude. I am informed that he has begun to behave even more oddly than usual. He has taken to locking the church, I hear. From the *inside*. He also appears to be engaged in some form of renovation work for which he is temperamentally and vocationally ill suited. His congregation has heard him digging, and hacking at the stones within, although I am told that there are, as yet, no obvious signs of damage to the chapel itself.'

'What would you have me do?' I asked.

'You are practised in the art of dealing with broken men. I have heard good reports of your work at Brayton, reports that lead me to believe that you are perhaps ready to return to more conventional duties. Let this be your first step towards the living for which you ask. I want you to talk to your brother cleric. Comfort him. Try to understand his needs. If necessary, have him committed, but I want this to stop. Do I make myself clear, Mr Pettinger? I want no more trouble from Mr Fell.'

And with that, I was dismissed.

The next day, my replacement arrived at Brayton: a young man named Mr Dean, with the instructions of his tutors still ringing in his ears. After an hour in the wards he retreated to the bathroom. When he eventually emerged his face was considerably paler, and he was wiping his mouth with a handkerchief.

'You'll get used to it,' I assured him, although I knew he would not. After all, I never did.

I wondered how long it would be before the bishop was forced to replace Mr Dean as well.

The train brought me to Evanstowe. From there, a car arranged by the bishop collected me and brought me ten miles west to Chetwyn-Dark, depositing me, after a cursory farewell from the driver, at the entrance to Mr Fell's garden. It was raining and I could smell salt on the air as I walked up the path to the minister's house, the sound of the departing car gradually fading as it returned to Evanstowe. Beyond, accessible by another paved pathway, was the church itself, silhouetted against the evening sky. It stood, not at the centre of the village, but about half a mile beyond it, and there were no other dwellings within sight of it. It had once been a Catholic church, but it was sacked during the reign of Henry and then later claimed for the new faith. Small, and almost primitive in construction, it still retained something of Rome about it.

A light burned in the depths of the house, but when I knocked no one came. I tried the door and it opened easily, revealing a wooden hallway leading to a kitchen straight ahead, with a flight of stairs to the right and a doorway to the left into a living room.

'Mr Fell?' I called, but there was no reply. In the kitchen, some bread lay on a plate covered by a tea-cloth, a jug of buttermilk beside it. Upstairs, both bedrooms were empty. One was tidy, with spare blankets laid out carefully at the base of a newly made bed, but the other bedroom was strewn with clothes and half-eaten food. The sheets upon the bed did not appear to have been laundered in some time, and there was a smell from them, as of an old man's unwashed body. There were cobwebs on the windows, and mouse droppings upon the floor.

Yet it was the writing desk that drew my attention, for it, and what lay upon it, had obviously been the focus of Mr Fell's interest for some time. I cleared some stained shirts from the chair and sat down to examine his labours. Under ordinary circumstances, I would not have intruded upon another man's privacy in such a way, but my duty here was to the bishop, not to Mr Fell. His cause was already lost. I did not want mine to join it.

Three old manuscripts, so yellow and worn that the writing had almost faded away, occupied pride of place at the centre of a storm of papers. The language was Latin, but the script was in no way ornate. Instead it was neat, almost businesslike. At the end, beside an illegible signature, was a darker stain. It looked like old, dried blood.

The documents appeared to be incomplete, with sections

missing or unintelligible, but Mr Fell had made a considerable job of translating what remained. In his neat script he had recorded three extended sections, the first of which related to the foundation of the original church at the end of the last millennium. The second appeared to describe the location of a particular stone formation on the floor, originally marked by a tomb of some kind. Beside it was a rubbing on thin paper, revealing a date – AD 976 – and a simple cross, behind which was a design of some kind. I could make out an eye at either side of the vertical trunk of the cross, and a great mouth segmented by the lower, as though the cross were resting upon the face beneath. Long hair streamed from its skull, and its eyes were huge with fury, but the features were not human. It reminded me of a gargoyle, but the impishness of such creatures was absent, and a grave malevolence appeared in its place.

I turned to the third part of Mr Fell's ongoing work. He had obviously encountered the greatest difficulty with this section. The translation was littered with gaps, or guessed words indicated by question marks, but he had underlined the terms of which he was certain. They included 'entombed' and 'malefic'. But there was one that had been repeated again and again throughout the text, and which Mr Fell had in turn emphasised in his translation.

That word was 'dæmon'.

I left my bag in the second, uncluttered bedroom and looked out of the window. It faced towards the chapel, and there I saw that a light burned. I watched it flicker for a time, then went downstairs and, remembering Mr Fell's reported habit of locking the church, searched until I found a set of dusty keys in a small cabinet. These in hand, I took an umbrella from the stand beside the door and made my way to the house of God.

The front entrance was locked, and through a gap in the

door I could see that a bar had been raised across it from within. I knocked hard and called Mr Fell's name, but there was no reply. I was walking to the rear of the church when, close by the east wall, but low, almost as if it came from beneath the ground, I heard a slight noise. It was the sound of someone tunnelling slowly, inch by inch. And yet, listen though I might, I could not discern the use of any tool. It was as if all the work were being done by hand. I continued quickly to the back door and tried each key in turn until the lock clicked and I found myself standing in an alcove of the chapel, with carved heads on the cornices above me. And as I stood, the sound of digging came again to me.

'Mr Fell?' I called, and I was surprised to find my voice catching in my throat, so that the words came out as almost a croak. I tried again, louder this time.

'Mr Fell?'

The digging from below stopped. I swallowed hard and moved towards a lamp that burned in a nook, my feet echoing softly on the stone floor. Rainwater and sweat mingled upon my face. The moisture tasted like blood upon my tongue.

The first thing I saw was the hole in the floor, beside which stood a second oil lamp, its fuel almost depleted, so that the flame was tiny and flickering. A number of stones had been removed and placed against the wall, leaving a gap big enough for a man to squeeze through. One of the stones, I noticed, was the model for the rubbing on Mr Fell's desk. Now, although the stone was worn, the face behind the cross could be more clearly discerned, and what I had taken to be flowing hair now appeared to be flames and smoke issuing from the features of the creature, so that the cross seemed to be branding it.

The hole itself was dark and dropped gently down, but I thought that I could discern another light deeper within. I was about to call again when the digging resumed, this time with greater urgency, and the sound made me stumble back in fright.

On the floor, the oil lamp was almost sputtering its last. I took the second lamp from the nook and knelt at the opening. I caught the smell that came from within, faint but definite, the stench of waste matter. I took my handkerchief from my pocket and wrapped it around my nose and mouth. Then I sat on the lip of the hole and gently lowered myself down.

The tunnel was narrow and sloped, and I felt myself sliding on stone and loose earth for a few feet, the lamp held low before me in case it might break upon the roof. For a moment, I feared that I might fall into some great chasm, with only darkness around me as I plummeted, never to be found again. Instead, I landed on stone, and found myself in a low tunnel, perhaps only four feet at its highest point, which curved ahead of me and to the right. Behind me, there was only a blank wall.

It was intensely cold in the tunnel. The sound of digging was stronger and more noticeable now, but so too was the smell of excrement. Holding my lamp ahead of me, I walked, crouching along the stone flags of the tunnel, following it as it sloped gently down, ever down. Where old supports had decayed, someone – I guessed that it was Mr Fell – had made improvements, adding new braces to hold the roof.

One support in particular caught my eye: it was larger than the others, and covered in carvings of writhing serpents, with the face of a beast at its highest point, tusks sprouting from either side of a snouted mouth, its eyes hidden beneath a thick, wrinkled brow. The face was reminiscent of that on the marker stone in the chapel, although better preserved and far more detailed in its depiction, for I had noticed no tusks before. Two heavy ropes snaked from either side of the brace, with a knot at each end. When I looked closely, I found them connected to a pair of iron rods hammered into a gap in the stone. The ropes were new, the rods old. From the look of them, if these ropes were pulled then the stones would collapse, taking the brace with them.

And I wondered why this tunnel had ever been built, and why someone had taken the precaution of contriving a mechanism to destroy it if the need arose.

The digging grew closer and closer, the tunnel ever cooler. It was narrower now, and far more difficult to negotiate, but I found myself hurrying, my curiosity briefly overcoming my unease. I was crouched almost double, and the stench was becoming unbearable, when I rounded a corner and my foot touched something soft. I looked down and heard myself moan.

A man lay at my feet, his mouth contorted and his face deathly white. His eyes were open, and there was blood in the corneas, where tiny vessels had burst under some dreadful pressure. His hands were raised slightly, as if to ward off something before him. The clothes of his ministry were tattered and filthy, but I had no doubt that I was in the presence of the late Mr Fell.

When I looked up, I saw what I thought at first was simply a stone wall, but at the centre of the wall was a hole big enough for a man's head to fit through. From behind it came that picking sound, and I knew then what I had been hearing.

It was not Mr Fell digging down, but something else digging up.

I raised the lamp and examined the breach in the wall. At first, I saw nothing: the wall was so thick that my light barely penetrated through the hole. I drew closer, and suddenly there was a gleam from within as the lamp caught a pair of eyes, entirely black, as if the pupils had permanently enlarged themselves over time, desperately seeking light in that dark place. There was a flash of yellow bone as those great tusks were revealed, followed by a hiss, like an exhalation of breath.

Then the image was gone, and a moment later the presence in the chamber struck the wall from behind. I heard it grunting with effort as it retreated and threw itself once more against the barrier. Dust descended upon me from the roof, and I thought I heard some of the stones in the wall shifting.

A claw appeared through the hole. Its fingers were long, impossibly so, and appeared to be jointed at least five or six times. Huge curved nails erupted from the ends, clouded with dirt. A grey scaling covered the bones, and thick, dark hairs protruded from cracks in the skin. It reached for me, and I felt its fury, its malevolence, its searing, desperate intelligence, and its absolute loneliness. It had been imprisoned here in the darkness for so long, until Mr Fell had commenced his translation and begun to explore, moving rock from where it had fallen, clearing debris and restoring braces as he drew closer and closer to the mystery of this place.

The fingers were withdrawn, and the beast hurled itself again at the wall. A fine tracery of cracks shot out from the hole at its centre, like threads on a spider's web. I retreated, backing further and further away from it, until the tunnel grew wide enough so that I felt that I could turn. For a moment, I thought that I had trapped myself in doing so, and found that I could go neither backwards nor forwards. Now the beast was howling, but in between its cries I thought I could discern words, although they were spoken in no language that I had ever heard.

With a final effort that tore my coat sleeve from my arm and ripped open a wound on my skin, I freed myself and ran. I heard stone falling behind me, and I knew that the creature was close to breaking through. Seconds later, my fears were realised, for I discerned the sound of its clawed feet upon the stones as it pursued me through the tunnel. I began to pray and cry at once, so terrified was I. My feet could not move fast enough, and the narrow, curving passageway arrested my pace. I could sense the thing growing nearer, could almost feel its breath on my neck.

I cried out, and considered using my lamp as a weapon, but I feared the thought of being trapped in darkness with the beast, and so I continued to run, never looking back, cutting my skin on the stones and stumbling twice on the uneven ground until I reached, once more, that ornate support, where I turned to face it at last. There came the sound of those talons scraping on the stone, moving faster and faster, as I groped for the ropes, found them, and pulled.

Nothing happened. I heard iron bolts falling, but no more. A clawed hand appeared at the edge of the tunnel, its nails scraping along the stones, and I prepared to die.

But as I closed my eyes, something rumbled above me, and I pushed myself back instinctively. The tunnel shook as the beast advanced, and a shower of rocks fell at my feet. I heard the thing roar, and suddenly it was lost from sight as the ceiling collapsed. Yet I thought that I could still hear it as the rocks descended, howling in rage and frustration as it retreated further and further in its efforts to escape burial beneath tons of rubble.

Then I too was running until at last I was hauling myself up into the blessed calm of the chapel, and dust was belching from the hole, and the sound of stones falling seemed to go on for ever.

* * *

I received my living. It is a small church, an old church. There is sunken ground nearby, and visitors sometimes stop and stare at this unexplained, and recent, phenomenon. Some damage to the floor of the chapel has been repaired and a new, larger stone set in the place where Mr Fell began his excavations. That stone now marks his burial site. I have few parishioners, and fewer duties. I read. I write. I take long walks by the seashore. Sometimes, I brood on Mr Fell, and the great thirst for proof of the existence of the Divine that led him to begin his excavation, as though by finding its opposite he might somehow have banished all of his doubts. I light candles for him, and I pray for his soul.

The documents have been taken away and now, I suspect, they rest in the bishop's safe, or in the care of his superiors. Perhaps their ashes lie in his fireplace, as he tamps tobacco into his pipe and lights its bowl in the darkness of his library. Where they were discovered, and how they came to be in Mr Fell's possession, remains a mystery. Their origins do not matter, and their confiscation does not trouble me. I do not need yellowed paper to recall the creature to mind. It stays with me, and it will always be thus.

For sometimes, when I am in the church alone at night, I believe that I can hear it digging, patiently and intently, moving tiny stone after tiny stone, its progress infinitesimally slow, yet still progress for all that.

It can wait.

After all, it has eternity.

The Erlking

How should I begin this story? Once upon a time, perhaps; but, no, that's not right. That makes it a story of long ago and far away and it's not that kind of story.

It's not that kind of story at all.

Better, then, to begin the tale as I remember it. After all, it is my story: mine to tell, mine in experience. I am old now, but I am not foolish. I still bar the doors and lock the windows at night. I still check in the shadows before I sleep, and give the dogs free roam through the house, for they will smell him if he comes again, and I will be ready for him. The walls are stone, and we keep torches burning. There are always blades to hand, but it is fire that he fears the most.

He will take no one from my house. He will steal no child from under my roof.

My father was not such a careful man. He knew the old stories, for he told them to me when I was a boy: tales of the Sandman, who tears out the eyes of small boys who will not sleep; and Baba Yaga, the demon witch, who rides in a chariot of old bones and rests her palms on the skulls of children; and of Scylla, the sea monster, who drags men into the depths and has an appetite that can never be appeased.

But he never spoke of the Erlking. All that my father would say was that I should not venture into the woods alone, and that I should never stay out beyond nightfall. There were things out there, he would say: wolves, and worse-than-wolves.

There is myth, and there is reality; one we tell, and one we hide. We create monsters, and hope that the lessons wrapped in their tales will serve to guide us when we encounter that which is most terrible in life. We give forged names to our fears, and pray that we may face nothing worse than what we ourselves have created.

We lie to protect our children, and in lying we expose them to the greatest of harms.

Our family lived in a small house, close to the edge of the forest at the northern end of our little village. At night, the moon would drench the trees with silver, relieving the dark expanse of woodland and creating silver spire upon silver spire, receding into the distance like a convergence of churches. Beyond were mountains, and great cities, and lakes as wide as oceans, so that a man might stand on one side and be unable to see land on the other. In my child's mind, I would picture myself passing through the barrier of the woods and into the great realm that they concealed from me. At other times, the trees would promise me shelter from the adult world, a cocoon of wood and leaves in which to hide myself, for such is the lure of dark places for a child.

I would sit at my bedroom window late at night, and listen to the sounds of the forest. I learned to distinguish the hooting of owls, the flapping of bat wings, the panicked scurrying of small things seeking to eat without being consumed in their turn. All of these elements were familiar to me, and they lulled me to sleep. This was my world, and for a time there was nothing in it that was not known to me.

Yet I recall one night when all seemed quiet, when it appeared that everything living in the darkness below had momentarily stifled a breath, and as I listened I sensed a presence moving through the consciousness of the forest, searching, hunting. A wolf howled, a quaver in its tone, and

I could hear the fear communicated in its cry. Within moments, the howl turned to a whine, rising in pitch until it resembled a scream, before it was suddenly cut off forever.

And the wind blew the curtains, as if the woods had at last released their breath.

It seemed that we lived our lives at the very edge of civilisation, aware always that beyond us lay the wildness of the forest. When we played in the schoolyard, our cries hung in the air for a moment then seemed to be sucked beyond the treeline, our childish voices wandering lost between the trees before fading at last into nothingness. But beyond that treeline, a creature waited, and it drew our voices from the air like a hand plucking an apple from a tree, and it devoured us in its mind.

There was a light dusting of snow upon the ground, the earliest fall of winter, when first I saw it. We were playing in a field by the church, chasing a red leather ball that stood out like blood upon the whiteness of the ground. A gust of wind arose where no wind had been before. It carried the ball upon it until it came to rest in a patch of young alders some distance into the forest. Unthinkingly, I followed.

As soon as I passed beyond the first of the great fir trees, the air around me grew colder and the voices of my companions were lost to me. Dark growths of fungus hung upon the shaded sides of the trees, close to the ground. I saw a dead bird lying at the base of one such cluster, its body collapsed in upon itself and seepage from the mushrooms frozen above it in a yellow, glotted mass. There was blood on its beak, and its eyes were tightly closed, as though the bird were lost forever in the remembrance of its final pain.

I moved further into the forest, the imprint of my passing trailing behind me like an unseen rank of lost souls. I parted a cluster of alders and reached for the ball, and as I did so, the wind spoke to me. It said:

'*Boy. Come to me, boy.*'

I looked around, but there was no one near me.

The voice came again, closer now, and in the shadows before me, a figure moved. I thought at first that it was the branch of a tree, so thin and dark was it, its frame wrapped in grey as if spiders had spun a thick skein across it. But the branch reached out, and the twigs of its fingers gathered and beckoned. Waves of strange desire emanated from it. They washed over me like the tides of a polluted sea, leaving me filthy and soiled.

'*Boy. Beautiful boy. Delicate boy. Come, boy, embrace me.*'

I grabbed the ball and backed away, but my foot caught on one of the twisted roots beneath the snow. I fell heavily on my back and a light thread touched my face: it was a gossamer strand of web, strong and sticky, which clung to my hair and seemed to coil around my fingers as I tried to push it away. Then a second fell, and a third, heavier now, like the filaments of a fishing net. Dim light speared through the trees, and thousands of floating strands were revealed. From the shadows where the grey being waited, line upon line of web floated, so that the figure appeared to be disintegrating, shedding itself upon me. I struggled and opened my mouth to cry out, but the threads were falling thickly now and they descended upon my tongue and tangled themselves around it so that I could not speak. The being advanced, silver web heralding its approach, and the mesh seemed to tighten upon me as I moved.

With all the strength that I had, I pushed myself backwards upon the ground and felt the strands catching on the roots, tearing apart and freeing me from their grasp.

Branches scratched my face and snow gathered in my boots as I burst through the treeline, the ball still in my hands.

And as I drew away, that voice came again:

'*Boy. Beautiful Boy.*'

And I knew that it wanted me, and that it would not rest until it had savoured me with its lips.

That night, I could not sleep. I recalled the web, and the voice from the darkness of the forest, and my eyes refused to close. I twisted and turned, but I could find no rest. Despite the cold outside, the room was unbearably warm, so that I was forced to kick the sheet from my body and lie naked upon the bed.

Yet I must have drifted into sleep, for it seemed that something caused my eyes to flicker open, and I found the light in the room was no longer what it had been. There were shadows in the corners where no shadows belonged. They shifted and twisted, but the trees outside remained undisturbed, and the curtains on the windows hung still and unmoving.

And then I heard it: a soft, low voice, like the rustling of dead leaves.

'*Boy.*'

I rose up suddenly, my hands reaching for the sheet to cover my body, but the sheet was gone. I looked around and saw it lying discarded beneath the window. Even in my worst thrashings, I could not have sent it so far from my bed.

'*Boy. Come to me, boy.*'

In that corner, a presence seemed to hover. At first it was almost shapeless, like an old blanket that has begun to rot, and strands of spider-web filigreed themselves upon it. The moonlight illuminated folds of faded, wrinkled skin that hung across its stick-thin arms like old bark. Ivy curled around its limbs and wreathed the thin fingers that now beckoned to me from the shadows. Where its face might have been, there were only dead leaves and darkness – except at its mouth, where small, white teeth glistened.

'*Come to me, boy*,' it repeated. '*Let me hold you*.'

'No,' I said. I curled my legs up before me, trying to make myself as small as possible, to expose to it as little of my body as I could. 'No. Go away.'

At the ends of its fingers, an oval shape glittered. It was a mirror, its frame carefully ornamented, with shapes like dragons chasing each other around its edges.

'*Look, boy: a gift for you, if you let me embrace you*.'

The mirror's face was turned to me and, for an instant, I saw my own face reflected in its surface. For that single, fleeting moment, I was not alone in the mirror's bright reaches. Other faces crowded around mine, tiny faces – tens, hundreds, thousands of them, a whole legion of the lost. Small fists beat at the glass, as if hoping to break through to the other side. And among them, its eyes huge with terror, I saw my own face, and I knew that this was how it could be.

'Please, leave me alone.'

I was trying not to cry, but my cheeks burned and my sight grew misty. The thing hissed, and for the first time I became conscious of the smell, a dense, loamy stench of rotting leaves and still, dank water. A lighter, less foul odour drifted in and out of my senses, curling through the stink of decay like a snake through the undergrowth.

It was the scent of alder.

The stick hand gestured again, and this time a puppet danced at the ends of its fingers: a small infant, carefully carved, so lifelike that it looked like a tiny person, an homunculus, silhouetted against the moonlight. It jerked and danced as the fingers moved, yet I could see no strings controlling its limbs and, when I looked closer, I could discern no joins at its elbows or legs. The creature's arm extended, moving the puppet closer to me, and I could not help but give a little moan of fear when the true dimensions of the marionette became clear.

For it was not a toy, not in any sense that we might mean. It was a human baby, tiny and perfectly formed, with wide, unblinking eyes and dark, ruffled hair. The thing gripped it by the skull, applying pressure to which the child responded by moving its arms and legs in protest. Its mouth was open, but it made no sound, and no tears fell from its eyes. It was dead, it seemed, and yet somehow alive.

'*A beautiful toy*,' said the shadow being, '*for a beautiful boy*.'

I tried to shout out then, but it seemed as though fingers had grasped my tongue and gripped it tightly. I could taste the thing in my mouth, and for the first time in my life I knew what it would be like to die, for the tang of death was upon its skin.

The hand moved in a flash, and the child was gone.

'*Do you know me, boy?*'

I shook my head. Perhaps it was a dream, I thought. Only in dreams were you unable to cry out. Only in dreams could a sheet spring unbidden from a bed.

Only in dreams could a being that smelled of leaves and stagnant water hold a dead child before you and make it dance.

'*I am the Erlking. I have always been, and I will always be. I am the Erlking, and I take what I desire. Would you deny me my desire? Come with me, and I will give you treasures and toys. I will give you sweet things to eat, and I will call you "beloved" until the day you die.*'

From where its eyes should have been, two black butterflies fluttered forth, like tiny mourners at a wake. Then the mouth opened wide, and its knotted fingers reached for me, and something caught in its voice as desire overwhelmed it. The Erlking advanced, and I saw him in all his terrible glory. A cloak of human skins hung upon his shoulders, falling almost to the floor, and in place of ermine it was fringed with scalps, yellow hair and dark hair and red hair all interwoven like the colours of autumn trees. Beneath the cloak lay a silver breastplate, intricately carved with details of naked bodies intertwining, so many of them that it was impossible to tell where one individual began, and another ended. There was a crown of bone upon his head, each tine the remains of a child's finger bound with gold wire, curling inward as though beckoning me to add to their number. And yet I could see no face beneath the crown. All that was visible was that dark mouth with its white teeth: appetite made flesh.

With all the strength of will that I could muster I sprang from my bed and leapt for the door. From behind me came the sound of leaves rustling and branches scraping. I twisted the door handle, but the sweat of my palms made it slippery and treacherous. I fumbled once, then again. The stench of rotting vegetation grew stronger in my nostrils. I let out a little whine of panic, and then the doorknob was turning, my feet were on the passageway, and branches were scraping at my naked back.

I wrenched myself away and, with one twisting motion, pulled the door closed behind me.

I should have run to my father then, but some instinct sent me to the fireplace where the last flickering embers of the fire still remained. I took a stick from the woodpile, wrapped a rag around it, and soaked it in oil from the lamp. I plunged it into the fire and watched as the flames leapt before me. I lifted a hearthrug from the floor and wrapped it around my body. Then, my bare feet slapping softly on the cold flagstones, I made my way back to my room. I listened silently before turning the handle of the door and pushing it open slowly before me.

The room was empty. The only shadows that moved came from the flickering of the flame. I made my way to the corner where the Erlking had stood, but now there were only cobwebs and the drained husks of dead insects. I stood at the window, but the woods beyond were quiet. I pulled the window closed but, as I stretched to do so, I became aware of a pain in my back. I reached behind me, and my fingers came back with blood at the tips. In the small shard of mirror that hung above my jug and bowl, I could see a series of four long slashes across my back.

I thought that I screamed, except that no noise came from my lips. Instead, the scream came from the room where my father and mother both slept, and I followed the sound.

In the sputtering torch light I saw my father at the open window and my mother on her knees beside the overturned cradle where my younger brother slept each night, swaddled in blankets. Now there was no sleeping infant, the blankets were strewn across the floor, and a dense, loamy smell, as of rotting leaves and still waters, hung in the room.

My mother never recovered. She cried and cried, until at last she could cry no more, and then body and spirit surrendered themselves to eternal night. My father grew old and quiet, and the sadness hung about him like a mist. I could not confess to him that I had denied the Erlking, and that he had taken another in my place. I carried the blame inside me, and vowed that I would never let him take another being who was under my protection.

Now I lock the windows and bar the doors to the outside,

and give the dogs free roam of the house. My children's rooms are never locked, so that I can reach them quickly, day or night. And I warn them that if they hear the knocking of branches at their window, they must call me and never, ever open the window themselves. And if they see a bright and shiny object dangling from a tree branch, then they must never reach for it, but should continue on their way, always remaining on the true path. And if they hear a voice offering them sweet things to taste for the promise of an embrace, then they should run and run and never look back.

And, in the light of the fire, I tell them tales of the Sandman, who tears out the eyes of small boys who will not sleep; and of Baba Yaga, the demon witch, who rides in a chariot of old bones and rests her palms on the skulls of children; and of Scylla, who drags sailors into the depths and has an appetite that can never be appeased.

And I tell them of the Erlking, with his arms of bark and ivy, and his soft, rustling voice, and his gifts to trap the unwary, and his appetites which are so much worse than anything they can imagine. I tell them of his desires, so that they will know him in all his forms, and they will be ready for him when he comes.

The New Daughter

In truth, I cannot recall the first time that I noticed the change in her behaviour. She was always developing, altering – or so it seemed – with each passing day. It is the element of being a parent that is most difficult to explain to those without children of their own: the fact that every day brings something new and unexpected, revealing some previously unsuspected facet of their personalities. It is harder still for a father bringing up a daughter alone, for there will always be some part of her hidden from him, unknowable to him. As she grows older, the mystery of her intensifies, and he is forced to rely on love and memories in an effort to remain close to the little girl that was once his own.

Or perhaps I can talk only about myself, and other men have no such fissures in their understanding. After all, I was married once, and thought that I understood the woman who shared my bed, but her dissatisfaction with the life she had made for herself must have been simmering for many years before it revealed itself to me. I was shocked when it emerged, but not as shocked as I might have been. I suppose, looking back, that her discontent must have communicated itself to me in a thousand subtle ways, and that I had already been preparing myself to receive the blow long before it landed.

That makes me sound like a passive element in all that occurred, but I am not, by nature, an aggressive man. I am not even terribly proactive in most matters and, when I look back on the path that led my wife and me to the altar, it was she, not I, who made most of the running. Still, I was prepared to fight her for the children, even though my legal advisers, and my instincts, told me that the courts rarely decided in favour of the father in such cases. To my surprise, my wife decided that the children were a burden that she wished to relinquish, at least for a time. They were very young – Sam was one, Louisa six – and my wife did not feel that she could take advantage of the opportunities she sought in the wider world while carrying two children in her arms. She left them with me, and there was an end to it. She calls them a couple of times each year, and sees them when she passes through the country. Sometimes, she talks about them coming over to join her at some point, but she knows that it will never happen. They are settled, and doing well in their lives. They are – or were – I think, happy.

Sam is gentle and quiet, and likes to stay close to me. Louisa is a more independent spirit, inquisitive and testing of the constraints placed upon her, and as she approaches adolescence, these aspects of her character have become more and more pronounced. And so it may have been that she had already become something different, even before we took the house for the summer. I do not know. All I can say for certain is that I awoke one night to find her standing in the darkness by my bedside, my son asleep beside me. I said to my daughter – or what used to be my daughter: 'Louisa, what's the matter?'

And she replied: 'I'm not Louisa. I am your new daughter.'

But I move ahead of myself. I should explain that this announcement was preceded by some tumultuous months. We moved, abandoning our life in the city for what we hoped would be a more peaceful one in the countryside. We sold our house for what still seems to me an obscene sum of money, and bought an old rectory on five acres by the outskirts of the town of Merrydown. It was a beautiful property, and absurdly underpriced, leaving me with a considerable nest egg with which to provide for our comforts, and for the education of my children. Both Louisa and Sam were due to transfer to new schools anyway, and their friends would be scattered. Neither objected to the prospect of a move and my ex-wife, after the obligatory grumblings, decided to raise no formal objection. In any case, I informed them that nothing was written in stone: we would try it for a time and, if we were not all happy by the end of the trial period, we would return to the city.

The house had five bedrooms, four of them quite substantial in size, so the children were able to claim spaces for themselves far larger than had previously been available to them in the city. Two remained unoccupied, while I took possession of a third to the rear of the house. In addition, there was a large kitchen which overlooked the rear garden, a dining room, a study which I annexed for my own use, and a spacious living area lined with bookshelves. To the right of the house were some old stables. They had not been used in some time, but the faint smell of hay and horses still hung about them. The stables were gloomy and damp and, after a cursory investigation, the children decided that they would provide little scope for play.

It appeared that the rectory had been on the market for some time, although I did not learn why this was so until some months after it was sold. Apparently, it had never provided a good living, and the care of the village's flock now lay with clerics from the larger town of Gravington, who took it in turns to hear services in the old chapel.

An artist, an illustrator of children's stories, had lived in the rectory for a time after the last cleric had departed, but she did not stay very long and had since died in a house fire far to the north. I suspected that she had trouble keeping up the modest rent on the rectory, if the nature of her work was anything to go by. I came across a box of hers amid a heap of rubbish and dead branches at the back of the house. Some attempt had been made to burn the whole pile, but either the fire had not taken or rain had doused it, for the box was wet and the ink had run on many of the drawings. Still, it was clear from what remained that her true vocation probably did not lie in working with material for children. The illustrations were uniformly horrific, I felt, dominated by pale half-human creatures with melted features, their eyes narrow oval slits, their nostrils unusually wide and their mouths agape, as though they relied predominantly on smell and taste for their survival. Some had long tattered wings extending from bony nodes upon their backs, the membranes punctured and torn, like those of dead dragonflies rotting on a spider's web. I kept none of the drawings, for fear that the images might disturb the children if found, and the addition of a little paraffin to the fire ensured that, this time, all was burned.

There was nothing structurally at fault with the rectory itself, and the introduction of new paint and furnishings meant that the previous dark hues and heavy drapes were quickly replaced by summer tones, brightening our surroundings considerably. There were apple trees at the end of the back garden, from which a series of small, sloped fields descended gradually towards a stream overhung by thick green trees. It was good land, but none of the locals appeared anxious to pursue grazing rights upon it for their cattle, despite repeated offers on my part.

The reason for their reluctance could be traced to a mound in the third field, equidistant from our house and the stream. It was perhaps twenty feet in circumference, and a little over six feet in height. Its origins were unclear: some in the village referred to it as a fairy fort, a former dwelling place for some older, mythical race. Others said that it was a burial mound, although it went unmentioned as such in archaeological records of the area and no one appeared to have any idea of who, or what, might be buried beneath it. Louisa liked the idea of having a fairy castle on our land, and so she chose to regard it as such. Frankly, I was happy to do the same, little people being infinitely less troubling to my slumbers than the possibility of large numbers of old bones slowly decaying beneath green grass and daisies. Sam, by contrast, avoided the mound, preferring that we take a circuitous path through adjoining fields rather than pass close by it, while his more adventurous sister took the direct route, frequently choosing to wave at us from her perch upon its topmost point as we passed.

Sam was always a little in awe of his sister and her mercurial qualities, while Louisa in turn remained protective of her brother while simultaneously urging him to be less of a little boy and more of a man. The result was that Sam, against his better judgement, would find himself in awkward, and sometimes painful, situations, from which his sister would have to extricate him. These inevitably ended in tears, recriminations, and a temporary respite from his sister's dares, before slowly she would set to work on him again. There was always something new with which to tempt him, some shiny aspect of herself with which to fascinate him. Once again, perhaps that was why I failed to spot the changes in her, for they took place against a constantly shifting backdrop of moods and humours.

Yet, now that I consider the matter more closely, I do recall an incident two weeks after we arrived. I woke to feel a cool breeze flowing through the house, accompanied by the sound of a window beating against its frame. I left my bed and followed the sound to my daughter's bedroom. She was standing at the window, reaching out to the sill.

'What are you doing?' I asked.

She turned quickly from the window, pulling it closed behind her.

'I thought I heard someone calling to me,' she said.

'Who would be calling to you?' I said.

'The people in the fort,' she replied, but she was smiling as she said it, and I took it for a joke, even as I noticed that she appeared to be concealing something from my view as she climbed back into bed. I went to the window and looked out, but I could see only blackness beyond. On the window-sill itself I spied some fragments of painted wood, torn from the frame close by the lock, but then a wind rose and blew them away into the night.

I returned to Louisa. She had drifted back to sleep almost immediately, as though she were wearied by her efforts, her hands hidden beneath the blankets. There was a leaf caught in her hair, perhaps blown in through the window, and I removed it gently, brushing the rest of her hair away from her brow so that it would not tickle her in her sleep. As I did so, my fingers touched something rough close by her shoulder. Gingerly, I drew back the blanket. Her doll, Molly, which she always kept close to her in bed, was gone. In its place was a rough form made of straw and twigs. It resembled a person, except that its arms were unusually long and its torso was distended, the belly enormous. Six matted strands of woven hair hung from its head. There was a circular hole where its mouth might have been, and oval sockets for eyes. Four dandelion leaves intersected at its back, in a crude imitation of wings.

I saw movement inside the hollow of its abdomen. I looked closer and discerned a large spider trapped beneath the branches and straw. It could not have found its way inside by accident, for the figure was too tightly woven. Instead, whoever was responsible for its construction had deliberately placed the creature within. It probed at the gaps, attempting to escape from its prison. As I removed the figure from my daughter's grasp, the spider seemed to shudder once, then curl in upon itself and die.

I carried the primitive form from my daughter's room and placed it on a shelf in my study, before returning to bed. When I went back to check upon it the next morning, it had fallen to pieces. No trace of its previous form remained, and the spider that had once dwelt within it was now merely a ball of dry, withered limbs.

It was almost midday when I at last had a chance to talk to Louisa about the incident of the night before, but she could recall nothing of our conversation, nor could she tell me where Molly had gone, or how the straw figure came to be in her place. I left her scouring the house for her lost doll. The sky had darkened and the promise of rain hung in the air. Sam was napping, and our housekeeper, a local woman named Mrs Amworth, was keeping one eye on him while working through a pile of ironing. Despite the prospect of the weather changing, I decided to take a walk and found myself, not entirely without design, making my way towards the mound in the third field. Even in bright sunshine it had a vaguely threatening aspect to it; now, beneath lowering skies and grey clouds, it seemed almost to have a palpable consciousness, as though something within were brooding and conspiring. I tried to dismiss the sensation, but Louisa's words from the night before kept returning to me. Her window faced out upon the mound. She could see it in the distance when she stood at the glass. Beyond it lay only the river, and empty fields.

I reached the mound and squatted silently at its base. I laid my hand upon it, the earth warm beneath my palm. I was experiencing no unease now. In fact, quite the opposite:

I found myself relaxing, my eyes closing, the scent of wildflowers and running water filling my nostrils. I wanted to rest, to lie upon the ground and forget my worries, to feel the grass against my skin. I think that I almost began to stretch myself upon it, when an image came unbidden to me. I both saw and felt a presence approaching fast from beneath the mound, ascending along a tunnel of earth and roots, segmenting worms and crushing insects as it came. I glimpsed white skin, as of a creature that had spent too much time away from the light; long-lobed ears that came to sharp points; wide, flattened nostrils beneath slitted depressions where once eyes might have been revealed, now concealed by a layer of veined skin; and a mouth set in a permanent grin, the lower lips drawn down to create a triangle of teeth, flesh and gum. Its ruined, wasted wings were held tight against its body, occasionally flapping tentatively against the earth walls as though desirous of the freedom of flight that had long been denied them.

And it was not alone. Others followed it, ascending towards where I knelt, drawn by my warmth and driven by an anger that I could not comprehend. My eyes snapped open, my mind emerging from its torpor, and I snatched my hand away and threw myself back from the mound. But for a brief moment I felt a disturbance beneath my palm, as though some force had tried to thrust itself through the crust of the earth in order to grasp me to itself.

I rose to my feet and wiped the grass and dirt from my hands. Where my palm had rested only moments before, I now glimpsed a patch of red. Warily, I stabbed at it with a twig. It tumbled down the slope of the mound, a little pile of disturbed earth beneath it exposed by the movement, and came to rest at my feet. It was a doll's head, separated from its body, worms coiling through its thick red hair and beetles scurrying from the hollow of its neck. It was the head of Molly, my daughter's doll, and it was only when the first drops of rain began to strike my face that I found the strength to pick it up and take it home.

Later, I went to Louisa's room and attempted to speak to her, but she grew agitated and tearful, denying with increasing force that she had done anything wrong and appearing genuinely shocked when I showed her the remains of her doll. In fact, she became so distraught at the possibility that Molly was lost beneath the earth that I was forced to remain with her until at last she fell asleep. I myself locked her bedroom window, securing it with a little key that, until now, had remained unused, then deposited the key in my pocket and took it with me to bed once I had ensured that every other entrance to the house was also securely closed.

That night, a great storm arose, and all the windows and doors rattled and shook. I awoke to the sound of Sam crying, and brought him to my bed. I checked on Louisa, but she remained asleep, oblivious of the turmoil without.

The next morning, when I pulled the curtains, the sun shone brightly and there was no sign of any disturbance to the garden or its environs. The lids sat on the dustbins, the leaves remained upon the trees, and the flowerpots on the windowsill had not deviated so much as an inch from their positions.

And in the village, nobody could recall even the slightest breeze arising during the preceding night.

Days went by, and the summer sun grew warmer and warmer. We slept with the thinnest of sheets to cover us, and tossed and turned until tiredness overcame our discomfort and at last brought us rest. On one or two of the hottest nights, I awoke to the sound of a tapping at the glass in the room next door, and found Louisa standing, somewhere between sleeping and waking, scraping at the lock. I would approach her carefully, recalling vague warnings against waking those who walk in their sleep, and guide her gently back to her bed. In the morning, she would have no memory of what might have caused her to rise, and she never again spoke of the people from the fort. But marks began to appear on the outside of the glass: faint, parallel scratches, as though the tines of a large fork had been dragged roughly against it, and more wood was torn from the frame. My dreams were haunted by shadows of flying beings, their long-constricted wings now free once more to beat against the darkness. They surrounded the house, testing doors and windows, frantically trying to gain access to the children within.

Sam no longer went walking with me down to the stream. Instead, he preferred to stay in the house, spending more and more time in his own room, with its window grilles, or in my study which had narrow leaded panes that would open only an inch at the top. When I asked what was troubling him, he declined to say what had caused this change in his behaviour, and it seemed almost that some threat hung over him, requiring silence on all such matters if it were not to be put into action.

Then, one day, I was called away to unavoidable business in London, where I was forced to spend the might. Despite my repeated warnings to her that all windows and doors should remain securely locked at night, Mrs Amworth, who had agreed to stay with the children, left the window in Louisa's bedroom slightly ajar, so that air might flow through her room and give her some comfort.

And whatever dwelt within the mound took the invitation that was offered, and all was altered irrevocably.

* * *

It was Sam who first alerted me to the change in his sister. Previously adoring of her, he now kept himself apart from her, refusing to join in her games and remaining even closer to me than before. One night, after I put him down to sleep, I heard movement in his room and, upon attempting to enter, found my progress impeded by a chair and cushions, and Sam's toy box. When I asked him what he was doing, he at first refused to speak, instead pushing his lower lip out and looking at his feet. But slowly that lip began to tremble, and in the midst of a flood of tears he told me that he was frightened.

'Frightened of what?' I asked.

'Louisa,' he replied.

'But why? She's your sister, Sam. Louisa loves you. She wouldn't do anything to hurt you.'

'She asks me to go outside and play with her,' said Sam.

'You like playing with her,' I said, conscious suddenly that while this might once have been true, it was true no longer.

'At night,' said Sam. 'She wants me to go out and play with her at night. In the dark. *At the fort*,' he added, and then his voice broke altogether and he would not be consoled.

But when I questioned Louisa about her brother's fears, she would answer only that he was lying, and that she had no desire to play with him anyway. When I tried to pursue the matter, she would not reply and I eventually gave up, frustrated and uneasy. In the days that followed, I watched Louisa, noticing now a stillness about her, a wariness. She spoke less and less, and appeared to be losing her appetite. She would eat only the meat on her plate, leaving the vegetables piled to one side. When confronted about any aspect of her behaviour, she simply retreated into silence. There was little that I could do to punish her, and even then

I remained unsure of precisely what I was punishing her for, although one day I found her examining the metal screen that kept Sam from opening his window until he was older, testing the lock with her fingernail. For the first time, I lost my temper with her, demanding to know what she thought she was doing. She did not answer, and tried to slip by me, but I caught her by the shoulders and shook her hard, demanding a reply. I almost struck her, so furious was I at the change in her behaviour, until I looked into her eyes and saw something red flicker in their depths, like a torch suddenly igniting in the darkness of a deep chasm; and it seemed to me, although perhaps I merely imagined it, that her eyes were narrower than before, and now slanted upward slightly at the corners.

'Don't touch me,' she whispered, and there was a hoarse, filthy aspect to her voice. 'Don't you ever touch me again, or you'll be sorry.'

And with that, she wrenched herself from my grasp and ran from the room.

That night, I lay in bed and thought of fire, and recalled again my predecessor's drawings curling to black. I wondered at the manner of her death, and briefly envisaged her, tormented by her imagination, piling picture upon picture in the hearth in the vain hope that their destruction might bring her some peace. Her death was adjudged to have been a tragic accident, but I was not sure. Sometimes, there was only so much that a mind could take before it sought at last a final release from its sufferings.

There is only one further incident that remains untold, and one that frightened me more than any other. Last week, Sam complained about the loss of a toy, a small bear given to him by his mother for his third birthday. It was a mangy thing, with mismatched eyes and thick black stitches where its fur had parted and been inexpertly repaired by his father, but he loved it dearly. Its disappearance was discovered shortly after he awoke, for it always rested on the small table by his bed. I asked Mrs Amworth, who had just arrived, to help with the search, while I went looking for Louisa in order to ask if she had seen the bear. Louisa was not in her room, or in any other part of the house. I went out into the garden, calling after her, but it was only when I reached the orchard that I saw her in the distance, kneeling by the foot of the mound.

I do not know what instinct made me decide not to alert her to my presence. I stayed under cover of the trees to the east until I was close enough to see what she was doing, but as I neared her she rose, cleaned her hands on her dress, and ran back towards the house. I let her go until she had entered the orchard and was lost from sight, then approached the mound.

I suppose that I already knew what I would find. There was a newly dug hole, and as I scraped away the earth I felt fur beneath my fingers. The eyes of the bear stared blankly up at me, even as I pulled it free. There was a ripping sound, and I came away with the head alone. When I dug further for the rest of the bear, it could not be found.

I stepped away from the mound, aware more than ever before of its strangeness: the regularity of its lines, suggesting a plan to its construction; the way it flattened at its peak, as though inviting the careless to rest upon it, to lose themselves against its warmth; and the rich colour of its grass, so much greener than its surroundings that it appeared almost unreal.

I turned around and saw a figure in white standing at the edge of the orchard, watching me, and I no longer knew the girl who used to be my daughter.

* * *

Now I have caught up with myself, and the details are almost entirely known. I am once again lying on my bed, my daughter standing beside me in the darkness, a red cast to her eyes as she says:

'I am your new daughter.'

And I believe her. Close by me, Sam sleeps. I keep him with me every night, even as he asks why I will no longer let him sleep in his own room, like a big boy. Sometimes, I wake him with my dreams, dreams in which my real daughter lies buried beneath a mound of earth, alive yet not alive, surrounded by pale things that have taken her and now keep her close to them, both curious and hateful of her, her cries smothered by the dirt. I have tried digging for her, but I hit stone within inches. Whatever lies under the mound has secured itself well.

'Go away,' I whisper to her.

The red lights flicker briefly as she blinks.

'You can't keep him safe for ever,' the new daughter says.

'You're wrong,' I reply.

'Some night you'll fall asleep with a window open, or a door unlocked,' she whispers. 'Some night you'll be careless, and then you'll have a new son, and I will have a new brother.'

I grasp the bundle of keys tightly in my fist. They hang from my neck, secured by a chain, and they never leave my sight. Only at night are we at risk. Only when the sun has departed do they come, testing the security of our home. I have already put it up for sale, and soon we will leave. Time is pressing, for them and for us.

'No,' I tell her, and I watch as she retreats into a corner and sinks slowly to the floor, the red lights shining in the darkness as unseen figures pull at the windows and the doors and my son, my real son, sleeps softly beside me, safe.

For now.

The Ritual of the Bones

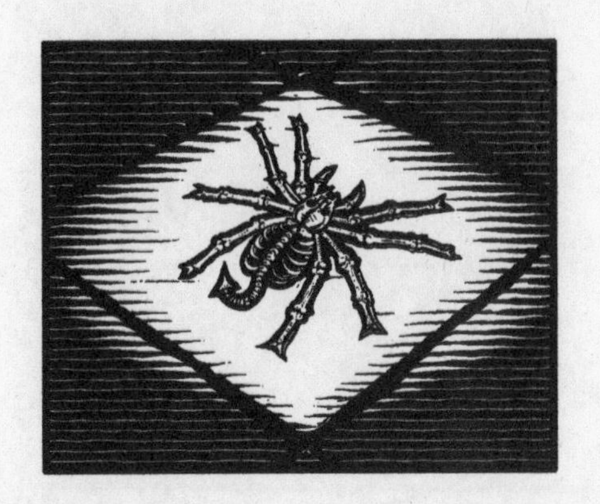

The headmaster's voice was the voice of God. 'You there, Johnston Minor, stop running. Bates, my office, ten AM. Be prepared to explain why you were studying the form on the two-thirty at Kempton during Latin One yesterday. In *Latin*, boy, since you're obviously so adept at the language that you no longer feel obliged to study it. You there, boy, what's your name?'

And, for the first time, or so I thought, I found his attention turned upon me.

'Jenkins, headmaster. The scholarship student.'

'Ah, Jenkins the scholarship student.' He nodded, as if everything had suddenly slotted into place. 'I trust you're not too intimidated by your surroundings, Jenkins the scholarship student.'

'A little, headmaster,' I lied. The Montague School, with its mahogany walls, its elaborate busts, its legions of dead men in powdered wigs staring down from the walls – prime ministers, bankers, captains of industry, diplomats, surgeons, soldiers – was just about the most intimidating place I had ever encountered.

'I shouldn't let it trouble you, Jenkins,' said the headmaster. He placed a hand on my head and briefly ruffled my hair, before cleaning his fingers carefully with a large white handkerchief. 'I feel certain that you're going to make a fine contribution to the Montague School. You know, in many ways, scholarship students are the life-blood of this establishment . . .'

* * *

The Montague School for Boys had been in existence for almost four centuries. So many great men had passed through its portals that it had become almost a microcosm of the Empire, a byword for all that was once great about Britain. It stood amid rolling hills and green playing fields, its buildings elaborate constructions of towers and battlements, as though the school were in a state of constant readiness to repel the great masses envious of the privilege it represented. Its Old Boys' network spread through the upper echelons of British society like a great unseen web, permitting only its favoured sons to trip lightly across its strands on the way to wealth and glory, while trapping those less worthy of ascension and draining them of hope and ambition. Their hollow forms littered the hallways of the Civil Service, the Foreign Office, and the lower echelons of the foremost institutions in the land, an object lesson in the power of good breeding and better connections.

It was surrounded by a vast high wall, and although its great iron gates remained open from early in the morning until late in the evening, few without business at the school dared to venture beyond them. Relations with the natives of the neighbouring villages were strained at best, for the school appeared to evoke feelings of intense dislike among those whose children would never experience the benefits of such an establishment (feelings exacerbated by the knowledge that, in all likelihood, their children would be subject to the whims of some of its graduates in later life, just as they themselves were). As a result, trips to the villages were carefully monitored and supervised by the school, although the older boys were permitted greater latitude in their wanderings and took a perverse pleasure in taunting the local merchants, certain in the knowledge that however much they despised these wealthy interlopers, they could ill afford to turn down their custom.

Still, occasionally groups of local urchins would mount an assault on the school's property, hoping to inflict some minor vandalism on the statuary, or steal apples and pears from the orchard. If they were very lucky, they might encounter an unfortunate student who had drifted too far from the safety of the herd, and a beating would be administered. But this was a risky business, for the grounds were regularly patrolled by porters in night-blue uniforms who meted out their own brand of justice upon those who fell prey to them; and, on at least one occasion, potential marauders had found themselves facing the combined might of the school's First Fifteen, and were fortunate to leave the grounds without medical assistance.

Yet the Montague School appeared to recognise, in some small and infinitely patronising way, a vague duty towards those less fortunate than its fee-paying elite. Every ten years, a scholarship examination was held in the school's Great Hall, and this test, along with a subsequent interview, was used to determine the identities of those lucky few who would be plucked from a life once destined to be littered with disappointment and unhappiness, and instead be allowed to glimpse the possibility of a better future (even if that future was never really on offer, for the ignominious reek of charity would hang about them for the rest of their days, and dirt would forever cling to their boots, leaving a trail behind them so that the wealthy and privileged might not, however briefly, mistake them for their own).

Like all such great institutions, the Montague School had its own unique traditions and rituals. There were particular dress practices to be followed, certain directions in which to walk, and peculiar hierarchies of students and teachers that appeared to have little to do with age or merit. Those with the strongest familial ties to the school were permitted dominion over those with less secure links, and with great wealth came the freedom to inflict pain and humiliation with impunity. There were songs to be learned, and histories to be recited. There were games with no rules, and rules without purpose.

And then there were the bones, and with them went the strangest ritual of all.

That morning, following my first face-to-face encounter with the headmaster, I saw them for the first time. A selection of the final year boys were presented with them at assembly, each one stepping onto the stage in turn to receive a bone locked in a small velvet box. In most cases their fathers had held the bones before them, and their fathers in turn, back, back for hundreds of years. When a family line died out, there was always another great name waiting to take its place, and so possession of the bones remained the preserve of only the bluest of bloodlines. It was an old Montague tradition, this ritual of the bones. When at last the final student received his token, all the boys turned to face their younger fellows and we were permitted – nay, instructed – to cheer loudly three times.

I wondered where the bones had come from, but when I tried to catch more than a glimpse of them as their new owners were proudly displaying them I found myself shunted roughly away, and a sea of backs closed before me, denying me even that small concession. Later that night, as I lay in my dormitory bed, I imagined my father, devoted but impecunious, discovering to his surprise that he was the lost heir to a great fortune, with a title to his name that would eventually be passed on to his son. Overnight, I would find myself elevated to a position of influence and respect in the school. I would perform heroic deeds on the sporting field, and my academic achievements would dwarf those of my peers. As my reward, the school would ignore the submissions of better-known families in order to make up for earlier injustices, and I would take my place on the stage and receive into my hand a small velvet box containing a single, yellowed bone, the symbol of a new life to come.

It was a brief fantasy, driven sharply away by the flicking of a towel at my face and a burst of laughter from the culprits. I knew that there would never be a relic for a scholarship boy, that they were not for the likes of us.

But I was wrong for, in a way, they were all for us.

One week later, I was standing in the rain watching a dispiriting rugby match when a small, untidy-looking boy with dirty blond hair approached me.

'Jenkins, isn't it?' said the boy.

'Yes?' I replied. I tried to sound detached and unconcerned, but secretly I was quite grateful to be approached. I had found it difficult to make friends among the other students. In fact, I had made no friends at all.

'I'm Smethwick, the other scholarship student.' He smiled uneasily. 'I've been a bit ill, so I started term late. Crumbs, it's quite a place, isn't it? So big, and old, but everyone's being jolly kind, even the older boys, and they were the ones who scared me the most.'

For a brief moment, I was jealous of Smethwick. Why had the older boys spoken to him, but not to me?

'Scared you?' I said at last. 'Why?'

'Oh, you know, in case they'd try to bully me. And then there are the stories.'

'The stories?'

'Crikey, Jenkins, you're like an echo. The *stories*. You must have been told some of them? Ten years ago, a scholarship boy died during some kind of prank. It was all hushed up, of course: they said he wandered off and got hit by a passing train, but they say he was dead before the train even left the station.'

Smethwick's face betrayed mingled terror and fascination at the tale. I wasn't sure what to feel. I was finding it hard enough to settle into the routine of life here without adding stories of mysterious deaths to my woes. I had already been regaled with tales of wandering spirits and creatures that lived in the eaves, and on my second day at the school my head was covered with a pillowcase and I was locked in a dark cupboard beneath the stairs until the housemaster heard my cries and finally released me.

'But don't worry.'

Smethwick smiled and patted my shoulder.

'We'll be fine.'

But we were not going to be fine. We were not going to be fine at all.

In the weeks that followed I grew closer to Smethwick, even though we had little in common. It was natural that I should do so, for I was without allies or support in that place, and Smethwick offered both. Yet I found myself distanced from him by the actions of the older boys. It was as though they had chosen to take Smethwick under their wing, for he was not subjected to the same little humiliations and hurts that marked my first months at the school. Instead, they joshed with him and permitted him to run small errands for them, in return for which he was allowed to conduct his business without fear of casual violence. He seemed to become almost a mascot for them, a totem of some kind. I took to staying close to him, in the hope that some of the goodwill directed towards him might extend to me. Smethwick, to his credit, did all that he could to protect me, even to the extent of placing himself between me and those who would have harmed me otherwise. On one such occasion, he received a gash to his forehead that required treatment by the school nurse. The headmaster was called, and although he spent some time with both Smethwick and me in an effort to discover the identities of those responsible, we both remained silent. Nevertheless, the fifth formers who had perpetrated the assault were quickly found, and their punishment was both savage and public as an example to others. The result was that, gradually, I was left in peace, although less out of a regard for my wellbeing than a greater reluctance to cause Smethwick any harm.

Things continued that way for some months. For my part, I neither understood nor trusted the motives of the older boys in taking Smethwick under their wing, but Smethwick himself was too grateful to be suspicious.

When at last they came for him, I believe that he cried as much out of sorrow as dread.

On the night of the ritual, I remember waking as a long line of sixth formers entered our dormitory, some with candles but all holding their little velvet boxes in their hands. They moved silently, and none of the other boys appeared to be awake to see them or, if they were, they chose not to reveal the fact. The sixth formers slapped their hands over Smethwick's mouth so that he couldn't scream, while four or five of them lifted him from his bed. I could see Smethwick thrashing in his pyjamas, his eyes full of fear and panic. Perhaps I should have cried out, but I knew that it would do no good. Perhaps also I should have left Smethwick to his fate and remained content in my ignorance, but I did not. I was anxious to see what they were going to do to him. It pains me to say it, but I was glad that it was him instead of me.

I shadowed the group at a distance, following them down corridors and stairs until they came to an oaken door bound with iron bands that stood open in a corner by the staff common room. I can't say that I remembered ever seeing the door before. Perhaps it had been hidden by a tapestry or a suit of armour, for there were many such relics in the Montague School.

The door was pulled closed behind the boys, but not locked. I opened it gently and felt cool air on my face. Stone steps wound down in front of me. In the quickly fading light from the candles of the group, I descended until I found myself in a huge, cold room with stone walls and a low, vaulted ceiling. There were more candles here, and more figures waiting. I hid in the shadows behind a stone column, and watched.

On a raised stone platform below me stood the male teaching staff of the school. There was Bierce, the games master, and James, who taught Latin and Greek, and Dickens and Burrage and Poe. Before them all stood Mr Lovecraft, the headmaster, dressed in a red tartan night-gown and matching slippers.

'Bring him forward, boys,' said the headmaster. 'Gently now, that's it. Tie him down well, Hyde, we don't want him running off on us, do we? Oh, do stop whimpering, Smethwick. It'll soon be over.'

They tied Smethwick to four iron rings set into the stone slab, binding his arms and his legs tightly with strong rope to each ring. Smethwick was wailing now, but nobody seemed to be paying him much attention and the stone walls simply threw his cries back at him.

'All right, you older boys,' said the headmaster, beckoning them with his right hand. 'Up you come, one at a time. You know what to do.'

The sixth formers stood in an orderly line facing the platform. On the floor beside Smethwick I could make out a pattern, perhaps a foot long and six inches wide, marked in a stone that was darker and older than those surrounding it. It looked like fossil remains, except concave, as if whatever fossil had once been entombed there had been expertly removed, leaving only the impression of what it had once been.

And as I watched, each of the boys stepped forward, opened his little velvet box, and placed his bone in a section of the hollow pattern, filling it bit by bit, until at last the skeletal remains of some kind of insect lay on the floor, although it was like no insect I had ever seen. It seemed to have eight legs, like an spider, but its skeleton was obviously internal, not external. I could see its rib cage and a tiny, pointed skull, and a kind of short, barbed tail that followed a groove in the stone.

The headmaster smiled as the last bone was positioned, then removed a small, ivory-handled knife from the pocket of his dressing gown. 'Hyde, as head prefect, the honour of bleeding Smethwick falls to you.'

Hyde, a dark-haired, smug-looking youth, stepped forward in his brocade gown. He accepted the knife from the headmaster with a small bow, then turned to Smethwick. The cries of the spreadeagled boy rose an octave.

'Please, let me go,' sobbed Smethwick. 'Please, headmaster. I won't tell. Please, please, Hyde, don't hurt me.'

The headmaster shook his head in exasperation. 'For goodness sake, Smethwick, stop whining. Be a man about it. It's no wonder your family never made anything of itself. Hyde's brother died at the Somme, leading a charge of two hundred men. They all died with him, and were grateful for the chance to go out like soldiers behind their beloved captain. Is that not correct, Hyde?'

'Yes, headmaster,' replied Hyde, with the kind of misplaced pride that only the relative of a bloodthirsty lunatic could show.

'You see, Smethwick? Hyde's the kind of chap that other men follow to their deaths. Who'd follow a whiner like you, Smethwick? Nobody, that's who. Who'd vote for you, Smethwick? Not a soul. Would tribes of natives break their ranks and flee in terror from the sight of your sword? No, Smethwick. They'd laugh at you, then cut your head off and stick it on a pole. You are of no value as you are, and you would be of no value in the future. This way, you'll bring a whole new generation of Montagans together. That will be your legacy. Hyde, continue, if you please.'

Hyde leaned over and made a long, deep incision in Smethwick's left arm. Smethwick immediately cried out in pain. Blood flowed quickly from the wound and dripped onto the skeletal remains of the insect-thing below.

And, as I watched, a red membrane began to form over the creature. I saw veins and arteries appear, and a tiny dark heart began to pump blood. The bones on the beast's skeletal legs, which had lain curled over what had once been its abdomen, now bonded and began to twitch, testing the air. A yellow substance flowed over its little skull as the spined tail moved on the stone with a thin, raking sound.

The creature twisted where it lay, then coiled its body in on itself and stretched suddenly, the springing movement ejecting it from its bed and bringing it to rest on the ends of its long, jointed legs. It stood about ten inches tall, the semi-transparent skin on its back a whitish-yellow and sectioned like a caterpillar's. In the candlelight, six round black eyes of varying sizes gleamed at the front of its skull. It raised its head, and I caught a glimpse of a long mouth, perhaps an inch or two in diameter, flanked at either side by small, thick palps.

The headmaster took a careful step back, then raised his left hand like a conjuror displaying his latest illusion.

'Gentlemen,' he said, his voice quavering with pride, 'I give you . . . *the school mascot!*'

There was a round of applause from the assembled boys. On the stone slab, Smethwick's whole body twisted and shook as he tried to wrench his limbs free.

'No, *pleeeaase*,' he pleaded. 'Let me go! I'm sorry for whatever I've done. I'm sorry. What did I do? Tell me! What did I do?'

The headmaster looked at him with what might almost have been pity.

'You, Smethwick, were born into the wrong class.'

Then the creature found at last the source of the blood. Its jaws opened and its mouth expanded and contracted as it swallowed the drops. It tensed its body again, its abdomen lowering until it almost touched the ground, and sprang up onto the slab. I heard Smethwick scream as the thing scuttled across his chest, arched its back and, with a single scorpion thrust, plunged its tail into Smethwick's neck. There was a jet of red which was quickly stopped by the creature's mouth as, slowly, it sucked the life from the boy. I tried to block my ears from the soft, rasping noise that it made, and I felt my gorge rise as its horrid body began to expand, stretching to store the blood of the unfortunate boy dying beneath it.

At last, the thing was sated. It drew away from Smethwick and staggered slowly onto the slab itself. Smethwick lay still, his eyes open and his face pale. There was a round, bloody hole at his throat. His left hand spasmed once, twice, then was still.

Gingerly, the headmaster lifted the beast by its sides and raised it high into the air, its legs flailing gently and blood dripping from its jaws.

'By this ritual of the bones, we are bonded together, all complicit, all united in the great family that is our class,' he declared. 'Generations of men have learned their most valuable lesson from this little creature. The blood of the lower classes is also our life blood: without it, we cannot be great and, if we cannot be great, our country cannot be great. Now, three cheers for the Montague School.'

All the boys shouted 'Hip-hip hooray!' as the headmaster lowered the creature and placed it in a small cage, then handed the cage to Mr Dickens.

'You know what to do, Dickens,' he said, his voice carrying in the echoing chamber. 'In a few days it'll be skin and bone again, then you can disassemble it and put the pieces back into the boxes.'

Mr Dickens held the cage away from his body and stared at its occupant, now drowsy and gorged with blood.

'It is the damnedest thing, isn't it, Head?'

For the first time, what might almost have been disgust showed itself on the headmaster's face.

'Indeed it is: the *damnedest* thing. Hyde, you and two boys take Smethwick here and dispose of him. I suggest a walk along the cliffs, but be sure to weight him down before you drop him off. Now, Mr Bierce will lead the rest of you boys in a chorus of the school song.'

But I didn't wait to hear it. I ran back to my room and packed my bags, and by morning I was gone. My parents were surprised to see me, and wanted to take me back to the school. My father was angrier than my mother, conscious, I think, of the opportunity that I was rejecting, and the future hardships attendant upon this decision. I cried and screamed, even vomiting with distress, until they relented. I think, perhaps, that my mother guessed that something was very wrong, although she never said anything about it and I never told her what I had witnessed. After all, who would have believed me?

And so a letter was sent to Mr Lovecraft announcing my

withdrawal from Montague. A place was found for me at a local school, one to which every child brought with him his own sandwiches and milk, and in which lice were rumoured to be a constant irritant. I was surrounded by those who were like me, and I quickly found my place among them.

One week after my leaving the Montague School, the headmaster came to the house for a visit and a talk. My father was at work. My mother gave him tea and scones, but politely declined to return me to his care.

'We'll be sorry to lose him, Mrs Jenkins,' he said, as he shrugged on his long, blue overcoat. 'He could have made a wonderful contribution to the school. New boys are our life-blood, you know? Will you permit your son to walk me to the gate? I should like to say farewell to him.'

My mother gave me a push in the small of the back and I was compelled to follow the dark form of Mr Lovecraft to the garden gate. He paused on the footpath and looked closely at me.

'As I told your mother, Jenkins, we're sorry to lose you.'

He gripped my shoulder, and, once again, I could feel those fingers working at my flesh.

'But mark my words, Jenkins: in the end, you can't escape your destiny. One way or another, we'll have you.'

He leaned in close to me, so near that I could see tributaries of blood in his eyes.

'Because, Jenkins, like all the members of your sturdy, loyal class, you're full of the stuff that makes Britain great.'

The Furnace Room

The Thibault company once made locomotives and carriages for the railroads, famous names that ran on lines all across the northeast: green cars for Wicasset and Quebec; green and red for Sandy River; yellow and green for Bridgton and Saco. Then the railroads closed down – first the narrow gauge in the forties, then the standard gauge in the fifties – and the trains from Boston no longer made the journey north. Union Station, once the hub of the rail network in that part of the world, had disappeared from the map, to be replaced by an ugly shopping mall. The only reminder of the great trains that had once proudly left the yards were some disused tracks, their sleepers now rotted and overrun by dark weeds. The Thibault company closed its doors, and its buildings fell into disrepair. Windows were shattered, and holes were punched in roofs. Weeds sprouted in the yard, bursting through cracks in the concrete, while the gutters filled with filth and rainwater streaked the walls. Occasionally, there was talk of knocking the whole place down and building something new and impressive there instead, but the city was in decline and no investor could be found who was willing to pump money into the economic equivalent of an open grave. After all, there were malls being constructed on the outskirts of the city, and businesses were abandoning the center of town in favor of covered streets bathed in artificial light, so that elderly walkers could pretend to fend off mortality without being troubled by either the elements or fresh air.

Then, a decade or so ago, the city stopped dying. Someone with an ounce of intelligence and imagination noticed that the port, with its beautiful old buildings and its cobbled streets leading down to the working harbor, was pretty enough to warrant its preservation. True, not every business had closed up shop and headed for the suburbs. There were old bars, and a couple of general stores, even a diner or two. They soon found themselves side-by-side with chi-chi souvenir stores and microbreweries, and pizzerias that offered more than one kind of cheese. There was some whining, of course, and claims that the character of the port had been sacrificed for the tourist dollar, but, truth be told, the old character hadn't been much to write home about to begin with. That kind of nostalgia tends to come from folks who never had to scrape together nickels and dimes to pay the rent on a bar, or who never opened their store and sat there, all the long day, just for a couple of sales and a side order of chit-chat.

Soon, there were visitors on the streets for more than half of every year, and the old port became a curious mix of working fishermen and gawping tourists, of those who remembered the bad times and those for whom there were only good times to come. The developments began to expand beyond the natural boundaries of the old port, and it was decided to reopen the Thibault company yard as a business park. The old red-brick buildings were converted into specialized engineering works, and boatmakers, and a locomotive museum. A narrow gauge railway ran up and down the waterfront from early summer until close to Christmas, when the last of the tourists departed after seeing the city's festive lights. The place wasn't exactly bustling, since the kind of work it attracted was the low-key sort, done indoors and under cover. It was pretty quiet during the day, but even quieter at night, except for the wind that howled across the bay, bringing with it the sound of breaking waves and passing ships, their horns calling through the darkness, a sound that was either reassuring or lonesome depending upon your frame of mind when you heard it.

I don't recall much of how I came to the city. It was a bad time in my life. I didn't care about where I was, or where I was going. I'd done some things that I regretted. I guess most people do, somewhere along the line. It's hard to live any kind of life without building up a store of regrets. The important thing for me was just to keep moving. I thought that if I kept shifting from place to place then I could leave my past behind me. By the time I realized that I was bringing my past right along with me, it was too late to do anything about it.

There wasn't much work on offer when I arrived. The season was almost over, and the casual workers in the restaurants and the bars had already departed for Florida and California, or for the winter resorts in New Hampshire and Vermont. I found a cheap room in a rundown house, and spent my nights looking for two-for-one specials in bars desperate for custom, asking anyone who sat still long enough if they knew of somewhere I might pick up a job. But the people who frequented those kinds of places either didn't much care for work or would take the job themselves if they heard about it first, so I didn't have a lot of luck. After a week, I was getting pretty desperate.

I don't think I would even have found out about the job had I not been walking along the waterfront, smoking a cigarette and wondering if I hadn't made a mistake by coming this far north, but there it was: a handlettered sign covered in plastic to shield it from the rain:

NIGHTWATCHMAN WANTED. APPLY WITHIN.

With nothing else to do, and no other hope for employment on the horizon, I went inside to inquire in the main office about the job. A guy who was sweeping the floors asked my name, then advised me to come back the next morning, when the man in charge would be available to talk to me. I was told to bring along a resumé. I thanked him, but he kept his back to me the whole time. I never even saw his face.

The next morning, I sat in the offices of the Thibault company's administration department and listened as a man in an expensive gray suit explained my duties to me. His name was Mr Rone, but he told me that most folk just called him Charles. He said he used to be in the marine business, and still liked to keep his hand in. Transport, he explained: animals, sometimes, and people. Mostly people.

The nightwatchman's job would require me to patrol the complex, making sure that the vacant premises did not become homes for hobos and junkies, for there were still buildings unoccupied or under development. I was not being paid to sit in a chair and read the sports pages, or snooze. There were no electronic clocks, nothing to monitor my activity, or lack of activity but, if anything went wrong, then it was my ass that would be in a sling, yessir.

'Any questions?' said Charles.

I was confused.

'You mean I have the job, just like that?'

Charles gave me a forty watt smile. 'Sure, you seem like the guy we've been waiting for.'

He hadn't even asked for my resumé. I'd typed it up at the local Kinkos the night before, spending money I couldn't afford to waste. Now, I was feeling a little resentful at having spent my time preparing it. True, it maybe wouldn't stand up much to close examination, and the people included for reference purposes would be harder to track down than dodos, but I'd made the effort.

'I brought a resumé,' I said, and I was kind of surprised at how hurt my voice sounded. Hell, you'd think the guy had refused to hire me, way I was going on.

Charles's smile brightened maybe two watts.

'Hey, that's great,' he said.

I handed it over. He didn't even glance at it, just put it on top of a trayload of papers that looked as if they hadn't been touched since the last locomotive left the building. In fact, it was hard to see precisely what Mr Rone's company actually did. From what I could tell, we were the only people in the entire building.

Still, that was it. I had the job.

They gave me a brown uniform, a flashlight, and a gun. I was told the paperwork for the gun would be sorted out later, and I didn't question them. I didn't imagine that I'd ever have to use it, anyway. The worst that could happen, I thought, was that some kids might try to break in and I'd have to run them off. I figured that I could handle myself against kids. Just in case, I brought my own telescopic baton, and a can of Mace.

Each night, before I went to work, I filled a small flask with Wild Turkey, just to keep out the cold. Don't get me wrong: I'm not a big drinker, and never was, but a north-eastern waterfront gets pretty cold in the winter. When you're wandering around the yards, or checking out those unheated buildings, then there are times when you're pretty glad of something to warm the heart.

I never minded working alone. I'd read some – mystery stories, mainly – or do word puzzles, or watch late night TV. I didn't have a wife to worry about. I used to have a wife, but she's gone now. People think she left me, went to live in Oregon, but I know different.

It was the start of my second week when the noises began. There were two vacant buildings on the site, close by the main road. The larger one was three storys tall, and kind of run-down. The windows were covered with wire screens, so mostly I just checked the locks on the doors to make sure that they hadn't been tampered with, but I'd never gone inside. I'd never had any call to, until then.

I was doing my usual two AM round when I heard the sound of doors opening and closing inside the empty building, and thought I saw the flicker of flames. When I checked the doors and windows, they all seemed to be secure and I could hear no voices from within. I shone my flashlight onto the roof but, as far as I could see, it looked okay. There were no holes, no busted slates through which someone could have squeezed. But those flames were a worry: if some hobo had found a way in, then lit a fire and fallen asleep, the whole place might go up.

I took my keys from my belt and found the one that fitted the main door lock. I'd color-coded them all with Scotch tape, then learned off the colors so I'd know them immediately. The door opened easily and I stepped inside, finding myself in a low-ceilinged room that extended the entire length of the ground floor.

At the end of the room was an open doorway from which stairs ascended to the upper levels, while a single flight led down to the furnace room. The light was coming from there. I slipped the Taurus from its holster and, gun in my right hand, flashlight crossed under it, I headed for the door. I was maybe halfway there when footsteps sounded. A little warning noise was triggered in my head, and I twisted the Maglite to kill the beam while I waited, quietly, in the shadows.

Two people appeared in the doorway. They wore long, black coats over black trousers, and heavy-soled black boots. Their faces were hidden in shadow until they stepped into the warehouse itself. A single dusty bulb burned over the doorway, and its faint light briefly illuminated their forms. They were a man and a woman, but they were all wrong. Both were bald, with pale, almost grey, skulls, crisscrossed with thick veins that bulged against their skin. The man was bigger, with red eyes set into his hairless face, but he had no other features. There was no nose, no mouth, just a flat expanse of skin below those eyes. The woman stood beside him, the shape of her breasts visible beneath her coat. She had a mouth, and a small, button nose, but no eyes, just smooth skin from her hairline to her nose.

From their right came a sound, and two more figures came forward. The first was another tall man, dressed in black like the others. I couldn't see his face, but the back of his skull was perfectly round and pale. There were no ears to be seen. One hand hung by his side, but the other hand rested on the shoulder of a small, thin man wearing a brown shirt and pants. His back was to me, so I couldn't see his face, but there was a wound to his right temple and blood on the left side of his head and on the left shoulder of his shirt, as if a bullet had exited from his left temple.

I should have intervened, but I couldn't move. I was so scared that I forgot to breathe, and when I realized that I was holding my breath I gasped so loudly that I thought they would hear me and come for me too. For an instant, it seemed that the woman paused and tested the shadows, her eyeless gaze resting momentarily where I crouched before moving on. Then her fingers probed at the darkness, searching for the small, bloodied man. Her mouthless companion did the same and, when all three of the figures were touching him, they guided him gently toward the stairs and pulled the door closed behind them. After a moment's pause, I followed them.

The door was unlocked. Behind it were stairs, one flight leading to the upper levels of the warehouse, the other leading down. The furnace in the building shouldn't have been lit, but it was burning now. I could smell it. I could feel it.

And so I descended until I came to an iron doorway, almost rusted away on its hinges. It stood open, and I could see the light of flames flickering within, casting an orange glow on the walls and floor. From within, I could hear the roar of the fire. I moved toward it. There was sweat running down my back, and my palms were slick against the gun and the flashlight. I was almost at the doorway when the fire died, and now there was only the flashlight in my hand to guide me. I breathed deep, then slipped quickly into the doorway.

'Who's –?'

I stopped. The room was empty. Inside, I could see the great furnace, but it was unlit. I walked over to the system and, very gently, reached for it with my hand. I paused before touching it, conscious that if I was mistaken my hand would never be right again.

The furnace was cold.

I made a quick check of the room, but there was nothing else to be seen. It was uncluttered, with but one way in and out. I kept my back to the wall of the stairs, and my gun pointing toward the furnace room, until I reached the main warehouse, then left so quickly that I raised dust from the floor. I spent the rest of the night in my office, with my gun on the desk before me, my senses so heightened that my ears rang.

I didn't say anything to anybody about what I thought I had seen. In fact, when I woke up that afternoon and prepared for another night's work I thought that I might just have imagined it all. Maybe I fell asleep in my chair with one too many nips from the flask under my belt and then just dreamed my way into the warehouse and back to my desk, where I woke up with a memory of mutilated figures taking a small man with a hole in his head down to a furnace room that created heat without burning.

I mean, what other explanation could there be?

Nothing else happened for the rest of that week. I heard no more sounds from the warehouse. I even took the trouble of putting a lock and chain on the elevator door, and checked it twice each night, but it never moved. Still, that smell, the odor of burnt powder, lingered. I could detect it on my uniform and in my hair, and no amount of washing seemed to be able to shake it from me.

Then, one Sunday night, when I was making my usual rounds, I entered the warehouse and found the stairwell doorway gaping. The main door to the building had been closed and locked when I arrived. Nobody had been in or out of there in the past week except me. But now, the door was open and, once again, I could see the light of flames dancing on the walls. I drew my gun and called out:

'Hello, anybody there?'

There was no reply.

'Come out now,' I shouted, sounding braver than I felt. 'You come out now, or I swear I'll lock you in here and call the cops.'

There was still no reply but, in the shadows to my right, a figure moved behind some old crates to the right of the door. I shone the flashlight and caught the edge of something blue as it slipped back into the darkness.

'Dammit, I see you. You come out now, y'hear?'

I swallowed once and the noise of it seemed to echo in my head. Although it was a cold night, there was sweat on my forehead and my upper lip. My shirt was soaked in it. Heat was coming from somewhere; intense, searing heat, as if the whole warehouse were ablaze with some hidden fire.

And I heard the furnace roar.

I kept the gun level with the flashlight as I stepped softly toward the crates. As I drew closer, the light revealed a bare foot, with filthy, twisted toenails and thick, swollen ankles marbled with blue veins. The hem of a dirty blue dress was visible just below the knee. It was a woman, a down-and-out taking shelter in the warehouse. Maybe she had been there all along and I had just never seen her. There must have been another way in and out for her: a busted window, or a concealed door. I'd find it, after I rousted her ass.

'Okay, lady,' I said, as I drew almost level with her, 'out you . . .'

But it wasn't a hobo. Like the old joke goes, it wasn't even a lady.

It was my wife.

Except I wasn't laughing.

Her dark hair had grown, obscuring most of her face, and the mottled skin seemed to have tightened on her bones, drawing back her lips and exposing long, yellow teeth. Her head was down, her chin almost resting on her chest, and she was looking at the wound in her stomach where the knife had entered, the wound I had made on the night I killed her. Then she raised her head and her eyes were revealed: the blue had faded from them, and they were now almost entirely white. The rictus that was her mouth stretched further, and I knew that she was smiling.

'Hi honey,' she said. I could hear the dirt moving in her throat. There was more beneath her broken fingernails, left there as she dug herself out of the shallow grave I had made for her, far to the south where dead leaves would cover her resting place and wild animals would scatter her bones. She moved forward in an awkward shuffle and I backed away from her: one step, then two, until my progress was halted by an obstacle behind me.

I turned my back on her and found myself staring into the pale face of the earless man in the black coat.

'You have to go with him,' said my wife, as the man in the black coat laid his hand upon me. I looked up into his face, for he was taller than me by a foot or more. In fact, he might just have been the tallest man I'd ever met.

'Where am I going?' I asked him, before I realized that he couldn't hear me. I wanted to run, but the pressure of his hand kept me rooted to the spot.

I looked over my shoulder to where my dead wife stood. This had to be a dream, I thought, a bad dream, the all-time worst nightmare I could ever fear to have. But instead of struggling, or crying out, or pinching myself awake, I heard the sound of my own voice speaking calmly.

'Tell me,' I said. 'Tell me where I'm going.'

The dirt in her throat shifted again. 'You're going underground,' she replied.

I tried to move then, but all the strength seemed to have left my body. I couldn't even raise my gun. In the doorway beyond, two figures now stood: the woman without eyes and the man without a mouth. The mouthless figure nodded to the man now holding me, and he began to guide me firmly toward the stairwell, oblivious to my words.

'No,' I said. 'This isn't right.'

But, of course, there was no sound from him, and at last I understood.

Earless, so that he could not hear the pleas of those for whom he came.

Eyeless, so that she could not see those whom she fed to the flames.

And the mute judge, the repository of sins, unable to speak of what he had seen or heard, merely required to nod his assent to the passing of the sentence.

Three demons, each perfect in its mutilation.

My feet were sliding on the dusty floor as I was dragged by the collar toward the waiting flames. I looked to the doorway of the warehouse and saw a man in a gray suit watching me. It was Mr Rone. I cried out to him, but he merely smiled his dim smile and closed the door. From outside, I could hear the sound of his key turning in the lock. I remembered the papers on his desk, old and dusty. I recalled the absence of a secretary, and a man sweeping the floors whose voice, now that I thought of it, might have sounded something like that of Charles Rone himself.

I was nearly at the doorway when I spoke for the last time.

I looked up at the demons standing before me and said simply: 'But I'm not dead.'

And at that moment, I felt my right hand start to raise my gun to my temple and saw, in my head, a small, thin man with blood on his shoulder walking to the stairs. Beside me, I heard my dead wife's voice beside my ear. There was no breath, only sound.

'Let me help you with that,' she whispered. Her hand closed upon mine, pressing my finger against the trigger as she lifted the gun to my skull.

'I'm sorry,' I said.

The sound of the furnace filled my head. Its heat rose through the floor and melted the soles of my shoes. Already, I could smell my hair burning.

'Too late,' she replied.

The gun exploded and the world was shrouded in crimson as I prepared to descend.

The Underbury Witches

Steam and fog swirled together upon the station platform, turning men and women to grey phantoms and creating traps for the unwary out of carelessly positioned cases and chests. The night was growing colder, and a faint sheen of frost could already be detected upon the roof of the ticket office. Through the steamed-up glass of the waiting room figures could faintly be discerned, huddling close to the noisy radiators that reeked of oil and smouldering dust. Some drank tea from cheap cups lined with spidery cracks, sipping urgently as though apprehensive that the crockery might yet disintegrate in their hands and shower them with tepid liquid. Tired children cried in the arms of weary parents. A retired major tried to engage two soldiers in conversation, but the men, new conscripts already fearful of the trenches, were in no mood to talk.

The station master's whistle sounded defiantly in the gloom, his lamp swinging gently high above his head, and the train slowly began to move away, leaving only two other men standing upon the suddenly deserted platform. Had there been anyone to see or to care, it would have become quickly apparent that the new arrivals did not belong in Underbury. They carried heavy bags, and were dressed in city clothes. One, the larger and elder of the two, wore a bowler hat, and a muffler around his mouth and chin. His brown coat was slightly frayed at the sleeves, and his shoes were built for comfort and long life, with few nods to fashion or aesthetics.

His companion was almost as tall as he, but slighter and better dressed. His coat was short and black, and he wore no hat, exposing a mass of dark hair that was a good deal longer than would ordinarily have been considered acceptable in his chosen profession. His eyes were very blue, and he might almost have been called handsome were it not for a curious aspect to his mouth, which curled down slightly at the edges and gave him an air of perpetual disapproval.

'No welcoming committee, then, sir,' said the older man. His name was Arthur Stokes, and he was proud to call himself a sergeant of detectives in what he did not doubt was the greatest police force in the world.

'The locals never like it when they're forced to accept help from London,' said the other policeman. His name was Burke, and he enjoyed the rank of inspector in Scotland Yard, if 'enjoyed' was indeed the right word. Judging by his expression at the moment in question, 'endured' might have been a more appropriate term. 'The arrival of two of us is unlikely to make them doubly grateful.'

They made their way through the station and onto the road beyond, where a man stood waiting beside a battered black car.

'You'll be the gentlemen from London,' he said.

'We are,' said Burke. 'And you would be?'

'My name's Croft. The constable sent me to collect you. He's busy at the moment. Local newspapermen. We've had some of the London boys on to us as well.'

Burke looked puzzled. 'He was told not to make any comment until we arrived,' he said.

Croft reached out to take their bags.

'And how's he supposed to do that, then, if he can't talk to them first to tell them that he can't make no comment?' he asked.

He winked at Burke. Sergeant Stokes had never seen

anyone wink at the inspector before, and he wasn't convinced that Croft was the ideal candidate to be the first.

'Fair point, I suppose, sir,' said Sergeant Stokes hurriedly, then added, for form's sake: 'Don't you think?'

Burke gave his sergeant a look that suggested he thought a great many things, of which few were complimentary towards the present company.

'Whose side are you on, sergeant?'

'The side of law and order, sir,' Burke replied happily. 'The side of law and order.'

The witch panic that gripped Europe for over three hundred years, beginning in the mid-1400s and ending with the death in Switzerland in 1782 of Anna Goldi, the last woman in Western Europe to be executed for witchcraft, claimed the lives of between fifty and one hundred thousand people, of whom eighty per cent were women, most of them old and most of them poor. Such panics were most prevalent in the German lands, which accounted for roughly half of all those killed. Fewer than five hundred died in England, but twice that amount were executed in Scotland, due in no small part to the Scotttish courts' greater tolerance for torture as a means of securing confessions, and the paranoia of its young monarch, James VI.

The most comprehensive guide to the identification, interrogation and, finally, immolation of witches was the Malleus Maleficarum, *the 'Hammer of Witches', co-authored by the German Dominican Heinrich Kramer and Father James Sprenger, the dean of theology at the University of Cologne. Kramer and Sprenger pinpointed the seed of witchcraft in the very nature of the female species. Women were spiritually, intellectually and emotionally weak, and motivated primarily by carnal lust. These fundamental flaws found their most potent expression in witchery.*

The coming of the Reformation did little to undo such beliefs. If anything, any existing tolerance for the so-called 'wise women' of village life was to be stamped out along with all other evidence of old pagan ways, leading Martin Luther himself to declare that they should all be burned as witches.

It would be 1736 before the crime of witchcraft would officially be removed from the books of law in England, almost 120 years after the capture, trial, and execution of the three women known as the Underbury Witches.

Croft drove the two policemen to the heart of the village of Underbury, where they checked into a pair of small but warm rooms at the back of the Vintage Inn. When they had refreshed themselves, and taken some sandwiches, the two policemen were brought to the local undertaker's. Waiting for them were the village doctor, Allinson, and the sole representative of the local constabulary, Constable Waters. Allinson was young, and a recent arrival to Underbury with his family following the death of his uncle, who had previously dealt with the births, illnesses and various manifestations of mortality in the area. Allinson walked with a slight limp, a vestige of childhood polio which had excused him from service in France. Waters, in Burke's view, was a typical village copper: cautious without being careful, and with a modest intelligence that had not yet evolved to the stage of wisdom. All four men stood by while the undertaker, a man seemingly composed entirely of creases and wrinkles, slowly uncovered the body that lay upon his slab.

'We haven't done much with him yet, on account of you gentlemen coming down from London,' he explained. 'Lucky it's been cold, or else he'd be on the turn more than he is already.'

The body revealed to them was that of a man in his early forties, with the bulk of one who laboured in the fields during the day, at the dinner table in the evening, and in the bar at night. His features, or what remained of them, were discoloured, and the men could smell the greater decay already taking place inside him. There were long vertical wounds across his face, and similar injuries on his chest and stomach. The wounds were deep, and penetrated far into his body, so that his innards were clearly visible to them. Rolls of torn intestine extruded from two of the cuts, like the larvae of some dreadful parasite.

'His name was Malcolm Trevors, or "Mal" to most people,' said Waters. 'Single man, no family.'

'Good Lord,' said Stokes. 'It looks as though an animal attacked him.'

Burke nodded to the undertaker, and said he would be called if he was needed. The little man exited quietly, and if he felt any sense of injury at his exclusion he was far too practised in his trade to show it.

Once the door to the embalming room was closed, Burke turned to the doctor. 'You've examined him?'

Allinson shook his head. 'Not fully. I didn't want to interfere with your investigations. I have taken a closer look at those wounds, though.'

'And?'

'If it's the work of an animal, it's like none I've ever seen.'

'We've sent out word to the circuses and fairs in the area,' said Constable Waters. 'We'll soon find out if they've lost one of their beasts.'

Burke nodded, but it was clear that he had little interest in what Waters had just said. His attention remained on Allinson.

'Why do you say that?'

The doctor leaned over the body of the dead man, and pointed to smaller abrasions to the left and right of the main cuts.

'You see these? In the absence of any other evidence, I'd say they were left by thumbs, thumbs with deep nails on the ends of them.'

He raised his hand, curled the fingers slightly as though grasping a ball, then raked them slowly through the air.

'The deep wounds come from the fingers, the ancillary, angled cuts from the thumb,' he continued.

'Couldn't someone have used some kind of farm implement on him?' asked Stokes. The sergeant was London through and through, and his knowledge of agriculture extended no further than washing the dirt from vegetables before cooking them. Nevertheless, he had a pretty fair suspicion that if one were to open up any barn between here and Scotland there would be enough sharp objects contained within to fillet a whole tribe of men such as Trevors.

'It's possible,' said Allinson. 'I'm no expert on farm tools. We may know a little more once I've taken a closer look at the body. With your permission, Inspector, I'd like to open him up. A more detailed examination of the wounds should confirm it.'

But Burke was once again leaning over the body, this time looking at the hands.

'Can you pass me a thin blade?' he asked.

Allinson took a scalpel from his instrument bag, then handed it to the policeman. Burke carefully placed the blade beneath the nail of the dead man's right index finger, and probed.

'Get me something to hold a sample.'

Allinson gave him a small specimen dish, and Burke scraped the residue from beneath the nail into it. He repeated the process with each nail of the right hand, until a small scattering of matter lay upon the dish.

'What is it?' asked Constable Waters.

'Tissue,' answered Allinson. 'Skin, not fur. Very little blood. Hardly any, in fact.'

'He fought back,' said Burke. 'Whoever attacked him should be marked.'

'He'll be long gone, then,' said Waters. 'A man scarred in that way won't hang around to be found out.'

'No, perhaps not,' said Burke. 'Still, it's something. Can you take us to where the body was found?'

'Now?' said Waters.

'No, the morning should do. In this fog, we'll risk trampling on any evidence that hasn't been crushed or lost already. Doctor, when do you think you might complete your examination?'

Allinson removed his jacket and began to roll up his sleeves.

'I'll start straight away, if you like. I should know more by morning.'

Burke looked to his sergeant.

'Right then,' he said. 'We'll be off for now, and we'll see you at nine tomorrow. Thank you, gentlemen.'

And with that, the strangers left.

The village of Underbury numbered barely 500 souls, half of whom lived on small farms some distance from the village itself, with its church, its inn, and its handful of stores, all set near the crossroads that marked Underbury's heart. A visitor might have noted that the central area in which the two roads met was considerably larger than one might have expected. It was perhaps sixty feet across, and was dominated by a raised grass circle upon which no flowers grew. Instead, to alleviate its dullness, a statue had been raised to the Duke of Wellington, although the cheap stone used for its creation had already begun to disintegrate, giving the Duke the physical appearance of one who was slowly succumbing to leprosy, or one of the more unmentionable social diseases.

To understand the nature of the circle at the crossroads required a knowledge of local history of which few visitors could boast. Underbury, once upon a time, was a far more populous place than it now appeared to be, and was, in fact, the commercial hub for this part of the county. A vestige of those former days still remained in the form of the weekly farmers' market held each Saturday in a field on the east side of the village, although in the past (and, indeed, in the present, in places other than Underbury) such markets traditionally took place in the very heart of the village. This practice came to an end in the latter half of the seventeenth century, when Underbury became the focus of the largest single investigation into witchcraft ever undertaken in the British Isles up to that point.

The reasons for the arrival of the witchfinders remain unclear, although an outbreak of illness among some of the children in the village may have provided the initial spur. Five children died in the space of a single week, all of them firstborn males, and suspicion fell upon a trio of women newly arrived in Underbury from parts unknown. The women claimed to be sisters of independent means, formerly resident in Cheapside. The eldest, Ellen Drury, was a midwife, and took over such duties in the village following the sudden drowning of her predecessor, one Grace Polley. Ellen Drury delivered the male children who subsequently passed away, and it was immediately said of her that she had cursed them as they passed from womb to world. Demands for the women's arrest and questioning grew louder, yet the Drury sisters had managed, in their brief time in Underbury, to make themselves popular with many of the local women, due to their facility with various medicines and herbs. It may also have been that the Drury sisters could have been described almost as 'proto-feminists', for they encouraged those who were victims of casual abuse from their husbands and male relatives to make a stand against such acts, and a number of men found their houses surrounded by groups of shouting women, invariably led by Ellen Drury and one or both of her sisters. In fact one resident, a farmer named Brodie, and a vicious man towards his wife and daughters to boot, was so badly beaten as he made his way home through his fields one night that it was thought he would not survive his injuries. Brodie subsequently declined to name his assailants, but gossip in the village intimated that the Drury sisters were abroad that night, and that their walking staffs were ingrained with Brodie's blood. While few wept for the victim of the assault, who was left with a useless right hand and an impediment to his speech as a result of the attack, this was clearly a state of affairs that could not be allowed to continue. The deaths of the children gave the men of the village the excuse that they sought, and a pair of witchfinders was despatched from London on the orders of the king to investigate the occurrences.

There is little that needs to be said about the manner of the witchfinders' enquiries, for their methods have been recorded elsewhere. Suffice it to say that the Drury sisters were sorely tried, along with ten other women from the village, of whom two were married, three very ancient, and one barely twelve years of age. Marks were found upon their bodies – patterns of warts, unexplained folds of skin in their private parts – that were construed as evidence of the women's diabolical nature. The young girl, under threat of torture, admitted to the practice of witchcraft, and claimed that she had seen Ellen Drury prepare the potion that took the lives of the newborn infants. She told her interrogators that the three women were not in fact sisters at all, although she did not know their true names. Finally, she added stories of debauches conducted in the women's cottage, in which she was forced to participate, and of treasons spoken against the Church of England, and even against the king himself. A confession thus secured, the women were presented to the circuit court judges, and sentence was passed.

On 18 November 1628, Ellen Drury and her sisters were hanged to death in the village square at Underbury, and their remains buried in an unmarked plot to the north of the cemetery, just beyond its walls. Their co-defendants were set to suffer the same fate, but the intervention of the king's physician, Sir William Harvey, who was curious about the nature of the 'witch marks' allegedly found upon the bodies of the convicted women, led to their transportation to London, where they were re-examined by the Privy Council, among whose members their fate was subsequently debated at leisure. Five of the prisoners passed away while imprisoned, and ten years went by before the survivors were quietly released to spend their final years in poverty and ignominy.

Ellen Drury was the last to die on the gallows. Even in her final agonies it was said of her that her eyes remained fixed on her tormentors, unblinking, until a relative of the unfortunate Brodie threw pitch upon her and set her alight, whereupon her eyes exploded in their sockets and her world went dark.

Dr Allinson worked into the early hours, examining the wounds left upon the body of Mal Trevors. The largest of them, as he later told Burke and Stokes over breakfast at the inn, extended internally from the man's belly all the way to his heart, which had been pierced in five places by long claws or nails. At this point, Sergeant Stokes briefly lost his appetite for his bacon.

'Are you telling us that a hand was pushed up through this man's body?' asked Burke.

'It would appear so,' replied the doctor. 'I inspected him closely in the hope that I might find a fragment of nail but none was forthcoming, which I find surprising under the circumstances. It is no easy thing to tear apart a man's insides in such a way, and some shattering would have been expected. It leads me to suspect that either the nails of the hand were unusually strong, or that the fingers had been artificially enhanced in some way, perhaps by the addition of metal talons which could be strapped on or removed as needed.'

The doctor could add nothing more to the sum of their knowledge, and retired to his bed at the behest of his wife, who had arrived to do a little shopping and encourage her exhausted husband to return home. She was a woman of striking looks, a tall blonde with flawed green eyes that caught the light as though they were emeralds inset with fragments of diamond. Her name was Emily, and Burke exchanged only a few words with her as he escorted her husband to the door.

'Thank you for your help,' he said, as Allinson buttoned his coat at the door of the inn, his wife remaining inside to exchange some pleasantries with the innkeeper's daughter.

'I'm sorry that I could not be of more assistance,' said Allinson. 'Nevertheless, it is most intriguing, in a dreadful way, and I should like to take one more look at Trevors later before we leave him to the gentle ministrations of the undertaker. It may be that, in my exhaustion, I missed some detail that could prove useful.'

Burke assented, then stepped aside in order to allow Mrs Allinson to pass.

And a most curious thing happened.

Directly across from Burke was a mirror, advertising some brand of whisky with which the policeman was unfamiliar. He could see himself reflected clearly in its surface, and, as she passed, so too was Emily Allinson, but through some distortion in the glass it appeared as though her reflection moved more slowly than she did, and Burke almost believed that it seemed to turn its face towards him even though the original stared fixedly ahead. That face, for an instant, was not that of Emily Allinson. Elongated and ruined, its mouth gaped and its face was grotesquely charred in places, the eyes like cinders in their sockets. Then Mrs Allinson stepped outside with her husband and the vision was gone. Burke stepped closer to the mirror and saw that it was deeply tarnished, as such cheap advertising tools tend to become. Its surface was mottled and uneven, so that even his own face shimmered and buckled like an image in a carnival tent. Yet he remained unsettled, even as he watched Mrs Allinson escort her husband down the street, the doctor seeming almost to lean into her for support as they went. There were few males under the age of fifty wandering through Underbury that morning, although this was by no means unusual. Most towns and villages were now sorely depleted of their stock of young men, and Burke had no doubt that when the present hostilities came to an end it would still be many years before places like Underbury found some balance restored between the sexes.

Burke returned to his sergeant, but he allowed the remainder of his breakfast to go cold and untouched.

'Anything wrong, sir?' asked Stokes, who had rapidly regained his appetite with the departure of the doctor.

'Just tiredness,' replied Burke.

Stokes nodded, and finished off the runny yolk with a swipe of his toast. It was a good breakfast, he thought; maybe not as good as the breakfasts Mrs Stokes cooked up for him, but very satisfying none the less. His good lady wife often offered the view that Inspector Burke could do with a little fattening up, but Burke was not one to accept invitations to dinner. In any event, Stokes understood that by 'fattening up' his wife meant that Burke should be married, with a good strong table beneath which he could rest his feet while a woman fed him cooked meals, but Inspector Burke appeared to have little time for women. He lived alone with his books and his cat, and while he was always courteous in his dealings with ladies, even with those for whom the term 'ladies' usually came with the appendage 'of the night', he remained distant, and even slightly uncomfortable, in female company. Such an existence would have proved insufferably lonely for Stokes, who fitted easily into the company of both sexes, but police work had made him conscious of the differences between people, and the complexity that lay beneath even the most apparently mundane of lives. Besides, he felt a great admiration, and even a fondness, for the inspector, who was a very good copper indeed. Stokes was proud to serve alongside him, and his private life was a matter for himself and no one else.

Burke stood and removed his coat from a hook on the wall.

'I think we need a little air,' he said. 'It's time to see where Mal Trevors died.'

Burke and Stokes stood at one side of the post, Constable Waters at the other. It was still possible to discern traces of the victim's blood upon the wood, and fragments of his jacket sleeve were caught in the barbs of the wire that formed a fence marking the verge of the property on which they stood. Beyond lay barren ground, then the low wall surrounding the church and the village cemetery.

'He was found against the post, his sleeves hanging from the wire,' said Waters. 'Poor beggar,' he added.

'Who found him?' asked Stokes.

'Fred Paxton. He remembered Trevors leaving the pub shortly before ten, and he followed about an hour later.'

'Did he touch the body?'

'No call to. Didn't need letters after his name to tell that he was dead.'

'We'll have to talk to Paxton.'

Waters proudly drew himself up a little.

'Thought you might say that. He and his missus live not half a mile up the road, and I told them to expect us this morning.'

Burke would happily have flayed Waters with the fence wire had he not taken this simple step, but the detective allowed the village policeman a muted 'Well done, Constable', which seemed to content Waters.

'Did you search the area?' Burke resumed.

'I did.'

Burke waited. Trevors was crossing the field when he was attacked, and it was a cold night. The temperature had not risen much since; in fact, if anything it had fallen. Burke could see his footsteps and those of his companions receding towards the road. Whoever attacked Trevors must have left some sign upon the grass.

'Well?'

'There were only two sets of footprints: Mal Trevors's, and Fred Paxton's. I tried to keep people away from the body, once I'd seen what had been done to it, so there wasn't as much disturbance as you might think.'

'Perhaps he was attacked on the road,' said Stokes, 'then attempted to escape across the fields and died on the fence when he could go no further.'

'Don't think so,' said Waters. 'There was no blood in the field between the road and the fence. I checked.'

Burke knelt and examined the ground at the base of the

post. There was still a great deal of dried blood visible upon the blades of grass. If what Waters said was true, and even Burke was forced grudgingly to acknowledge a certain level of competence on the part of the village copper, then Waters had been attacked on this spot, and had died here.

'Something must have been missed,' he said at last. 'No disrespect to you, Constable, but whoever killed Trevors didn't materialise out of thin air. We'll go over the ground on either side of the fence, inch by inch. There has to be some trail.'

Waters nodded his assent, and the three men spread out from the death post, Burke moving towards the cemetery, Stokes towards the road, and Waters in the direction of a cottage some way distant, which was, he informed the detectives, the home of the Paxtons. The policemen searched for an hour, until the cold had burrowed into their hands and feet, yet found nothing. It seemed that Mal Trevors had been attacked, quite literally, from out of nowhere.

Burke finished his examination of the ground and sat upon the low cemetery wall, watching his fellow policemen as they moved across the field, Stokes bent over slightly, his hands in his pockets, Waters less careful, but still doing his best. In his heart, Burke knew that it was a futile yet necessary effort. To have made a proper search would have required more men, and men were scarce, but then he remained unconvinced that anything would be found. Still, it made no sense to him that a big man like Trevors could be savagely murdered with no sign of a struggle.

He took a handkerchief from his pocket and wiped it over his face. He was sweating profusely, his brow was hot, and he was starting to feel a little ill. It's this place, he thought: it saps one's energy. He recalled Dr Allinson walking down the main street, virtually propped against his wife, and the earlier lassitude of Constable Waters, which seemed to have been arrested somewhat by the arrival of new blood in the form of the two London policemen. Underbury was a village emptied of its most virile men, all of whom were now fighting in foreign fields. Those that remained must have been aware of their status as flawed bodies, unsuited for combat or sacrifice, and that awareness hung like a miasma over their lives. Now Burke was feeling it too. If he stayed here too long, perhaps he also would end up like Allinson, exhausted after a few hours labour, for the doctor told him that he had retired to bed shortly after one in the morning. He had therefore rested for some six hours, but at breakfast Burke would have sworn that the man had not enjoyed sleep in many months.

Burke slipped down from his perch and went to rejoin his colleagues. As he did so, his foot struck stone. He stepped back, then knelt down and brushed the tips of his fingers along the ground. There was a slab there, almost entirely covered by long grass and weeds. The vegetation came away easily as Burke pulled at it, for some of it had merely fallen across the stone, or had been placed there to conceal it. There was no inscription upon it, but Burke knew its purpose. This was an old community, and he did not doubt that in times past the bodies of suicides, of unbaptised children, and of gallows fodder had been interred outside the walls of the cemetery. It was common practice, although it was rare to see a marker of any kind upon such graves.

Now, as he looked at the ground from this low angle, he could see two other similar raised slabs nearby. When he examined them, he discovered that the stone on one had been broken recently. Someone had taken a hammer and chisel to it, fragmenting the rock into a number of pieces and leaving a hole as big as Burke's fist at the centre. Burke leaned forward and slipped two fingers into the gap, expecting to touch earth below. Instead, there was only emptiness. He tried a similar experiment using his pen tied to a piece of thread from his coat, and again felt the instrument dangle in the space beneath the stone.

Curious, he thought.

He stood and saw Stokes and Waters watching him from the road. There was nothing more to be learned by the cemetery wall, so he joined them and made no argument when Waters suggested that now might be the time to talk to the Paxtons, and perhaps take some tea for their trouble.

'What kind of man was Trevors?' Burke asked Waters, as they made their way along the road.

The constable made a noise somewhere between a cough and a sigh.

'I didn't care much for him myself,' he said. 'He served time in a prison up north for assault, then came back down here when he was released and lived with his father until the old man died. After that, it was just him alone on that farm.'

'And the mother?'

'Died when Mal was a boy. Her husband used to beat her, but she never made a complaint. Constable Stewart, my predecessor, he tried talking to her, and to her husband, but nothing ever came of it. I reckon Mal picked up some of his old man's bad habits, because he was jailed for beating up a, well, you'll forgive me, sir, but a prostitute in Manchester. Near killed her, from what I hear. When he came back here, he took up with a woman named Elsie Warden, but she soon gave him a wide berth when he fell back into his old ways with her. There was an incident about a week ago, when he came to her house in the night and demanded to speak to her, but her father and younger brothers sent him on his way. They'd already given him a taste of his own medicine once, and he didn't fancy another spoonful.'

Burke and Stokes exchanged a look.

'Could the Wardens be suspects?'

'They were all in the bar when Trevors left, and they were still there when Fred Paxton came back with news of what he'd found. They never left. Even Elsie was with them. They're in the clear, as far as this is concerned.'

Waters reached into his pocket, withdrew a folded sheet of paper, and handed it to Burke.

'Thought you might want this. It's a list of all the people who were in the bar that night. A star marks the ones who were there from the time Trevors left until the time the Paxtons returned.'

Burke took the list and read it. One name caught his eye.

'Mrs Allinson was there that night?'

'And her husband. Saturday night's the big night in the village. Most people find their way to the inn, sooner or later.'

Emily Allinson's name was one of those marked with a star.

'And she never left,' he said, so quietly that nobody heard him utter the words.

The Paxtons, a young couple without children, were both relative newcomers to the area. Fred was born about twenty miles west of Underbury, and after a period of city living decided that it was time to return to the countryside with his wife. The land at Underbury had cost them comparatively little, and they were now raising cattle and hoping for a good crop of vegetables to sell in the coming year. They fed the detectives bread and cheese, and brewed up a pot of tea large enough to feed a field of labourers.

'I remember I was walking along, my mind on getting home, and I just happened to look to my right,' said Fred Paxton. His left eye was yellowy white, with tendrils of red criss-crossing upon it. It brought back to Burke an image from his childhood: a visit to his uncle's farm on the outskirts of the city, where his father had drunk milk fresh from the cow and the boy had seen blood in the creamy liquid.

'There was a shape draped across the fence,' Paxton continued. 'It looked like a scarecrow, but there's no scarecrow on that land. I climbed the gate and went to have a look-see. I never seen so much blood. I felt it under my boots. I'd say Mal hadn't been dead more than a couple of minutes when I found him.'

'Why do you say that?' asked Stokes.

'His innards were steaming,' replied Paxton, simply.

'What did you do then?' said Burke.

'I went back to the village, fast as I could. Ran into the pub and told old Ken the barman to send for the constable here. I think some people might have been on their way to take a look at the body for themselves, soon as they heard, but as it happened the constable was passing when they came out and he went with them.'

'And you also went back, I presume?' said Stokes.

'I did. When all was done, I went home to the missus here and told her what had happened.'

Burke turned his attention to the young woman seated to his left. Mrs Paxton had spoken barely five words since their arrival. She was a slight thing, with dark hair and large blue eyes. Burke supposed that she might even have been termed beautiful.

'Is there anything you can add to what your husband has told us, Mrs Paxton?' he asked her. 'Did you hear or see anything that night that might help us?'

Her voice was so low that Burke had to lean forward to hear what she was saying.

'I was asleep in bed when Fred came in,' she said. 'When he told me it was Mal Trevors, well, I just felt something turn inside me. It was terrible.'

She excused herself and rose from the table. Burke watched her go, then caught himself doing so and returned his attention to the men around him.

'Do you remember how the people in the inn responded when you told them the news?' he asked Paxton.

'Shocked, I suppose,' he said.

'Was Elsie Warden shocked?'

'Well, she was later, when she found out,' said Paxton.

'Later?'

'Dr Allinson said that Elsie'd taken ill not long before I returned. His wife was looking after her in old Ken's kitchen.'

Burke asked if he might use the toilet, so that he could have a little privacy in which to consider what he had learned. Fred Paxton told him the facilities were outside, and offered to show him, but Burke assured him that he would be able to find them alone. He walked through the kitchen, found the privy, and relieved himself while he thought. When he went back outside, Mrs Paxton was standing at the kitchen window. Her upper body was bare and she was washing herself with a cloth from the sink. She stopped when she saw him, then lowered her right hand so that her breasts were exposed to him. Her body was very white. Burke looked at her for just a second longer, then slowly she turned away, her back a pale expanse against the shadows, and disappeared from view. Burke skirted the side of the house, returning to the main room through the front door. Upon his return, Waters and Stokes stood and the four men walked together into the front yard. Paxton spoke to the constable about local matters, and Stokes ambled onto the road, taking the air. Suddenly, Burke found Mrs Paxton by his side.

'I'm sorry,' he said. 'I didn't mean to embarrass you.'

She blushed slightly, but Burke felt that the only real embarrassment was his own.

'It wasn't your fault,' she said.

'I do have just one other question,' he said to her.

She waited.

'Did you like Mal Trevors?'

It took a moment for the answer to come.

'No, sir,' she said eventually. 'I did not.'

'May I ask why?'

'He was a brute of a man, and I saw the way he looked at me. Our land adjoined his, and I made a point never to be alone in the fields when he was around.'

'Did you tell your husband of this?'

'No, but he knew how I felt, right enough.'

She stopped talking suddenly, conscious that she might have said something to incriminate her Fred, but Burke reassured her.

'It's all right, Mrs Paxton. Neither you nor your husband is a suspect here.'

She remained suspicious of him, though.

'So you say.'

'Listen to me. Whoever killed Mal Trevors would have been covered in blood after what was done to him. I hardly think that description applied to your husband that night, did it?'

'No,' she replied. 'I see what you mean. I don't think Fred has it in him to kill Mal Trevors, or to kill anyone, come to that. He's a good man.'

'But you felt distressed at Trevors's death, despite what you felt about him,' said Burke.

Again, there was a pause before the reply came. Burke could see her husband over her shoulder, no longer distracted by Waters but now coming to his wife's aid. There was little time left.

'I wished that he was dead,' said Mrs Paxton softly. 'The day before he died, he brushed against me when we were in

Mr Little's store together. He did it deliberately, and I felt him push into me. I felt his . . . *thing*. He was a pig, and I was tired of being afraid to walk in our own fields. So, for a moment, I wished him dead, and then a day later he was dead. I suppose I wondered . . .'

'If somehow you might have caused his death?'

'Yes.'

Fred Paxton was now beside them.

'Is everything all right, love?' he asked, placing a protective arm around his wife's shoulders.

'Everything's fine, now,' she said.

She smiled at her husband, but it was to reassure him rather than to express any real emotion on her own part, and Burke caught a glimpse of the real power behind their marriage, the strength hidden inside this small, pretty woman.

And he felt a surge of unease.

Everything's fine.

Everything's fine now that Mal Trevors is dead.

Sometimes, you do get what you wish for, don't you, my love?

By now it was growing dark. Stokes remarked that winter seemed to be extending its reach far into February, for although the winter solstice had long since passed, daylight was in short supply in Underbury and its surrounds. Constable Waters counselled the detectives against visiting the Warden family after dusk – 'They're an uneasy lot, and like as not the old man will have a shotgun in his hand to greet visitors at this hour' – and so the policemen returned to the village, where Stokes and Burke ate stew together in one corner of the inn, untroubled by enquiries after their health. Burke announced that he wished to visit Dr Allinson, and politely declined his sergeant's offer of company on the road. He wished to have some time alone, and although Stokes generally knew when to keep quiet in the presence of the inspector, Burke nevertheless found the presence of others distracting when he was trying to think. He secured a lamp from the innkeeper and then, once the directions offered were clear in his head, he took to the road and walked to the Allinsons' house, which lay about one mile north of the village. It was a starless night, and Burke was oppressed by unseen clouds.

All of the windows were dark when he arrived at the house, save one at the very highest eave. He knocked loudly and waited, expecting a housekeeper to open the door. Instead, after some minutes, and to his surprise, the lady of the house herself greeted him.

Mrs Allinson wore a very formal blue dress that extended from her ankles to her neck, where it ended in a faint ruffle beneath her chin. It was somewhat dated to Burke's eye, but she carried it off with aplomb, aided by her height and her fine features, not least of which were the flawed green eyes now regarding Burke with polite inquiry and, he felt, not a little amusement.

'Inspector Burke, this is a surprise,' she said. 'My husband had not told me to expect you.'

'I regret any imposition,' said Burke, 'I take it that your husband is not at home?'

Mrs Allinson stepped back and invited the policeman inside. After an almost imperceptible pause, Burke accepted the invitation and followed her into the drawing room, once Mrs Allinson had illuminated the lamps.

'I'm afraid he was called out suddenly. Such are the duties of a village physician. He shouldn't be very long. May I offer you tea?'

Burke declined.

'I rather expected you to have a housekeeper, or a servant

of some sort,' he said, as Mrs Allinson took a seat on a couch and waved him towards an easy chair.

'I gave her the night off,' said Mrs Allinson. 'Her name is Elsie Warden. She's a local girl. Have you met Elsie, Inspector?'

Burke replied that he had not yet had that pleasure.

'You'll like her,' said Mrs Allinson. 'A lot of men seem to like Elsie.'

Once again, Burke was aware of Mrs Allinson's distant amusement, an amusement that he believed she felt at his expense, although he was unable to guess why that might be so.

'I understand you were with her on the night Mal Trevors died.'

Mrs Allinson raised her left eyebrow slowly, an action followed closely by the hint of a smile on the left side of her mouth, as though a wire extended from eye to jaw, linking their movements.

'I was "with" my husband, Inspector,' she replied.

'Do you usually spend your Saturday nights at the village inn?'

'You sound almost disapproving, Inspector. Don't you believe that ladies should socialise with their husbands? Doesn't your good lady accompany you on the occasional evening?'

'I'm not married.'

'That is a shame,' said Mrs Allinson. 'I believe that a wife tames a man wonderfully. A good woman, like the alchemists of old, can make gold from the lead of most men.'

'Except the alchemists failed in their efforts,' said Burke. 'Lead remained lead. I expect the late Mal Trevors might have been construed as a man of lead, don't you think?'

'Mal Trevors was corrupted metal,' said Mrs. Allinson dismissively. 'In my view, he is of more benefit to the earth now that he lies beneath it than he ever was when he walked upon it. Now, at least, he will provide food for worms and nourishment for plants. Poor eating, admittedly, but sustenance for all that.'

Burke did not remark upon this display of feeling.

'It appears that few people have a good word to say about the late Mr Trevors', he said. 'I expect it will be a short eulogy.'

'I believe "succinct" is the word, and any eulogy would be more than he deserves. Do you have any theories yet on how he might have died? They talk in the village of a wild animal, although my husband scoffs at the possibility.'

'We are keeping an open mind on the subject,' said Burke. 'Nevertheless, we appear to have become sidetracked from the subject of Miss Elsie Warden. My understanding is that she was taken ill on the night that Mal Trevors died.'

'She had a moment of weakness,' admitted Mrs Allinson. 'I took care of her as best I could'

'May I ask the cause?'

'You may ask Elsie Warden, if you choose. It's not my place to tell you such details.'

'I thought it was only doctors who took the Hippocratic Oath?'

'Women have their oaths too, Inspector, and I doubt if even Hippocrates himself could rival them for their fastness, when they choose to be silent. I am curious, though, as to who it was that spoke to you of Elsie Warden's illness.'

'I'm afraid I can't say,' replied Burke. 'Policemen, too, have their secrets.'

'Never mind,' said Mrs Allinson. 'I expect I will find out soon enough.'

'Elsie Warden clearly trusts you a great deal, for one so recently arrived in the village.'

Mrs Allinson tilted her head slightly and regarded Burke

with renewed interest, rather like a cat that suddenly finds the mouse with which it is toying making an unexpected but ultimately doomed break for freedom, all the while with its tail pinned firmly beneath the feline's paw.

'Elsie is a strong young woman,' answered Mrs Allinson, with what Burke construed as a degree more caution than she had previously exercised. 'This is not a village known for its tolerance of strong women.'

'I'm afraid I don't understand,' said Burke.

'They hanged witches here, many years ago,' said Mrs Allinson. 'Three women died at the heart of the village, and more languished in jail until they too began to die. The hanged women still bear the name of Underbury when they are spoken of, and their bodies lie buried beyond the cemetery walls.'

'The three stones,' said Burke.

'So you've seen them?'

'I didn't know what they were, although I suspected that they marked graves of some kind,' said Burke. 'I was surprised to see plots beyond the wall commemorated in any way.'

'I don't believe the stones were placed there to commemorate three murdered women,' said Mrs Allinson. 'There is a cross carved in the underside of each stone, facing down. The superstition that caused their deaths followed them into the ground.'

'How do you know about the crosses?'

'The village records. In a small place like this, one has to entertain oneself as best one can.'

'Yet these are more enlightened times, and Underbury is no longer as it once was.'

'Would you have considered Mal Trevors an enlightened man, Inspector?'

'I never met him, except to look upon his remains. All I have is the testimony of others as to his character.'

'Why are you not married, Inspector?' asked Mrs Allinson suddenly. 'Why is there no woman in your life?'

Now it was Burke's turn to answer cautiously.

'My job takes up much of my time,' he began, uncertain why he was even attempting to explain himself to this woman, except that in doing so he might learn more about her. 'Perhaps, too, I have never met the right woman.'

Mrs Allinson leaned forward slightly.

'I suspect,' she said, 'that there is no "right" woman for you. I'm not entirely sure that you like women, Inspector. I don't mean in the physical sense,' she added quickly, 'for I am sure that you have appetites like most men have. Rather, I mean that you don't like their minds. You perhaps distrust them, maybe even despise them. You don't understand them, and that makes you fear them. Their appetites, their emotions, the workings of their bodies and their brains, all are alien to you, and you are afraid of them for that reason, just as the men of Underbury were afraid of the women whom they named "witches" and hanged amid the winter snow.'

'I'm not afraid of women, Mrs Allinson,' said Burke, a little more defensively than he had intended.

She smiled before she spoke again, and Burke was reminded of the faint smile on the face of Mrs Paxton as she reassured her husband earlier that day. He heard the sound of footsteps approaching the house, their rhythm slightly distorted, and knew that Dr Allinson had returned, yet he found himself staring only at Mrs Allinson, caught in the depths of those green eyes.

'Really, Inspector, I don't know if that's true,' she said, untroubled by any offence she might be causing him. 'In fact, I don't believe that's true at all.'

* * *

Dr Allinson joined them and, after a suitable period had elapsed, his wife announced that she was retiring for the evening.

'I know I'll be seeing you again, Inspector,' she said, as she left them. 'I look forward to it.'

Burke spent another hour with Allinson, learning little that was new but content to bounce theories back and forth with someone whose knowledge of physiology was so intimate. Allinson offered to take him back to the village, but Burke declined, consenting only to a little brandy to warm him on the journey.

Burke almost instantly regretted taking the brandy once he set out for the village, for while it was undoubtedly warming, it clouded his head, and the cold was doing little to sober him. Twice he almost slipped before he had even made it to the road, and once upon it he kept to the centre, fearing for his safety if he drew too close to the ditch. He had been walking for only a few minutes when he heard movement in the bushes to his right. He stopped and listened, but the presence in the undergrowth had also paused. Burke, like Stokes, was every inch the city dweller, and supposed that there must be a great many nocturnal animals in these parts, yet whatever was on the other side of the bushes was quite large. Perhaps it was a badger, he thought, or a fox. He moved on, the lamp raised, and felt something brush past his coat. He turned suddenly, and caught a flash of black as the creature entered the bushes to his left. It had crossed the road behind his back, so close to him that it had touched him as it went.

Burke reached behind himself and brushed at his coat. His fingers came back coated with something dark and flaking, like pieces of charred paper. He brought them closer to the lamplight and examined them, lifting them to his nose to sniff them as he did so.

They smelled of burning right enough, he thought, but not of paper. Burke recalled an incident, some years earlier, when he had been forced to enter a house about to be engulfed by fire in an effort to extract any survivors before the building collapsed. He found only one, a woman, and her body was already badly burned when he discovered her. She expired upon the road outside, but Burke remembered the way that fragments of her skin adhered to his hands, and the smell of her had never left him. It was why he rarely ate pork, for the smell of roasting pig was too close to that of human meat burning. That was the smell that now lay upon his fingers.

He brushed it away on his coat as best he could and continued towards the village, faster now, his footsteps slapping upon the road as he ran, and all the time he was conscious of being followed from the undergrowth, until at last he came to the margins of Underbury itself and the creature stopped before the first house. Burke was breathing heavily as he scanned the blackness in the bushes. He thought for an instant that he saw a darker shape within it, a figure within the shadows, but it was gone almost as soon as he registered it. Still, its shape stayed with him, and he saw it in his dreams that night: the shape of its hips, the swelling of its breasts.

It was the figure of a woman.

The next morning, Stokes and Burke, accompanied by Waters, drove across the village to the farmhouse occupied by Elsie Warden and her family. Burke was quiet on the journey. He did not speak of what had occurred the night before on the road back to the village, but he had slept badly and the stink of charred meat seemed to cling to his pillow. Once he awoke to the sound of tapping at his window, but when he went to check upon it all was still and silent outside, yet he could have sworn, for a moment, that the smell of roasted fats was stronger by the sill. He dreamed of Mrs Paxton watching him through the glass with her breasts exposed, but in his dream her face was replaced by that of Mrs Allinson, and the green of her eyes had turned to the black of cinders.

Elsie Warden's brothers, too young to enlist, were out in the fields, and her father off on some business of his own in a neighbouring town, so only Elsie and her mother were in the kitchen when the policemen arrived. They were offered tea, but they declined.

In truth, Burke was not entirely certain why they had come, except that there had clearly been bad blood between the Warden family and the late Mal Trevors. Mrs Warden remained sullen and unresponsive in the face of their questions, and Burke saw her glance occasionally through the window that looked out over the family's fields, hoping to catch sight of her sons returning from their labours. Elsie Warden was more forthcoming, and Burke was a little surprised at the level of assurance exhibited by a young woman brought up in a household largely composed of menfolk.

'We were all in the pub that evening,' she told Burke. 'Me, my mum and dad, and my brothers. All of us. That's the way around here. Saturday nights are special.'

'But you knew Mal Trevors?'

'He tried to court me,' she said. Her eyes dared Burke to dispute any man's reasons for pursuing her. The detective was not about to argue with her. Elsie Warden had lush dark hair, fine features, and a body that Sergeant Stokes was doing his very utmost not to notice.

'And how did you respond to his advances?'

Elsie Warden pursed her lips coyly.

'Whatever do you mean by that?' she asked.

Burke felt himself redden. Stokes appeared to be suddenly afflicted by a fit of coughing.

'I meant –' Burke began, wondering what exactly he *had* meant, when Stokes came to the rescue.

'I think what the inspector means, miss, is did you like Mal Trevors, or was he barking up the wrong tree, so to speak?'

'Aaah,' said Elsie, as if she were only now beginning to understand the direction the conversation was taking. 'I liked him well enough, to begin.'

'She always was attracted to bad sorts,' said her mother, speaking a full sentence for the first time since they had arrived.

She kept her head down as she spoke, and did not look at her daughter. Burke wondered if the old woman was scared of her. Elsie Warden seemed to radiate life and energy, and it was clear that she had the capacity to arouse strong feelings in men. There was something fascinating about her, especially seeing her seated next to the worn-out figure of her mother in the gloomy kitchen.

'Was Mal Trevors a bad sort?' asked Burke.

Elsie tried the coy look again, but it faltered a little on this occasion.

'I think you know what Mal Trevors was,' she said.

'Did he hurt you?'

'He tried.'

'What happened?'

'I struck him, and I ran.'

'And then?'

'He came looking for me.'

'And got a beating for his troubles,' said Burke.

'I wouldn't know anything about that,' she replied.

Burke nodded. He took his notebook from his pocket and flicked through the pages, although he had no need of its contents to guide his thoughts. Sometimes, he found that the very act of checking the written word was enough to disconcert an individual under police scrutiny. He was pleased to see Elsie Warden crane her neck slightly, as though in an effort to discern what might be contained within.

'I'm told you took ill the night Mal Trevors was killed,' he said.

Elsie Warden flinched. It was a small reaction, but enough for Burke. He waited for an answer, and watched as Elsie appeared to analyse the possible answers she might give. Burke felt a shift in her, and was aware of the charm slowly seeping out of her, disappearing between the cracks on the floor to be replaced by what he could only regard as a form of restrained ferocity.

'That's true,' she said.

'Before or after you heard about Mal Trevors?'

'Before'

'May I ask what ailed you?'

'You may ask,' she said, 'if you want to embarrass yourself.'

'I'll take that chance,' said Burke.

'I had my visitor,' she said. 'The monthly guest. Are you happy now?'

Burke gave no sign of happiness or unhappiness. Underbury was giving him much-needed practice in hiding any embarrassment he might feel.

'And Mrs Allinson assisted you?'

'She did. She took me home later, and tended to me.'

'It must have been most severe, to require her ministrations.'

He was aware of a sharp intake of breath from Stokes, and even Waters felt compelled to intervene.

'Now, sir, don't you think we've gone far enough?' he said.

Burke stood.

'For the moment,' he said.

Suddenly, he staggered, overcome, it seemed, by a moment of weakness. He stumbled and brushed against Elsie Warden, then found purchase on the mantel.

'Are you all right, sir?' Stokes had come to his aid.

Burke waved him away.

'I'm fine,' he said. 'Just a little lightheadedness.'

Elsie Warden now had her back to him.

'I'm sorry, miss,' he said. 'I hope I didn't injure you.'

Elsie shook her head and turned to face him. Burke thought she was a little paler than before, and her hands were folded across her chest.

'No,' she said. 'You didn't.'

He took a breath, thanked the women, then left. Mrs Warden saw them to the door.

'You're a rude man,' she said to Burke. 'My husband will hear of this.'

'I don't doubt it,' he replied. 'I should tend to your daughter, if I were you. She looks ill.'

He said nothing to Stokes or the disapproving Waters as they returned to the village. Instead, he thought of Elsie Warden, and the look of pain that had crossed her face as he brushed against her body.

And of the new speckles of blood upon her blouse that were almost, but not quite, hidden by her folded arms.

Mal Trevors was buried in the churchyard the following day. Many turned out for his funeral, despite his reputed failings as a human being, for in a village such as Underbury a funeral served a greater social purpose than that represented by the mere interment of a body. It was an opportunity to exchange information, to gather, and to speculate. As Burke looked around the graveside he could see faces familiar to him from his brief time in the village. The Wardens were there, the family making its dislike of Burke clear only through hostile glances in his direction rather than outright force. So too were the Allinsons, and the Paxtons. As the ceremony concluded, Burke saw Emily Allinson leave her husband, who made his way over to join Burke and Stokes. Mrs Allinson walked by the wall of the cemetery, staring out over the fields towards the spot where Mal Trevors had died. She exchanged a few words with Elsie Warden as she passed her by, and they both looked for a moment in Burke's direction and laughed before going their separate ways. Mrs Paxton seemed to be keeping her distance from both of them, but Emily Allinson cornered her and laid a hand on her arm, a gesture simultaneously intimate and somehow threatening, for it effectively held Mrs Paxton in place while the tall, elegant Mrs Allinson leaned down to talk to her.

'What do you think that's about, sir?' asked Stokes.

'A little friendly greeting, perhaps?'

'Doesn't look too friendly to me.'

'No, it doesn't, does it? Perhaps we need to have another talk with Mrs Paxton.'

By now, Allinson was almost upon them.

'Any progress on your investigation?' he said.

'Slow and steady,' said Burke, who felt a small pang of guilt as he recalled the appearance of the doctor's wife in his dream.

'I hear you stirred up the Wardens.'

'They've spoken about our visit?'

'The mother has spoken of little else. She seems to think you're somewhat improper in your manner. She's suggesting that someone ought to teach you a lesson.'

'Any candidates for the role?'

'No shortage, apparently. The Warden family is large,

extended and very male. I'd watch my back, if I were you, Inspector.'

'I have Sergeant Stokes here to watch my back,' said Burke. 'It leaves me free to watch other people.'

Allinson grinned. 'Good. I'm rather hoping that you won't have any reason to call on my services in a personal capacity.'

'You know,' said Burke, 'I'm rather hoping that too. Tell me, does your wife know a little of medicine?'

'Many doctors' wives do. Mrs Allinson is trained as a midwife, and her skills now extend considerably beyond that. She can't practise medicine, of course, but she knows what to do in the event of a crisis.'

'The women of Underbury are fortunate to have her, then,' said Burke. 'Very fortunate indeed.'

The rest of the day added little to the sum of knowledge accumulated by the two policemen. With the help of Constable Waters, they completed their questioning of all those who had been present at the inn on the night of Mal Trevors's death, and began talking to many of those who were not present. While few had a good word to say about the dead man, there was nothing to link them to the events of that night, and by the time evening came Burke's natural silence had deteriorated into sullenness. He bid Waters a curt goodnight, paused for a time to exchange some words with his sergeant, and then ascended to his bedroom, where he remained seated on his bed for the rest of the evening, rising only to receive his supper at the door.

In time, he must have fallen asleep, for the room was darker than he remembered when he opened his eyes, and the inn was quiet. He was not even aware of why he had awoken, until he heard voices speaking softly beneath his window. Burke left his bed and walked to the glass, concealing himself in the shadows as best he could. Two women stood in the yard below, and in the dim light filtering from the inn he could make out the faces of Emily Allinson and Mrs Paxton. The women appeared to be arguing, for he could see Mrs Allinson's finger stabbing the air before the smaller, darker Mrs Paxton. Burke could not make out their words, but then Mrs Allinson abruptly walked away. Some seconds later, Mrs Paxton followed, but by then Burke was already on his way downstairs.

He left the inn, moved through the yard, and soon found himself following the two women along the road that led out of the village. They were heading towards the Paxton house, but as soon as Mrs Paxton caught up with Mrs Allinson they left the road and made their way across the fields. They seemed to be heading for the place in which Mal Trevors died, until Burke saw them reach a small gate in the fence, open it, and move towards the wall of the churchyard. The inspector kept low as best he could, aided by the clouds that obscured the moon. He was almost at the gate when the women stopped and turned to face him.

'Welcome, Inspector,' said Mrs Allinson. She did not look surprised to see him. In fact, Burke thought she looked rather pleased, and he knew then that he had stepped firmly into the trap they had set for him. Mrs Paxton said nothing, but kept her head down, unwilling even to look in his direction.

Burke heard footsteps approaching from behind. He turned to see Elsie Warden moving slowly through the grass, her hands brushing the tips of the weeds as she walked. She stopped when she was some twenty feet from him. Mrs Paxton in turn moved away from Mrs Allinson, so that Burke found himself at the centre of a triangle formed by the three women.

'Is this how you put paid to Mal Trevors?' he asked.

'We never laid a hand on Mal Trevors,' said Mrs Allinson.

'We didn't have to,' said Elsie.

Burke tried to keep turning, always holding two women in his sight and hoping that he might be fast enough to prevent an attack by the third.

'I suspect there are wounds on your chest, Miss Warden,' said Burke.

'And on my scalp,' she said. 'He fought back. He always was quick with his hands, was Mal.'

'So you attacked him?'

'In a manner of speaking.' It was Mrs Allinson.

'I'm afraid I don't understand.'

'Oh' said Mrs Allinson. 'But you will.'

Burke felt the ground shift slightly beneath his feet. He leaped away, fearful of plummeting into some terrible depths. Over by the cemetery wall, fragments of stone shot a foot into the air, leaving gaping holes where they once lay. He heard a howling sound, like wind rushing through a tunnel, and then something scratched his face, opening parallel wounds across his cheek and nose. He stumbled backward, raising his arms to protect himself, and watched as the front of his coat was torn open by unseen claws. He smelled foul breath, and thought for a moment that he caught a disturbance in the air, as of heat rising from summer ground. Slowly, its form became clearer, allowing Burke to see, however indistinctly, the shape of breasts and hips.

Faced with a target, Burke struck. He pounded his fist into the figure before him. There was slight resistance before his fist passed through it, but he saw Emily Allinson's head jerk backward. Blood spurted from her nose. Burke tried to punch again, but he was attacked from behind before he could do so. His scalp was torn apart, and he felt liquid warmth upon his neck. He tried to rise, but his right hand was wrenched away from him and forced into the air. A sharp pain ran through three of his fingers, and the impression of teeth appeared upon the skin of his knuckles. Over by the fence, he saw Elsie Warden's teeth gritted.

Elsie shook her head furiously, the pain increased, and the fingers were severed from Burke's hand. His eyes closed, and he prepared to die. Then, from somewhere in the darkness, he heard a booming sound, and a familiar voice said:

'That'll be enough, now.'

Burke's eyelids felt heavy, and blood dripped from the lashes when he finally managed to force them open. Sergeant Stokes stood by the cemetery wall, and he held a shotgun in his hands.

You took your bloody time, thought Burke.

He caught sight of a disturbance in the air, moving quickly towards Stokes. Once again, it seemed to him to approximate the shape of a woman. Its body was unblemished, and long fair hair trailed behind it as it crawled along the ground to attack Stokes. He tried to warn his sergeant, but no words came. Instead, his own head was pulled back by the hair, and he felt teeth upon his neck.

Stokes saw the presence when it was almost upon him. Instinctively, he swung the shotgun around and fired.

For a moment, nothing happened, then slowly Emily Allinson's mouth opened and a great gush of red poured from it. She rocked upon her feet, and the front of her green dress darkened. Burke heard a scream which seemed to come from the ground beneath him, echoed in turn by Elsie Warden. His hair was released and he fell to the dirt, a weight upon his back as he was used as a stepping stone by an unseen presence. Burke's left hand reached out and grasped a rock upon the ground. With the last of his strength, he rose up and straddled the thing, bringing the rock down with all the force that he could muster upon its head. He could feel it moving beneath him, although he saw it only as a shimmering in the air. The stone hit its target, and it spasmed beneath him.

Behind him, Elsie Warden's skull cracked. Her eyes rolled back in her head, and she fell down dead.

Stokes was running towards him now, reloading the shotgun as he came. He was watching Mrs Paxton, but she was retreating from them, her face a mask of horror and disgust. She turned from them and ran across the fields, making for the little cottage that she shared with her husband. Stokes shouted after her, warning her to stop.

'Let her go,' said Burke. 'We know where to find her.'

And then he fell back on the ground, unconscious.

Summer came, and the streets grew bright with the plumage of women.

The two men met in a bar close to Paddington. It was quiet, the lunchtime drinkers now departed, and the evening crowd yet to arrive. One man was thinner and perhaps a little younger than the other, and he wore a glove on his right hand. His companion placed two beers on the table before them, then took a seat against the wall.

'How is the hand, sir?' asked Stokes.

'It hurts a little still,' said Burke. 'It's odd. I can feel the ends of my fingers, even though they're no longer there. Strange, don't you think?'

Stokes shrugged his shoulders. 'To tell the truth, sir, I don't know any more what's strange and what isn't.'

He raised his glass and took a long draught.

'You don't have to call me "sir" any longer, you know,' said Burke.

'Doesn't seem natural calling you anything else, sir,' said Stokes. 'I do miss being called "Sergeant", though. I'm trying to get the missus to call me it, just so I can hear it again, but she won't agree.'

'How is the bank?'

'Quiet,' he said. 'Don't care much for it, to be honest, but it keeps me busy. The money helps, though.'

'Yes, I'm sure it does.'

They were silent, then, until Stokes said:

'You still think we did right, not telling them what we saw?'

The two men had not met in many months, but they had never been ones to dance around a subject of concern to them.

'Yes,' said Burke. 'They wouldn't have believed us, even if we had. Mrs Allinson had my blood and skin in her nails, and the bite marks on my hand matched those of Elsie Warden. They attacked me. That's what the evidence said, and who were we to disagree with the evidence?'

'Killing women,' said Stokes. 'I suppose they had no choice but to send us on our way.'

'No, I suppose they didn't.'

Burke looked at his former sergeant, and laid his good hand upon the older man's arm.

'But never forget: you didn't kill women. You never fired at a woman, and I never struck one. Let your conscience be clear on that score.'

Stokes nodded.

'I hear they let the Paxton woman go,' he said.

'She supported our story. Without her testimony, it would have gone much harder for us.'

'Doesn't seem right though.'

'She wished a man dead. I don't think she expected that wish to come true, and I don't believe that she wanted a part of what the other women were offering. She was weak, but she did nothing wrong. Nothing that we can prove, at any rate.'

Stokes took another draught from his glass.

'And that poor beggar, Allinson.'

'Yes,' said Burke. 'Poor Allinson.' The doctor had taken his own life in the weeks that followed the incident at Underbury. He had never uttered a word of blame towards Stokes or Burke for the part they played in his wife's death.

Burke spent most of his waking hours thinking about that night, juggling facts with suspicions but never able to make them fit to his satisfaction into a cohesive theory. A village depleted of its men; the arrival of a strong woman, Mrs Allinson, from outside; the threat posed to Elsie Warden and, perhaps, Mrs Paxton by Mal Trevors; and the response to that threat, which had led to Trevors's death and the subsequent attack on Burke and Stokes. Burke had not yet been able, or willing, to put a name to that response. He now knew more about the Underbury witches and their leader Ellen Drury, burned as she hanged. Possession, the term that Stokes had used in the aftermath, was one possibility, but it seemed inadequate to Burke. To him, it was something more. He believed with all his heart that it came from within the three women, not solely from some outside force, but then he had never enjoyed a great understanding of the fairer sex.

They finished their drinks, then parted on the street with vague promises to meet again, although both men understood that they would not. Burke walked in the direction of Hyde Park, while Stokes stopped at a flower stall to buy some carnations for his wife. Neither saw the small, dark-haired woman who stood in the shadows of a laneway, watching them closely. The air shimmered around her, as though distorted by the summer heat, and a faint smell of roasting meat could be scented by passers-by.

Mrs Paxton made her choice, and slowly began to follow Burke towards the park.

The Inkpot Monkey

Mr Edgerton was suffering from writer's block. It was, he quickly grew to realise, a most distressing complaint. A touch of influenza might lay up a man for a day or two, yet still his mind could continue its ruminations. Gout might leave him racked with suffering, yet still his fingers could grasp a pen and turn pain to pennies. But this blockage, this barrier to all progress, had left Mr Edgerton a virtual cripple. His mind would not function, his hands would not write, and his bills would not be paid.

In a career spanning the best part of two decades he had never before encountered such an obstacle to his profession. He had, in that time, produced five moderately successful, if rather indifferent, novels; a book of memoirs that, in truth, owed more to invention than experience; and a collection of poetry that could most charitably be described as having stretched the capacities of free verse to the limits of their acceptability.

Mr Edgerton made his modest living from writing by the yard, based on the firm but unstated belief that if he produced a sufficient quantity of material then something of quality was bound to creep in, if only in accordance with the law of averages. Journalism, ghostwriting, versifying, editorialising; nothing was beneath his limited capabilities. Yet, for the past six months, the closest he had come to a writing project was the construction of his weekly grocery list. A veritable tundra of empty white pages stretched before him, the gleaming nib of his pen poised above them like a reluctant explorer. His mind was a blank, the creative juices sapped from it to leave behind only a dried husk of frustration and bewilderment. He began to fear his desk, once his beloved companion but now reduced to the status of a faithless lover, and it pained him to look upon it. Paper, ink, imagination: all had betrayed him, leaving him lost and alone.

At first, Mr Edgerton had almost welcomed the opportunity to rest his creative muscles. He took coffee with those less successful than himself, safe in the knowledge that a brief hiatus in production was unlikely to damage his reputation among them as a prolific producer of adequate material. He attended the best shows, making sure that his presence was noted by taking his seat at the last possible moment. When questioned about his latest endeavours, he would merely smile mysteriously and tap the side of his nose with his index finger, a gesture employed by Mr Edgerton to suggest that he was in the midst of some great literary endeavour, but which instead gave the unfortunate impression that a particularly irritating fragment of snuff had stubbornly lodged itself in his nostril.

But after a time, Mr Edgerton stopped attending musical performances, and his peers were forced to find other sources of amusement at the city's coffee houses. Conversations about writing began to pain him, and the sight of those whose creative juices flowed more freely than his own compounded his agony. He found himself unable to keep the bitterness from his voice as he spoke of such blessed souls, arousing immediately the suspicions of his fellow, less prolific, scribblers, for although they were more than willing to skewer another's reputation with a barbed witticism or unflattering anecdote, they avoided the use of brute insults or, indeed, any form of behaviour that might lead a casual listener to suspect that they were not their rivals' superiors in talent, success and critical acclaim. Mr Edgerton came to fear that even his silences now gave him away, clouded over as they were with brooding and frustration, and so his social appearances grew fewer and fewer until at last they ceased altogether. In truth, his colleagues were not unduly troubled by his absence. They had reluctantly tolerated his modest success. Now, with the taint of failure upon him, they relished his discomfort.

To further complicate matters, Mr Edgerton's wallet had begun to feel decidedly lightweight of late, and nothing will dampen a man's ardour for life more than an empty pocket. Like a rodent gripped in the coils of a great constricting snake, he found that the more he struggled against his situation, the tighter the pressure upon him grew. Necessity, wrote Ovid, is the mother of invention. For Mr Edgerton, desperation was proving to be the father of despair.

And so, once again, he found himself wandering the streets, trawling the city's great rivers of people in the hope of netting a single idea. In time, he came to Charing Cross Road, but the miles of shelved books only depressed him further, especially since he could find none of his own among their number. Head down, he cut through Cecil Court and made his way into Covent Garden in the faint hope that the vibrancy of the market might spur his sluggish subconscious into action. He was almost at the Magistrates Court when something caught his eye in the window of a small antique shop. There, partially hidden behind a framed portrait of General Gordon and a stuffed magpie, was a most remarkable inkpot.

The inkpot was silver, and about four inches tall, with a lacquered base adorned by Chinese characters. But what was most striking about it was the small, mummified monkey that perched upon its lid, its clawed toes clasped upon the rim and its dark eyes gleaming in the summer sunlight. It was obviously an infant of its species, perhaps even a foetus of some kind, for it was no more than three inches in height, and predominantly grey in colour, except for its face which was blackened around the mouth as if the monkey had been sipping from its own ink. It really was a most ghastly creature, but Mr Edgerton had acquired the civilised man's taste for the grotesque and he quickly made his way into the darkened shop to enquire about the nature of the item in question.

The owner of the business proved to be almost as distasteful in appearance as the creature that had attracted Mr Edgerton's attention, as though the man were somehow father to the monkey. His teeth were too numerous for his mouth, his mouth too large for his face, and his head too great for his body. Combined with a pronounced stoop to his back, his aspect was that of one constantly on the verge of toppling over. He also smelled decidedly odd, and Mr Edgerton quickly concluded that he was probably in the habit of sleeping in his clothes, a deduction that briefly led the afflicted writer to an unwelcome speculation upon the nature of the body that lay concealed beneath the layers of unwashed clothing.

Nevertheless, the proprietor proved to be a veritable font of knowledge about the items in his possession, including the article that had brought Mr Edgerton into his presence. The mummified primate was, he informed the writer, an inkpot monkey, a creature of Chinese mythology. According to the myth, the monkey provided artistic inspiration in return for the residues of ink left in the bottom of the inkwell. As he spoke, the dealer placed the inkpot on the counter before him, like an angler skilfully spinning a lure before a hungry fish in the hope of drawing it onto his hook.

Mr Edgerton's limited ability, like that of so many of his

kind, was inversely proportionate to his sense of self-regard, and he was therefore generally unwilling to entertain the possibility that his genius could be attributed to any outside agency. Nevertheless, he was a man profoundly in need of inspiration from any source, and had recently been considering opium or cheap gin as possible catalysts. Having heard the story of the inkpot, he required no further convincing. He paid over money he could ill afford for the faint hope of redemption offered by the curiosity, and made his way back to his small apartments with the inkpot and its monkey tucked beneath his arm in a cloak of brown paper.

Mr Edgerton occupied a set of rooms above a tobacconist's store on Marylebone High Street, a recent development forced upon him by his straitened circumstances. While Mr Edgerton did not himself partake of the noble weed, his walls were yellowed by the fumes that regularly wended their way between the cracks in the floorboards, and his clothing and furnishings reeked of assorted cigars, cigarettes, pipe tobaccos, and even the more eyewatering forms of snuff. His dwelling was, therefore, more than a little depressing, and would almost certainly have provided him with the impetus necessary to improve his finances were he not so troubled by the absence of his muse.

That evening, Mr Edgerton sat at his desk once again and stared at the paper before him.

And stared.

And stared.

Before him, the inkpot monkey squatted impassively, its eyes reflecting the lamplight and lending its mummified form an intimation of life that was both distracting and unsettling. Mr Edgerton poked at it tentatively with his pen, leaving a small black mark on its chest. Like most writers, he had a shallow knowledge of a great many largely useless matters. Among these was anthropology, a consequence of one of his earlier works, an evolutionary fantasy entitled *The Monkey's Uncle*. (One newspaper had described it as 'largely adequate, if inconsequential'. Mr Edgerton, grateful to be reviewed at all, was rather pleased.) Yet, despite searching through three reference volumes, he had been unable to identify the origins of the inkpot monkey and had begun to take this as a bad omen.

After another unproductive hour had gone by, its tedium broken only by the spread of an occasional ink blot upon the paper, Mr Edgerton rose and determined to amuse himself by emptying, and then refilling, his pen. Still devoid of inspiration, he wondered if there was some part of the arcane ritual of fuelling one's pen from the inkpot that he had somehow neglected to perform. He reached down, and had gently grasped the monkey in order to raise the lid when something pricked his skin painfully. He drew back his hand immediately and examined the wounded digit. A deep cut ran across the pad of his index finger, and blood from the abrasion was flowing down the length of his pen and congregating at the nib, from which it dripped into the inkpot with soft, regular splashes. Mr Edgerton began to suck the offended member, meanwhile turning his attention to the monkey in an effort to ascertain the cause of his injury. The lamplight revealed a small raised ridge behind the creature's neck, where a section of curved spine had burst through its tattered fur. A little of Mr Edgerton's blood could be perceived on the yellowed pallor of the bone.

The wounded writer retrieved a small bandage from his medicine cabinet and bound his finger before resuming his seat at his desk. He regarded the monkey warily as he filled his pen from the well, then put pen to paper and began to write. At first, the familiarity of the act overcame any feelings of surprise at its sudden return, so that Mr Edgerton had completed two pages of close script and was about to embark upon a third before he paused and looked in puzzlement first at his pen, then at the paper. He re-read what he had written, the beginnings of a tale of a man who sacrifices love and happiness at the altar of wealth and success, and found it more than satisfactory. It was, in fact, as fine as anything he had ever written, although he was baffled as to its source. Nevertheless, he shrugged and continued writing, grateful that his imagination had apparently woken from its torpor. He wrote long into the night, refilling his pen as required, and so bound up was he in his exertions that he failed entirely to notice that his wound had reopened and was dripping blood on to pen and page and, at those moments when he replenished his instrument, into the depths of the small Chinese inkpot.

Mr Edgerton slept late the following morning, and awoke to find himself weakened by his efforts of the night before. It was, he supposed, the consequence of months of inactivity, and after tea and some hot buttered toast, he felt much refreshed. He returned to his desk to find that the inkpot monkey had fallen from its perch and now lay on its back amid his pencils and pens. Gingerly, Mr Edgerton lifted it from the desk and found that it now weighed considerably more than the inkpot itself and that physics, rather than any flaw in the inkpot's construction, had played its part in dislodging the monkey from its seat. He also noted that the creature's fur was far more lustrous than it had appeared in the window of the antique shop, and now shimmered healthily in the morning sunlight.

And then, quite suddenly, Mr Edgerton felt the monkey move. Its arms and legs stretched wearily, as if it were waking from some long slumber, and its mouth opened in a wide yawn, displaying small blunt teeth. Alarmed, Mr

Edgerton dropped the monkey and heard it emit a startled squeak as it landed on the desk. It lay there for a moment or two, then slowly raised itself on its haunches and regarded the writer with a slightly hurt expression before ambling over to the inkpot and squatting down gently beside it. With its left hand, it raised the lid of the inkpot and waited patiently for Mr Edgerton to fill his pen. For a time, the bewildered writer was unable to move, so taken aback was he at this turn of events. Then, when it became clear that he had no other option but to begin writing or go mad, he reached for his pen and supplied it from the well. The monkey watched him impassively until the reservoir was filled and Mr Edgerton had begun to write, then promptly fell fast asleep.

Despite his unnerving encounter with the newly animated monkey, Mr Edgerton put in a most productive day and quickly found himself with the bulk of five chapters written, none of them requiring more than a cursory rewrite. It was only when the light had begun to fade and Mr Edgerton's arm had started to ache that the monkey awoke and padded softly across a virgin page to where Mr Edgerton's pen lay in his hand. The monkey grasped his index finger with its tiny paws, then placed its mouth against the cut and began to suck. It took Mr Edgerton a moment to realise what was occurring, at which point he rose with a shout and shook the monkey from his finger. It bounced against the inkpot, striking its head soundly against its base, and lay unmoving upon a sheet of paper.

At once, Mr Edgerton reached for it and raised it in the palm of his left hand. The monkey was obviously stunned, for its eyes were now half closed and it was dazedly moving its head from side to side as it tried to focus. Instantly, Mr Edgerton was seized with regret at his hasty action. He had endangered the monkey, which he now acknowledged to be the source of his new-found inspiration. Without it, he would be lost. Torn between fear and disgust, Mr Edgerton reluctantly made his decision: he squeezed together his thumb and forefinger, causing a droplet of blood to emerge from the cut and then, his gorge rising, allowed it to drip into the monkey's mouth.

The effect was instantaneous. The little mammal's eyes opened fully, it rose on its haunches, and then reached for, and grasped, the wounded finger. There it suckled happily, undisturbed by the revolted Mr Edgerton, until it had taken its meal, whereupon it burped contentedly and resumed its slumbers. Mr Edgerton gently laid it beside the inkpot and then, taking up his pen, wrote another two chapters before retiring early to his bed.

Thus it continued. Each day Mr Edgerton rose, fed the monkey a little blood, wrote, fed the monkey once again in the evening, wrote some more, then went to bed and slept like a dead man, his rest only occasionally troubled by the memories being dredged up in the course of his work, as old lovers and forgotten friends found their place in the narrative now taking shape upon his desk. The monkey itself appeared to require little in the way of affection or attention beyond its regular feeds of blood and the occasional ripe banana. Mr Edgerton, in turn, decided to ignore the fact that the monkey was growing at quite an alarming rate, so that it was now obliged to sit beside him on a small chair while he worked and had taken to dozing on the sofa after its meals. In fact, Mr Edgerton wondered if it might not be possible to train the monkey to do some light household duties, thereby allowing him more time to write, although when he suggested this to the monkey through the use of primitive sign language it grew quite irate and locked itself in the bathroom for an entire afternoon.

In fact, it was not until Mr Edgerton returned home one day from a visit to his publisher to find the inkpot monkey trying on one of his suits that he began to experience serious doubts about their relationship. He had noticed some new and especially disturbing changes in his companion. It had begun to moult, leaving clumps of unsightly grey hair on the carpets and exposing sections of pink-white skin. It had also lost some weight from its face; that, or its bone structure had begun to alter, for it presented a more angular aspect than before. In addition, the monkey was now over four feet tall and Mr Edgerton had been forced to open veins in his wrists and legs in order to keep it sated. The more Mr Edgerton considered the matter, the more convinced he became that the creature was undergoing some significant transformation. Yet there were still chapters of the book to be completed, and the writer was reluctant to alienate his mascot. So he suffered in silence, sleeping now for much of the day and emerging only to write for increasingly short periods of time before returning to his bed and collapsing into a dreamless slumber.

On the twenty-ninth day of August, he delivered his completed manuscript to his publisher. On the fourth day of September, which was Mr Edgerton's birthday, he was gratified to receive a most delightful communication from his editor, praising him as a genius and promising that this novel, long anticipated and at last delivered, would place Mr Edgerton in the pantheon of literary greats and assure him of a most comfortable and well-regarded old age.

That night, as Mr Edgerton prepared to drift off into contented sleep, he felt a tug at his wrist and looked down to see the inkpot monkey fastened upon it, its cheeks pulsing as it sucked away at the cut. Tomorrow, thought Mr Edgerton. Tomorrow I will deal with it. Tomorrow I will have it taken to the zoo and our bargain will be concluded for ever. But as he grew weaker and his eyes closed, the inkpot monkey raised its head and Mr Edgerton realised at last that no zoo would ever take the inkpot monkey, for the inkpot monkey had become something very different indeed.

Mr Edgerton's book was published the following year, to universal acclaim. A reception was given in his honour by his grateful publishers, to which the brightest lights of London's literary community flocked to pay tribute. It would be Mr Edgerton's final public appearance. From that day forth, he was never again seen in London and instead retired to the small country estate that he purchased with the royalties from his great, valedictory work.

That night, speeches were made, and an indifferent poem recited by one of Mr Edgerton's new admirers, but the great man himself remained silent throughout. When called upon to give his speech, he replied only with a small but polite bow to his guests, accepting their applause with a gracious smile.

And while all those around him drank the finest champagne and feasted on stuffed quail and smoked salmon, Mr Edgerton could be found sitting quietly in a corner, stroking some unruly hairs on his chest and munching contentedly on a single ripe banana.

The Shifting of the Sands

The decision to reopen the rectory at Black Sands was not one taken lightly. The Church of England, it was felt, was not welcome in that place, although antipathy was not directed towards the King's Church alone. The community had resisted the presence of organised religion since its inception some four hundred years earlier. True, chapels had been built there, both Catholic and Protestant, but without worshippers what was a chapel? One might as well have erected a small hut close to the shore, for at least then bathers could have made some use of it.

The small Catholic church had been deconsecrated at the turn of the century and subsequently demolished after a fire consumed its roof and turned its walls as black as the very grains that gave the village its name. The Protestant house of worship remained, but was in a state of shameful neglect. There was no living to be had at Black Sands. The people of the village, when asked, pointed out that they had no need of clergymen, that they had survived and even prospered through their own efforts, and there was some truth to what they said. This was a treacherous coastline, with riptides and hidden, fatal currents, yet in its entire history not one soul from Black Sands had fallen victim to the sea, and not a single ship from its small fleet of fishing vessels had been lost to the depths.

Without the support of the community, the chapel at Black Sands had to be resourced entirely from diocesan funds, and only the worst and most desperate of clergymen were dispatched there to eke out a miserable existence by the sea. Most drank themselves quietly into oblivion, troubling the natives only when they were found unconscious by the side of the road and had to be carried back to their beds. There were exceptions, of course: the last rector, the Reverend Rhodes, had approached his assignment with a veritable missionary zeal for the first six months, but, slowly, communications from him became less and less frequent. He indicated that he was having trouble sleeping and, while he had experienced no outright hostility, the lack of enthusiasm from his prospective parishoners was wearing him down. Finally, in the last letter he ever sent, he confessed that the loneliness and isolation were taking their toll on his sanity, for he had begun to hallucinate.

'I see shapes in the sand', he wrote in that final letter. 'I hear voices whispering to me, inviting me to walk upon the shore, as if the very sea itself is calling my name. I fear that if I stay here any longer, I will do as they request. I will take that walk, and I will never return.'

Yet still he persisted in his efforts to encourage the villagers to change their ways. He began to take an interest in the history of the community, to inquire about its past. Packages arrived from bookshops, packed with obscure tomes. They were found in his study after his death, the pages prodigiously marked and annotated.

The Reverend Rhodes's body washed up upon the shore at Black Sands one week after his last missive was received, but the circumstances surrounding his death were never fully explained. For, you see, the Reverend Rhodes had not drowned, but suffocated. When his body was opened, his lungs were found to contain not water, but sand.

But that was decades ago, and now the decision had been taken to reopen the church at Black Sands. There was a duty upon the church and its clergy not to allow a community to exist without the light of the true faith to guide it. Even if the villagers chose to turn their backs to it, yet still that light would shine upon them, and it was given unto me to be its bearer.

The chapel stood on a rocky promontory close by the seashore. Scattered around it were the weathered graves of those clergymen who had come here down the centuries, and had breathed their last against the sound of the waves crashing. The Reverend Rhodes was buried close by the western wall of the church, a small granite cross marking his final resting place. A path led from the rear of the chapel to the rectory itself, a modest two-storey residence built from local stone. From my bedroom window, I could see the ghosts of the waves descending upon the dark shore, white on black. When they broke, it was as if the very sands had devoured them.

The village itself was little more than a huddle of small houses spread over five or six narrow streets. There was a shop devoted to the sale of whatever the residents might require, from a clothes peg to a cartwheel. Beside it stood a small inn. I gave my custom to each in that first week, and found that I was treated with a respectful caution, but made to feel neither welcome nor unwelcome. Both premises were owned by the unofficial mayor of Black Sands, a Mr Webster. He was a tall, cadaverous man, with the manner of an undertaker measuring up a particularly impoverished client for a cheap casket. He politely declined my request to post times of services in both the inn and the shop.

'As I said to your predecessor, Mr Benson, we have no need of your presence here,' he informed me, with a half-smile, as he walked with me along the main street of the village. He was greeted warmly as we made our way. I, on the other hand, received only cursory nods. On occasion, when I glanced over my shoulder, I caught those who had passed us watching me, and exchanging words.

'I disagree,' I said. 'Those who exist without God in their lives are always in need, even if they are unaware of it themselves.'

'I am no theologian,' said Webster, 'but it seems to me that there are many religions, and many gods.'

I stopped short. This, after all, was heresy.

'Yes, there are many gods, Mr Webster, but only one true God. All else is superstition and the misheld beliefs of ignorant men.'

'Really?' said Webster. 'Am I an ignorant man, Mr Benson?'

'I, I cannot say,' I stammered. 'In most things, you seem to me to be a most cultured man, yet in matters of religion you exhibit an almost wilful blindness. The people of this village look up to you. Were you only to use your influence to—'

'To do what?' he interrupted, and for the first time I saw real anger in his eyes, although his voice remained frighteningly calm. 'To encourage them to follow a god that they cannot see, who promises nothing but pain in this life in exchange for the hope of some idyll in the next? As I have said, perhaps there are other gods than yours, Mr Benson. *Older* gods.'

I swallowed.

'Are you telling me that the people of this village are engaged in pagan worship?' I asked.

The anger left his eyes, to be replaced by his customary calm.

'I am telling you no such thing. All I am trying to say is that you have your beliefs, and others have theirs. Each has a place in the order of things, that I do not doubt. Unfortunately, the place for yours is not here.'

'I choose to stay,' I replied.

He shrugged. 'Then we may yet find a use for you.'

'That is my fervent hope,' I concluded.

Webster's smile widened, but he said no more.

I held my service that Sunday in an empty church, as was my duty, and I sang 'The Lord is My Shepherd' accompanied only by the cries of seagulls. That night I sat by the window of the study, staring down on the strange, black sand that gave the village its name, surrounded by my predecessor's meagre possessions, now coated in many years of dust. Unwilling yet to retire to my bed, I spent an unproductive hour rummaging through old seafaring histories, topographical studies and anthologies of supposedly factual supernatural encounters more suited to the archives of penny dreadfuls than the library of a clergyman.

It was only when I began to search the writing desk that I discovered the notebook. It had been placed flat at the end of one of the drawers, among the corpses of dead insects. No more than twenty of its pages contained writing, but the neat script clearly matched that of the Reverend Rhodes contained in the various church documents bequeathed to me.

The notebook was an account of Rhodes's investigations into the history of the area. Most of it was of only passing interest: tales of foundation, of feuds, of myths. Rhodes had learned that Black Sands was far older than a casual perusal of its history might have suggested. True, the village itself had only been in existence since the early seventeenth century, but the lands had been in use for long before that. Rhodes believed that he had ascertained the location of a stone circle that had once stood close by the shore, its position now marked by a raised slab that might once have served as an altar. But what purpose had the altar served? It seemed that to this question Rhodes was willing to offer an answer.

What Rhodes had discovered was this: once every twenty years, within one week either side of the anniversary of the community's official founding on 9 November 1603, somebody drowned in the waters off Black Sands. The records were incomplete, and there were years for which Rhodes had been unable to provide entries, but the pattern was clear. Every two decades, a stranger, somebody from outside the community, died at Black Sands. True, there were other drownings in the intervening years, other accidents, but there was a strange consistency to the November deaths. The final entry in the notebook was for one Edith Adams, on 2 November 1899, but hers was not the last such death at Black Sands. That distinction would fall to Rhodes himself.

That night, I did not sleep, but found myself listening to the sound of the sea. At other times, it might have lulled me to rest, but not at this time, and not in this place.

The whispering began on the night of 1 November, the day of the saints. At first, it sounded like the wind in the grass, but when I went to my window the branches of the trees appeared unmoving. Still it came, sometimes soft, sometimes keening, speaking words I could not understand. I returned to bed and clasped my pillow to my ears, but the noise did not begin to fade until first light.

And each night thereafter, as the anniversary of the foundation of the community approached, I heard those voices, and it seemed to me that they grew louder and more insistent. I found myself awake in the dead of night, my blanket wrapped around me as I stood at my window and stared out at the black shore. And though the air was still, I thought I saw trails of sand rise up from the shore, twisting sinuously in the air like wraiths.

I tried to make up for my lost rest during the day, but the resources of my body and mind were not to be so easily replenished. I was troubled by headaches, and strange waking dreams in which I stood on the black sands and felt a presence behind me, only to turn and see the empty strand stretching towards the sea. One of these dreams was so disturbing that I awoke, thrashing at my sheets, and was unable to resume my rest. I rose and went to my little kitchen, in the hope that some warm milk might restore my composure. As I sat at my table, I glimpsed a light moving on the promontory to the north, where the old stones lay, a testament to earlier beliefs. Leaving my milk, I dressed hastily and, wrapped in my dark coat, made my way through the fields towards the path that led to the ancient site. I was almost within sight of the track when some instinct made me fall to the ground. Two shadows fell across me, the forms of men marching silently in the direction of the stones. I followed them, staying away from the path, until I came within sight of the altar. There Webster stood waiting, a lantern resting upon the stone. He was dressed in his usual tweeds, the tails of his overcoat flapping in the breeze.

'Do you have it?' he said.

One of the two men who had joined him, a dour farmer named Prayter, handed over a brown paper bag. Webster reached inside and removed something white: a stole. One had gone missing from my laundry basket earlier in the week, and I had been driven almost to distraction trying to guess what might have happened to it. Now I knew.

Webster picked up his lantern. Instantly, his face was illuminated, but it seemed to me that I saw regret there, or so I now hope, in light of what was to occur later.

'It has to be done,' said Prayter. 'It's the way of things.'

Webster nodded. 'There will come a time when it will no

longer be possible,' he said. 'Soon, it will be too dangerous to continue.'

'And what then?' asked the third man, whose name I did not know.

'Then perhaps the old gods will die,' said Webster simply, 'and we will die with them.'

He picked up the stole and he and his companions walked down to the beach. There, they dug a hole in the sand and placed the vestment within, before carefully filling in the depression once again. Then they returned to the village.

I stayed where I was for a time, until I was certain that they would not return, then followed the path that they had taken down to the shore. It was the work of only a few moments to find the little mound they had left, beneath which lay the remains of my church garment. I stood there for a time, uncertain of how to proceed. I believed in God, my God, and yet images from my troubling dreams came back to me, and the deaths discovered by my predecessor and referred to by Webster. I was terribly afraid, and prayed for guidance, but none came.

And so, feeling that I was betraying the very faith that I had so ardently defended to Webster, I began to dig with my hands until I found my stole. I removed it from the hole, shook the black sand from it, and was about to make my way back to the rectory when I turned and refilled the hole once again. As I did so, I became aware of the sands gently drifting around me, forming shapes and patterns that to my troubled mind appeared almost purposeful, and I redoubled my efforts to disguise my recovery of the garment.

For the rest of the night, I did not sleep, but mulled over what I had seen, and what I had heard.

* * *

The next day, I rose early and made my way into the village. I bought some bread and cheese, then stopped by Webster's inn as he was making his preparations for the day. He found it hard to meet my gaze, but I gave no indication that I recognised his unease.

'I was wondering,' I said, 'if I could trouble you for a cup of tea? I must confess, I feel a little weak this morning, and in need of something to fortify me for the walk home.'

Webster grinned.

'I could give you something stronger than tea, if you like,' he said.

I declined his offer.

'Tea will be fine,' I said, and watched as he disappeared into the kitchen behind the bar in order to heat the water. He was gone for only a couple of minutes, but in that time I did all that I needed to do. From the pocket of his jacket, which always hung on a hook behind the bar, I removed a worn white handkerchief, praying to God to forgive me as I did so. Then, once Webster returned, I sat with him and drank my tea, maintaining a pretence of normality while fearing throughout that he might sniffle or sneeze, causing him to search for his handkerchief. When I was done, I offered him money for the tea, but he refused.

'On the house,' he said. 'Just to show there are no hard feelings.'

'None whatsoever,' I said.

I left him, and took a walk upon the beach. Only when I was certain that I was unobserved did I get down upon my knees and commence digging a hole in the coarse, dark sand.

I did not sleep that night, so that when I heard my name being called I was almost expecting the summons.

'Mr Benson, Mr Benson! Wake up!'

Webster was below my window, a lamp in his hand. 'You must come quickly,' he shouted. 'There is a body on the seashore.'

I left my bed, pulled on my clothes and shoes, and descended to the door, but Webster was already running ahead of me by the time I got it open. I could see the light bobbing as he moved across the grass towards the sands themselves.

'Come on,' he cried. 'Hurry!'

I paused and drew a stout birch stick from my umbrella stand. I liked to carry it when I walked, enjoying the feel of the bark on my hand, but now its weight and heft offered me a kind of reassurance. I followed Webster's light until I stood at the edge of the dunes looking down on the beach. Where the waves were breaking, a black bundle lay. It looked like a child's body. Perhaps I was wrong to doubt Webster, and there really was someone hurt or dead. Laying aside my fears, I stepped onto the strand. The sand felt soft and yielding, and my feet sank unpleasantly into it to the depth of about an inch. I began to walk. Ahead of me, Webster was beckoning, calling me closer, but the bundle at his feet remained unmoving, even when I knelt down beside it in the light and probed gently at it. Slowly, my hands shaking, I drew back the damp black cloth that covered it.

Beneath the cloth was hair, and a muzzle, and a long pink tongue. It was a dog, a dead dog. I looked up to find Webster's light beginning to recede from me as he tried to leave me alone on the beach.

'Mr Webster?' I said. 'What does this mean?'

I was about to stand when I was momentarily distracted by a stinging sensation against my face. I brushed at the spot, and my fingers came away with a coating of black sand. All around me, the grains were moving, shifting. Shapes rose and fell, forming columns that held their shape for an instant before disintegrating into dark clouds that fell upon the beach below. They might almost have been human, except that they were strangely hunched, their features hidden beneath thick folds of hair. I thought I discerned horns emerging from their heads, warped and twisted growths that appeared to curl around their skulls, ending almost at their necks. The whispering began and I understood that it was not language that I had heard on past nights, but the movement of the sands, the individual molecules brushing against each other, reconstituting themselves in strange configurations, briefly uniting to create, for a moment, ancient, lost forms.

Now Webster was running, making for the safety of the dunes and the raised stone slab that rested on the promontory, his light held high before him so that he might not stumble on seaweed or driftwood. I followed him, my progress arrested by the strange, sponge-like quality of the terrain. Behind me, I sensed a form rising high and then sand was filling my eyes and mouth, like fingers clasped suddenly across my face. I spat and wiped at my face with my sleeve, but did not look over my shoulder or stop running.

Ahead of me, Webster was tiring. I was closing on him, but I would not reach him before he gained the dunes. I waited, narrowing the gap between us by another five or six feet, then threw my stick with all the force I could muster. It struck him firmly on the back of the head and he fell awkwardly to the ground, the lamp tumbling away from him and the oil it contained igniting on the beach. In the sudden glare I saw his eyes grow wide and staring, yet he was looking not at me but at what lay behind. He tried to rise but I caught him a glancing blow with my foot as I leaped over his prone form. He fell again, and then I was approaching a steep rise, my feet sliding in the lighter sand of the dunes. I clutched at a patch of marram grass, drew myself up, and looked down on the black sands.

'You can't escape,' he called. 'These are the old gods, the true gods.'

He stood and rubbed the sand from his clothes. He appeared wary of the approaching forms, but not fearful.

'Embrace it,' Webster continued. 'This is your destiny.'

'No,' I cried. 'It is not my destiny, and these are not my gods.'

I removed from my pocket the bundled form of my stole, and displayed it to him.

'Check your pockets, Mr Webster. I think you'll find you're missing something.'

And as realisation dawned, Webster was surrounded by what appeared to be five or six columns of swirling grains. I saw him try to break through, but the intensity of their movement increased, blinding him and forcing him back. And then, of a sudden, they disappeared and all was still. Webster's thin form was left standing alone in the dying light from the burning oil. All movement had ceased on the beach. He raised his head uncertainly to me and reached out a hand. Instinctively, I stretched out my own hand to him in return. Whatever he had tried to do to me, I could not leave him in peril.

Our fingers were almost touching when a shape appeared close by Webster's feet. I saw an oval of sand rise up with two holes about midway down its form, like the sunken sockets of eyes. The bridge of a ruined nose stretched between them, framed on either side by a pair of jagged cheekbones. And then, around Webster's feet, a maw opened: I saw lips, and a brief glimpse of what might have been some kind of tongue, all carved from black sand. Webster looked down and started to scream, but the thing began to suck him down. He struck at the shape, his fingers clawing as he attempted to arrest his descent, but soon he was submerged to his chest, then his neck. His mouth opened wide once more, but any further sound he made was silenced by the grains that filled his mouth as his head disappeared beneath the sand.

And then the face collapsed, leaving only a shallow depression where the hole had swallowed the life of a man.

There is no salvation without sacrifice. God Himself sent His only son to prove the truth of that lesson, but there are others who have learned it in their own way. An archaeological dig at the site of the stone altar revealed a mass of bones, dating from before the time of Christ to the foundation of the village, an appeasement to whatever strange gods these people worshipped.

The chapel at Black Sands once more lies empty, and the village has a new leader. A German bomb landed on the beach in 1941, but it failed to explode. Instead, it sank into the sands, and attempts to recover it proved fruitless. If a bomb could sink into those sands, the argument went, then why not a person? So barbed wire has since been erected around the beach, and warning signs have been posted advising people to stay away.

Webster was wrong: the old gods will not be so easily forgotten. Sometimes, the wind blows along this desolate stretch of coastline and causes shapes to rise up from the beach, phantasms of sand that hold their form for just an instant too long before falling in small heaps to the ground. It may take years, even decades, to complete the process but they will succeed.

For slowly, and surely, they are obscuring the warning signs.

Some Children Wander by Mistake

The circus seldom came to the towns in the north. They were too scattered, their populations too poor, to justify the expense of transporting animals, sideshows and people down neglected roads in order to play to sparsely filled seats for a week. The bright colours of the circus vehicles looked out of place when reflected in the rain-filled potholes of such places, and the big top itself seemed to lose some of its power and vibrancy when set against grey storm clouds and relentless drizzle.

Occasionally some forgotten television star would pass through for a week of pantomime season, or a one-hit wonder from the seventies might attempt to rustle up a weekend crowd in one of the grim, boxlike clubs that squatted in the larger suburbs, but the circus was a rare visitor. William could not recall a circus ever coming to his town, not in the whole ten years of his life, although his parents sometimes spoke of one that had played early in the year of his birth. In fact, his mother said that she had felt William kick in her womb as soon as the lights went down and the first of the clowns appeared, as though he were somehow aware of the events taking place outside his red world. Since then, no great tent had occupied the big field out by the forest. No lions had passed through here, and no elephants had trumpeted. There had been no trapeze artists, no ringmasters.

No clowns.

William had few friends. There was something about him that alienated his peers: an eagerness to please, perhaps, that was the flipside of something darker and more troubling. He spent much of his spare time alone, while school was a tightrope walk between a desire to be noticed and a profound wish to avoid the bullying that came with such attention. Small and weak, William was no match for his tormentors, and had developed strategies to keep them at bay. Mostly, he tried to make them laugh.

Mostly, he failed.

There were few bright spots to life in that place, and so it was with surprise and delight that William watched the first of the posters appear in shop windows and upon lampposts, adding a splash of colour to the dull streets. They were orange and yellow and green and blue, and at the centre of each poster was the figure of a ringmaster, dressed in red with a great top hat upon his head and moustaches that curled up at the ends like snail shells. Surrounding him were animals – lions and tigers and bears, oh my – and stilt walkers, and women in spangled costumes soaring gracefully through the air. Clowns occupied the corners, with big round noses and painted-on smiles. Sideshows and rides were promised, and feats never before witnessed in a big top. 'From Europe,' announced the posters, 'For One Night Only: Circus Caliban!' The performance would take place on, of all dates, 9 December, the date of William's tenth birthday.

It took William only minutes to track down the circus folk responsible for distributing the posters. He found them on a sidestreet, using a stepladder to put up the advertisements for their great show. A cold north wind threatened to make off with a dwarf in a yellow suit who teetered at the top of the ladder as he tried to staple a pair of posters together around a lampost, while a strongman in a vinyl cape and a thin man in a red coat held the ladder steady. William sat on his bicycle, watching them silently, until the man in the red coat turned to look at him and William saw those great curly moustaches above a pair of bright pink lips.

The ringmaster smiled.

'You like the circus?' he said. His accent was funny. 'Like' became 'lak', and 'circus' became 'sow-coos'. His voice was very deep.

William nodded, awestruck.

'You don't speak?' said the ringmaster.

William found his voice.

'I like the circus. At least, I think I do. I've never been.'

The ringmaster staggered back in mock surprise, releasing his hold upon the ladder. The dwarf at the top stumbled a little, and only the actions of the bald strongman prevented the ladder from coming down, dwarf and all.

'You have never been to the circus?' said the ringmaster. 'Well, you must come. You simply must come.'

And from the pocket of his bright red coat he produced a trio of tickets and handed them to William.

'For you,' he said. 'For you, and your mother, and your father. One night only. Circus Caliban.'

William took the tickets and held them tightly in his fist, unsure of the safest place in which to put them.

'Thank you,' he said.

'You're welcome,' said the ringmaster.

'Will there be clowns?' asked William. 'There are clowns on the posters, but I just wanted to be sure.'

The strongman stared at him silently, and the dwarf on the ladder grinned. The ringmaster leaned forward and gripped William's shoulder. For a moment, William felt a stab of pain, as though the ringmaster's sharp nails were needles piercing his skin, injecting him with unknown toxins.

'There are always clowns,' said the ringmaster, and

William thought that his breath smelled very sweet, like bullseyes and gum drops and jelly babies all mixed together. 'It would not be a circus without clowns.'

Then he released William as the dwarf descended from the ladder and the three men moved on to another lamppost and another street. After all, they were here for 'One Night Only', and there was much work to be done if that night was to be as special as it could possibly be.

Over the course of the next week, more and more circus folk began to arrive in the town. Rides were assembled, and sideshow booths appeared. There was the stink of animals, and many children gathered at the edge of the field to watch the circus take shape, although the circus folk kept them back behind the wall by warning them that the animals were dangerous, or by telling them that they did not want the surprise to be spoiled. William tried to spot the clowns, but they were nowhere to be seen. He supposed that they looked like ordinary people most of the time, until they put on their makeup and their big shoes and their funny wigs. Until they did that, there was no way of telling if they were clowns or not. Until they dressed up and made you laugh they were just men, not clowns.

On the night of the performance, while his tummy was still full of birthday cake and fizzy drinks, William and his mother and father drove into town and parked their car at the edge of the great field. People had come from all around to see the circus, and a 'House Full' sign stood beside the ticket caravan. William could see the grown-ups clutching yellow admission tickets. William's tickets – the special free tickets given to him by the ringmaster – were blue. He did not see anyone else holding blue tickets. He suspected that the ringmaster couldn't afford to give out too many tickets without charge if the circus was only in town for one night.

The big top itself stood at the centre of the field. It was black with red trim, and a single red flag flew from the topmost support. Behind it were the performers' caravans, the animal cages, and the vehicles used to transport everything from town to town. Most of them looked very old, as though the circus had somehow transported itself from the middle of one century to the beginning of the next, travelling through time and space, its animals ageing but unchanging, its trapeze artists now ancient but blessed with the bodies of younger people. William could see rust on the bars of the empty lions' cage, and the interior of one of the caravans, glimpsed through an open door, was all red velvet and rich, dark wood. A woman looked out at William, then pulled the door closed to prevent him from seeing anything more, but William briefly caught a glimpse of others within: a sullen fat man whose naked body was reflected in a mirror as a young girl bathed him by candlelight, her own figure barely concealed by the thinnest of slips. For an instant, William locked eyes with the girl as her hands moved upon the older man, and then she was gone and he was left with an unfamiliar feeling of disgust, as though he were somehow complicit in the commission of a bad deed.

He followed his parents through the sideshows and rides. There were shooting ranges and hoop toss, games of skill and games of chance. Men and women called out from behind the stalls promising wonderful prizes, but William saw nobody carrying the big stuffed elephants and teddy bears that stood arrayed on the topmost shelves of the game booths, their glass eyes gleaming emptily. In fact, William saw nobody win anything at all. Shots were missed by those who regarded themselves as fairground marksmen. Darts bounced from playing cards, and hoops failed to land around goldfish bowls. All was disappointment and broken promises. William could almost see the smiles beginning to fade, and the cries of unhappy children carried on the breeze. The hucksters exchanged glances and sly grins with one another from their booths as they called to the new arrivals, the ones who still had hopes and expectations of success.

William was not aware of drifting away from his parents. One minute they were beside him, and the next it was as if the whole circus had shifted slightly, moving silently in a great circle so that William no longer stood among the rides and games but at the very periphery of the performers' caravans. He could see the lights of the sideshows and could hear the sound of the children on the merry-go-round, but they were hidden from him by vehicles and tents. These looked more dirty and worn than those close to the big top, the fabric of the tents shabbily mended where it had torn, the panels of the caravans slowly decaying into rust. There were puddles of waste on the ground, and a stale smell of cheap cooked meat hung in the air.

Uncertain, and a little afraid, William began to pick his way carefully back to his parents, stepping over guy ropes and avoiding the tow bars of the caravans, until at last he came to a single yellow tent which stood apart from the others. Outside stood a red jalopy decorated with balloons, its wheels misshapen and its seats balanced on huge springs. William could hear voices speaking inside the tent, and knew that he had found the clowns. He crept closer and lay down on his belly so that he could peer beneath the bottom of the tent, for if he was seen at the entrance then they would surely send him away and he would learn nothing more about them.

William saw battered dressing tables with brightly lit mirrors above them, the bulbs powered by a humming, unseen generator. Four men sat at the tables, dressed in suits of purple and green, yellow and orange. They had oversized shoes on their feet. Their heads were bald, but they wore no makeup. William was faintly disappointed. They were just men. They were not yet clowns.

Then, while William watched, one of the men took a cloth and doused it in liquid from a black bottle. He looked at himself grimly in the mirror, then drew the cloth across his face. Instantly, a line of white appeared, and the rim of a big red mouth. The man wiped himself again, harder now, and circular red cheeks appeared. Finally, he hid his face in the cloth, rubbing furiously, and when the cloth came away it was covered in flesh-coloured makeup and a clown stared back from the mirror. The other men were engaged in similar activities, rubbing away the cosmetics that concealed the clown faces beneath.

But those faces were not in the least bit funny or engaging. True, the men *looked* like clowns. They had big smiling mouths, and oval shapes around their eyes, and big red circles fixed on their cheeks, but their eyeballs were yellow and their skin looked puckered and diseased. Their bare hands were very white, reminding William of cheap sausages, or lengths of uncooked dough. The clowns moved listlessly, and they spoke in a language William had never heard before, more to themselves than to one another. The tongue sounded very old, and very foreign, and William felt himself grow increasingly afraid. A voice in his head seemed to echo their words, as though someone close by were translating for his benefit.

Children, the voice said. *We hate 'em. Foul things. They laugh at what they doesn't understand. They laugh at things they should be afeared of. Oh, but we know. We know what the circus hides. We know what all circuses hide. Foul children. We make them laugh, but when we can . . .*

We take 'em!

And then the nearest clown turned and stared down at

William, and the boy felt moist hands gripping his own as he was dragged beneath the canvas and into the tent. Two clowns, unseen until now, knelt by him, holding him down. William tried to cry out for help, but one of the clowns placed a hand over William's lips, stilling any sound within.

'Quiet, child,' he said, and although he still spoke in that strange language William understood each word. The clown's painted mouth smiled, but his other mouth, his *real* mouth, remained grim. The other clowns crowded around, some with a little of their old make-up still in place, so that they seemed half-human and half-other. Their irises were entirely black, and their eye sockets were rimmed with bright red flesh. One of them, now with an orange wig upon his head, placed his face very close to William's and sniffed at the boy's skin. Then he opened his mouth, revealing very white, very thin, and very sharp teeth. They curved inward at the bottom, like hooks, and William could see great spaces of red gum between them. A tongue emerged, long and purple and covered with tiny barbs. It unfolded like a fly's, or the end of a paper whistle, slowly uncurling from deep in the clown's mouth. The tongue licked at William, tasting his tears, and it felt to William like having a thistle or a cactus rubbed against his face. The clown stepped back, readying his tongue to lick again, but another clown with blue hair, bigger and taller than his fellows, grabbed the tongue between his thumb and forefinger and squeezed it so hard that his stubby nails punctured the flesh and yellow liquid dripped from the wound.

'Look!' said the clown.

The others drew closer, and William could see a streak of something pink upon the orange clown's tongue before it was released to slide back into its owner's mouth with a slapping sound. The blue clown raised his finger so William could see what was upon it.

It looked like pink make-up.

Instantly, William was dragged to his feet and brought to one of the dressing tables. He was forced into a chair, and an old cloth handkerchief was stuffed into his mouth. William struggled and tried to cry out, but the cloth smothered the sounds and the clowns held him in place. There were hands on his shoulders, on his legs, on the top of his skull and beneath his jaw, keeping his mouth closed on the gag.

And then the clowns descended upon him, their long tongues unfolding from their mouths, their breaths stale with the lingering taste of tobacco and alcohol. He felt their tongues upon him, licking his face, scouring his eyelids and his cheeks with their tiny barbs, exploring his ears and his lips and his nostrils as they covered him with their saliva. William closed his eyes tightly as his skin began to burn, the pain like the stinging of nettles. Just as he felt sure that he could take no more, the clowns stopped. They stared down upon him, and now there were real smiles beneath the painted ones as their tongues withdrew into the cages of their mouths. They backed away, revealing William's reflection to him.

Another William stared back at him from the mirror, this one pale-faced and yellow-eyed, with a fixed smile and rosy-red cheeks. The blue clown rubbed William's head gently, and a handful of William's dark hair came away in his hand. The other clowns joined in, running their sharp nails through William's hair until there was nothing of it left but a few stray strands. William's face crumpled, the tears flowing freely now, but the clown smile never left his face, so that he seemed to be laughing even as he cried, crying harder than he had ever cried before, crying for all that he had now lost and that would never be his again.

'I want my mum,' whimpered William. 'I want my dad.'

'No need,' said the blue clown. His accent was thick and foreign, like the ringmaster's. He looked very old. 'No need for family. New family now.'

'Why are you doing this to me?' said William. 'Why have you done this to my face?'

'Done?' asked the blue clown, and there was real surprise in his voice. 'What done? Done nothing. Clown not learned. Clown chosen in the mudderwomb. Clown does not become: Clown *is*. Clown is not made: Clown is *born*.'

And the show went on that night, while William's parents searched and searched for him; and the police came, and laughter rose from the circus tent as the clowns drove on in their happy jalopy and gave balloons to the children, the hated children, and when they left there were smiles on the faces of nearly all of those in the audience, except for the very clever children who sensed that there was more to clowns than bright suits and funny cars and oversized feet, and that if you were wise you didn't laugh at them, and you stayed out of their way, and you never pried into their business, for clowns are lonely and angry and want company in their misery. They are always seeking, always searching, always looking for new clowns to join them.

The Circus Caliban was gone the next day, and there was no sign that it had ever visited the town. The police looked, but William was never seen again, and a new clown was added to the act of the Circus Caliban when next it appeared at the edge of a forest in a country far, far from this one. He was smaller than the rest, and seemed always to be looking into the laughing audience, searching for the parents that he still hoped would find him, but they never came.

And his teeth fell out and were replaced by sharp, white hooks that were kept hidden behind shields of plastic; and his nails decayed to hard yellow stumps at the end of soft, pale fingers. He grew tall and strong, until at last he forgot his name and became only 'Clown', and a great clown he was. His tongue grew like a snake's, and he tasted children with it as they laughed, for clowns are hungry and sad and envious of humanity. They travel from town to town looking for those that they can steal away, always marking the child that kicks in the womb, and always finding him upon their return.

For clowns are not made.

Clowns are *born.*

Deep Dark Green

We should never have gone near Baal's Pond. We should have stayed far away from it as we were told, as we had always been told, but young men will follow young girls and do their bidding. That is the way of things, and it will always be the way. Hindsight is worse than blindness, and pleasure and regret walk hand in hand.

And so we had gone to that place, Catherine and I. I had been blinded by the promise in her eyes, deafened by the demands of my own appetites. I was young. I did not understand what those appetites could create, how they could be transformed, mutated, degraded.

How they could find form in the being that dwelt in Baal's Pond.

I think of Catherine often, now that the hour of my own passing approaches. I find myself staring at my reflection on the surface of the lake near my home. I throw a stone and watch my face come apart in ripples, one visage briefly becoming many as I am drawn back to the last day that I spent with her. It becomes harder and harder to depart from such places now, for since her death part of me has always been lost in dark water. The pain of the disease that is eating away at my insides is relentless, but I think that I shall not wait for my body to betray me. Instead, I will join her in the depths and hope that she will come to me, her mouth against mine as I breathe my last, and yet I have lived with her loss for so long that the thought of being reunited with her is almost too much to bear.

There have been other women since Catherine, although none remained by my side for very long. I was not entirely sorry to see them go. In truth, I found that I came to fear them, and so was unable to open myself fully to them. I was afraid of their desires, their rapaciousness, their ability to draw a man inside them and make him lose himself in the promise of their flesh. Is that not a terrible confession for a man to make? Sometimes I feel that it is. At other times, though, I believe that perhaps I am merely more honest than most of my fellows. My eyes have been opened, and I have seen the worm that coils in the apple of temptation.

So I am alive and Catherine is dead, and her body will never be found. It lies at the bottom of Baal's Pond, far in the tainted reaches, down where it is green.

Deep, dark green.

There had always been something strange about that place. A long time before, so long ago that none of those responsible, or their children, or their children's children, remained alive to tell of it, the river was redirected through a small glen. Somehow – it was said that stolen kegs of gunpowder were used – the banks were blown apart and the waters rushed downhill into the little valley, flooding it completely before resuming their original course half a mile further on. People from distant villages gathered to watch the event, and the only sound to be heard before the gunpowder exploded was the soft uttering of prayers, the rattle of the beads, and the dull clanking of a chain from the cottage far below as a presence within tried desperately to free itself.

Those who stood, listening and praying, had lost children to what lay below. It had drawn them in through its small, wooden gate, luring them with the wondrous colours of its flowers and their strange, intoxicating scents. Like flies attracted to a pitcher plant, they had entered and died, drowning in strange desires that they could not comprehend. Afterward, their bodies were interred in the garden, and the flowers grew sweeter still.

Then, as the tale would have it, the prayers stopped, a fuse was lit, and a great mass of earth exploded into the air. The waters surged forth, exploiting the breach, and descended into the glen. Whatever had once lived in that place – the animals, the insects, the trees and plants, every living thing – had died on that day in a brown muddy torrent.

Or so they must have hoped. Now, this place that they named Baal's Pond was deeper than any other stretch of the river. No sunlight penetrated to its depths, and no fish swam there. The water was so dark as to be almost black, like oil. It even felt different on the skin: it was viscous, and when clasped in cupped hands it dripped like honey through one's fingers. Nothing could live in such an environment. I still do not believe that anything lives down there.

For whatever is down there is not alive.

It exists, but it is not alive.

I was sixteen years old on the morning that we went there together for the last time, Catherine and I. She too was sixteen, but so far beyond me that the months between us were really years, and I felt awkward and powerless around her. I know now that I was already in love with her, with what she was and with the promise of what she would become. She stood at the edge of that dark place, and her brightness appeared to mock it. Her hair was blond and hung loosely on her back and shoulders, and the sunlight made her tanned skin glow. But when I looked into the water there was no reflection of her on its surface, as though she had already been devoured by the blackness.

She turned to me as she cast aside her clothing and said: 'Are you afraid?'

And I was afraid: I was afraid of the stillness of the water. It should have moved swiftly, fast as the flow that poured into it from the higher ground above, but it did not. Instead, there was a sluggishness about it, a lethargy. At its eastern extreme, where the flooded glen ended and the slope of the hill began, the river regained some of its lost energy, but it seemed that the water had been tainted by its contact with this place, for a thin film of oil was now revealed by the sunlight upon it.

I was afraid, too, of what our parents would say if they discovered that we were in this place, if they knew what we were planning and if they suspected what my thoughts of her were. That, in its turn, led me to my greatest fear: my fear of her. I wanted her badly, so very badly. My stomach tightened every time I looked upon her. Now, seeing her naked for the first time, it was all that I could do to stop myself from trembling. I shook my head.

'I'm not afraid,' I said.

In my mind, I replayed fantasies of a life we might have together, of marriage and children, and love, and the touch of her skin against mine. We had kissed, Catherine and I, and I had felt her in my mouth before she pulled away from me, laughing. Yet with each kiss she lingered a little longer, her laughter a little more uncertain, her breath a little shorter.

And I lived and died in every kiss.

'Are you sure?'

She stood on the bank and glanced at me over her shoulder. She was smiling, and there was that promise in her smile. She could tell what I was thinking. She could always tell. Then, with one short peal of laughter, she took a deep breath and arced into the pond. There was no splash.

The surface simply separated to allow her passage, then bound itself together again behind her. No ripples appeared, and the rhythm of the water lapping at the bank remained undisturbed.

But I did not follow her. I looked into that black pool, and my courage left me. Instead, I waited for her, shivering, the grass sharp beneath my feet, the wind cold against my skin, and willed her to emerge once again from the water, her laughter baiting me and her eyes calling me to her.

But she did not return. Seconds passed, then an entire minute. I stared into the pool, hoping to see her golden form just below the surface, but there was nothing. There was not even birdsong in this place, and no flies buzzed. I thought of the warnings, the old tales. Others had descended into those depths, and some had never been seen again. The river banks had been searched in the hope that the waters might yield up their bodies, but they never did. Now only the bravest or most foolhardy came here, young men who hoped that their youthful displays would be rewarded by an embrace, or more. And when at last they walked away from this place, their hands entwined with those of another, they promised themselves that they would never return, for they were the lucky ones. They knew that others had not been so fortunate.

And so my love for her overcame my fear, and I closed my eyes and followed her into the depths.

The water was unimaginably cold, so cold that I felt my heart would stop beating and freeze within my body, and its strange thickness made it difficult to swim. I looked up and could not see the sun, yet there was a light of sorts. I could perceive my hands in front of my face, but the palms were lit from below, not above. I twisted in the water, facing the bed of the pond, and kicked back with my legs, moving towards the source of the illumination.

There was a house at the bottom of the pond.

It was built of stone and had two windows, one at either side of the door, and a roof that might once have been thatched but was now no more than slats and struts. The remains of a low stone wall curled like arms around what might once have been a garden, a gap in the middle where a gate had once hung, and a ruined chimney stack pointed an accusing finger towards the bright, blue, unseen world above. The light came from behind the windows of the dwelling, moving slowly from side to side as if what was bearing it were somehow trapped and, like a caged animal, had bound up its madness in relentless motion. Around the house, tall thick weeds grew, each fifteen or twenty feet in length and swaying gently in the flow. I had never seen anything like them before. It seemed to me that there was something wrong with them, and their swaying made me uneasy. It took me only seconds to realise what it was about them that troubled me.

Their rhythm was not being dictated by the current of the river. Instead, they moved independently of it, seeking, probing, spreading themselves through the dark waters like the tentacles of some great sea creature searching for prey. And at the end of one weed, something golden thrashed, and a broad halo of hair was briefly burnished by the light from below. Catherine looked up at me, her cheeks swollen as she tried to hold in the last of her air, and shook her head desperately. Her hands reached for me, the fingers grasping. I began to swim to her, but the weed wrapped itself once more around her body, twisting her in a circle as it did so, tightening its grip upon her. Catherine's mouth opened, sending a stream of precious bubbles towards me. Her eyes grew wide and her lips seemed to form my name as the dark green water entered her body. Her thrashings increased in intensity and her hands lashed out at the weed, her fingers wrenching wildly at it. Then her lungs flooded, her struggles became feeble, and she grew still as she drowned. She hung in the depths, her arms outstretched and her eyes open, staring into eternity.

Even then, I thought that I could save her, that somehow I could bring her to the surface and pump that foul water from her, that I could fill her with life from my body and taste once again her breath in my mouth. But as I tried to swim to her, she began to recede from me. I thought at first that it must be some illusion, that the water was simply deeper than it at first seemed, but the ruined house continued to grow nearer even as she drew further away from me. I watched helplessly as the weed pulled her deeper and deeper down until, with one final jerk, she was yanked through the doorway, and I understood at last that the weeds were growing not around the house, but from within it.

Inside the cottage, the light stopped moving. Through the wreckage of the roof, I saw Catherine anchored to the bed of the river, the weed still tight around her waist. There came the muffled, distorted sound of an old chain clanging on stones as the light approached and surrounded her, then wrapped her in its embrace. It assumed a shape: arms and legs formed, thin and pale, the muscles wasted and the skin hanging loose upon the bones. I saw long white hair writhing in the water. I caught a glimpse of naked flesh, wrinkled by the relentless flow of the river and pitted with ugly red sores. Old female breasts, flat and lifeless, pressed themselves against the still form of my beloved Catherine, as it bent as if to kiss her.

I was almost within reach of the roof now and, for the first time, the being seemed to sense my approach. It twisted towards me, raising its face to mine, and I saw its mouth. Where lips and teeth should have been, there was instead the round, sucking hole of a lamprey, red and engorged. It opened and closed, pulsing quickly, already tasting the girl it had ensnared. Above the mouth, black lidless eyes regarded me blankly before its hunger finally overcame it and it turned away to begin its work. I tried to wrench one of the struts from the roof to use as a weapon, but my strength was failing and my head ached from the effort of holding my breath. I felt certain that I had only seconds of air left, but I would not leave Catherine to this thing.

Yet as I gripped the wood, I sensed movement around me. White things shimmered at the periphery of my vision. I looked to my left and found that the length of weed closest to me no longer moved gently in the flow. It could not, for the burden it held constrained it. Strands of green had wrapped themselves around the legs of the boy, holding him in place even as he seemed to be reaching for the surface, but this one was long dead. There were dark patches around his unseeing eyes, and the edges of his bones showed like knives beneath his skin. His lips were torn and bruised where that lamprey mouth had attached itself to his for one final kiss.

All around me, boys and girls hung unmoving in the water, each anchored securely by the weeds which emanated from the ruined house below. Some were naked, while tattered clothing still clung to the bodies of the others. Their hair shifted softly in the current, and their hands moved in small strokes, imitating life even in death. They were all here: all of the lost, all of the young dead, their shades lingering in the depths, waiting to welcome another to their ranks.

I felt a huge surge of pity and fear, and my mouth opened with the shock of what I was seeing. Immediately, water rushed into my nose and mouth. I panicked and thrashed my legs, Catherine now forgotten in the urge to save my own life. I did not want to die down there, to be touched in my final moments by the thing that dwelt in the old house, before joining the ghosts of children in the waters of that place.

It was my panic that saved my life. I felt something rubbery lashing at my heel as the weed tried to gain some purchase on my body, but I was already leaving it behind as the light below me faded and the dark water filled my lungs, until the sky at last exploded above me and the sweetness of the air dazzled my senses.

For two days they dragged the river and probed with poles the depths of Baal's Pond, but they never found her. She was lost to us, lost to me, and she dwelt thereafter in a place where black waters flowed and the ghosts of the young hung in the current and watched her, unspeaking. She still waits for me there, and I will join her, soon enough. I have been back there many times since, although now it is fenced and gated, and the land around it has been sown with briars and poisonous plants to discourage the incautious. The surface of the pool still devours the light, and the thing below still waits, pacing hungrily, a being of pure appetite, as it was in life, as it is in death. It lives in a world of only two colours: red, the colour of lips and lust.

And green.

Deep, dark green.

Miss Froom, Vampire

To begin, it is a matter of record that Miss Froom enjoyed a reputation as a gardener of some note. Her roses were the envy of many a retired army man who, after a lifetime of inflicting destruction on others, now believed that he had found an outlet for his hitherto unexplored creative urges, the impulse to cultivate roses being one that traditionally strikes males in the autumn of their years, and is generally encouraged by their weary spouses as it gets their husbands out of the house for long periods of time. It is a little-remarked fact that many a retired gentleman has unwittingly avoided a messy death at the hands of his wife by the simple expedient of picking up a pair of pruning shears and departing for greener spaces.

Had Miss Froom's expertise extended solely to roses, she would still have been assured a permanent place in the gardening lore of the county. But the lady in question also produced wonderful marrows, marvellous carrots, and cabbages with the otherworldly beauty of alien sunsets. At the annual fair in Broughton, which was to the county's gardeners what Cruft's is to besotted dog owners, Miss Froom was the yardstick by whom others measured their successes, and their failures.

Curiously, Miss Froom's accomplishments aroused little envy among her male peers, a circumstance not unrelated to her general attractiveness. Her age was largely indeterminable, but most suspected that she was in her early fifties. Her hair was very dark, and unstreaked with grey, a condition that led the more uncharitable women of the village to suggest that her colour was only natural if the good Lord had a palette that included Midnight Haze or Autumn Night. Her face was quite pale, with full lips and eyes that appeared alternately dark blue or deep green, depending upon the light. Her body was full, although she tended to dress rather conservatively and rarely exposed more than an ivory neck and the faintest hint of bosom, a restraint that merely added to her allure. Miss Froom was, in short, the kind of woman of whom men spoke favorably when they were freed from the constraints of censorious female company. She was also the kind of woman of whom other women spoke, and perhaps not always kindly, although there were those among them who might have felt something of their menfolk's baser admiration of Miss Froom, were they capable of admitting it to themselves.

A lane ran behind Miss Froom's cottage on the outskirts of the village, from which she could sometimes be glimpsed in her garden, digging and pruning in order to maintain the quality and beauty of all that grew there. She would always refuse offers of male help with even the most taxing of labours, arguing with a smile that she liked to believe that whatever awards accrued to her as a result of her work were entirely hers, and hers alone. The men would tip their hats and go about their business, regretting that an afternoon spent in the company of the very lovely Miss Froom was to be denied them once again.

And so it might have come as a surprise to these gentlemen, had any of them been present to witness the occurrence, when Miss Froom hailed a young man who was bicycling by her garden one bright spring afternoon. The young man, who came from the neighbouring village of Ashburnham and was largely unfamiliar with matters horticultural, and therefore with the reputation of Miss Froom, stopped and leaned his bicycle against the wall. Peering over, he saw a woman in beige trousers and a white shirt resting on a spade. The young man, whose name was Edward, allowed himself a brief moment to take in the woman's appearance. Although the sun was shining it was still a chilly day, but the woman seemed untroubled by the cold. Her hair was tied up loosely on her head, and her lips were very red against the pallor of her complexion. She was quite stunningly attractive, Edward thought, for a woman three decades his senior. In fact, her face looked vaguely familiar, and Edward wondered if one of his more private fantasies had somehow come to life before him, for he felt certain that a woman with just such a face had occupied his imagination in a most pleasant way at some point in the past.

'I was wondering,' said the woman, 'if you might have a moment to spare. I'm trying to break the soil in order to sow, but I'm afraid there's still a touch of winter to it.'

Edward dismounted, opened the gate, and entered Miss Froom's garden. As he drew closer, she seemed to grow in beauty, so that Edward felt his jaw drop slightly in her presence. Her lips parted and Edward caught a glimpse of white teeth and a hint of pink tongue. He tried to speak, but only a hoarse croak emerged. He coughed, and managed to compose a relatively coherent sentence.

'I'd be happy to help you, ma'am,' he said. 'It would be my pleasure.'

Miss Froom seemed almost to blush. At least, she approximated the movements of one who was a little embarrassed, but only the faintest rose of blood bloomed at her cheeks, as though she had only a little to spare.

'My name is Miss Froom,' she said, 'but you can call me Laura. Nobody calls me "ma'am." '

Laura was Edward's favourite name, although he could

not recall himself ever noticing that before. He gave Laura his own name and, introductions complete, she handed him the spade.

'It shouldn't take long,' said Miss Froom. 'I do hope I'm not keeping you from anything.'

Edward assured her that she was not. By now he could not even remember why he had come to the village to begin with. Whatever it was, it could wait.

And so they worked, side by side, in Miss Froom's garden, sharing small details of their lives but largely silent, Edward occupied mainly by thoughts of the woman close beside him, and the faintest scent of lilies which emanated from her person.

And Miss Froom?

Well, suffice it to say that Miss Froom was thinking of Edward in return.

As the light began to fade, Miss Froom suggested that they finish up, and enquired if Edward might like to step inside for some tea. Edward readily agreed, and was about to take a seat at Miss Froom's kitchen table when she asked him if he wouldn't like to wash his hands first. Now it was Edward's turn to be embarrassed, but Miss Froom hushed him and led him by the hand up the stairs, where she showed him into her spotlessly clean bathroom and handed him a towel, a cloth, and a bar of clear soap.

'Remember,' she said. 'Right up to the elbows, and don't neglect your face and neck. You'll feel better for it.'

Once she had left the room, Edward removed his shirt and cleaned himself scrupulously. The soap smelled a little funny, he thought, rather like a hospital floor after it has been disinfected. Nevertheless, it was undoubtedly effective, for Edward believed that he had never been cleaner once he had finished drying himself off. There came a knock at the door and a hand appeared, at the end of which hung a crisp, white shirt.

'Put this on,' said Miss Froom. 'No point in being clean in a dirty shirt. I'll let the other soak while we eat.'

Edward took the garment and put it on. It felt a little rough against his skin, and there were small rust-coloured stains upon the sleeve and the shoulders, but compared to his own shirt it was spotless. Truth be told, Edward's shirt had not been entirely fresh *before* he began his labours on Miss Froom's behalf, and he rather hoped that the lady in question would ascribe its unfortunate state to his exertions in her garden and not to any lapse in personal hygiene on his own part.

When he returned to the kitchen, Edward saw that there was an array of cheeses and cold meats displayed upon the table. There were also assorted pastries and biscuits, and a large fruit cake that still steamed slightly from the oven.

'Were you expecting someone?' Edward asked.

Actually, it looked to Edward as if Miss Froom was expecting a whole team of someones, and that he had seen less lavish spreads at the end of village cricket games.

'Oh,' said Miss Froom. 'You never know when company will drop by.'

She poured him some tea and Edward, famished, began to eat. He was finishing his third sandwich before he noticed that the woman on the other side of the table was not joining him.

'Aren't you eating?' he asked.

'I have a disorder,' said Miss Froom. 'It limits what I can eat.'

Edward didn't press the lady further. He was largely ignorant about the female body, but he had learned from his father that such ignorance was only right and proper. There was, he gathered, nothing worse for a man than to inadvertently set foot in the minefield marked 'Women's Troubles'. Edward decided to make for less dangerous territory.

'You have a nice house,' he said.

'Thank you,' said Miss Froom.

There was another lull in their discourse. Edward, unused to taking tea with strange ladies in their kitchens while wearing unfamiliar shirts, was struggling to keep the conversation going.

'You're not, er..?' he began. 'Um, I mean, is there a—'

'No,' said Miss Froom, cutting him off at the pass. 'I'm not married.'

'Oh,' said Edward. 'Right.'

Miss Froom smiled at him. The temperature in the kitchen appeared to Edward to rise a couple of degrees.

'Have a bun,' said Miss Froom.

She extended the plate of pastries toward him. Edward opted for a lemon tart. It disintegrated as soon as he bit into it, showering him with crumbs. Miss Froom, who had stood to pour him some more tea, placed the teapot back on its stand and brushed softly at Edward's shirtfront with the palm of her hand.

Edward nearly choked on his tart.

'Let me get you some water,' said Miss Froom, but as she turned she staggered slightly, apparently about to fall. Edward rose swiftly and held her shoulders, then helped her back to her seat. She looked even paler than before, he thought, although her lips were redder yet.

'I'm sorry,' she said. 'I've been feeling a little weak lately. The winter was hard.'

Edward enquired if she needed a doctor, but Miss Froom told him that she did not. Instead, she asked him to go to the refrigerator and retrieve from it the bottle that stood beside the milk. Edward did as he was told, noting as he opened the door that the interior of the fridge was very cold indeed, and returned with a red wine bottle.

'Pour me some, please,' said Miss Froom.

Edward poured the liquid into a cup. It was more viscous than wine, and had a faint but decidedly unpleasant smell. It reminded Edward of the inside of a butcher's shop.

'What is it?' he asked, as Miss Froom took a long mouthful.

'Rat's blood,' said Miss Froom, wiping a little dribble from her chin with a napkin.

Edward felt certain that he had misheard, but the stench from the cup told him that he had not.

'Rat's blood?' he asked, unable to keep the disgust from his voice. 'Why are you drinking rat's blood?'

'Because it is all that I have,' said Miss Froom, as though the answer was obvious. 'If I had anything of higher quality, then I would be drinking that instead.'

Edward wondered how hard it could be to acquire something tastier than rodent's blood, and decided that it couldn't be very difficult at all.

'What about, er, wine?' he suggested.

'Well, wine isn't blood, is it, dear?' said Miss Froom gently, in the tone teachers are accustomed to use with the slower children in the class, the kind who sup from inkwells and misjudge the time it takes to get to the toilet.

'But why blood at all?' asked Edward. 'I mean, you know, it's not what people usually drink.'

Miss Froom was now sipping delicately, if distastefully, from her glass.

'I suppose you're right, but it is all that I *can* drink. It's all that gives me sustenance. Without it, I would die. Any blood will do, really, although I don't care much for goat's blood. It tastes a little strong. And rat's blood, naturally, is a last resort.'

Edward sat down heavily.

'All a bit much for you, is it?' asked Miss Froom. She patted his hand lightly. Her skin was almost translucent. Edward thought he could see bones through it.

'What kind of person drinks blood?' asked Edward. He shook his head at the awfulness of it.

'Not a person,' said Miss Froom. 'I don't think I can call myself that any longer. There is another word for what I am, although I don't like to hear it used. It has such . . . *negative* connotations.'

It took Edward a moment to figure out the word for himself. He wasn't very smart, but then Miss Froom liked that about him.

'Is the word—?' Edward began, but Miss Froom interrupted him before he could speak it, flinching slightly as she did so.

'Yes,' she said. 'That's the one.'

Edward quickly moved away from Miss Froom, putting as much distance between them as he could, until he realised that he had backed himself into a corner.

'Stay away from me,' he said. He rummaged under his shirt and removed a small silver cross. It was about half an inch long, and he had trouble holding it between his thumb and forefinger without hiding it altogether.

'Oh, don't be silly,' said Miss Froom. 'I'm not going to hurt you. And put that away. It doesn't work anyway.'

Edward kept the cross outstretched for a moment or two more then, rather sheepishly, put it back inside his shirt. Nevertheless, he stayed as far away as possible from the now faintly threatening woman at the table. His eyes cast around for possible weapons to use in the event of an attack, but the only heavy object he could see was the fruit cake.

'So it's not true then, about crosses and suchlike?' he said.

'No,' said Miss Froom. She sounded a little offended.

'What about only being able to come out at night?'

'Edward,' she said, patiently. 'We've just spent an afternoon working in the garden.'

'Oh,' said Edward. 'Right. Stake through the heart?'

'That'll work,' said Miss Froom. 'But then, it would work on anybody, wouldn't it? I expect the same would go for cutting my head off, but I can't say I've tried that either.'

'What about swift flowing water?'

'I have swimming medals,' said Miss Froom. 'From when I was a girl.'

'Garlic?' asked Edward hopefully.

'Never cared for it,' said Miss Froom, 'except in casseroles.'

'Sleeping in a coffin?'

'Be serious,' said Miss Froom.

Edward thought for a moment.

'Look,' he said, 'apart from the drinking blood thing, are you sure you're a, well, a "you-know-what"?'

'Well,' said Miss Froom, 'the "drinking blood thing" as you put it, is rather a large part of being a "you-know-what". In addition, I'm very old, older than I look, older even than this village. I am what I am, and have been for a very long time.'

'But, er, "your kind" attack people, don't they?'

'Not me,' said Miss Froom. 'I like a quiet life. You start biting people and drinking their blood and, frankly, someone is going to notice after a while. It's easier to prey on forest animals, the odd cat, maybe even sip from the neck of a cow or two, although it's not very hygienic.'

She sighed loudly.

'Unfortunately, my scruples about preying on people mean that my strength has been gradually failing over these last decades. I'm not sure I could even hold on to a cow any longer, so now I'm reduced to rats. You know, it takes about fifty rats to equal the nutritional value of even one pint of human blood. Do you know how hard it is to trap fifty rats?'

Edward opined that it was probably very hard indeed.

'But I can live for a few months on a pint, if I'm careful,' she said. 'At least, I could in the past, but I am weaker now than I have ever been. Soon, I will begin to age, and then . . .'

She fell silent. As Edward watched, a single tear trickled down her pale cheek. It left only a trace of moisture behind it, like a diamond slowly sliding across a patch of ice.

'Thank you for your help with my garden,' she said softly. 'Perhaps you'd better leave now.'

Edward stared at her, unsure of how to respond.

'And Edward?' she added, 'I beg of you to say nothing of this to anyone. I felt that I could trust you, but it was weak and unfair of me to do so. All I can hope is that you are as honourable as you are handsome, and as decent as you are kind.'

And with that she buried her head in her hands and spoke no more.

Edward left his corner and walked to her. He laid a hand gently on Miss Froom's shoulder. She felt very cold.

'A pint?' he said at last.

Miss Froom slowly stopped sobbing.

'What?' she asked.

'You said that a pint of blood could keep you going for months.'

His voice was very soft, and a little hesitant.

'A pint's not much, is it?' he said.

Miss Froom looked at him, and he drowned in her eyes.

'I can't ask you to do that,' she said.

'You didn't ask,' said Edward. 'I offered.'

Miss Froom didn't speak. Instead, she ran a cold hand across Edward's face and touched his lips with her fingers.

'Thank you,' she whispered. 'Perhaps there's something I can offer you in return.'

Her hand touched her chest and a button on her shirt popped open, exposing a little more of the fabled bosom that had kept many a frustrated rose grower awake at night. Edward swallowed hard as, gently, she made him sit down once again on the kitchen chair.

'Would you mind if I drank a little now?' she asked.

'No, not at all,' said Edward, although his voice trembled slightly. 'Where do you want to take it from?'

'It doesn't matter,' said Miss Froom. 'The neck is good, but I don't want to leave a visible mark. Perhaps . . . your wrist?'

And she rolled up his sleeve, revealing his clean, freckled arm.

Edward nodded.

'Will it hurt?' he asked.

'Just a sting at first,' said Miss Froom. 'Then you won't feel anything else.'

Miss Froom's mouth opened, and he saw that her canines were a little longer than a normal person's. Her tongue flicked at them, and Edward felt a surge of fear. Her mouth descended on him and twin needles of pain shot through his forearm. He gasped, but then the pain faded and he felt a kind of warmth, and a sleepy pleasure. His eyes closed and beautiful images came to him. He dreamed that he was with Miss Froom, together in a wonderful intimacy, and that she loved him dearly, even as he drifted into a deep, shadowy redness.

When Edward was dead, Miss Froom, her strengh now restored, carried him to the cellar. There she worked on him, removing the major organs before placing his body in a large wine press. When he was fully drained, she removed what was left of him, separated the bones, and put them through a grinder. She took the fine powder and placed it in jars, so that she could mix it into the soil over the coming weeks, assuring herself of another fine crop of vegetables and roses for the coming year. Lastly, she disposed of Edward's bicycle by tossing it into a patch of marshland a short distance from her home. When all was done, she treated herself to a little tipple from her new stock, her fingers lingering at her neck as she recalled her first taste of the young visitor.

Men, thought Miss Froom to herself: they really were the sweetest of creatures.

The Wakeford Abyss

The truth of nature lies in
deep mines and caves.

Democritus

The two men stared down into the void below. Behind them, the sun was slowly rising, a counterpoint to the journey that they were about to undertake. Larks called, but the sound of them seemed to come from far away. Here, among these desolate hills, no birds flew. The only sign of life that they had encountered upon their ascent was a single goat that had somehow found itself alone on the side of Bledstone Hill and was now making a concerted effort to rejoin its fellows in more hospitable surroundings. They could still see it moving gingerly among the rocks and scree when they turned towards the sun. Sure-footed as it was, it seemed to evince a distrust of the ground beneath its feet, and with good cause: both of the men had taken nasty tumbles on their approach, and Molton, the older and stouter of the two, had lost his compass during one particularly painful fall.

It was Molton who now removed his cap and, holding it firmly by the brim, began to fan himself gently.

'Feels like it's going be a hot one,' he said.

From where they stood, they could see green fields and stone walls slowly emerging from the night's gloom as the light rose. The distant spire of Wakeford's only church was revealed to them, surrounded by the small, redbrick houses of its worshippers. Soon there would be people moving, and the noise of carts upon its narrow streets, but for now the village was still. Molton, who was born and raised in London and considered himself very much the city gent, wondered how anyone could live in such a place. It was too quiet for him, too provincial, and without any of the distractions on which he depended for his amusement.

A bleating noise came to him, and he shielded his eyes as he attempted to assess the goat's progress. He saw it poised on a small rock, testing the ground ahead with its hoof. Each time it tried to place its weight down, shingle slid away, raising dust as it went.

'Poor beggar,' said Molton. 'He'll be hungry soon.'

He tugged at his moustaches and, finding them colonised by small pieces of grit, began to clean them with a small comb.

The other man did not take his eyes from the maw at their feet. He was smaller than Molton by about six inches, and his face was clean shaven but, like his companion, his bearing betrayed his military origins. His name was Clements, and it was largely at his instigation that the two men had made their way to Wakeford. Both had some experience of climbing, mainly in the Alps, but it was Clements who had suggested that those skills might serve them just as well below ground as above.

'Who's a poor beggar?' asked Clements.

'The goat,' said Molton. 'Looks as if he's stuck up here.'

'He'll find his way down. They always do.'

Molton looked doubtful. He had always been the more cautious of the two men, and sedentary by nature, at least when compared with Clements's more robust approach to life. Nevertheless, the two men had found a common bond in their fascination with ascents and descents, a bond strengthened by their shared belief in the value of a good, strong rope.

The skills required by mountaineers, and the equipment they used, had advanced little in three hundred years of climbing. A stout alpenstock was essential, while the continentals also favoured crampons. Britons, Clements and Molton among them, eschewed crampons in favour of two rows of triple-headed tacks in the soles of their boots, but most parties agreed that ropes simply weren't the sort of thing that a gentleman ought to be using. They were considered vaguely unmanly, as well as potentially dangerous.

Clements and Molton had become believers in the merits of rope following an encounter with the legendary Irish scientist and climber, John Tyndall, in London some years earlier. In 1858, Tyndall had successfully completed his first solo ascent of Monte Rosa without the aid of guides, porters or provisions, and with only a ham sandwich and a bottle of tea to sustain him. Only the most foolhardy of critics would dare to impugn the bravery of such a man. In 1860, he had aroused considerable controversy when he ascribed the blame for the deaths of two Englishmen and a guide on the Alpine slope of Col du Geant to inadequate use of ropes. Clements and Molton had read Tyndall's letter to *The Times* concerning the accident, and the correspondence that quickly followed. When, in the spring of 1861, Tyndall invited the Alpine climber and guide, Auguste Balmat, to speak at the British Museum, the two men were in attendance, and later enjoyed a supper with Tyndall. By the time he was finished with them, it was all that they could do not to seek out the nearest ropemaker and set him to work on miles of stout hessian.

Thus it was that Clements and Molton were clad in what was, for the time, considered more than suitable attire for a descent beneath the earth: stout boots, strong tweeds and stiff leather gloves. Lengths of rope lay coiled at their feet, alongside two packs filled with water, some roast chicken, two loaves of freshly baked bread, and a flask of burgundy. They had brought four lanterns with them, and enough fuel to give them light for about twelve hours, although they expected to be below ground for no more than half of that time.

Molton's gaze drifted across the rocky landscape, then alighted like a crow on a vertical wooden stave that stood off to his right.

'I say, what do you think that is?' he said, pointing with his right hand.

Clements squinted, then walked towards the pole. It was about three feet in height, and was set deeply into the ground. A metal ring hung from the top, adorned with strands of old rope.

'It looks like a tethering post,' said Clements.

'Odd place to tether an animal,' Molton replied.

Clements shrugged.

'They're odd people.'

He rubbed his hands together and headed back to the opening in the rock.

'Right then,' he said. 'Let's get started.'

While Clements anchored the rope, Molton checked the kit and tested the lamps.

'How deep did you say this was?' he asked.

'Don't know,' Clements replied. 'Couple of hundred feet, maybe.'

'Huh. A few hundred feet doesn't sound like much of an abyss.'

'It's merely an estimate,' said Clements. 'It could be more. Nobody knows. It's virgin territory.'

The Wakeford Abyss, as it was known locally, extended for about fifty feet along the south face of Bledstone Hill, like a scar in the earth that had never quite healed. At its widest point it opened to about twenty feet, narrowing at either extreme to mere inches before losing itself among the bare rocks. By standing on its very edge, it was possible to see only the first fifteen feet of the interior, before the curvature of the rock blocked out the sunlight.

It was not entirely clear what had caused this geological anomaly and, in truth, few in the region cared much to discover more about it. Clements and Molton had dined at Wakeford's sole inn the night before, and made efforts to plumb the depths of local knowledge about the hole torn in the hillside. For their troubles they received a hodge-podge of myth, tall tales and regional superstitions. The abyss was said to be the lair of a dragon in ancient times, according to one regular at the bar. Another claimed that it was formerly known as The Devil's Hole, a name as much bound up with the locals' penchant for earthy humour as with any satanic origins. There was talk of druidic sacrifices, of long-dead lords tethering animals to the rocks as a means of appeasing the appetites of whatever lay within. As the evening wore on, and the beer flowed more freely, the stories grew more and more extreme in their details, until a credulous listener might have felt that Bledstone Hill contained every form of devilment known to man, and more besides.

Finally, while they were finishing their ales in preparation for bed, a farmer took the seat nearest to the two ex-soldiers. He was a small man, with the dark, worn features of one who has spent most of his life out of doors confronting the harshest of elements. The other men and women at the bar did not greet him by name, although they followed his progress carefully as he crossed the floor to join the two strangers.

'I hear you gentleman are intent upon visiting the abyss tomorrow,' he said.

Molton advised him that, yes, that was indeed the case.

'Have you another tall tale to add to our collection?' asked Clements. 'We seem to be accumulating quite a number.'

The impatience was audible in his voice. Clements had earlier hoped for some useful information that might have aided them in their exploration, but two hours spent in the best company that Wakeford could offer had left him no wiser than before, although slightly poorer and considerably more weary.

'No, I'm not much of a one for telling tales,' replied the farmer. 'But my fields lie at the base of Bledstone Hill, and you'll be passing through them tomorrow on your journey, I don't doubt.'

'We'll take care to close the gates,' said Molton. 'You don't have to be concerned.'

The farmer took a sip of his beer.

'It's not about gates that I'm concerned,' he said. 'Like I said, I don't have any tall tales to share with you, but I do know this: there was a time when flocks grazed on the lower reaches of Bledstone. They do so no longer.'

Clements shrugged. 'We've seen it from afar. It doesn't look as if there would be much grazing there.'

'Sheep, and goats more, will find food in the barest of places,' said the farmer. 'This is hard land, and we can't be choosy about how we fill the bellies of our livestock. But I've lost animals on Bledstone, and never found them again, and now I'd be hard pressed to make even sheep graze on that hill. They don't like it, so I leave them where they are.'

Molton and Clements exchanged a glance, and the farmer picked up on their scepticism.

'I don't expect you gentlemen to listen to much that I have to say. You're from the city. Army men, too, I should say. You think you've seen it all, and it may be that you've seen much, it's true. But I've found substances on the rocks, sticky in the morning sun, as though something had passed that way in the night. I've found the bodies of birds drained of life. You talk to other people here, the ones who kept their own counsel tonight, and you'll hear the same from them.'

'Nonsense,' scoffed Clements.

Molton, ever the diplomat, attempted a more conciliatory tone.

'Has anyone ever *seen* anything?' he asked. 'I mean, it's all well and good telling us these things, but Clements here has a point: there could be a hundred explanations for what you've just told us, and none of them stranger than the next.'

The farmer shook his head. He seemed untroubled by the doubts expressed by the two men, as though he were so certain of the truth in his own mind that he had long since learned to hide his frustration with those who chose not to listen.

'No,' he said. 'I've not seen anything, and anyway there are precautions taken now to keep it at bay. Whatever's down there knows better than to show itself too, for fear of being exposed or hunted. I'd say it tries to venture out only when it's desperate, and can live long on the poorest of suppers. It's been in the abyss for a long, long time, and must be old now, older than any of us can imagine. Why should that be so hard for you to believe? From what I hear, they're finding new creatures all the time, animals that nobody could ever have imagined existed living quietly in remote places. Why not here, under the ground?'

Despite his better judgement, Clements found himself drawn into the debate.

'I accept that such things can be,' he said, 'but why has nobody ever encountered one? Surely such an animal would be glimpsed, even at a distance. Even the shyest of nocturnal creatures exposes itself to view at some point.'

'Because it's not like them,' said the farmer simply. 'They're poor dumb animals. Some may be more cunning than others, but in the end they're just no match for us. Whatever's down there has learned to keep hidden. I'd say it's sensitive to us. It's learned how to wait.'

And with that he departed, leaving Molton and Clements to finish their beer alone before tipping a small bow to the landlord and heading to bed.

Now they were on the brink of the abyss, and the tales of ribald drunks and fearful farmers were almost forgotten. When Clements had completed his work, the two men exchanged roles, each examining the other's preparations. Upon finding that all was in order, Molton took to the rope and, after pausing for a moment or two upon the lip of the chasm, slipped over the edge. After some time had elapsed, Clements felt a double tug on the rope. He moved to the rim and shouted down.

'All well?'

'Splendid,' came the reply.

Molton was invisible to him, due to the nature of the incline at the entrance to the abyss, although Clements thought he could discern the faintest hint of artificial light.

'You have to see this, old chap,' continued Molton. 'In your own time, of course.'

Within minutes, Clements had joined his companion on a wide lip of rock that jutted out from the side of the chasm, the twin lights of their lamps hanging in the blackness. Neither man spoke, both overawed by their surroundings.

They were in a cathedral of stone. The abyss, narrow at its entrance, began to widen at the point where no further sunlight could penetrate, quickly extending to hundreds of feet in circumference. In the light of their lanterns they saw wondrous stalactites hanging like melted wax. Crystals gleamed, surrounded by great frozen waterfalls of stone. It was wonderfully cool, with a hint of moisture to the air.

'Careful, old man,' said Molton, as his companion drew perilously close to the edge of the shelf. Clements stopped, his heels almost on the very rim of the stone. His eyes shone brightly in the flickering light.

'My God,' he whispered. 'Look.'

The walls of the cavern were covered in paintings, reaching almost to the cleft in the earth that had enabled them to enter. Clements could see images of men and women, some running, others lying torn and half consumed, their remains shaded in pale yellows and faded reds. The depictions were crude, almost symbolic. There were triangles for faces and blurs for clothing, so that seen from close up the images would have been almost unintelligible. But seen at some distance, they were clear.

Molton joined the smaller man, his own lantern lofted. The combined light revealed more of the paintings, confirming the great extent of the work.

'Who did this?' asked Molton.

'More to the point: how was it done?' said Clements, as he began walking to his left, attempting to find the limits of the artwork. 'These look very old. A man would need scaffolding to paint that rock face, maybe even—'

He stopped. He was now at the farthest extreme of the outcrop, yet the paintings continued. Despite a sheer drop barely inches from where he stood, the images extended both vertically and horizontally.

'Incredible,' he said.

'What a find!' said Molton. 'It's amazing, simply amazing.'

Clements didn't reply. Instead, he lay on his belly, attached a rope to the ring of his lantern, and slowly lowered it down. After another fifty feet, the lantern came to rest upon what they could see was a much larger ledge, which appeared to run around at least half the circumference of the cavern.

'What do you think, old man?' he asked Molton. 'Do you want to go on, and did you get that smell as we were descending?'

'Like oil, but worse,' said Molton. 'Nasty stuff.'

'It was fresh, as though it had been poured over the rim recently. Now why do you suppose someone would do that?'

He hefted his axe in his hand.

'To discourage us?' Molton suggested.

'To discourage something,' answered Clements. 'Perhaps that's what was meant by "precautions".'

'It would take us a long time to get back to the village,' said Molton. 'Even then, what would we tell them?'

'Nothing that they don't already know, I expect,' said Clements.

'Well, we're here now,' Molton concluded. 'Might as well take the shilling tour as the tuppeny one.'

Once again, he assumed the lead, puffing slightly as he made his way down the rope. Clements watched his light grow smaller and smaller, like a lifeforce slowly dwindling. He swatted the thought away. Nearly there now, he thought. Another ten feet, another five—

Suddenly, the rope was wrenched from his hands, almost dragging him over the side with it. Pressing the sole of his boot against a hollow in the base of the rock, he attempted to arrest his progress, the smell of burning leather assailing his nostrils. Somehow, Molton must have fallen. Perhaps he had missed the ledge, or they had misjudged its weight-bearing capacity.

'Hold on!' he shouted. 'Hold on, Molton! I've got you.'

But then, almost as soon as it had begun, the rope stopped its movement. Breathing hard, Clements tied it firm around a stalagmite and scrambled to the edge. He leaned over, the lantern in his hand, and saw Molton's light on the ledge below. The rope was there too, winding into the shadows where the lantern could not reach.

'Molton?' he shouted.

There was no reply.

He tried again, and thought he detected sounds of scuffling from below.

'Hullo! Molton!'

The noise ceased.

Clements thought for a moment. It was clear now that Molton was injured, or worse, although Clements had no idea how the accident had occurred. He would have to descend and tend to his companion as best he could before seeking assistance from the world above. Most of the food was in Molton's pack, but Clements had the first aid kit, as well as some of the chicken. He would leave it all with Molton before ascending, he thought, as he checked the rope before making his way down to his friend.

He descended carefully, wary now of what lay beneath. Three feet from the ledge, he paused. The stone face of the chasm was more uneven here, with hollows and crevasses. The ledge itself, though, was relatively smooth. Molton's cap rested upon it beside the remains of his lantern, which had shattered upon impact.

Clements allowed himself to slide down the remaining feet of rope and touched the rock gingerly with his feet. It felt firm, as he had expected it would. After all, he had heard no sound of collapse when the rope began to burn through his hands. Whatever had occasioned the accident, it was not the ledge giving out beneath Molton's weight.

Clements placed his feet firmly on the rock, then tried to find some trace of his friend. He picked up the rope and began to follow it, tracing it across the ledge and behind a rocky outcrop. There, it disappeared into what appeared to be a narrow cavern, accessible through a cleft in the rock face.

Lantern raised, Clements approached the entrance.

'Molton?' he called.

Again, he heard sounds of movement. He extended his arm, attempting to illuminate the space within—

And caught sight of the upper half of Molton's body, lying flat upon the ground. His face was turned towards Clements, and his eyes were wide open. Blood flowed from the corners of his mouth, but his lips appeared largely gummed up by a white, sticky material. Molton reached out his right hand, and Clements was about to enter the cavern to take it, when the older man's body shuddered and he slid some inches to his right. As Clements raised the lantern, he saw that Molton's legs had almost entirely disappeared into a hole at the base of the cavern wall, drawn inward by some unseen force. There were more paintings here, but Clements barely registered their presence as he laid down the lamp and gripped his companion beneath the arms. Neither did he take time to examine the bones strewn upon the floor, the corrosion upon them a testament to the age of those from whom they had come.

'I've got you,' he said. 'I've got you.'

There came another tug on Molton's body, this time drawing him forward almost to the level of his waist, where any further progress was arrested by his girth. Whatever was pulling him towards it paused in its efforts, either disturbed by the sound of Clements's voice or by the fact that it was unable to haul its catch further into its lair.

Molton held on tightly to Clements's arm.

'Its not taking you anywhere, old man,' said Clements. 'Don't worry, I won't let you go.'

He took a firmer grip on Molton's chest.

'On three,' he said. 'One. Two.'

Molton tensed himself as Clements pulled.

'Three!'

A warm spray struck Clements's face and he was momentarily blinded as Molton was freed. The two men stumbled back against the wall, Molton shaking uncontrollably as Clements struggled to clear his vision. Slowly, Clements felt Molton grow still. He looked down and saw the life leave the remains of his companion.

Whatever was drawing Molton into the hole had proved reluctant to cede its prey, for his lower body was almost entirely missing, apart from a section of his left leg which already appeared to be rotting on the bone, turning to fluid even as Clements watched.

Clements scrambled away, trying hard to keep his breakfast down.

'Christ!' he shouted. 'Oh, Christ.'

And in the light of the lantern he glimpsed motion through the hole at the base of the rock. A sprinkling of black eyes gleamed, and Clements saw palps test the air, and venom drip from elongated fangs. A great stink seemed to rise from inside the chamber, and then legs appeared, spiny and jointed, each more than a foot long, as the spider began to force its way through the gap. Clements could see others moving behind it, could hear the dull scraping of their bodies as they brushed against one another. He responded with the best weapon he had to hand. Gripping the lantern, he flung it as hard as he could at the emerging creatures. The lantern shattered instantly, sending flames shooting up the cavern wall and dousing the spiders in burning oil as Clements fled, using the light from the flames to spy the rope dangling before him. He gripped it and began to climb, listening for any sounds coming from below, until he felt the upper ledge beneath his fingers. There he paused, and with his pocket knife he cut the rope that led down before lighting his remaining lantern in preparation for the last ascent back to the world he knew. He stood and gave the dangling rope a single pull. There was a momentary resistance before it fell from above and landed in a heap at his feet.

Clements looked up, and heard a goat bleating.

Poor beggar. He'll be hungry soon.

Sounds rose from below, the faintest contact of flesh upon stone, and he knew the creatures were starting to scale the rock face. He clutched his axe to his chest as a scratching noise came from above him. Clements looked up and thought he could detect movement in the shadows. A rock dislodged far to his right, and although he listened hard he could not hear it strike the base of the cavern. Now there was movement all around him, slowly drawing closer to the ledge upon which he sat. In the light of the lantern he fell to his knees and listened to the spiders approach, venom already dripping upon him from unseen fangs above.

Clements rose to his feet. He sensed the creatures had stopped, and knew that they were preparing to strike. He thought of Molton, and their times together.

'We should have stayed in the mountains, old man,' he said aloud. 'We should have stayed where there was daylight.'

And with that he stepped from the lip of the ledge, the lantern still clutched in his hand as he brought light at last to the depths of the Wakeford Abyss.

Nocturne

I don't know why I feel that I must confess this thing to you. Perhaps it is because I do not know you, and you do not know me. You have no preconceptions about me. We have not spoken before, and it may be that we will never speak again. For now, we have nothing in common, except words and silence.

Lately, I have been thinking a lot about silence, about the spaces in my life. I am, I suppose, a contemplative man by nature. I can only write when there is quiet. Any sound, even music, is an unwelcome distraction, and I speak as one who loves music.

No, let me rephrase that. I speak as one who *loved* music. I cannot listen to it now, and the quiet that has taken its place brings me no peace. There is an edge to it, a constant threat of disruption. I keep waiting to hear those sounds again: the lifting of the piano lid, the notes rising from the vibration of the strings, the muffled echo of a false key being struck. I find myself waking in the darkest spell of the night, just to listen, but there is only the threatening stillness.

It was not always this way.

Audrey and Jason died on 25 August. It was a sunny day, so the last time I saw them alive Audrey was wearing a light yellow summer dress and Jason was dressed in shorts and a T-shirt. The T-shirt was yellow too. Audrey was taking Jason to swimming class. I kissed Audrey goodbye and ruffled Jason's hair, and she promised to bring back something for lunch. Audrey was thirty-five. Jason was eight, just one year older than his brother David. They died because a lorry driver swerved to avoid a fox while he was coming around a bend, only a mile or two from our home. It was a stupid thing to do but, looking back, almost understandable. He ran straight into their car, and they were killed instantly.

About a month ago, shortly after the second anniversary of their deaths, a job was offered to me. A local council had received an unexpected boost to its arts funding, in that it had gone from having no arts funding to having a little. Fearing that even this small allowance might not materialise the following year if it were not used in this one, the wise burghers advertised for someone to teach their citizens the rudiments of creative writing, to speak at local schools, and to edit, in the course of the year, a volume of work reflecting the talents that the presence of a writer in the town would undoubtedly uncover and nurture. I applied for the post, and was duly accepted. I thought that it might help us. Every day, on his way to school, David had to pass the place where his mother and brother had died. I had to pass it too, whenever I was required to leave the house. I thought that taking a break from it all might be good for us both.

But it wasn't, of course.

Our troubles began about two weeks after we arrived at the new house; or, rather, at the old house, for it was a little dilapidated. The cost of its rental was to be paid in addition to my salary, and a local man was engaged to take care of some basic refurbishments. It had been sourced for us by an estate agent back in the city, who assured us that it was a fine property at a price that would not exceed the council's budget. The labourer, a man named Frank Harris, had already commenced his renovations before we arrived, but it was still a work-in-progress. It was built of grey stone on two levels, with a kitchen, living room, and small toilet downstairs, and three bedrooms and a bathroom upstairs. Most of the walls remained unpainted, and some of the floors were still tacky with varnish. We brought some furniture with us, but it looked lost and uncomfortable in this unfamiliar setting, like guests that had somehow wandered into the wrong party.

Yet, in the beginning, David seemed to enjoy the experience of moving to a new place. Children are so very adaptable in that way. He explored, made friends, decorated his room with paintings and posters, and climbed the great trees at the bottom of the garden. I, by contrast, was seized with a terrible loneliness, for I found that the absence of Audrey and Jason was exacerbated rather than reduced by the strangeness of my surroundings. I took to writing in the garden, in the hope that sunlight might dissipate my mood. It worked, sometimes.

I can remember clearly the first night that it occurred. I woke in darkness to hear the piano being played in the living room. It was one of only a few pieces left by the house's previous owner, along with the great oak table in the kitchen and a pair of handsome mahogany bookshelves that occupied twin alcoves in the living room. I arose, my head fuzzy with sleep and the noise of the out-of-tune piano hammering at my nerves, and went downstairs to find David standing in the room alone. I thought that he might have been sleepwalking, but he was awake.

He was always awake when it happened.

I'd heard him talking to himself as I descended, but he stopped as I reached the room, and so too did the piano music. Still, I caught snatches of his conversation as I descended, mainly 'Yes' and 'No', as if somebody were asking him questions and he were giving out reluctant answers in return. He talked the way he talked to people he didn't know very well, or of whom he was shy, or wary.

But the one-sided conversation wasn't the strangest part of it. It was the piano playing that was so strange. You see, David never played the piano. It was Jason, his lost brother, who had played. David didn't have a note in his head.

'David?' I said. 'What's going on?'

He didn't reply for a moment and, had the room not been empty apart from we two, I would have said that someone had just warned him to say no more.

'I heard music,' he said.

'I heard it too,' I said. 'Was that you playing?'

'No,' he said.

'Then who was it?'

He shook his head as he pushed past me and started back up the stairs to his bedroom. His brow was deeply furrowed.

'I don't know,' he said. 'It's nothing to do with me.'

The next morning I asked David, over breakfast, what he had seen when he was in the room. In the daylight, he seemed more willing to talk of what had occurred.

'A little boy,' David replied, after a time. 'He has dark hair and blue eyes and he is older than me, but only a little. He talks to me.'

'You've seen him before?'

David nodded. 'Once, at the back of the garden. He was hiding in the bushes. He asked me to join him. He said he knew a game we could play, but I wouldn't go. Then last night I heard the piano, and I went down to see who was playing. I thought it was Jason. I forgot—'

He trailed off. I reached out to him and ruffled his hair. 'It's okay,' I said. 'Sometimes, I forget too.'

But my hand was trembling as I touched his head.

David laid his spoon in his bowl of untouched cornflakes, and resumed his story.

'The boy was sitting at the piano. He asked me to come and sit with him. He wanted me to help him to finish a song. Then he said we could go away and play together. But I didn't go to him.'

'Why, David?' I asked. 'Why didn't you go?'

'Because I'm afraid of him,' said David. 'He looks like a boy, but he isn't.'

'David,' I asked. 'Does he look like Jason?'

David's face froze as he looked at me.

'Jason's dead,' he replied. 'He died with Mum in the crash. I told you, I just forgot.'

'But you miss him?'

He nodded. 'I miss him a lot, but the little boy isn't Jason. He maybe looks like him sometimes, but he isn't Jason. I wouldn't be frightened of Jason.'

With that, he stood and placed his cereal bowl in the sink. I didn't know what to say, or to think. David was not the kind of boy who made up stories, and he was a very bad liar. All I could guess was that he was enduring some kind of delayed reaction to his brother's death. It was frightening enough, but nothing that we could not deal with. There were people we could talk to, experts who could be consulted. Everything would work out in the end.

David stayed at the sink for a time, then turned to me, as if he had decided something.

'Dad,' he said. 'Mr Harris says that something bad happened in this house. Is that true?'

'I don't know, David,' I replied, and it was the truth. I had seen David talking to Frank Harris as he went about his work in the house. Sometimes, he allowed David to help him with little tasks. He seemed like a nice man, and it was good for David to work with his hands, but now I began to have second thoughts about leaving my son alone with him.

'Mr Harris says that you have to be careful with some places,' David continued. 'He says they have long memories, that the stones hold those memories and sometimes, without meaning to, people can make them come alive again.'

I tried to keep the anger from my voice as I responded.

'Mr Harris is employed as a handyman, David, not as a professional frightener. I'm going to have a talk with him.'

With that, David nodded unhappily, picked up his jacket and sports bag from the hallway, and walked down the garden path to wait for the bus. The local school, where David would begin studying in the autumn, was running summer events for children three days each week, and David had enthusiastically embraced the opportunity to play cricket and tennis in the sun.

I was about to join David when I saw another figure kneeling beside him, obviously talking to him, his face serious and concerned. He was an elderly man with silver hair, and there were paint stains on his blue overalls. It was Frank Harris, the handyman. He stood and patted David's head gently, then waited with him until the bus pulled up and whisked David away.

I intercepted Harris as he opened the front door with the spare key. He looked a little confused as I began to speak.

'I'm afraid that I have to talk to you about a serious matter, Mr Harris,' I said. 'It's these stories you've been telling David about the house. You know, he's been having nightmares, and you may be the cause of them.'

Mr Harris laid down his paint pot. He regarded me evenly.

'I'm sorry you feel that way, Mr Markham. I never meant to give your son bad dreams.'

'He says you told him that something bad had happened here in the past.'

'All I told your son was that he should be careful.'

'Careful of what?'

'Just that, well, older houses have histories, some good, some bad. And as new people enter them, and bring new life into them, the history of the house is altered and modified. That way, bad histories can slowly, over time, become good histories. It's the way of things. But the house where you now live hasn't experienced that kind of change. It hasn't had time.'

Now it was my turn to look confused. 'I don't understand,' I said.

'The people who found this property for you didn't check on its history,' said Harris. 'It was just in the right area at the right price, and the local agent was so happy to rent it he didn't see any point in spoiling a good deal by opening his mouth. Nobody from around these parts would ever have considered renting or buying this house, or even recommending it to a non-local. In fact, I was the only person who would agree to work on it. It's not a good house in which to be raising a child, Mr Markham. It's not good to allow a child to live its life in a house where another child had its life ended.'

I leaned back against the wall. I welcomed its support. 'A child died in the house?'

'A child was *killed* in the house,' he corrected me. 'Thirty years ago this November. A man named Victor Parks lived here, and he murdered a child in his bedroom. The police caught him trying to bury the remains down by the river.'

'Lord,' I said. 'I didn't know. I've never even heard of Victor Parks.'

'Nobody told you, Mr Markham, so you couldn't have known,' continued Harris. 'By the time you'd rented the house, it was already too late. As for Parks, he's dead. He had a heart attack in his cell on the very night he was sentenced to life imprisonment. He had lived in this house all his life, and the house had been in his family for two generations before that. Maybe the thought of an existence spent trapped in a small cell, far away from what was familiar to him, was too much for him to bear. I could only hope that his punishment would last longer in the next life.'

Something changed in his voice. It tightened, as if fighting off some unwanted emotion.

'He was an unusual man, Victor Parks,' he said. 'He worked as a verger in the church, and helped train the local football team. In many ways, he was a model citizen. People respected him. They trusted him with their children.'

He paused, and those old eyes were filled with a remembered grief. What he said next caused my hands to tense involuntarily.

'He also gave lessons, Mr Markham. He taught piano to the children.'

I couldn't speak. I didn't want to hear this. It was foolishness. Harris had told David this story, and David had picked up on some details of it to create a fantasy that mixed up his dead brother and the victim of this Victor Parks.

I tried to salvage some semblance of sense from all of this, to return us to reality.

'All of this may be true, but it doesn't change the fact that these stories are obviously troubling David. Last night, I found him in the sitting room. He thought there was a little boy at the piano, and that the boy spoke to him.'

Harris bent down to pick up his paintpot. I was about to tell him not to bother, that his services were no longer needed, when he spoke again.

'Mr Markham,' he said, as he straightened. 'I didn't tell David what happened in this house. He doesn't know anything about Victor Parks or what was done here. If he's heard something about it, then it was told to him by someone else. David says he sees a little boy, and you think that he believes that it's the child who was killed, but Parks didn't kill a boy. He killed a little girl. Whatever your son is seeing, Mr Markham, figment of his imagination or not, it isn't the girl Parks murdered.'

I stood aside to let him pass, and the next question came so unexpectedly that I thought for a moment that an unseen third person had asked it.

'What was her name, Mr Harris? What was the name of the girl who died here?'

But even as the words left my lips, I already seemed to know part of the answer, and I understood at last why it was that he had agreed to do the work on this house.

'Lucy,' he replied. 'Her name was Lucy Harris.'

I did not ask Frank Harris to leave. I could not, not after what he had told me. I could not even imagine what it must be like for him to work in the place in which his daughter had lost her life. What brought him back here, day after day? Why would he torment himself in this way?

I wanted to ask him, but I did not. In a way, I think that I understood. It was the same instinct that made me find excuses to drive past the spot where Audrey and Jason had died. It was a means of maintaining some kind of contact with what they once were, as if some part of them remained there and would find a way to reach out to me.

Or perhaps I hoped that some day I would drive by and see them, however briefly, caught between living and dying, before they faded away for ever.

For a time, David had no more bad dreams, and there were no more nocturnal wanderings. Frank Harris finished most of his work on the house and departed temporarily, but not before he tried to speak to me once again of his concerns for David. I brushed them away. It was over. The trouble had passed, and David was himself once more, helped by warm days spent playing with other children in green fields, far from the house in which a little girl had died. I taught my classes, and my own writing progressed. Soon, David would commence school, and the normal rhythms of our new life would be established at last.

But the night before school began, David came to me and woke me to listen to the sound of the piano.

'It's him,' he whispered.

I could see his tears glistening, even in the darkness.

'He wants me to follow him into the dark place, but I don't want to go. I'm going to tell him to go away. I'm going to tell him to go away for ever.'

With that, he turned and ran from the room. I jumped from my bed and followed him, calling to him to stop, but he was already racing down the stairs. Before my foot even hit the first step, he had entered the living room, following the sound of the piano, and seconds later I heard his voice raised.

'Go away! You have to leave me alone. I won't go with you. You don't belong here!'

And a second voice answered. It said: 'This is my place, and you'll do as I tell you to do.'

When I reached the bottom of the stairs, there was a boy seated on the piano stool. David was right: he looked somewhat like Jason, as though someone had been given a fleeting description of my lost son and had constructed an imperfect imitation on that basis. But all of the good in Jason, all of the brightness, was gone from this being. Instead, there was only the shell of a boy who might once have been mine, and something dark moved inside it. He wore the same yellow T-shirt and shorts that Jason had been wearing on the day he died, except they didn't fit quite right. They looked too tight, and there was dirt and blood on them.

And the voice wasn't a child's voice. It spoke in a man's tone, deep and threatening. It sounded obscene, coming out of this small figure. It said: 'Play with me, David. Come, sit beside me. Help me finish my song, then I'll show you my special place, my dark place. Do as I tell you, now. Come to me and we can play together for ever.'

I stepped into the room, and the child looked at me. As it did so, it changed, as if by distracting it I had somehow broken its concentration. It was no longer a boy. It was no longer anything human. It was old and stooped and decayed, with a balding skull and pinched white skin. The shreds of a dark suit hung on what was left of its body and its eyes were black and lusting. It raised its fingers to its lips and licked the tips.

'This is my place,' it said. 'The children come to me. Suffer the children that come unto me . . .'

I grabbed David and pushed him behind me, back into the hallway. I could hear him crying.

The thing smiled at me, and it touched itself as it did so, and I knew what I had to do.

There was a sledgehammer in the hallway. Harris had left it there, along with some other tools that he planned to take away later. I reached for the sledgehammer, my eyes never leaving the thing on the piano stool. It was already fading away when I took the first swing, and I saw the hammer pass through it as it hit the piano. I struck at the wood and ivory, again and again and again, screaming and howling as I did so. I kept swinging the hammer until most of the piano lay in pieces on the ground. Then I took the remains outside and, in the darkness, I set them alight. David helped me. We stood side by side and we watched it turn to ash and blackened wood.

And I thought, at one point, that I saw a figure writhing in the flames, a man in a dark suit slowly burning in the night air, until at last he was dispersed by the wind.

Now it is I who have the nightmares, and I who lie awake listening in the dead of night. I hate the silence, but more than that I fear what may disturb it. In my dreams I see a thing in a ragged suit luring children into dark places, and I hear the sound of nocturnes playing. I call to the children. I try to stop them. Sometimes, Frank Harris is with me, for we share these dreams together, and we try to warn the little ones. Mostly they listen to us, but sometimes the music plays, and a little boy invites them to play a game.

And they follow him into the darkness.

The Reflecting Eye
A Charlie Parker Novella

The soul's dark cottage, batter'd and decay'd
Lets in new light through chinks that time has made;
Stronger by weakness, wiser men become,
As they draw nearer to their eternal home.
Leaving the old, both worlds at once they view . . .

Edmund Waller, 'Of the Last Verses in the Book'

I

The Grady house is not easy to find. It lies on a county road that winds northwest from 210 like a reptile crawling off to die, the road dragging itself between steep banks of pine and fir, gradually becoming harder and harder to navigate as Tarmac gives way to cracked concrete, concrete to gravel, gravel to dirt, as if conspiring to discourage those who would look upon the blue-gabled house that waits at its end. Even then there is a final barrier for the curious to overcome, for the pitted trail that leads at last to its door has become wild and overgrown. Fallen trees have not been cleared and creepers and vines have exploited the natural bridges, thorny briers and stinging nettles joining with them to create an ugly wall of green and brown. Only the most tenacious will make their way farther, carving a path through the vegetation or working their way over ditches and rocks, tripping over roots that seem barely to cling to the earth, the trees they sustain prey to the mildest of storms.

Those who progress will find themselves in a yard of gray soil and foul-smelling weeds, the edge of the forest ending in a remarkably uniform tree line some twenty feet from the house, so that nature itself appears reluctant to extend its reach any closer. It is a simple, two-story arrangement, with a gabled attic window above the second floor. A porch runs along three sides, a decrepit swing chair to the east hanging askew by a single rope. Dead leaves lie curled inward like the remains of insects, piled up against the windows and doors. The mummified husk of a wren is buried beneath them, its body sunken and its feathers fragile as ancient parchment.

The windows of the Grady house have long been covered over with wood, and the front and back entrances have been fortified by the addition of steel doors. Nobody has damaged them, for even the most daring of pranksters steer clear of the building itself. Some come out to look, and to drink beer in its shadow, as if to goad its demons into taking action against them, but like small boys taunting a lion through the bars of its cage they are brave only as long as there is a barrier between themselves and the presence in the Grady house.

For there is a presence there. Perhaps it does not have a name, or even a form, but it exists. It is composed of misery and hurt and despair. It is in the dust on the floors and in the fading paper that peels slowly from the walls. It is in the stains on the sink and in the ashes of the last fire. It is in the damp upon the ceiling and in the blood upon the boards. It is in everything, and it is of everything.

And it waits.

It is strange how John Grady's name is rarely spoken, except in reference to killings committed by others. No books have been written about him, even in this age of insatiable curiosity about the darkest among us, and the nature of his crimes remains unexplored in the popular imagination. True, if one is prepared to delve into the journals of criminology or the textbooks of violent crime then there will be attempts to come to grips with John Grady, but all of them will fail. John Grady is inexplicable, for to explain him one must first *know* about him. There must be facts: a background, a personality. There must be schoolmates and fellow workers; an absent father, an overbearing mother. There must be trauma and conflicted sexuality. For John Grady, there are none of these things.

He arrived in Maine in 1977, and he bought a house. His neighbors dropped by, and he invited them inside to take a look around. The house was old, but John Grady clearly had some experience in construction for he was tearing out walls, laying new floors, filling in cracks, and replacing old plumbing. His neighbors never stayed long, as John Grady was clearly a busy man, albeit one with dubious taste. The original expensive wallpaper was already gone, and a cheap, unadorned replacement had been put up in its stead. The paste Grady used was of his own creation, and it stank, giving visitors another reason not to prolong their stay. Grady was doing all the work alone. He would talk about his plans for the house, and it was clear that he had already created it in his mind. He spoke of red drapes and deep velvet couches, of claw-toed bathtubs and mahogany dining tables. It was, he said, a labor of love, yet people looked up at that cheap paper, and smelled the rank substance that he had used to raise it, and quickly put Grady down as a fantasist.

John Grady stole children. He took the first, little Mattie Bristol, from North Anson in the autumn of 1979; the second, Evie Munger, from Fryeburg in the spring of 1980; the third, Nathan Lincoln, from South Paris, in the summer of 1980; Denny Maguire, the fourth victim, and the only one to survive, was taken as he walked from school in Belfast in the third week of May 1981; and his final victim, Louise Matheson, disappeared while she was walking from her home in Shin Pond to the house of her best friend, Amy Lowell, on 21 May 1981.

That was his mistake, for Amy was so excited about her friend's impending arrival that she was hiding in the woods at the verge of her house, hoping to leap out and surprise her. She watched Grady's Lincoln pull up alongside her friend, saw the man inside lean over to speak to her, and then found herself unable to move as Grady's big hand grabbed Louise by the hair and dragged her into the car. Amy's parents heard her screaming, and within minutes the police were on their way, already mounting a search for a red Lincoln.

They did not have to look far. The abduction of Louise Matheson was a crime of opportunity for John Grady. His previous victims had been taken from towns elsewhere in the state, then brought west to be killed, but Shin Pond was barely ten miles from the Grady house. John Grady's appetites had become increasingly hard to sate, and the release that he gained from their appeasement did not last as long as it once had. It is possible to imagine him, on the day that Louise Matheson was abducted, prowling the roads, his hunger gnawing at him, perhaps promising himself that he was only trying to distract himself from his appetites by taking a ride, that he did not really intend to seek out another victim.

John Grady was a tall, thin man. His hair was graying prematurely and cut close to his scalp, which served only to make his face seem even longer than it was. A calcium deficiency in his youth had given his chin an unfortunate prominence, one that he tried to hide by keeping his head low. He always wore a suit when out in public, set off by a bright bow tie and dark suspenders. There was something dated about him. His suits, though clean, gave the impression of having dwelt for some time in an attic or a thrift store. The shirts were a little frayed at the collars and cuffs. The bow ties looked faded rather than fresh, and bore wrinkles and stains that suggested many years of use.

John Grady had long fingers and large hands. Amy Lowell told the police that, when he gripped her friend's head, the man's fingers had closed on it entirely like the talons of a great bird, extending almost to her eyes.

Despite her shock, Amy Lowell gave the police a good description of the individual who had taken Louise Matheson, and the vehicle that he drove. There were those who recalled John Grady's ownership of a red Lincoln, and the police arrived at the Grady house and found the car. Nobody answered their knocks to the door, and a debate ensued on the porch steps of the Grady house concerning the nature of probable cause. It was curtailed by the sound, real or imagined, of a child's cry, and the door was kicked in.

John Grady was standing in the hallway of his house. His great work remained uncompleted, and there were ladders and drapes everywhere. His left hand was on the handle of the door to his basement, and he held a gun in his right. Before he could be stopped, he darted through the basement door and locked it behind him. He had reinforced it specifically for such an eventuality, replacing the flimsy original with sturdy oak and strengthening it with steel bands and a security bar. It took the police twenty minutes to break it down.

When they entered the basement, Louise was dead. Slumped on the floor beside her was another child, a little boy. He was still alive, but unconscious from hunger and dehydration. This was Denny Maguire.

John Grady stood over them both with his gun to his head. His last words, before he pulled the trigger, were:

'This is not a house. This is a home.'

II

Winter was here. The north wind had almost stripped the last of the leaves from the trees, leaving only a sprinkling of foliage to threaten the dominion of the evergreens. Clusters of young beeches trembled beneath the canopy, and sugar maple seedlings lay sprinkled through the forests like lost gold. There was a kind of silence now in the woods, as animals prepared to slumber, or to die.

In Portland, the trees of the Old Port were festooned with white lights, and a Christmas tree burned brightly further up on Congress. It was cold, although not as cold as the winters I recalled from my childhood. When I was young, we would drive north to spend New Year's at my grandfather's house in Scarborough. He and my father would share whiskey and war stories, for they were both policemen, although my grandfather had retired many years before. My mother would listen indulgently to tales that she had heard told over and over again, then hustle me off to my bed. Outside, the snow would gleam with a blueish tinge, lit by a bright moon in a clear, dark sky. I would sit at my window, wrapped in a blanket, and stare at it, following its contours, basking in the otherworldliness of it. Even on the darkest of nights, when the moon was invisible, the snow seemed to hold light within it. To the child gazing at it from his window, it glowed from deep inside, and I would fall asleep with the curtains open so that its unsullied beauty was the last thing I saw before my eyes closed, the voices of those whom I loved distantly rising and falling in low cadence.

In time, those voices from my past would be stilled. My grandfather, my parents, all were gone now. I found that I became that which I had most feared when I was a child: a man whose blood ran only in his own veins, a figure without visible ties to those who had brought him into this world. And when I tried to anchor myself with a family of my own, that too was taken from me, and I drifted, and was lost for a time in places without names.

Yet at last I learned to recognize that I was not entirely adrift, and that there were deep connections binding me to all that I had known. I had to come back to this place to find them, to reveal them where they had always lain, waiting beneath fallen leaves and compacted snow in the memory of a child seated by a window. My past and my present were here in this northern place, and, I hoped, my future too. Soon, I would be a father again, for my lover Rachel was due to give birth in the coming weeks. I felt part of a circle, slowly completing itself in this region of my childhood, and I thought that I would always remain here. During the long winter months, I would bitch and moan with the best of the old men. I would complain when my wheels became mired in mud during the spring thaw, or when filthy piles of iced snow upon street corners continued their slow melt into March, sullying the streets in a futile rearguard action against the coming of spring. I would strike out at mosquitoes and greenheads during the summer, and watch my lawn disappear beneath brown leaves in fall.

Occasionally, even now, I would hear one of my neighbors joke about heading for Florida, that this was the last damn winter he could endure in the cold northeast, but I knew that the speaker would never leave. It was part of the game that we all played, the dance of which we were all a part. I could not live without seasons, for in seasons are reflected the rhythms of our existence: of birth and maturity, of decline and decay, yet always with the promise of renewal for those who remain. Perhaps I would alter my attitude as I grew older, as the winters took a greater toll upon me and the north wind brought with it a reminder only of my own mortality. I wondered, sometimes, if that was part of the appeal of Florida or Arizona for those in their later years: cut off from the seasons it was possible to forget the rhythm that governed one's life, even as one's feet still moved to complete the final steps of the dance.

My prospective client was late, but I didn't really care. Up on Middle Street, the Half Moon Jug Band was playing carols to cheer the shoppers. I could hear the music from where I sat in JavaNet on Exchange, surrounded by kids playing with the computers. I kind of liked JavaNet, even if the geek quotient tonight was a little greater than I would have preferred. It had decent coffee, and some comfortable armchairs. It was also a pretty good place to meet people, as most of those sharing space were too caught up with Internet dating or their e-mail games to bother with what was happening around them. Its window was also a good spot for people-watching, and outside of Newbury Street in Boston or just about anywhere below 14th Street in Manhattan, the window of JavaNet on Exchange was one of my favorite places from which to watch the world pass by. I had already counted at least three women who, if I hadn't been perfectly happy with Rachel, would probably have refused to have anything to do with me, and rightly so. I had also seen Maurice (pronounced 'Maur-*reese*') Gardner, who was something of a local celebrity among those of us with a blacker than average sense of humor, since Maurice had once shot and superficially wounded a Santa Claus at the mall. Maurice claimed that Santa had snuck up on him, while Santa, when he gave evidence at Maurice's trial, claimed that he had merely been heading for the men's room beside the mall office. Since Maurice was hopped off his head at the time on coke riffed with Persian Brown, a combination likely to make even Buddha a little edgy, the judge sided with Santa Claus and Maurice was locked up for a while for his own protection and to ensure that Christmas did not become a time of mourning for traumatized junior patrons of the mall stores. Maurice was now clean, taking his medication, and working as second mate on a lobster boat. In a nice circularity of events, he volunteered each Christmas to play Santa Claus at some out-of-town children's charity. From what I heard, he felt it was the least that he could do to make up for his past sins.

I like Portland. It has all the advantages of a city, but still feels like a small town. There's an eccentricity to it, and a strength of character. It has more coffee shops than maybe any city its size rightfully needs, and there are one or two bars that could slide into the sea and make this a classier place by their absence, but that's okay. It has a little art-house theater, and the downtown Nickelodeon has promoted itself back to first-run movies. The Public Market is still going, and there are decent bookstores and a big library. All told, it's not such a bad place to have on your doorstep, and when it preyed on my nerves – as it sometimes did – I had the reassurance that I didn't actually live here. I could retreat back to my house on the Scarborough marshes within minutes, and watch the sun set on still waters.

Some clown in a bad suit waved at me from the street, and I gave him a non-commital nod in return. It took me about three minutes to recall him as the real estate salesman who had once tried to convince Rachel and me that our lives would be improved by living in his sinkhole new development out Saco way. Since then, he had experienced some misfortune in his life. He had been screwing his secretary on the side, and when his wife found out she screwed him. His business went to the wall and he was threatened with jail when it emerged that he had been frugal with the information he had provided to the IRS. Both his wife and his secretary gave evidence against him, which says a lot about the kind of person that he was. A couple of the Saco houses had also subsided when a passing child sneezed too loudly, and all kinds of legal storms were now brewing on that front as well. But there he was, a shopping bag from Country Noel in one hand, waving to a man he barely knew but had once tried to rip off with a bad property deal.

Really, you had to love Exchange Street.

My client was now twenty minutes late, and counting, but it still didn't matter. There was life around me; life, and the promise of new life to come. Most of those on the streets were locals, reclaiming the Old Port from the tourists now that summer was gone and the leaf-watchers had departed. I could see a group of skater kids dressed in hooded sweats and oversized jeans trying to pretend that the encroaching cold wasn't bothering them. I guessed that about half of them would be receiving antibiotics and TLC from their moms before the week was out, but they wouldn't share that fact with their buddies.

I had dropped some cash over at Bullmoose earlier, and now flicked idly through my purchases. Some of them would probably be okay with Rachel, I guessed: the Notwist, and maybe Thee More Shallows. I wasn't too sure how she would feel about . . . And You Will Know Us By The Trail Of Dead, but I'd heard some of their stuff on one of the more vibrant local radio stations, and liked it a lot. It was also a cool name for a band, which counted for something. I figured that if I could find a T-shirt with the band's name on it, I might be allowed to hang out with the slacker kids for a while, at least until the cops came by and decided to haul me in for my own safety.

My client arrived at 6.25 PM. I knew him by his clothing. He had told me to expect a man in a gray suit with a gray-black tie, a black overcoat protecting him from the cold, and that was what I got. He looked younger than I expected, although I guessed that he was probably close to seventy by now. I decided not to share my . . . Trail Of Dead CD with him. I thought it might be pushing things a little on our first meeting. I raised a hand to let him know who I was, and he threaded his way through the computer stations to take a seat with me at the window, casting some suspicious glances at some of the, well, more 'sheltered' patrons.

'It's okay,' I said. 'They won't hurt you.'

He looked a little uncertain, but gave them the benefit of the doubt. 'Frank Matheson,' he said, stretching out his hand. It was a big hand, scarred in places. A huge callus stretched across his palm from the base of his thumb. I could feel it as I shook his hand. Matheson owned a machine tool company over in Solon, and was a reasonably wealthy man, but he had clearly come by it through hard graft. I bought him a coffee – black, no sugar – and rejoined him at the window.

'I'm surprised that you don't have an office,' he said.

'If I had an office I'd have to paint it, then buy chairs and a desk. I'd have to think about what to put on the walls. People would judge me on the quality of my furnishings.'

'And what do they judge you on now?'

'The quality of other people's coffee. It's pretty good in this place.'

'You meet all your clients here?'

'Depends. If I'm not sure about them, I meet them in Starbucks. If I'm really not sure about them, I meet them at a gas station, maybe offer them a couple of Milk Duds to break the ice.'

A look of confusion crossed his face, as though a small warning light had just tripped in his brain. I get that look a lot.

'You come highly recommended,' he said, apparently to reassure himself rather than to compliment me.

'Probably people I brought to this place.'

'Plus I've read about you in the newspapers.'

'Yet still you're here.'

He made a wavering gesture with his right hand. 'I'll admit that not all of it was complimentary.'

'I believe it's called "balanced reporting." '

Matheson allowed himself a smile, although I still wasn't certain that the little warning light had extinguished itself entirely. He sipped his coffee, lifting the cup with that callused right hand. It trembled slightly. His left had never ceased clutching the leather attache case on his lap.

'I should tell you why I'm here,' he said. 'I suppose I should start with my family. My—'

I interrupted him.

'Is this about your daughter, Mr Matheson?'

He didn't look too surprised. I guessed that it happened a lot. It probably took a little while for the name to register with some people, but they'd get there in the end. I imagined Frank Matheson, sitting in his office with a prospective customer, seeing the eyes narrow, the hands move awkwardly.

Was your daughter Louise Matheson? Jesus, I'm sorry, that was a terrible thing that happened. Death was too good for that guy, what was his name? Grady, yeah.

John Grady.

'In a way,' said Matheson.

He opened his case.

'I brought some material along, just in case you didn't know about what happened, or needed some background.'

Inside, I could see a plastic folder. It contained copies of newspaper clippings, and photographs. He didn't remove it.

'I know about it,' I said.

'It was a long time ago. You must have been very young when it occurred.'

'It was a famous case, and people here don't forget things like that too easily. They stay in the memory, and get passed along. Maybe it's right that they should.'

He didn't reply. I knew that his daughter was always in his memory, frozen in death at the age of ten. I wondered if he ever tried to picture what she might have been like had she lived, how she might have looked, what she might be doing with her life. I wondered if he ever saw other young women on the street, and in their faces caught glimpses of his own departed child, a faint trace of her as though she were briefly inhabiting the body of another, trying to make contact with her family and the life denied her.

Because I saw my own dead child in the children of others, and I did not believe that I was alone in experiencing my loss in such a way.

'I know about you as well,' said Matheson. 'That's why I want to hire you. I believe you'll understand.'

'Understand what, Mr Matheson?'

He reached into his case and withdrew a brown envelope. He slid the envelope toward me. It was unsealed. Inside was a single sheet of unfolded paper, glossy on one side. I removed it and looked at the copy of the black and white photograph on the sheet. It showed a child, a little girl. The photo had been taken from a distance away, but the child's face was clear. She was holding a softball bat, her attention focused on an unseen ball beyond the limits of the picture. The girl wasn't wearing a helmet, and her brown hair hung loose around her shoulders. Even at a distance, and allowing for the relatively poor quality of the photo, she was a beautiful child.

'Who is she?' I asked.

'I don't know.'

I looked at the photograph again. There was nothing in it to indicate where it might have been taken. There was just the girl, the bat, and grass and dark trees in the distance. I turned the sheet over, but the reverse side was blank.

'Where's the original?'

'The cops at Two Mile Lake have it.'

'You want to tell me how you came by it?'

He took the photograph from me and carefully placed it on the counter ledge, before putting the envelope on top of it so that it was entirely covered.

'You know who owns the Grady house?'

'No, but I could hazard a guess.'

'Which would be?'

'That you own the Grady house.'

He nodded. 'The bank put it up for sale about two years after my Louise's murder. There were no other bidders. I didn't pay very much for it. Under other circumstances, you might even have said that I got a bargain.'

'You left it standing.'

'What would you have expected me to do: raze it to the ground?'

'It's what a lot of folks would have done.'

'Not me. I wanted it to remain as a monument to what was done to my daughter and to those other children. I felt that, if it was removed from the earth, then people would start to forget. Does that make sense to you?'

'It doesn't have to make sense to me. It doesn't have to make sense to anyone but you and your family.'

'My wife doesn't understand. She never has. She thinks that all traces of John Grady should have been wiped away. She doesn't need anything to remind her of what happened to Louise. It's always with her, every single day.'

Matheson seemed to retreat from me for a moment, and I watched his relationship with his wife reflected in his eyes like a rerun of a desolate old movie. In some ways, it was a miracle that they had stayed together. Both as a policeman and as an investigator, I had seen marriages disintegrate under the burden of grief. People speak about a shared sorrow, but the death of a child is so often not apportioned in the same way between a father and a mother. It is experienced simultaneously, but the grief is insidious in its individuality. Couples drown in it, sinking beneath the surface, each unable to reach out and touch the other, incapable of seeking solace in the love that they feel, or once felt, for each other. It is particularly terrible for those who lose an only child. The great bond between them is severed, and in some cases they simply drift away into loneliness and isolation.

I waited.

'Can I ask you what you did with your house, after what happened?' he asked.

I knew the question would come.

'I sold it.'

'Have you ever been back there?'

'No.'

'You know who lives there now?'

'A young couple. They have two children.'

'Do they know that a woman and a child were killed in that house?'

'I guess that they do.'

'You think it troubles them?'

'I don't know. Maybe they feel that what happened there once can never happen again.'

'But they'd be wrong. Life doesn't abide by such simple rules.'

'Do you feel that way about the Grady house, Mr Matheson?'

His fingers trailed across the envelope, seeking to find the lineaments of the face of the unknown girl hidden beneath. I thought again of new fallen snow, and how I once believed I could see the outlines of faces beneath it, like the shapes of skulls beneath white skin. That was later, when I left behind the child I once was and those whom I loved began to fall away.

'You asked me where I found the photograph, Mr Parker. I found it in the mailbox of the Grady house. It was in a torn envelope. The envelope had been sealed, then opened by someone to get at what was inside. Judging by the marks on the envelope, I'd guess there was more than one photograph in it originally. The shape of the remaining photograph didn't quite match the marks of the bulge in the envelope. That's how I knew.'

'Do you check the mailbox often?'

'Nope, just occasionally. I don't go to the house much anymore.'

'When did you find the photograph?'

'One week ago.'

'What did you do?'

'I took it to the police.'

'Why?'

'It was a photograph of a little girl, placed in the mailbox of a house once owned by a childkiller. At the very least, someone has a sick sense of humor.'

'Is that what the police think?'

'They told me that they'd see what they could do. I wanted them to go to the newspapers and the TV people, get this little girl's picture shown across the state so that we could find out who she is, and—'

'And warn her?'

He drew a breath, and his eyes closed as he nodded.

'And warn her,' he echoed.

'You think she's in danger, because someone put a photo of her in Grady's mailbox?'

'Like I said, at the very least the person who put that picture there has a disturbed mind. Who would even want to link a little girl with that place?'

I slipped the envelope away and looked at the print of the child's picture again.

'Was the photograph old, Mr Matheson?'

'I don't think so. It looked recent to me.'

'And the photograph itself was black and white, not just the copy that you made?'

'That's right.'

'Anything on the back to indicate that it came from a lab? You know, any identifying marks, brand names?'

'It was Kodak paper, that's all I know.'

That paper could be purchased in any camera store in the country. Whoever took the photograph had probably developed it in his own home or garage. It was simple enough to do, with the right equipment. That way, there was no chance of a curious lab worker spying suspicious photographs of playing children and calling in the cops to investigate the individual behind the camera.

The child really was beautiful. She looked happy and healthy, and the intensity of her concentration on the ball about to head her way made me smile.

'What would you like me to do, Mr Matheson?'

'I want you to see if you can discover who this girl is. I want you to talk to her parents. I'll come with you, when you find them. They should know about this.'

'That's going to be difficult.'

Matheson placed the palm of his right hand very deliberately upon the envelope, as if afraid that the wind might try to steal it from him, taking with it all hope of identifying the girl within.

'I've done some business in Japan,' he said. 'The Japanese don't like to say "no." If they don't want to do something, they say "That will be difficult." If it's impossible, they say "That will be *very* difficult." So which is it for you, Mr Parker?'

'We're not in Japan, Mr Matheson, we're in Maine. Japan is easy by comparison. They're inscrutable, but we're stubborn. Difficult here is just difficult. Maybe the police have found her already. Have you spoken to them?'

'They won't tell me anything, except that it's under investigation and that I shouldn't worry. They said, it was probably nothing.'

Maybe they were right. There were those who might find amusing or arousing the idea of associating a little girl's image with the memory of a childkiller, but their actual potential for harm was likely to be limited. And yet someone had gone to the trouble of snapping at least one photograph of an unsuspecting little girl, and if Matheson was right in his suspicions then there were probably more photos, some perhaps of this child, but some possibly of other children.

'I was also wondering if you might watch the Grady house for a while, just in case the person who left this picture comes back.'

Wintering at the Grady house didn't sound like the best way to get into the Christmas spirit. I tried not to let my reluctance show, but it was hard. In fact, had I been Japanese I would have said it was 'very difficult.'

'Have you seen any signs of damage to the house', I asked, 'any indications that someone might have tried to get inside?'

'Nope, it's sealed up good and tight. I have a set of keys, and the police at Two Mile have another set. I gave it to them after some lunatic tried to get onto the roof and start a fire there a couple of years back. I don't know if they've been inside since I gave them the photograph.'

I touched the picture of the little girl with my fingertips. My fingers brushed the image of her hair.

'It's kind of an obvious question, but have you seen anybody hanging around the property, or has anyone displayed excessive interest in what went on there?'

'Well, we had some trouble with a man named Ray Czabo, but the chief warned him off. I don't think he's been back since. You know him?'

Matheson couldn't have missed the pained look that crossed my face. Voodoo Ray Czabo was a death tourist from Maine, a haunter of crime scenes. He liked taking pictures of places in which people had died. When the cops were finished with their work, he would sometimes remove 'souvenirs' from the location and try to hawk them on the Net. Ray Czabo and I had history. He had visited the house in Brooklyn in which my wife and daughter were killed, and had stolen from outside the door the carved wooden block upon which the house number was engraved.

I got it back, though.

Since then, Ray had kept out of my way, even though he now lived up in Bangor, in a small house off Exit 48 close by Husson College.

'Yeah, I know Ray Czabo,' I said.

The Grady house would appeal to someone like Ray. I felt pretty certain that he'd been down there on more than one occasion. He must have found it galling to be denied access to its secrets.

'Was Ray the only one?'

Matheson was holding something back. I wasn't sure

why. Perhaps he wanted to be certain that I was going to take the case before he told me, but I'd learned that lesson the hard way. Now I liked to know what I was getting into *before* it all began to fall down around my ears.

'There was another man, a few days ago. He came to the plant. You should understand, Mr Parker, that very few people know about my ownership of the Grady house. Officially, the title is held by a shelf company, and the company shares its address with a particularly litigious firm of lawyers in Augusta. They're not even my own lawyers. They were sourced independently. Yet this man arrived at my office and told my secretary he was interested in placing a large order. He seemed to know what he was talking about, so she called me. I was out on the floor at the time, and I came back to meet him.

'The first thing that struck me was that he wasn't there to buy anything from my company. He was dressed in a threadbare coat, there were stains on his trousers, and the sole was coming away from his left shoe. I couldn't tell the last time his shirt had been properly washed, and he wore a dead man's tie. Don't get me wrong: in my business, I see a lot of people who work with their hands, and I'm not afraid to get my own skin and clothes dirty. But that's, I don't know, *honest* dirt, hard won and nothing for a man to be ashamed of. This guy, though, he was just plain filthy. I almost threw him out of my office before he had a chance to open his mouth. Maybe I should have.'

'What did he look like?'

'Tall. Taller than you. His hair was black, and long. It was hanging over his shirt collar. He was receding pretty badly, and he hadn't shaved in a couple of days. His skin was very white. Don't recall the color of his eyes, if that's the kind of detail you need to know. His fingertips and nails were stained yellow. I guess he was a smoker, but he didn't light up while he was with me.'

'He give you a name?'

'No. I introduced myself, shook his hand – although I kind of regretted doing it – but he didn't give me a card or a name. He just told me he had come about a delicate matter.'

'*I believe that you are the owner of the Grady house.*'

'*I don't know what you're talking about.*'

'*I think that you do. There is a debt outstanding upon the house. An opportunity is about to arise for its payment.*'

'*I told you: I think you have the wrong man.*'

'I tried to convince him, but the guy just didn't want to listen. He knew that the Grady house belonged to me. I don't know how, but he did. When I checked with the lawyers, they told me that there had been no formal enquiries about the house for years, apart from a couple of media hounds howling down the phone on the anniversary of Grady's death. Next thing I know, he's rattling off details of the purchase: the price, the date the final agreement was signed, even the name of the bank manager at the time. It was like he had a file in front of him and was just reading the stuff from it. I was so surprised, I couldn't even speak for a minute. Then I started to get angry. I mean, what business did this guy have coming in to my office and demanding payment for bills that were nothing to do with me anyway? It was all that I could do to stop myself climbing over the desk and dragging him out of the office by his collar.'

'Why didn't you?' I asked. Matheson looked as if he could still handle himself.

'I'm not that kind of man,' he replied, but there was an unspoken 'and' hanging in the air.

I waited. It came.

'He didn't look like much: thin, dirty, unhealthy, but I got the feeling that he was stronger than he looked. I think that if I'd tried to lay a hand on him he would have hurt me. Not badly, maybe, but he would have enjoyed humiliating me. There was a malice to him, y'know? This all probably sounds cockeyed to you, but once my anger started to die down I began to get worried. Scared, even.'

I told him it didn't sound cockeyed at all, that I had met men like that. They wanted you to descend to their level, and once you were down there they would try to finish you. If you were going to take them on then you had to be prepared to take some pain, and to inflict it back in spades.

Matheson continued: 'So I told him that even if what he said was true, he should call up the Farmers' Mutual Bank and ask them about it. Payments owing to him from John Grady were no business of mine. He didn't seem to agree.'

'*I am a collector, Mr. Matheson. I collect debts, but I also have an interest in other items. In lieu of the debt left outstanding by the previous owner, I will accept some small item of furniture from the house. It will barely cover my expenses, but in this case a token gesture will be sufficient. The house contains a number of ornate mirrors. If you give one of them to me, I will consider you to have discharged any responsibilities you may have in this matter.*'

'That was exactly how he spoke,' said Matheson. 'He spoke like a damn lawyer. Well, I'd had enough of him by then, so I told him to get the hell out of my office or I'd call the cops. He had any more questions, he could discuss them with my legal people, or with the Farmers' Mutual, but I didn't want to see him again.'

'What did he say?'

'He didn't move. He just looked at his fingernails for a while before he stood, said that he was sorry I felt that way, and told me that he would deal with the matter through "other channels". Then he left.'

'Did you get a look at his car?'

'There wasn't one. He left on foot.'

'And he gave you no contact name, no number?'

'Nothing. He just told me he was a collector.'

'Did you talk to the police about this?'

'I told Chief Grass over in Two Mile, but he said there were probably a whole lot of debts left unpaid when John Grady died. He took down the description I gave him, but he said there wasn't much that he could do unless the collector came back, or used threats.'

'Did you feel as if he was threatening you in your office? He did speak of going through "other channels" for his payment.'

'I suppose it could have been a threat. I didn't take it that way.'

'And he never mentioned what the debt was, or whom he was representing?'

'No.'

'Do you think this man might be the one responsible for placing the photograph in the mailbox?'

'It's possible, but I can't see why he would do it. He certainly didn't mention anything to do with pictures.'

Matheson asked if I wanted another coffee. I said yes, if only to give me a little time to think. His story about the collector made me uneasy, and I didn't particularly want to sit in my car watching an old house night after night, waiting for some lowlife in old clothes who got kicks from planting the pictures of children in a dead child-murderer's mailbox, but something about that photograph of the girl was drawing me in. I had this much in common with Matheson: both of us had lost a daughter, and neither of us was prepared to stand idly by if another child was potentially in danger. Looking back, I guess I knew I would take the case as soon as he showed me the picture of the little girl with the bat in her hands.

When he came back, I told him my rates. He offered to pay me in advance, but I explained that I'd bill him after the first week. If I was making no progress after two weeks, then I'd have to leave it to the cops. Matheson agreed and prepared to depart. He left the photograph of the unknown girl with me.

'I made lots of copies,' he said. 'If you hadn't agreed to do this, I was going to post them in stores, on telephone poles, anywhere they might be seen.'

'How many copies did you make?' I asked.

'Two thousand,' he replied. 'They're in the trunk of my car. You want some?'

I took one hundred of them, and left him with the rest. I just hoped that we wouldn't have cause to use them.

III

The house was silent and dark when I returned home. Rachel was attending a meeting of the Friends of the Scarborough Public Library, and I didn't expect her back until later. I stood at the door for a moment and looked out upon the marshes. The great migratory exodus was almost complete, and the quiet of the grasses was now relatively undisturbed for much of the day. The sounds of the birds that remained with us stood out more clearly than before as a consequence, and in recent days I thought I had heard grackles and cowbirds and goldfinches. I wondered if there was an added lightness to their calls now, triggered by an awareness that the population of raptors was now depleted, as some of the hawks and harriers would inevitably have followed their prey south. Then again, the hunters that had stayed would now be competing for a more limited food supply. When the snows came, hunger would start to gnaw at them.

The move here, following the sale of my grandfather's old house a few miles away, was a good one, tarnished only by an incident earlier in the year that had led to the drowning of a man out on the marshes. Rachel didn't like to talk about it, and I didn't push her on the subject. I wanted very badly for us to be happy here. Perhaps, after all that had gone before, I wanted that happiness too much.

As I opened the door Walter, our Lab retriever, emerged guiltily from my little office, where I was pretty certain he'd been curled up on the couch, then tried to divert my attention by covering me with dog spit. I briefly considered shouting at him for putting hairs on my favorite resting place, then realised from his slightly shameful posture that he already knew he wasn't supposed to be on it and that, frankly, we both understood that if he hadn't been deep in dog sleep when I arrived he would have been smart enough to make a dash for his basket before I even managed to get my key in the lock. Instead, I contented myself with letting him out into the yard, then closing the door behind him while I made a sandwich from cold cuts.

I put, 'A History of Sport Fishing', the album I'd bought by Thee More Shallows, on the CD player in the kitchen before sitting down at the table to eat, until the sound of Walter's paw plaintively scratching at the glass caused me to relent and head out on to the porch instead. Walter had me down pat. He knew I couldn't stay mad at him for long. Pretty soon, he'd be throwing sticks and I'd be running to fetch them. I fed him about a quarter of my sandwich, even as I recalled Rachel reading me an article about dog training which said that you shouldn't feed your dog scraps from the table, or allow him to jump up and lick you, because that made him believe he was the alpha male.

'Walter doesn't think he's the alpha male,' I protested at the time, sort of lamely now that I come to think of it. I looked to Walter for confirmation, which probably wasn't the smartest move on my part if I was trying to claim superiority. Walter, hearing his name, was looking back and forth between us, as if trying to figure out which one of us was going to relent first and just hand over a set of keys and the deeds to the house.

'Hah!' was Rachel's response. She has a way of saying 'Hah!' that pretty much skewers any possible dissent, like a skeptical python that's just been told to cough up the rabbit and send it merrily on its way.

Rachel had patted her bump and said: 'I hope you're listening to this. That's your daddy talking. He thinks he's the alpha male, but just shoot goo-goo eyes at him and he'll buy you a car.'

'I didn't buy you a car,' I pointed out, 'and you shot goo-goo eyes at me all the time.'

'I didn't want a car,' she said. 'I have a car.'

'So why did you shoot goo-goo eyes at me?'

'Because I wanted something else.'

'And what was that?'

'I wanted you.'

I thought for a moment.

'You know,' I said, 'that would be really cute if it wasn't kind of sinister.'

'Yes,' she said, smiling. 'It would, wouldn't it?'

I glanced at my watch. Rachel would be back soon. The house always felt very empty when she wasn't around. In the background, a track from the album faded out, the singer repeating over and over something about the people we choose to leave being the ones whom we see all time, all the time. I fed Walter my last piece of sandwich.

'Just don't let Rachel know I did that,' I told him. 'Please.'

The Grady house was quiet. A breeze stirred the trees, and disturbed the pile of dry leaves beneath which the dead wren rested. Matheson stood at the bottom of the steps leading up to the porch, and shined his flashlight upon the house. He checked the locks on the doors, and the wood that covered the windows. There was a SIG Compact in a holster on his belt. He had begun carrying it shortly after the man he now thought of as the Collector came to his office and demanded payment of an old debt.

The sound of approaching footsteps came to him, but he

did not turn around. The beam of a second flashlight joined his own.

'Everything okay?' asked the patrol cop. He had seen Matheson pull up at the Grady house, and had offered to accompany him up the dark road. Matheson had been grateful for the offer.

'I think so,' said Matheson.

'It's getting colder.'

'Yes. Snow's coming.'

'It'll make it easier to tell if anyone's been snooping around here.'

Matheson nodded, then turned to go. The cop followed him, then stopped short. He turned his flashlight upon the woods.

'What is it?' asked Matheson.

'I don't know.'

He inched forward, his hand already drawing his gun. Matheson added his own light to the cop's and together they scanned the trees. Suddenly there was the sound of movement in the undergrowth, and a gray shape with red underparts darted through the low greenery before disappearing into the shadows.

Both men let out a long, relieved breath.

'Fox,' said the cop. 'That wasn't good for my nerves.'

He replaced his pistol and headed back to his car. Matheson remained staring into the woods for a moment more, then followed him. They made their farewells, and both cars drove away.

There was silence for a time, before the figure of a man detached itself from a bank of pines in the darkest reaches of the woods and approached the Grady house. He stood at the very edge of the tree line then began circling the building, never once straying from the safety of the woods, as though the ground beyond them was somehow unsafe to tread upon. He made one full circuit of the property, then a second, slower this time, seemingly searching for something that had been lost. Eventually, he stopped as he faced the eastern side of the house. He knelt, and using a pocket knife commenced digging beneath a small cairn of pebbles that lay almost hidden by grass at the verge of the yard. After he had dug about six inches into the earth, a pale totem was revealed: the skull of a dog. Symbols and lettering had been carved into the bone.

The man sat back on his haunches, but he did not touch the skull. Instead, he let out a suppressed hiss of anger and disgust. Carefully, making sure that his hands did not come into contact with the dog's remains, he replaced the earth upon it, then folded the knife and put it back in his pocket. In total, the Collector had counted eight such cairns, each representing a compass point.

It was as he had suspected: the house was impregnable. He retreated into the forest, and then was gone.

Later that night, I watched from our bed as Rachel undressed in the moonlight. She eased the straps of her slip over her shoulders and let it fall to the ground, then stared at her reflection in the mirror, turning first to one side, then the other. The moonlight touched the swelling of her belly, and cast the shadow of her breasts upon the wall.

'I'm big,' she said.

'Bigg*er*.'

I ducked my head just in time to avoid being hit by a shoe.

'I look like a whale.'

'Whales are loveable. Everybody loves whales, except the Japanese and the Norwegians, and I'm neither. Come to bed.'

She finished undressing and slipped under the covers, then lay awkwardly on her side, looking at me.

'Did you meet your client?'

'Yep.'

'Did you take the job?'

'Yep.'

'Want to talk about it?'

'Not tonight. It's nothing bad, so don't start worrying. It'll keep until the morning.'

Rachel grinned.

'So whatcha wanna do now?' she said.

She leaned forward and kissed me lightly on the lips. Softly, I kissed her back.

'It's okay,' she said. 'I can't get pregnant.'

'Very funny.'

'I'll even let you be the alpha male.'

'I *am* the alpha male.'

Her hand moved slowly down my chest and on to my stomach.

'Of course you are, darling,' she whispered. 'Of course you are . . .'

IV

The town of Two Mile Lake lay in the middle of hardscrabble land, three miles northeast of the towns of Bingham and Moscow. Here the Kennebec River fed into Wyman Lake before proceeding on its way toward the coast, enlarged further by countless small streams and tributaries. This area was part of the 'Bingham purchase', named after a Philadelphia landowner named William Bingham who owned so much of the state at the end of the eighteenth century as to be able to bequeath his heirs sufficient territory to cover half of Massachusetts. There was even a dam named after him on the Kennebec, which put him right up there with Hoover.

North of Two Mile Lake, up by the confluence of the Kennebec and Dead rivers, lay The Forks, one of those strange Maine places where the past and the present appeared to have reached an uneasy accommodation. The Forks was still technically a plantation – in Maine terms, an unorganized township – and had once been the center of a resort area in the nineteenth century. Now rafters came here, attracted by the effect of the Harris Hydroelectric Station on the water flow. New inns and stores stood alongside the old Marshall Hotel, with its neon 'Cocktails' sign, and the stuffed animals in Berry's General Store. From The Forks, 201 headed north to Canada along the Arnold Trail, striking out into the wilderness just like old Benedict himself did on his way to Quebec at the end of the eighteenth century, with Jackman as the only decent-sized stop along the way.

Two Mile Lake must have envied some of the comparative prosperity enjoyed by its northern neighbor. It wasn't entirely clear how the town had come by its name, as there was no body of water worthy of the name closer than Wyman Lake. Two Mile had a kind of standing pond on the northern edge of town, and if you were particularly foolhardy you might take a chance on swimming in it, or eating something that came out of it, but it was no more than a couple of hundred feet at its widest point. Instead, the only conclusion that anyone could reach about the town's name was that if you headed north from it then you'd head right back south again after two miles, because there was nothing there to see. In essence, Two Mile Lake was two miles away from nowhere.

I followed 16 through Kingsbury and Mayfield Corner, then headed up Dead Water Road a ways until I reached the town's southern limits. I kept my foot to the pedal and pretty soon I was at the town's northern limits. In between I passed a couple of stores, a school, a pair of churches, a police station, and the remains of a dead dog. I wasn't sure what had killed the dog, but boredom seemed like a good guess.

I parked beside the gray police building and headed inside. The local cops shared the premises with the town council, a fire truck, a garbage truck, and what looked like a charity store, its windows grimly festooned with old men's suits and old women's bingo dresses. At the little office inside the door I gave my name to the elderly secretary who looked old enough to remember William Bingham in pantaloons. Then I gave it to her again, as she'd managed to forget it somewhere between hearing it and looking for a pen with which to write it down. Behind her, an overweight woman with frizzy black hair typed slowly on a computer, the expression on her face suggesting that someone had forced her, on pain of death, to suck repeatedly on a sour lemon. They seemed like the kind of women who considered it their sacred duty to be unhappy and regarded anyone with a smile on his face as mired in unimaginable vice. I smiled, and tried to give the impression that I only engaged in imaginable vices. In return, the secretary directed me to an uncomfortable plastic chair. When I sat on it, it teetered to the left, forcing me to shift my weight to the right or tumble straight back out the door.

After a couple of minutes, a man appeared in the doorway of the room to my left. He wore a brown uniform shirt and neatly pressed brown trousers. According to the badge at his breast, his name was Grass. The local stoners probably laughed themselves blue in the face, at least until Grass got up close and personal with them. He was a big man in his fifties, and he still looked fit. There was no paunch, and when he shook my hand I felt one of my knuckles pop. His face was deeply tanned, making his gray mustache and hair seem all the more startling. He should have lost the mustache, I thought: without it, and wearing a hat, he could have passed for early forties.

'I'm Wayne Grass,' he said. 'Chief of police'.

'Charlie Parker,' I said. 'I'm a private investigator.'

'I know who you are,' he said. 'Pleased to make your acquaintance.'

I followed Grass into his office. It was tidy, with flowers growing in pots on the windowsill. There was a picture of a woman and two children on his desk. The woman was very pretty and looked a lot younger than Grass. The kids, a boy and a girl, were in their early teens.

'My family,' he said, spotting the direction of my glance.

'Recent picture?'

'Just last year. Why?'

'No reason,' I said.

'My wife is a little younger than I am, if that's what you mean.'

'Nice work,' I said.

Grass grinned and reddened. He offered me coffee. I declined, and he settled back into his chair.

'So what can I do for you, Mr Parker?'

'I've been hired by a man named Frank Matheson. He's worried about a photograph that he found in the mailbox of a house that he owns. It's the photograph of a child. The house is the old Grady house.'

I waited, watching the smile on Grass's face melt away.

'I'm disappointed,' he said at last.

'Why would you be disappointed?'

'I told Frank Matheson that I'd take care of it, and I will, but I'm not going to let him scare some little girl and her parents half to death, and maybe start a panic among others, just because he found a picture in a mailbox.'

'You think that's what he wants to do?'

'I don't know what he *wants*, but that will be the result. We need to tread softly on this thing. We'll circulate the picture, see what comes up. Hell, it may not even have been taken in the state. That photograph could have come from anywhere. But if Frank Matheson or anyone else goes to the newspapers and the TV stations and starts telling them that this little girl's picture was placed in a dead child-killer's mailbox, what do you think is going to happen?'

'Maybe you'll find the girl.'

'Or maybe we'll be accused of starting a panic over nothing, of overreacting to what's probably just a sick practical joke. Next thing, I've got the media down here showing images of the Grady house, and then the freaks will start to arrive. Maybe the whole shitstorm will give one of them an idea, and then we really *will* be looking for an endangered child. Like I said, we're going to work at getting the photograph out to local and state law enforcement, then school boards. We find that little girl, then we can just take her parents quietly to one side and tell them what we know, which is squat.'

In one way, I knew Grass was right. The whole affair had to be handled delicately, and there was no point in frightening a little girl and her family over what might be nothing. But I realized that Grass was approaching the issue from one perspective, and Matheson was approaching it from another: Grass believed that the child probably wasn't in any danger, because there was no evidence to suggest otherwise, but, heightened (or, perhaps, tormented) by his own loss, Matheson's instincts told him that the child was at risk. I was stuck in the middle, wanting to believe Grass, but half persuaded by Matheson's concerns.

'Were there any prints on the envelope?'

'None, apart from Matheson's, and we don't suspect him of putting an envelope in his own mailbox and then bringing it to us.'

I agreed that it didn't sound likely, mainly in an effort to diffuse what felt like growing tension between us. Small-town cops don't like people questioning their decisions. Even big-city cops don't like it very much, but they tend to be less protective of their patch.

'Have you been out to the Grady house recently?' I asked Grass.

'We check it pretty regularly. The place is locked down tight. I was back there after Frank Matheson found the photograph. There was nothing out of the ordinary.'

'When you say "we" . . .?'

'We have four officers in total, myself included: three male, one female. They're good people.'

'So sometimes one of them will go by there and open up the house?'

'Well, occasionally. Mostly, I do it myself. Easier that

way. I don't have to worry about the keys getting lost, or someone getting spooked.'

'Spooked?'

'You know what happened in that house. It's not a place to visit unless you have to. It's got a bad feel about it, and always will have. It stinks too. Something in the paints and pastes that Grady used. It just seems to get worse and worse. After twenty years, I'm used to it. It doesn't get to me so much. Someone else, someone new . . .'

He trailed off.

We sat like that, in silence, until I stood and thanked him for his time.

'Like I said, it was my pleasure, but I don't know what more you can do for Mr Matheson.'

'I'm not sure either,' I said. 'I think I'll just nose around. If I find out anything, I'll let you know. I'd appreciate it if you could see your way clear to doing the same.'

I gave him a card. He placed it carefully in his wallet, then gave me a card of his own in return from a little dispenser on his desk.

'You going to take a look at the Grady house while you're up here?' he asked.

'I think I will, seeing as I've come all this way.'

'You want me to go out there with you?'

'I believe I'll be okay.'

He nodded to himself, like a man who feels secure in the conclusion that he has just reached.

'I guess this is the point in the conversation where you tell me that you don't scare easy,' he said.

'Being scared isn't the problem,' I replied. 'It's not running away that's the hard part.'

The Grady house was much as I remembered it from the news reports of the time: a little more overgrown with ivy, perhaps, its windows now boarded up and a pair of locked steel doors preventing access through either the front or back of the house, but these were relatively cosmetic changes. The Grady house was ugly when it was built, even foreboding in its way, although I felt certain that this impression was mostly a consequence of my knowledge of its past. I circled the house, checking the windows and the doors to see if they had been tampered with in any way, then returned to the mailbox and gave it a cursory check. It was empty, apart from some dead insects and a faded flyer offering free soda and fries with every pizza delivery.

I walked back up to the house and took a set of keys from my pocket. Frank Matheson had given them to me when I agreed to take on the job. I unlocked the outer steel door and pulled it open. The door behind it had a fan of stained glass dominating its upper third, and opened easily to the touch. Inside, the hallway was covered with a coating of dust, and cobwebs draped the chandelier in the center of the ceiling. There were no bulbs in its sockets. To my right, I caught my reflection in the mirror on a battered coatstand, the sole furnishing in the hallway. Footsteps had disturbed the dust relatively recently. I guessed that Grass or Matheson had left them when they came to check on the house.

To my left was what would once have been a receiving room. It contained no furniture, but an ornamental marble fireplace against the far wall had been left untouched. There was another mirror here, although its reflection was slightly off. I approached it and saw that it was angled toward the covered window. A length of shiny new chain led from the back of the mirror to an old nail driven into the plaster. Maybe the original chain had broken, and someone had seen fit to rehang the mirror. It seemed like an odd thing to do.

A pair of sliding doors led into what was probably once

the dining room, again empty of furnishings apart from a fireplace matching the one in the drawing room, and another mirror, this time angled to the floor and once again with a new chain. There were mirrors too, I discovered, on the back of the kitchen doorway facing into the hallway; in the kitchen itself; on the first and second landings of the upper floors; and in every bedroom. There were mirrors on the walls of the upper floors, in the bathroom, and even in the attic when I checked it using a rickety stepladder. Most were old, but some looked like more recent additions, untainted by the decay of the nitrates.

I went back downstairs and checked the kitchen and the downstairs bathroom. The sink in the kitchen was stained and reeked of stagnant water and rotting matter in the pipes. By contrast, the sink in the bathroom was comparatively clean. Nobody would be drinking from it in a hurry, but compared to the kitchen sink it was a model of good hygiene. Someone had wiped it down in recent months, or had at least allowed the faucets to run. Maybe someone had used it to wash up after checking the house, because my own hands were already black with dust and filth.

The only door in the entire house that appeared to be locked was the door leading down into the basement where John Grady had made his last stand before shooting himself. I tried all of my keys on the lock, with no result, then made a mental note to ask Frank Matheson about it when next we spoke. A full-length mirror hung on the basement door. I checked my reflection in it. I was going kind of gray, I thought. Old age was going to be a gentle slide for me.

As I turned, I felt my head swim a little. I had been conscious of a vague, chemical scent in the air when I entered the house but now it seemed to have suddenly grown stronger. This would be a bad place to stay for any length of time, I thought. With the windows boarded up, and the doors sealed, there was no fresh air to dispel whatever miasma hung about the house. After only fifteen minutes, I was already experiencing the beginnings of a headache.

I was about to leave when a noise from the front of the house alerted me. There was a man on the step, his hand on his gun. It took a moment for my eyes to distinguish his brown uniform against the afternoon sun. He was in his forties, and running to seed. His stomach bulged over his belt, and there were sweat stains beneath his armpits.

'Who are you?' he said.

Instinctively, I raised my hands.

'My name's Charlie Parker. I've been employed by Frank Matheson, the owner of this house, to look into some things. I spoke to Chief Grass earlier today. He'll vouch for me.'

'Okay, I want you to step outside here.'

He backed away from me, his hand still poised on the butt of his gun. 'You got some ID?'

I nodded, walking slowly toward him, my hands still raised.

'It's in my jacket pocket, outside left.'

I always kept it there. At the risk of being pickpocketed, it meant that I was never in danger of making a nervy cop or security guard any more nervous than he already was by reaching inside my coat. I got to the doorway, moved on to the porch, then took the three steps down to the yard.

'Take your ID out,' said the cop. 'Slowly.'

The cop still hadn't drawn his gun.

I took out my wallet, flipped through it to my PI's license, then let him take a good look at it. When he was satisfied he allowed his hand to drift from his weapon for the first time. He introduced himself as Ed O'Donnell, one of the part-timers from Two Mile Lake.

'Chief Grass told me you'd been asking questions,' he said. 'I just didn't expect to find you in the house so soon. I got the impression the chief would be happier if you didn't spend too much time nosing around in there either.'

'Why would that be?'

'I think he'd prefer it if this house was gone. It's a reminder of the past.'

'You go in a lot?'

'Nah, although I met Frank Matheson here last night when we were both taking a look over the place. I saw your car parked down the road as I was passing. You seen enough?'

'Pretty much,' I said. 'Cellar door is locked, though. You wouldn't know anything about that, would you?'

'Nothing, except that it's where they found Grady's body. The other kid he took, Denny Maguire, was down there too. I suppose it's something that Grady didn't kill him as well. It was Chief Grass who took him out of the house, wrapped up in his jacket. He was just a state trooper then. A photographer got a snap of them coming out. It's kind of a famous picture around here. Since then, the chief has always kept an eye on this place. It's personal for him, after what he saw.'

'You have any idea what happened to the Maguire kid?'

'Denny? Sure, he works down in Moscow at a bar called the Desperate Measure. It's over on Main. He doesn't talk much about what happened that day, though.'

'No, I don't imagine he would.'

I looked back at the house. Its boarded-up windows reminded me of closed eyes on the brink of an awakening.

'You ever see anyone hanging around here?'

He shrugged. 'Kids, mostly, but they tend to stay away from the house itself.'

'Mostly?'

'What?'

'You said "kids, *mostly*." Sounds like there might have been others.'

'Tourists. Thrill-seekers.'

'Ray Czabo?'

'Couple of times. He's harmless.'

'What about a guy taller than me, thin, long dark hair? He probably looked kind of dirty.'

O'Donnell shook his head.

'Doesn't ring any bells.'

I thanked him for his time. He watched me lock the door then waited until I was in my car and driving away before he followed me from the property.

The Desperate Measure was the kind of bar in which most people wouldn't set a fire, not to mention a foot. A green shamrock barely stood out from the dirty white of the illuminated sign outside, and its windows were small bevelled panes of blue and orange. It was a place where men went to drink and think about hitting other men, and where women went to drink and think about hitting men as well. Inset into the door was a small square of glass, barred like the entrance to a keep, presumably so those within could check on anyone seeking entry once the door was locked. It wasn't clear why they felt the need to check. Nobody outside could be any more threatening than the kind of people who were already inside.

Half the seats at the bar were already taken, although it was not yet four in the afternoon. The customers were mainly men between their late thirties and late fifties, seated alone or in pairs. There was no conversation. A TV was bolted to the wall at the far end of the bar, further anchored in place by a pair of steel rods that partially obscured the edges of the screen. It was tuned to a news channel, but the sound was down. Most of the people in the Desperate Measure looked as if they'd already heard all the bad news they wanted to hear in their lives.

A sad line-up of domestic beers stood above the register like deserters waiting for the firing squad, with a single dusty bottle of Zima bringing up the rear, as out of place here as one of the patrons might have been on Castro Street during Gay Mardi Gras. There was a pretty good selection of bourbon, a couple of bottles of brandy, and one bottle of Tia Maria that didn't appear to have been touched since the Cold War.

I took a seat at the end of the bar nearer the door, two stools away from a man in a lumberjack shirt who kept flicking at the loose fingernail of his middle finger with the end of his thumb. Each time he did so, the nail raised up from the skin, barely held in place at the cuticle. I wondered if it hurt. In another life, I might have been tempted to ask, but I'd learned that a man who doesn't care much about idly inflicting pain on himself sometimes considers it a pleasant change to inflict pain on somebody else. I figured the nail would come out eventually, and then he could start on another finger. It would never be the same, though. There's nothing like losing your first nail.

The barman made his way down the counter.

'What can I get you?'

'You got coffee?'

'We got it, but you don't want to drink it.'

He indicated a pot of something stewing away on a hot plate. It looked as though it might have gone on fire at some point in the past, and was currently considering reigniting just to break the monotony.

'OJ is fine, then.'

He poured my juice into a clean glass and placed it before me.

'I'm looking for Denny Maguire,' I said. 'He around?'

'You found him,' said the barman.

I tried to keep the surprise from my face. My guess was that Denny Maguire must be in his thirties by now, but the guy behind the bar looked twenty years older than that again. In a way, he was the flipside of Chief Grass. If the chief, like Dorian Gray, had a bad portrait of himself hidden in the attic, then Denny Maguire's appearance gave some indication of what it might look like.

'My name's Charlie Parker,' I said, for the third time that day. 'I'm a private investigator. You need to see some ID?'

I asked because when you're in a place like the Desperate Measure, then producing anything that might lead the customers to mistake you for a cop and showing it to the barman was likely to lead to some awkward questions, or worse, for both of you.

'I believe you,' he said. 'Why would a man lie about something like that?'

'I could be doing it to gain the esteem and respect of strangers.'

'It'll take a little more than a piece of card and some attitude to get that here.'

'Maybe I should have shot a bear.'

'Maybe. You want to tell me why a private investigator is asking after me?'

I could see that Fingernail Man had found something to divert his attention from his own decaying fingers, so I suggested to Maguire that maybe we could talk somewhere away from the bar. He agreed, and summoned a woman who was reading a magazine at one of the deuces over by the men's room.

'I got five more minutes!' she said.

'Bill me,' said Maguire.

The woman shook her head in disgust, killed her cigarette and made her way slowly to the bar.

'You have to keep them motivated,' I said.

'Motivated? It's all I can do to keep her moving.'

He made his way along the bar, grabbed a soda from the cooler, and patted the woman on the ass as he went by.

'I'm gonna bill you for that an' all,' she said.

'Uh-huh,' said Maguire. 'You got change of a dollar?'

'Asshole.'

Maguire took a seat across from me, lit up a cigarette, and laid its tip beside the still-smouldering remains of the waitress's butt.

'So?'

'I've been hired by a man named Frank Matheson,' I said.

Maguire gave me nothing.

'You know who Frank Matheson is?' I said.

'I know. What's it to me?'

'He's concerned that someone with knowledge of the history of the Grady house may have gotten some ideas from what happened there in the past. He's afraid that the someone in question may have targeted a child.'

'Like I said, what's it to me?'

'What happened there took place before my time. I got some of it from the newspapers, a little more from Matheson, a little less from the chief over in Two Mile Lake. I was hoping you could tell me more.'

'Because I was there, you mean?'

'Yes. Because you were there. You were there when John Grady died.'

Maguire waited for a while before answering. He watched the woman moving behind the bar, joshing sourly with one or two of the regulars who had perked up some now that they were being exposed to a little female company. He seemed to take in the grim walls, the faded posters on the walls, the hole that someone had punched in the door of the men's room.

'You know, I own this place,' he said at last. 'Bought it three years ago from a man named Gruber. He was a German Jew. Never could understand why he had a shamrock on the sign. When I asked him, he told me that nobody ever lost money on a bar that looked Irish. Didn't matter what happened once you got inside. Kind of people who come into a place like this, they're not too concerned about decor. They want to drink, drink some more, have one for the road, then stagger home and be left to themselves from start to finish, so when Gruber said he was going to retire, I bought it, because it suited my disposition. I like being left to myself. I don't like people asking about my present or my past. Why do you think I'd make an exception for you?'

Now it was my turn to pause before answering. There was a game being played, and I think Maguire knew it. I had come here in part to find out what he could tell me about the Grady house, because to understand the present you have to understand the past. But I also wanted to take a look at him. He was the only child to have entered the Grady house and survive, and I didn't like to think about the kind of scars that experience had left upon him. While those who have been abused in the past, or have suffered in the way that he had, do not automatically themselves become abusers, it does happen and it was something that needed to be considered.

'I came here to look into your eyes,' I said.

Maguire met my gaze levelly.

'And what do you see?'

'I know what I don't see: I don't see a man who has been transformed by his own pain into the very thing that caused that pain to begin with.'

'You thought I might have been behind whatever is troubling Frank Matheson.'

He said it softly, but without blame or anger.

'I had to consider it.'

He took a long pull on his cigarette, releasing the smoke slowly through his nostrils. Along with the fumes, some of the suspicion seemed to ease from his body.

'What made him hire a private investigator?'

I handed him one of the copies of the photograph, the unknown girl caught in her pose, ready and waiting for the ball to be released, for her chance to strike at it. Maguire picked it up and examined it for a time.

'Do you recognize her?' asked.

'No. Where did it come from?'

'Matheson found it in the mailbox of the Grady house. He doesn't know why it was left there. He thought that it might be some kind of tribute to John Grady.'

Maguire was quiet for a long time. I knew that at the end of his silence, he would either stand up and tell me to leave, or open up to me. The decision would be his to make, and if I spoke before he reached it I felt certain I would get nothing from him.

'An offering,' said Maguire.

'Maybe.'

'He used that word, you know, when I was with him. He called the Matheson girl that. He said she was an "offering." '

'An offering to what?'

'I don't know. Maybe to whatever he believed made him do the things that he did. He talked all the time I was there, but only some of it was addressed to me. I don't remember so much of it. I was too scared to listen while I was conscious, and when I came to he was dead. I've blanked out most of the rest. I didn't do so good in high school so they sent me to a doctor, a shrink, and he said I needed to confront what happened in that house, but I prefer it the way it is. Hidden. Locked up, just like I was.'

It wasn't for me to comment on how he chose to deal with what he had endured, but I had a brief flash of a barred cellar door, and inside a small boy was being tormented by John Grady, over and over again. Whatever front he presented to the world, that was the reality of what was hidden inside Denny Maguire's head.

He retrieved his cigarette from the ashtray, took a drag on it, and continued.

'Mostly,' he said, 'he spoke to something that I couldn't see.'

'What else do you remember?'

'The mirrors. There were mirrors on every wall. I could see him reflected in them. It was like the room was filled with John Gradys. I remember that, and I remember the remains of the other children. They were sitting over by the far wall. I don't like to recall how they looked. He talked to them too, sometimes, in a way.'

'Do you recall anything about Louise Matheson?'

He shook his head.

'I think I heard the shot that killed her, but I was pretty far gone by then.'

'Why did he keep you alive?'

Maguire pretended to think about the question, but I guessed it was one that had troubled him all his life, ever since Grass had led him from that terrible place.

'I was the only boy he took,' he said. 'He spoke to me some, told me about himself, about the house he wanted to create. He hated the little girls, but me, I was different. I still think he'd have killed me, in the end, or maybe just let me fade away and die. Could be he saw something of himself in me. I hope to Jesus he was wrong, but I think that's what he believed.'

The cigarette had almost burned down to the filter. A column of ash toppled like a condemned building and exploded into dust upon the tabletop.

'Can you remember anything else that he said?' I asked.

He looked at me, then stubbed out the cigarette and rose.

'Like I told you, I don't remember the details. I do recall that he didn't talk directly to the other children,' he said.

It sounded as if there was dust caught in his throat.

'He talked to their reflections in the mirrors. He talked to them like they were inside the mirrors, and if those policemen hadn't come, then he'd have been talking to me that way too. I'd have been lost in there with them.'

And in the gloom of his grim little bar, Denny Maguire began to cry.

The streets around the Desperate Measure were quiet as I walked back to the parking lot at the rear of the bar. I wasn't sure that I was learning much that I hadn't already suspected: John Grady was a vile human being, and all those who had come into contact with him remained tainted by his touch.

When I turned the corner, I saw a man leaning against the hood of my Mustang. He was smoking a cigarette in his right hand while the fingers of his left tapped a delicate rhythm against the bodywork. I knew who he was, even as he watched my approach, his eyes lost deep in his domed skull and his lank hair hanging like an afterthought at the back of his head.

'Can I help you?' I said.

The Collector had turned to watch my approach. He looked sickly and ill in the yellow glow of the single light that illuminated the lot, and appeared to be dressed in the same clothes that he had worn to his interview with Matheson. I could see the sole of his shoe gaping like a fish's mouth.

'I think you can,' he said, 'and perhaps I can help you in return.'

'I can give you the address of a good tailor,' I said. 'He might also know someone who can fix your shoe. After that you're on your own.'

The Collector looked down, as if noticing his ruined sole for the first time.

'Well, well,' he said. 'Look at that.'

He shot a plume of smoke into the night air. It went on for a long time, as though he were manufacturing it deep inside his lungs.

'You want to step away from my car?'

The Collector considered it for a moment. Just when it seemed as if I'd have to drive off with him draped across the hood, he tossed his cigarette to the ground and stamped it out with his good shoe, then moved a couple of feet away from my car.

'My apologies,' he said. 'You work for Mr. Matheson.'

'I think we have a misunderstanding,' I said. 'I wasn't offering to exchange information in return for you finding someplace else to rest.'

I stood by the Mustang, but I didn't take out my keys. If I tried to open the car door then I might have to take my eyes off the man in the lot for an instant, and I didn't want to do that. Matheson was right. The Collector's appearance, his greasy hair combined with his filthy clothes, was a distraction, a ruse to fool the unwary. His movements were slow and precise because he chose to make them that way. When he wanted to, I sensed that he could move very quickly indeed, and that his old coat and tattered trousers concealed strong bones and lean, stringy muscles.

'I suspect Mr. Matheson told you about me.'

I didn't reply. I wasn't going to reveal anything to him.

'I know about the picture,' he said.

Everything changed.

'What picture?'

'The picture of the little girl.'

'Do you know who she is?'

He shook his head.

'Do you know who took the photograph?'

Again, he shook his head.

'Then you're no use to me. Go find another dark place to haunt.'

I made a show of fiddling with my keys.

'She's at risk,' said the Collector. 'If you give me what I want, some of that risk will diminish.'

I wondered if he had taken the photograph, if its placement in the mailbox was all part of his efforts to receive payment for whatever old debt he believed he was owed.

The Collector was smart. He was waiting for me when I reached that conclusion.

'But she is not at risk from me,' he said. 'I have no interest in children. I merely want my debt paid.'

I took a couple of steps toward him. He didn't appear threatened.

'And what debt is that?'

'It's a private matter?'

'Are you working for somebody?'

'We all work for somebody, Mr. Parker. Suffice it to say that John Grady attempted to secure a certain asset before he died. He partially succeeded. A token gesture will be enough to undo the damage. Your client is unwilling to make that gesture.'

'The debt is not his to pay. He has no obligation to you, and even if he had, I don't see how paying it diminishes the "risk" to the girl in the photograph.'

The Collector lit another cigarette. In the flare of the match, his eyes filled with flames.

'This is an old and wicked world. John Grady was a foul man, and the Grady house is a foul place. Such places retain a residue which can pollute others. If you help me, then some of that pollution may be removed.'

'What do you want?'

'A mirror, from the Grady house. It has many mirrors. One will not be missed.'

'Why don't you just take one yourself?'

'The house is secured.'

'Not so secure that a man couldn't get into it, if he wanted something badly enough.'

'I am not a thief,' said the Collector.

It was more than that. For the first time, his eyes shifted from mine. He was scared of the house. No, not scared, but wary. For whatever reason, he was unable to enter the house himself.

'I think you need to talk to the lawyers, or the bank,' I said. 'Talk to somebody, anybody, but just don't talk to me again. I can't help you.'

As I spoke, I opened the car door. He remained standing, isolated in the middle of the lot, watching me.

I closed the door and put the key in the ignition. When I looked up, the Collector was gone, or so I thought until the tapping came at my side window. He was close to the glass, so close that I could see the lines in his face and the veins running beneath his pale skin. It looked too thin, as though only the slimmest of membranes concealed the bloody redness beneath.

'I will collect,' he said. 'Remember that.'

I gunned the engine and pulled out so quickly that he was forced to throw himself back against the big Toyota in the next space. He hung in the rear-view mirror like an infected wound in the flesh of the night, and then I turned the corner and he disappeared from my sight.

* * *

There was no moon upon Scarborough as I drove home. Great swathes of cloud hid the light. Soon the marshes would flood, and a fresh round of feeding and dying would begin. I wondered what effect that cycle might have on me, and if the water in my own body might somehow be prey to the revolutions of a chunk of dead rock in space. Perhaps it affected my behavior, making me act in odd and unpredictable ways. Then I thought of Rachel, and what she might say if I shared those thoughts with her: she would tell me that my behavior was odd and unpredictable anyway, and that nobody would notice a difference if they tried to make a lunar connection.

Our first child was due, and every time my cell phone buzzed I half expected to hear her voice telling me that it was time. I had long given up cosseting her, for not only was she fiercely independent but she saw in my actions an attempt to guard against the loss of another child. My daughter and my wife had been stolen from me only a few years before. I was not sure that I could live if another was taken from me. Sometimes, that made me overprotective of those I now held dear.

I stopped my car before entering the driveway to our home. I thought of Matheson and his wife: how did they see themselves now, I wondered? Was one still a father, a mother, when one's child was dead? A wife who has lost her husband becomes a widow, and a husband bereaved of his wife a widower, but there was no name for what one became when one's only child was wrenched from this world. But perhaps it didn't matter: in my own mind I was still her father, and she was still my child, and regardless of the world in which she now dwelt, that would always be. I could not forget her, and I knew that she had not forgotten me.

For she came to me still. In the lost time, in the pale hours, in those moments between waking and sleeping when the world was still forming around me, she was there. Sometimes her mother was with her, cloaked in shadows, a reminder of my duty to them, and to those like them. I used to dream of being at peace, of no longer experiencing these visions. Now I know that it is not meant for me, not now, and that my peace will only come when I close my eyes and at last take my place beside them in the darkness.

Rachel was lying on the couch, reading, her hand resting on her belly and her long red hair descending in a braid across her left shoulder. I kissed her forehead, then her lips. She placed my hand alongside hers, so that I could feel the child within.

'You think the kid is planning to leave anytime soon?' I asked. 'If the baby stays there any longer, we can start charging rent.'

'Get used to saying that,' she said. 'You'll be asking the same question until our child goes to college. Anyway, I'm the one who has to carry another person around inside me. It's about time you started shouldering some of the burden.'

I went to the kitchen and took a soda from the fridge. 'Yeah, what about all the ice cream I have to keep bringing home? It doesn't float here on its own.'

'I heard that.'

I stood at the kitchen door and waved a carton of Len Libby's orange sherbet at her.

'Tempted? Huh? Do we want a little spoonful for the road?'

She threw a cushion at me.

'How I ever allowed you to get close enough to impregnate me I really don't know. I guess it was a moment of weakness. Literally a moment, in your case.'

'Harsh,' I said. 'You're not including cuddling time.'

I sat down beside her and she folded herself into me as

best she could. I shared my soda with her, despite her hurtful comments about my perceived lack of stamina.

'So how did it go?' she asked.

I told her about my day: the cops, the Grady house, my conversation with Maguire. None of it added up to very much. Rachel had spent some time going through the files Matheson had left with me. Now that the birth was imminent, she was not taking on any new academic or professional work, and consequently the Grady case offered her an opportunity to stretch some underused psychologist's muscles.

'Mirrors,' said Rachel. 'Conversations with an unseen other. A display of victims yet without any real interaction. No actual sexual or physical abuse of the children, beyond the actual act of taking their lives. Even then, he seemed determined to put them through as little pain as possible: a single blow to the head to render them unconscious, then suffocation.'

'Then there's the house,' I said. 'He had great plans for it, yet never did much to improve it from what I can see. All he did was start wallpapering and put too many mirrors on the walls.'

'And what do you think he saw in them?' asked Rachel.

'He saw himself. What does anyone see in a mirror?'

She pursed her lips and shrugged. 'Do you see yourself when you look in a mirror?'

I had the feeling that I often got with Rachel, that she had somehow moved three steps ahead of me while I was being distracted by a passing cloud.

'I—'

I stopped as I tried to consider the question properly.

'Well,' I said at last. 'I see a version of myself.'

'Your reflection is informed by your own self-image. In effect, you create part of what you see. We are not as we are.

We are as we imagine ourselves to be. So what did John Grady see when he looked in the mirror?'

I saw again the house. I saw its unfinished walls, its filthy sinks, its decaying carpets. I saw the cheap sticks of furniture, the empty bedrooms, the warped boards.

And I saw the mirrors.

'He saw his house,' I said. 'He saw his house as he wished it to be.'

'Or as he believed it to be, in another place.'

'In the world beyond the glass.'

'And maybe that world was more real to him than this one.'

'So if the house was more real in that world, then . . .'

'Then so was he. Perhaps that's who he was talking to while he was waiting to kill Denny Maguire. Maybe he was talking to John Grady, or what he perceived to be the real John Grady.'

'And the children?'

'What did Denny Maguire say: that he never spoke directly to them?'

'He said that Grady spoke to their reflections in the glass.'

Rachel shrugged. 'I don't know. I've never heard anything quite like that before.'

She moved in closer to me.

'You will be careful, won't you?' she asked.

'He's dead,' I said. 'There's a limit to the harm dead men can do.'

In the Grady house, something stirred. Dust was raised in ascending spirals. Papers rustled in empty grates. It was the north wind, whistling through rotting frames and broken boards, that created the sense of movement in the silent rooms. It was the north wind that made doorknobs rattle, and doors creak. It was the north wind that caused coathangers to jangle against one another in locked closets, and dirty glasses to clink in closed kitchen cupboards.

And it was the north wind that made the trees move, creating faint shadows that fell through cracks in the boarded windows, their shapes drifting across the old mirror above the fireplace in the dining room, the world reflected in its depths subtly different from our own, the shape moving within it finding no companion in the old house. There should have been photographs on the mantel, for there were photographs in its reflection in the glass. Instead, the mantel within the house itself was empty.

It was the wind, then, that had carried these black and white images of unknown children through the glass and into another world.

It was the wind, just the wind.

V

Surveillance is difficult work. Even the worst doughnut head, the kind of guy who wore a hockey helmet to school in case he fell over, is going to catch someone who's watching him regularly for any length of time. The cops are lucky. It's harder for a suspect to spot a handful of people on his tail than just one, and cops can split the job up between them, give one another a break, and generally help the other guy to remain on alert throughout, because surveillance, as well as being difficult, is also tedious and the mind tends to wander. A good surveillance detail therefore requires a lot of manpower, which is why even the cops tend to sit on their hands some when the subject comes up. Taking two or more cops off regular duties to watch some mook who may or may not be worthy of the attention has a knock-on effect on morale, overtime, and probably crime in general.

Private investigators generally don't have the luxury of surveillance teams, and their clients aren't always so wealthy that they can afford to hire a whole bunch of operatives to cover a job, so checking up on someone can be difficult work. The Grady house detail was different. The house wasn't about to go anywhere, or attempt to make a break for freedom through the woods. Nevertheless, watching it continuously was going to be a problem, which meant that someone would have to be found to share the burden. To be done well, even a simple task like monitoring an empty old house required someone with patience, self-discipline, a steady nerve, and an eye for detail, someone who didn't spook easily and who would know how to handle himself if anything went down.

In the absence of such an individual, I needed someone with a lot of time on his hands.

I knew just the person.

'Surveillance, huh?' said Angel.

Angel and his boyfriend Louis were the closest thing to real friends that I had. Admittedly they were morally suspect, and Angel had the kind of temperament that might have been helped by a little pharmaceutical intervention, but then I couldn't claim to be perfect either. Most men end up with the friends that they deserve, but I figured that I could probably get away with a lot during the rest of my life and still have some cause for complaint about the ones that I'd been handed. Most of the time, they lived together in an apartment on the Upper West Side, where Louis's natural tendency toward order and minimalism fought a valiant but losing battle against his partner's fascination with clutter and bargain clothing. It was all very Yin and Yang, but when I offered that theory to Angel he pretended that I was talking about Siamese twins and regaled me with anecdotes of a sexually fascinating, if politically incorrect, nature. When I shared a similar view with Louis, he threatened to send Angel to stay with me, just to see how long Rachel and I would tolerate a little of Angel's Yang. Given that Rachel sometimes made Louis look like a slob, I imagined that wouldn't be very long.

I could hear music playing in the background as Angel and I spoke. It sounded terrible.

'What the hell are you listening to?'

'A progressive rock compilation. I'm trying to get in touch with my muse by listening to music from my past.'

I was almost afraid to ask. Almost.

'You have a muse? What is she, some kind of community service muse? Did the court order her to help you?'

Angel chose to ignore me.

'I'm considering writing my memoirs. I mean, I'm gonna have to change some shit around, maybe alter names to protect the guilty, play with dates and timescales and stuff. I bought a book, one of those "How to Write A Bestseller" guides. There's some good advice in there. Guy who wrote it is a bestselling writer himself, knows what he's talking about.'

'You ever hear of the guy who wrote it?'

There was a pause.

'Nope, least not until I bought his book.'

'So why do you think he's a bestselling writer, if you haven't heard of him?'

'There's a lot of people I haven't heard of, doesn't mean to say that they're not what they say they are. Says on the cover he's a bestselling writer.'

'So what's he written?'

There came the sound of pages being flipped in a thin, overpriced book.

'He's written—'

'Yep?'

'Hey, I'm looking. He's written . . . Okay, he's written a bestselling book on how to write bestsellers. That what you wanted to hear? Happy now?'

I heard the sound of a book being cast to one side with some force. Still, I figured he'd retrieve it as soon as I hung up the phone, but he probably wouldn't get much farther on his memoirs than the first chapter. I certainly hoped that he wouldn't.

'This surveillance thing you want me to do, it's on a house?'

'Uh-huh.'

'An empty house?'

'Yes.'

'What did the house do: spy on its neighbors?'

'I suspect it of stealing underwear from clothes lines.'

'Knew a guy who did that once. He'd steal them, clean them, fold them, then deliver them back to the house with a note describing all the work that he'd done, with some care tips for the owners. He told the judge he was worried about hygiene. Judge advised the prison governor to let him work in the laundry. We had the cleanest overalls in the state. Starchy, too.'

Angel had spent too long in prisons; a lot of hard time. He rarely spoke about them, and it was rarer still that he joked about them. It meant that he was happy in his life, for the moment, and for that I was grateful. He had endured a lot in recent times.

'That's a nice story. You about done?'

'Doesn't sound like a job looking at an empty house has too many prospects.'

'If you turn out to be good at it, we'll promote you to a job watching *occupied* houses. Look, no offense meant, but you've burgled enough properties. You must have some experience of watching them.'

'Nice. You call me up, ask for my help, and now you insult me. Got any other skeletons from my past you want to throw in my face?'

'It would be like emptying a crypt. I don't have that kind of time.'

'How much does this job pay?'

'A dollar a day and all the peanuts you can eat.'

'Salted, or roasted?'

'Salted.'

'Sounds good. When can I start? And, hey, can I bring a friend?'

* * *

My next call was to Clem Ruddock. Clem retired from the state police a couple of years back and, like some cops do, bought himself a bar in a place where the temperature never dipped below seventy in winter. Unfortunately for Clem, he was living testament to my belief that some people are just born to die in Maine. He never quite settled in Boca so he sold a half share in the bar to an ex-cop from Coral Gables and headed back north. Now he divided his time between Florida and a duplex in Damariscotta, near his daughter and his grandchildren. Clem's answering machine told me that he wasn't home, but left me with a cell phone number to try instead.

'What are you, a surgeon?' I asked him, when I eventually got through to him. 'What does a retired guy need a cell phone for anyway?'

He was driving. I could hear the purr of his engine in the background.

'I guess you didn't hear,' said Clem. 'I took up pimping to make ends meet. Got me some girls in a trailer off 295. I'm thinking about franchising, you got some money to spare.'

'I'm sorry, my money's all tied up in monkey porn. It's a growing market. You got time to talk?'

As it turned out, Clem was on his way down to Portland to meet with his lawyer. Sometimes, things work out that way. I arranged to meet him for a hamburger lunch in Rosie's down in the Old Port. He told me I was cheap. I told him that he was paying, so I was even cheaper than that. After all, I wasn't the one with two homes and a bar in Florida.

Rachel was sitting at the kitchen table, flicking through a magazine and nibbling on a bagel. Walter was waiting midway between his basket and Rachel, clearly keen to try his luck at scamming some food from her plate but reluctant to risk being shouted at for his trouble. When I came in, he seemed to decide that the balance had suddenly tipped in his favor, and used sniffing my hand as a pretext to close in on the table.

'You've been feeding him scraps again,' said Rachel, without looking up.

'What did you do, shine a light on him until he broke down and confessed?'

'We're sending out mixed signals. It's confusing him.'

'He's just confused by why you don't love him as much as I do,' I said.

'Oooh, that's low. Is that how you plan to earn the love of your child, with bribery and treats?'

'Start as you mean to continue. It worked with the dog. And with you.'

I leaned over and kissed her on the lips.

'I have to go,' I said. 'I'll be back for dinner, and I'll keep the cell on.'

Her eyes drifted toward the inside of my jacket. The butt of the gun was just visible to her, but she made no comment.

'Just be careful,' she said, and returned to her magazine. As I left the house, I looked back and saw her slip a piece of bagel into Walter's mouth. He rested his head on her lap in return and she stroked him gently, her eyes no longer on her reading but staring through the kitchen window at the marshes and the trees beyond, as though the glass had turned to water and she could see once again the face of the drowning man beneath its surface.

The Collector was looking for Ray Czabo. The name had come up in the course of the Collector's own investigation into the Grady house, and he was anxious to talk to the man in question. He made no moral judgements on Voodoo Ray's gruesome hobby: in his experience, human beings were capable of far worse than stealing mementoes from crime scenes. What interested him was the possibility that Ray had found a way into the house, and that perhaps he had managed to secure a trinket for himself in the process. If it was the right kind of souvenir, then the Collector's work would be done.

But Ray Czabo was proving difficult to find, and there was now a stranger in his house. The Collector usually believed in adopting the direct approach, but the young man who appeared to be servicing Mrs Czabo in her husband's absence looked troublesome. More to the point, the Collector had discovered that this was a case of 'like father, like son', and that Mrs Czabo's lover enjoyed the protection of a small but efficient criminal operation.

The Collector had been careless, assuming that his old car and his rundown appearance would allow him to pass unnoticed unless he chose otherwise. He was beginning to wonder if Mrs Czabo might have conspired with her boyfriend to remove her husband from the scene, whether through threats or actual violence. He was thinking this over as he returned to his car, having followed the lover back to his father's base, when a man emerged from behind a Dumpster and blocked his progress.

'You want to tell me what you're doin'?' said the man. He was slightly overweight, and wore a black leather jacket and blue jeans. His face bulged in all the wrong places, as though every bone had been broken and then badly reset. His name was Chris Tierney, and he had a reputation as a hard man, an enforcer. The Collector had no time for this. He tried to slip by but Tierney pushed him back, advancing a step as he did so.

'I asked you a question,' he said.

The Collector remained silent.

'Fuck you,' said the man, finally. 'You're coming with me.'

He moved in on the slim, greasy-looking individual with the yellowed fingers, this stick figure dressed in rags who had tried to bulldoze his way past him, but instead of backing away the raggedy man moved forward to meet him. Tierney felt an impact at his chest and his body was raised up until only the tips of his toes remained on the ground. He curled over his attacker's hand as the shock of the blow began to dissipate, only to be replaced by a sharp pain. Tierney tried to speak, and blood ran from his mouth and flowed over his lips and chin. His fingers clutched at the Collector's hand and found the hilt of the knife. He tried to say something, although there was nothing to be said.

The Collector touched his left hand to the dying man's lips.

'Shhh,' he said. 'Hush. It's all right. Nearly there, now. Nearly there.'

The knife thrust hard once more, and the life left Tierney in a rush of air and blood.

Clem hadn't changed since last I saw him. His hair had turned white while he was in his thirties, so he appeared not to have aged much apart from the wrinkles around his eyes and mouth. He still had the remnant of a tan from his most recent trip south, and he'd lost a little weight.

'You look good,' I said.

'I eat healthy, when I have no other option,' he said, then ordered a cheeseburger with extra fries, hold the mayo. 'It's the mayo that kills you,' he added.

Clem was one of a network of cops who had remained friends with my grandfather after he left the force, and who had extended their good will to his grandson. Back in Manhattan, there were cops who would cross the street to avoid me, even if that street was mined. Up here, there were other, older loyalties to be considered.

We spoke about nothing in particular until after we had eaten, then sat back in our chairs by the window and watched the cars and people passing by. Nobody seemed in too much of a hurry to get anywhere, and it was still early enough in December for the prospect of Christmas to seem more welcome than stressful.

'You remember John Grady?' I said, at last.

It struck me that I hated saying his name. It seemed to pollute the very air, seeping out through the window frame to poison the festive atmosphere outside.

'John Grady,' said Clem.

He took a mouthful of beer, then held it for a time, as though using it to wash the mention of Grady from his mouth.

'You have a habit of resurrecting old ghosts,' he said. 'I think you have a morbid interest in dead killers.'

'Well, some of them didn't turn out to be quite as dead as people believed'

'You do seem to enjoy a gift for waking them, that's for sure. John Grady, though, he's not coming back. I watched him die.'

'You were there?'

I knew Clem had been involved in the investigation, but not that he'd witnessed Grady's final moments.

'When the little Matheson girl was taken, we got the first half-decent lead in months. It was a foolish thing for him to have done, pulling her like that, but I guess by then he couldn't control his appetites anymore. We got to the house, but it was too late for her.'

He took another sip of beer and looked beyond me to where his own reflection lay suspended in the window.

'That one stays with me. I can't remember more than a

handful of cases in twenty-five years that make me want to break my fist against a wall, but that's one of them. Too many "if onlys." If only we'd been quicker to make the connection with Grady's car. If only we'd been able to break that door down. If only . . .

'Anyway, we got there, and found Grady with the gun already pointed at his head. If it wasn't so horrible, it might almost have been funny. After all, there we were with our guns pointed at him, threatening to shoot, and there he was with a gun in his hand ready to blow his own head off and save us the trouble. Only one way it was going to end, I guess.

'I remember what he said before he died: "This is not a house. This is a home." Still don't know what he meant by that. The place looked less like a home than anywhere I've ever been. Sticks of furniture, half-painted walls, cheap wallpaper already starting to peel. There was dust and filth and damn mirrors everywhere. Those mirrors, they completely threw me. It seemed like there was movement everywhere: our reflections, the *reflections* of our reflections. I've never been so jumpy in all my life.

'I was pretty close to Grady when he pulled the trigger. I recall his face, and his eyes. You know, what he did was beyond belief, as terrible a thing as I've seen in all my life, but he was a tormented man. I could see it on him. His skin was covered with some kind of rash. There were sores all over his mouth, and his eyelids were swollen and puffy. He was just this haunted, sick creature. I was the closest man to him. I saw myself reflected in his eyes and, I swear, I knew what he was about to do and I wanted to stop him: not because I cared if he lived or died, but because I had this feeling that if he died at that moment then, somehow, he'd take a part of me with him, because I was trapped in his gaze. Makes no sense, does it? I was so wired at the time, so freaked out by all those mirrors, that the fear just kind of hit me. I didn't think it through. Suddenly, it was just there.

'Anyway, he kind of looked to his right and saw his reflection in the mirror, and his face changed. He looked almost relieved. Then he pulled the trigger, and the mirror just disappeared in a shower of blood and glass. That was it for him. We found the bodies with him in the basement, and the little Maguire kid, who was drifting in and out of consciousness. The best thing that can be said about what happened to those kids is that the M.E. figured they died quickly, but this is children we're talking about. Jesus, what are we reduced to when we have to console ourselves with the idea of a fast end to their sufferings?'

He raised his bottle for another beer. I was on coffee. I don't drink much anymore. I don't have the taste for it.

'I can't believe all that stuff just came out,' said Clem. 'Strange what you keep inside, almost without knowing.'

I thought of Denny Maguire, carried from the house in the arms of a policeman, wrapped in a stranger's coat. I got the feeling that he probably hadn't slept well after he closed up the bar on the night that we spoke. Then again, I guessed Denny Maguire had rarely slept peacefully since the day John Grady stole him from his family and brought him to that house. He had kept it all inside too, and it had turned him into an old man before his time.

Clem's beer arrived, but he didn't touch it.

'I just told you all that, and I don't even know why you're asking about him.'

I briefed him on Matheson, and the photograph of the little girl.

'Children,' he said, quietly. 'It's always children with you.'

I didn't respond. I didn't want to.

'Some cops, they have a thing,' he continued. 'Cases of

one kind just seem to come their way more than others. They don't go looking for them. They just kind of happen upon them. With some, it's domestics; others, it's rapes. They develop a way of looking at them that's different from the rest, and then it's like they attract them. With you, I guess it's children. Must be hard for you, after what happened.'

'Sometimes,' I said.

'You believe in God?'

'I don't know. If He exists, then I don't understand what He's doing.'

'If He doesn't exist, then we're lost. I look around, I think about men like Grady and what he did, and I wonder sometimes if there's anybody beyond this who really cares. And, then, it's like the fog clears for a couple of seconds, and I see a pattern. No, not even a pattern, just the possibility of one.'

'You see the hand of God?'

He laughed, and tapped his cheekbone with his finger.

'Cop's eyes: I see his fingerprints. I see patterns on the glass. You get older, you start thinking about these things. If there is a God, then you and He are going to be having a serious talk in the near future, so you start thinking about what you might say. Mostly, you figure you're going to be saying "sorry." A lot.'

Clem seemed to remember what he was doing here.

'I'm rambling. You say Grass is looking into this thing?'

'He's skeptical. He says he wants to be discreet, in case he freaks out some family for no good reason, or starts a panic among parents.'

'Grass is a straight arrow. He was a young man when the Grady thing happened but, like me, he was there at the end. I don't think it will ever leave him. From what I hear, he takes his stewardship of the place pretty personally. He doesn't want to remind people of what happened there, and I suppose he's right to take that view. Next thing you know, it's on a death trip tourist trail, or somebody takes it into his head to torch the place. No bad thing, if you ask me. I don't understand why Matheson wanted to keep the house to begin with. But, like I said, the Grady house is now Grass's patch. He's taken on the burden of it.'

I wondered if Clem was right. Grass, Denny Maguire, even Clem himself, all seemed to carry with them some remnant of what had taken place in the Grady house, like a splinter in the soul. Perhaps wiping it from the earth would help to bring some relief to them and to all those whose lives had been touched by John Grady. Even Matheson must have begun to reconsider his urge to preserve it as a monument, now that it had found a way to extend its reach into an unknown girl's life.

'Anything else you can tell me?' I asked.

'There's not much more to tell,' he said. 'Grady was a blank slate. I don't even know if that was his real name. His fingerprints weren't on record, and nobody came forward after his death to claim his body. He cost the state a funeral and a cheap cross.'

He pushed the bottle of beer away from him.

'Don't know why I ordered this. I drink more than one bottle in the afternoon and I'm napping for the rest of the day. I'm already finding it hard to think of details that might be helpful to you. I suppose the only thing I can add is that we took some material from the house – books, mostly – that was kind of odd.'

'Odd how?'

'It was woo-woo stuff. You know: witchcraft, demons, pictures of those star things.'

'Pentagrams.'

'Yeah, trust you to know the name for them. It wasn't

low end stuff, either. Some of those books were pretty old. I hear they made some money for the widows and orphans when they were sold.'

'They were sold off?'

'Well, there was no reason to hold on to them in the first place, since Grady was dead, and it wasn't like there was going to be a trial or anything. Someone put them to one side and forgot about them, and they lay around in a basement for twenty years. Then there was that big clearout last fall. I went over to take a look, just in case there was anything worth holding on to as a souvenir. Those books turned up, and someone decided to get a valuation on them. The word went out to some of the dealers in the state, and literally the next day a guy showed up to take a look at them. He offered a thousand dollars for the lot, and walked out with them five minutes later.'

'Do you know who bought them?'

'I can find out for you right now, if you want.'

He took out his cell and tapped in a phone number.

'See, I did have a use for this after all,' he said, as his call was answered. 'Hi, can you put me through to Detective Brian Harrison, please?'

I didn't know Harrison. He came on the line and he and Clem exchanged greetings for a while and caught up on news of mutual friends. Eventually, Clem asked him about the sale of the Grady books. After a lot of 'uh-huhs' he thanked Harrison, promised to meet him for a drink, then hung up.

'Wouldn't you know it?' he said. 'There had to be a woo-woo angle. The guy who bought the books claimed to be working for Bowe & Heinrich. He said he was Milton Bowe's nephew.'

Bowe & Heinrich was a well-known firm of rare book dealers based in Bangor.

'Let me guess,' I said. 'Bowe & Heinrich never heard of him.'

'Milton Bowe arrived at state police headquarters a day later to take a look at the books himself, but they were already gone by then. He was pretty pissed at what happened. He didn't like the idea of some weirdo impersonating his nephew, or stealing books from under his nose.'

'Weirdo?'

'He looked like a tramp. Some of these collector types do, I hear. They spend more money on books and antiques than they do on clothes. This guy had an old coat, and a shoe that was speaking to him. He paid in cash, though: ten hundred-dollar bills, which was probably more than Bowe would have paid, the cheap bastard. If this guy committed a crime, it was a victimless one.'

I didn't need to ask Clem any more about the buyer. I knew who he was.

'You decided how you're going to handle this thing?' Clem asked.

I gave a non-commital reply. I wasn't sure yet what I could do, other than dig up old memories and watch as the dust they raised settled itself on the Grady house.

'Well, you need help, you let me know,' said Clem.

We stood to leave. I picked up the check, despite ribbing Clem earlier about his wealth.

'It's taken care of,' he said. 'I left my credit card behind the bar.'

'You didn't have to do that.'

'Hey, it was good to see you. I don't get to talk to someone thirty years younger than me so often now. Makes me feel like less of an old fart.'

The weather had turned chill. My breath hung like an unfulfilled promise in the afternoon air.

'Have you ever been back to the Grady house?' I asked Clem, as we walked to our cars.

'Nope. No cause to go there. Even if I had to go back, I wouldn't stay too long. There's something unhealthy in the atmosphere of the place. You've been there, you know what I'm talking about. I didn't know better, I'd say that there were chemicals in the walls and the floors. In the days after Grady killed himself, most of the men who spent time in the house complained of nausea and vomiting. I had headaches for weeks afterward. That was more than twenty years ago. It could be that it's not as strong now, but I don't doubt that it's still there.'

His words brought back my own disorientation after spending a little time in the Grady house. Clem was right. Whatever had infected the house was still present, engaged in a process of slow decay like the half-life of radioactive waste.

We parted on Commercial. Clem gripped my hand tightly in both of his.

'No "if only," ' he said. 'Remember that. Don't let anything happen to that little girl. There are too many lost children. You know that better than anyone else. There are just too many lost children . . .'

VI

I drove up to Brewer that afternoon. Voodoo Ray Czabo and his wife had moved back up to Maine so that she could be closer to her mother, which proved that not only was Ray kind of unpleasant, he was also dumb as well. When a woman like Edna Czabo says she wants to be closer to her mother then you might as well start packing your bags and looking for a bachelor apartment, because no good can come of it. The talk was that Ray Czabo's marriage was on the rocks.

Ray was a skinny guy who dressed neatly, smelled nice, and could be superficially charming when the necessity arose, but his fascination with suffering and the vicarious pleasure – and actual profit – he derived from it left him a couple of rungs below blowflies on the moral ladder. I'd never had the distinction of making Mrs Czabo's acquaintance, but from what I heard she made Ray seem like good company.

There were two vehicles in the driveway, a sensible Nissan and a souped-up Firebird, when I pulled up outside the Czabos' nondescript single-story house, surrounded by similarly anonymous houses with marginally newer paintwork. The grass in the yard was patchy and unkempt, and the trees and bushes that bordered their property hadn't been pruned that year. Light was already fading as I walked up to the door and pressed the buzzer. After a couple of minutes, the door was opened by a woman in a pale blue bathrobe. Her feet were bare, her hair was tousled, and she had the smoking butt of a cigarette in her hand. I picked out the remains of lipstick at the corners of her mouth, and her chin and cheeks were red and irritated.

'Mrs Czabo?' I said.

'That's me.'

She finished the cigarette, seemed to look for somewhere to put it out, then contented herself with tossing it onto the step by my feet. I stamped it out for her.

'I was looking for your husband.'

'Who are you?'

I showed her my license.

'My name's Charlie Parker. I'm a private—'

'Yeah, I know all about you. You broke Ray's nose.'

'I didn't break his nose. He ran into a wall.'

'He ran into a wall because he was running away from you.'

I conceded the point.

'I still need to talk to him.'

'What's he done now? Dug up a corpse?'

'I just have some questions for him. He's not in any trouble.'

'Yeah, well, Ray don't live here no more. He moved out a couple of months ago.'

'You know where he is?'

She picked at something between her teeth. Her fingers emerged clutching a short hair. I tried not to think of its possible origins.

'He does his thing, I do mine. I don't pay no heed to his business.'

I heard a toilet flush in the house and a man appeared in the hallway with a towel wrapped around his waist. He was younger than Mrs Czabo by a decade, which made him about my age, but he looked bulkier and stronger than I was. He glanced at me, then asked her if everything was okay.

'I'll holler if I need you,' she said. Her tone made it clear that it would be a sorry day when she needed his help.

'I just want an address,' I said.

She shook her head.

'Cocksucker,' she said. 'You hear me?' Her voice was low, and I could smell the staleness on her breath.

'Ray said you were a cocksucker, and he was right. That's all you are. So why don't you just get the fuck out of here and leave us all in peace?'

'Gee,' I said, 'You're a nice lady.'

She made a gesture using her tongue and her right hand, just in case I wasn't clear on what being a cocksucker entailed, then closed the door in my face.

My cell phone rang as I walked down Edna Czabo's garden path. I didn't recognize the number on the caller display. It turned out that it was Denny Maguire.

'Can you talk?' he asked.

I leaned against my car and looked at the Czabo house. A drape twitched in one of the front windows.

'Sure,' I said.

'Look, this could be nothing. You asked me if I remembered anything that Grady said while I was in that basement. Like I told you, I was pretty out of it before they rescued me, so most of it's a blur, but I do recall him telling me that he was afraid.'

'Afraid of what?'

'He said that he was going to be punished for what he'd done to those kids, and for what he was going to do to me eventually, I guess. He said that he was damned, but that he wouldn't go without a fight. He told me that he'd taken precautions. I didn't know what he meant. I thought later that he was talking about the way he'd reinforced the basement door, but now I'm not so sure.'

The drape twitched again in the front window, this time with a little more force.

'There was always black paint on his hands,' Denny continued, 'and he was hanging paper and working on the house all of the time. I remember that most of the walls had been covered while I was kept in the basement, because he'd nearly finished the job when the police came for him. There were other things, odd things. During the first days, there was a pile of bones in the corner of the basement. He told me that they came from dogs. Later, he took them away and buried them.'

'He told you this?'

'Yeah. His hands were dirty, and he must have seen me looking at them. He said that he'd been working in his yard, burying the bones. That was when he first began talking about the precautions he was taking, and about how he wasn't going to be pulled from his home without a fight.'

The front door of the Czabo house opened, and the bulky young man appeared on the step. He was now dressed in baggy jeans and a hooded sweat top. There were scuffed sneakers on his feet.

'I don't know if any of that is helpful,' said Denny.

'It may be,' I said. 'Listen, Denny, I have to go, but thanks for that. I'll let you know how things work out.'

I killed the connection just as the man I took to be Edna Czabo's lover reached the end of the path.

'Who were you talking to?' he asked. His voice was a little higher and softer than I'd expected.

'Your mother,' I replied. 'She says you're to come home and stop screwing around with other men's wives. Oh, and she wants you to pick up some milk along the way.'

He didn't look too pleased at the reply, but he didn't make a move either, although I could see his hands almost involuntarily tense into fists. He was probably smarter than he looked, which made me wonder what he was doing with Edna Czabo.

'Why are you looking for Ray?' he asked.

'I have some questions for him. He hasn't done anything he needs to worry about. I hope.'

'Ray doesn't come around here much.'

'Did you scare him away?'

'It's all over between him and Edna. He moved out.'

'So she told me. Do you know where he is?'

'Edna says he's in Bangor someplace. I don't know where.'

'That's not very helpful,' I said. 'So if you didn't come out here to help, why did you come out?'

His head jerked back slightly in the direction of the house, and the woman within.

'Did she send you out to frighten me?' I asked.

He had the decency to look embarrassed.

'We just don't want any trouble. *I* don't want any trouble.'

I sized him up. A man who says he doesn't want trouble has usually experienced trouble before, and has a pretty good expectation of experiencing it again. If Ray Czabo had done something wrong, then I could just be the first of any number of people who might come knocking on his wife's door, the cops among them.

'You got a name?' I said.

'Tillman,' he said. 'Casey Tillman.'

'Anything to Gunnar Tillman?'

He nodded. 'He's my old man.'

'I thought I saw a resemblance.'

Gunnar Tillman was bad news, the kind of minor-league hood that places like Bangor threw up occasionally like a piece of rotten fish. He was involved in drugs, prostitution, and maybe a little smuggling of immigrants across the

Canadian border, if the stories were to be believed. I could understand now why his son didn't want the cops sniffing around his affairs.

'You see much of him?' I asked.

'As little as I can.'

I didn't know if that was true. From what I'd heard of Gunner Tillman, he made the decisions on the extent of his involvement in people's lives. It seemed unlikely that he'd accept any form of rejection from his own son.

I handed Casey Tillman my card.

'You think of anything, or if you hear from Ray, let me know. I wasn't lying to you: Ray's not in any trouble that I know of, but I do need to talk to him. If you're being straight with me, then I won't say anything about you to the cops unless circumstances change and there's no way to avoid it.'

Tillman slipped the card into a pocket of his jeans.

'Nice car,' he said, pointing with his chin at my Mustang. 'I run an auto shop in Orono. You ever need some work done, you give me a call. It's under my name in the book.'

With that, he turned and walked back to the house. Edna Czabo met him at the door. I wondered if we should have staged a fight, just for appearances' sake. I settled for trying to look shaken. She seemed happy with that, but shot me another orally suggestive gesture before she slammed the door, just in case I'd forgotten my place.

I got Ray Czabo's new address from a detective named Jeff Weis over in the Bangor PD. Ray had a habit of leaving his business cards around in the hope that someone might give him a call if something juicy came up. They rarely did, as most Maine cops regarded Voodoo Ray as low enough to ride a rat, but you had to admire his capacity for optimism. Since his separation, he had been living in a first-floor apartment over by the Bangor municipal golf course. It was the kind of place where kids rode bicycles down the hallways and there was a constant smell of burnt fat in the air. There was no reply when I rang his doorbell, so I headed around to the front of the building and peered in through his window. I saw a TV, some true crime magazines on a coffee table, and stacks of cardboard boxes filled with files. Some of the top boxes had been overturned, and their contents left on the floor. That wasn't like Ray Czabo. He was a meticulous man. I knew that from my own personal encounter with him, when I had forced him to hand over the souvenir he had taken from my house, his nose still bleeding upon the floor. There had been nothing out of place in his office then. Everything was clean and dusted.

The top window was open to allow a little air in. I looked around to make sure nobody was watching, then slipped on my gloves and hoisted myself up on to the sill. I reached in to open the latch on the main window, then entered Voodoo Ray's apartment. It was cold inside. The bed in the apartment's sole bedroom was neatly made, and the kitchen was tidy apart from a cup soaking in the sink. The dish cloth on the rack was bone dry, and so was the towel hanging on the back of the bathroom door. Maybe Ray didn't take a lot of showers, or maybe he hadn't been home in a while.

I examined the papers on the floor. They were mostly reports of serious crimes clipped from newspapers and magazines, some of them with handwritten pages of notes appended by Ray. One or two of the cases were familiar to me. Most, being out-of-state, were not. Apart from the disordered files, there was nothing suspicious about Ray's apartment. I closed the window and went to the front door to let myself out. My foot hit something light which spun across the carpet and bounced against the wall.

I picked up the black plastic case from the floor. It was an empty film canister.

Papers spilled on the floor, and a film canister by the door; they were small things, and could be dismissed as the carelessness of a man in a hurry. If it was Ray's doing, then I wondered why he had been in such a rush to leave, and if the photographs he had taken included one of a little girl with a baseball bat in her hand. I hadn't seen any developing equipment in Ray's closet, but that didn't mean that he wasn't responsible for the picture. The other possibility was that someone had searched Ray's house before me, and that among the items that person had removed was at least one roll of photographic film.

I left the apartment, closing the door gently behind me, then stuck my card underneath it in case Ray came back. I still had questions I wanted to ask him about the Grady house. As I stood, the door across from Ray's opened and an elderly man in a clean blue shirt peered out from across a security chain.

'I'll call the police,' he said.

'Why?' I said.

He squinted at me.

'You shouldn't be in there. That's Mr Czabo's apartment.'

I had to admire the old guy. There were few neighbors in this kind of place with the courage to stand up for those around them.

I showed him my ID.

'I'm a private investigator. I got no reply from inside, so I thought I'd leave my card for Ray.'

The old man gestured with his hand. I handed him my wallet. He looked at it for a time, pursed his lips while he considered its authenticity, then handed it back to me.

'I guess you're straight,' he said.

'Thanks,' I said. 'Have you seen Mr Czabo around lately?'

The old guy shook his head.

'Not for a while. Last time I saw him, it was when he had the trouble.'

'Trouble?'

'Two men came. A little fella and a big fella. The little fella was older, but younger than me. They shouted some at Mr Czabo, then went outside and kicked in the side of his car. I was going to call the police then as well, but Mr Czabo told me not to. He said it was a misunderstanding.'

'When was this?'

'A while back. Could have been three weeks, maybe more.'

'Do you remember anything else about the men involved?'

'The older one was small, with white curly hair and too many gold chains for a man his age. The other one was just huge. No neck. Looked like a throwback to the cavemen.'

The older man sounded like Gunnar Tillman. I figured his companion for the hired help.

I thanked Voodoo Ray's neighbor again.

'Well,' he said, as his door began to close. 'I give a damn. This place will go to shit if people don't look out for each other.'

'You're a dying breed,' I said.

'Maybe, but I'm not dead yet,' he replied, and then he closed the door.

About two minutes from Ray's place was a strip mall, anchored by a large drugstore. It was a slim chance, but I pulled into the lot and parked up outside the store. The photo desk was beside the registers, manned by a bored-looking teenager in a bright yellow polo shirt.

'Hi,' I said. 'I think my wife left some photos in here maybe a week ago. We can't find the receipt, but we'd really like our pictures.'

'You sure she left them in here?'

I did my best impression of a frustrated husband.

'She thinks this is where she left them to be developed. She's distracted at the moment. We're expecting our first baby.'

I wasn't sure which was worse: lying, or embellishing the lie with the truth. The photo guy didn't seem to care much either way.

'What's the name?' he said.

'Czabo.'

He flicked wearily through the envelopes behind the counter. About halfway through, he stopped and removed two of them from the cabinet.

'Czabo,' he said. 'Two rolls.'

He didn't ask for ID. I thanked him and paid him, then walked out of the store feeling like a spy.

I opened the envelopes in the car. One batch of photographs contained pictures of Ray's buddies in a bar, a couple of empty landscapes which might have been a crime scene or an attempt by Ray to get in touch with nature, and two photos of some damage to the wing of a green car that was probably Ray's. I guessed it was the result of Gunnar and his goon kicking in the wing. The damage didn't look too serious, and the pictures were probably for insurance purposes.

The second set of photographs began with five scenes of Ray's house, the one currently occupied by his wife and her toy boy. Casey Tillman was in each of the pictures, mostly getting into or out of his car, or greeting Edna Czabo with a kiss and an embrace. It looked as if Ray wasn't as happy about staying out of his wife's affairs as she appeared to be about staying out of his.

Casey was also in two more photographs, this time taken outside the garage that bore his name. There were two other men in the pictures with him. One looked like the Missing Link, assuming the Missing Link had learned to tie its own shoelaces. The other was Gunnar Tillman. He was much smaller than his son, and any weight he was carrying was still more muscle than fat. His hair was white and curly, and contrasted nicely with his winter tan. He was wearing a golf sweater and shiny sweat pants. Gold jewelry glittered in the sunlight at his wrist and around his neck. Gunnar Tillman clearly shopped at Hoods-R-Us.

It wasn't a good idea for Ray Czabo to be shooting clandestine photographs of Tillman, but maybe he hoped to win back his wife by showing her that her lover hadn't entirely cut off relations with his criminal father. Somehow, I felt Ray was clutching at straws. Edna Czabo had a new man in her life, one that was a lot younger than the old one, and with a little grit to him. Since she wasn't running for the Presidency, or leading her local Girl Scout troop, I didn't think she would be too concerned about him meeting up with his old man occasionally.

The last photographs were all images of the Grady house, taken from every possible angle short of dangling upside down from the drainpipe. According to the digital date imprinted in the right hand corner of the frames, they were all shot a couple of weeks before, in the space of about fifteen minutes. Ray had even managed to photograph the interior of the house through cracks in the window boards. I quickly flicked through them once, and saw nothing to make them stand out in any way. I went through them again, this time more slowly, and found a detail in the second last photo that made me pause.

It was the photograph Ray had taken by pressing the camera to the boards. Most of the image was obscured by the reflection of the flash on the glass, but the left-hand side was relatively clear. It showed the mirror on the wall of the reception room, the same mirror that I had seen when I first entered the house.

Reflected in the glass was the shape of a man. I could just make out his back, which was clothed in a dark jacket, but his face was not visible. His reflection was turned away from the camera. I flicked back through the images one more time, to confirm what I had seen, then laid them to one side.

In Ray Czabo's photographs, all the doors and windows in the Grady house were clearly locked from the outside. There was no way that anyone could be inside.

Yet someone was.

That night Rachel complained of pains in her stomach, so I took her to Maine Medical and spent two hours in the waiting room while the doctors looked her over. I read the newspapers for a time, but they seemed to be filled with suffering and I didn't need to read about people dying while Rachel was in pain.

Eventually, the doctors let her out. They told us that there was nothing to be concerned about, and that everything looked fine. We got home at about 2 AM, and Rachel began crying shortly after. I couldn't console her, and she couldn't seem to bring herself to speak, so I held her in my arms until her crying stopped and she at last fell asleep, her final moments of wakefulness punctuated by small hiccuping sobs.

The next morning she acted as if nothing had happened, and I didn't know what else to do except to let her be.

VII

They arrived at the Portland airport shortly after 10 AM. Its official title was the Portland International Jetport, which had a kind of Buck Rogers ring to it, although futurism and Portland weren't concepts that sat easily together. I kind of liked it that way.

They were getting older, I realized. We all were. True, the changes in Angel, the new pain lines in his face and the creeping gray in his previously soot-black hair, were too sudden to go unnoticed, but his partner was also graying slightly. Louis's satanic beard was slowly speckling with white, and there was now also a considerable dusting of it in his hair. He caught me looking at him.

'What?' he said.

'You're going seriously gray,' I said.

'I don't think so.'

'Hate to break it to you.'

'Like I said, I believe you're mistaken.'

'You can take steps. You don't have to just sit back and let it happen.'

'I don't have to sit back and do nothin', because there's nothin' to *let* happen.'

'Okay, if you say so. But you know, you let that hair grow out some and you can sign on as Morgan Freeman's stunt double.'

'He has a point,' chipped in Angel. 'Morgan ain't as young as he used to be. Studios would probably pay good money for a younger guy who just *looks* as old as Morgan Freeman.'

Louis stopped at the door leading out of the terminal building.

'You going to sulk?' I asked him.

'Maybe he's just forgotten where he's going. That happens as you get—'

For an older man, Angel could still move pretty quickly when he wanted to, so Louis's Cole Haan missed him by an inch.

The first time.

We sat at a table in the Bayou Kitchen, a tiny little diner over on Deering that until recently had only opened for lunch but now did weekend dinners as well. It could seat maybe twenty people, and its counter was piled high with sauces that carried warnings advising that they shouldn't be used by pregnant women or people with heart complaints. The food was good, and in winter it was mainly locals who went there.

Angel was still rubbing his shin occasionally and casting hurt glances at Louis, so it was left to me to do most of the talking. I told them a little more of the history of the Grady house, and about my encounters with Chief Grass, Denny Maguire, and Gunnar Tillman's boy, among others.

'You sure Maguire's clean?' asked Louis.

'I didn't get anything bad from him.'

'You tell Matheson about him?'

'No.'

I had spoken with Matheson that morning. He told me that he had a key for the basement in the house, and he thought that the cops had one too, but he hadn't realized that there was no copy on the set of keys he had given to me. He promised to get one to me by the end of the day. He also told me that he'd had a shouting match with Chief Grass, after Grass had questioned the wisdom of hiring me.

'Matheson is edgy enough as it is,' I said. 'The last thing I need is for him to start bothering Maguire about the past.'

'What about Czabo?'

'I'd call him a suspect, but there hasn't been a crime. Still, the photo in the mailbox isn't his style. He's a watcher, not a doer.'

'And the antiques guy?'

'The Collector?' I had begun to think of him by that name. After all, I had no other. 'He told me he had nothing to do with the photograph. He said he just wanted a mirror from the house, but he knows something.'

'Could be he's a graverobber, like Voodoo Ray,' said Angel.

'Maybe if you just gave him a mirror, he'd tell you what he knows,' suggested Louis.

'I don't think so. Anyway, nothing in the house is mine to give away.'

'You think he's a threat?'

I put my hands up in the air.

'A threat to what? To us? We haven't done anything. For once, we're free and clear. Nobody hates us on this case.'

'Yet,' said Angel.

'Always happens, though' said Louis.

'If only they took the time to get to know us a little better,' said Angel.

'I've taken the time to get to know you a little better,' I said, 'and look where it's gotten me. You're on the payroll, by the way, so it's not a charity case. Matheson signed off on the surveillance.'

Louis finished off his jambalaya, soaking up the last of the sauce and rice with some fresh bread.

'For how long?'

'As long as it takes, was what he said. I told him we'd give it a week, then review our options.'

'Sounds like it could be nothing,' said Louis. 'A photograph in a mailbox, that's all you got?'

'That's all.'

I reached into my pocket and removed a copy of the Matheson picture. I carefully unfolded it, then pushed it slowly across the table.

'But do you want to take the chance?'

The two men looked at the image of the young girl. Angel answered for both of them.

'No,' he said. 'I guess not.'

Later that afternoon they stopped by the house to say hi to Rachel. She was a little distant, but neither of them remarked upon it. I thought that she was just tired after the night before, but it was the first sign of troubles to come. The pain and danger that she had endured by remaining with me, and the fears that she felt for herself and our child, seemed to her to be rendered more acute by the presence of two men who were friends yet who always carried with them a potential for violence. They reminded her of what had befallen her in the past, and what might befall the child she carried. Looking back, perhaps they also caused her to reflect on my own capacities, and the possibility that I might always draw violent men to me. She had attempted to explain these things to me before, and I had tried to reassure her as best I could. I hoped that, in time, her worries would fade. I think she hoped so too, even though she feared that they would not. I wanted to ask her again about the visit to the hospital, and the tears that followed, but there was no time. Instead, I held her and told her I'd be home before midnight, and she squeezed me and said that would be fine.

I drove to Two Mile Lake as the afternoon light began to dim, Angel and Louis following behind. It was dark by the time we arrived, and the bare trees slept over us as we passed the Grady house and took the next turning on the right. The road led up to a run-down, single-story farmhouse. Like the Grady house itself, it had been bought by Matheson after his daughter's disappearance. It seemed to me that he wanted to seal off the whole area from the possible depredations of strangers, as though his loss were inextricably tied up with the very fabric of the Grady house, with its surrounding fields and with the buildings that had silently borne witness to the events that had occurred in their purview. Perhaps he envisaged her, lost and alone, desperately trying to seek a doorway back into the world that she knew, and felt that any change to the place from which she had vanished would make it impossible for her to return; or maybe this was all simply one great monument, an ornate offering upon which her name and the names of the other children were deeply inscribed yet never seen.

I opened the door to the farmhouse and led Angel and Louis inside. It had been cleaned recently, for there was little dust on any of the surfaces. Most of the rooms remained empty, apart from the kitchen, where there was a table and four chairs, and the sitting room, which contained a sofa bed and a radiator. In one of the bedrooms there were some ladders and tins of varnish and paint. An envelope on the table, addressed to me, contained a set of keys to the Grady house for Angel and Louis, and a single key with a note from Matheson identifying it as the one for the basement.

'Nice,' said Angel, as he took in his surroundings. 'Very minimalist.'

'Who knows that we're here?' asked Louis.

'We do, and so does Matheson.'

'The cops?'

'No. Anyone asks, you tell them you're here to do some work on the house and Matheson will back you up, but this place is pretty much invisible from the road so we shouldn't be bothered. You two will take the lion's share of the duty – twenty-four on, twelve off. There's a motel about three miles out of town. I've rented a room there for the next week. This place has no hot water, and we can't risk too many lights. There are blackout shades in the kitchen, so if you want to read then that's the place. There's a radio and TV in there too.'

I led them to the back bedroom. There, a single window looked down upon the Grady house, framed by a gap in the trees. It would be hard for anyone to approach it from north, south or east without being seen, and the west side of the house had no point of entry.

'There it is,' I said.

'You been in there?' asked Angel.

'Yes. Do you want to check it out?'

Among the items left by Matheson was a plan of the house. Louis spread it out on the floor and examined it.

'Is this accurate?'

I looked it over.

'Looks like it. There's not much to add. Mirrors on the walls. Some old furniture, but most of it is stacked away, so the floors are clear.'

Louis shrugged. 'Maybe we'll take a look in daylight if we get bored.'

We watched the shape of the house, darker yet against the night sky.

'So we wait,' he said.

'We wait.'

Nothing happened that night. I drove home to Rachel after a couple of hours, then returned the following evening. It set the pattern for the week that followed. Sometimes, I would stay with them for a couple of hours after they arrived to relieve me, sitting at the window and talking with Angel while Louis rested or read, the Grady house before us like a dark hand raised against the sky.

Conversations with Angel were not always a good idea.

'Are me and Louis the only gay men you know?' he asked, on the second night.

'You're certainly the most irritating gay men I know.'

'We bring color into your life. Seriously, you got any other gay friends?'

I considered the question.

'I don't know. It's not like you all wear lavender loon pants and Village People T-shirts, or introduce yourselves with "Hey, I'm Dan and I'll be your token homosexual for the evening." Just like I don't walk up to people, shake their hands and tell them, "I'm Charlie, and I'm proud to be a heterosexual." It worries people.'

'It would sure worry me.'

'Well, you wouldn't be my target market.'

'You have a target market? What is it: the needy? Needy heterosexuals. "The Needy Heterosexuals." It sounds like a band.'

'*Anyway*, in answer to your question, I don't know how many of my acquaintances are gay men. Maybe a couple. Plus I don't have "gaydar." I think that's a gay preserve.'

'I think gaydar's a myth. It's all kind of confusing, now that straight men are dressing nice and using skincare products. Kind of muddies the waters.'

I looked at him.

'But you're a gay man and you *don't* dress nice. Plus, if you use skincare products you're using them on a part of your body that I can't see, and you have no idea how happy I am to be able to say that.'

'You telling me I look straight? If I look straight, how come straight women never hit on me?'

'You're lucky anybody ever hit on you, looking the way

you do. Don't blame straight women for keeping their distance.'

Angel grinned.

'But still, you're happy to call me "friend." ' He reached over and patted my arm.

'I didn't say I was happy about it, and get your hands off me. I have a suspicion about where they've been.'

He backed off.

'You and Rachel okay?' he asked.

'We had a scare the other night. She had pains. The doctors took a look at her and told her she was fine.'

'She was kind of funny with us. Distant.'

'It was a long night.'

'You sure that's all it was?'

'Yes,' I said. 'Pretty sure.'

When I was alone, I kept myself alert with a radio and caffeine, or cleared my head a little by taking a walk around the property when I was certain everything was quiet. Once or twice I saw Officer O'Donnell make a cursory check of the Grady house, but he didn't even glance up at the farmhouse on the slope above.

On the seventh day, as I was heading home, I got a call from Detective Jeff Weis, the cop who had given me Voodoo Ray's new bachelor address.

'Bet you didn't have any luck finding Ray Czabo,' he said.

'How'd you know?'

'Because they just found him.'

I pulled over to the side of the road.

'Something tells me that he's not about to be talking to me anytime soon.'

'Not unless you're psychic. Somerset County Sheriff called it in about an hour ago. His body was buried over by Little Ferguson Brook, mile or two east of Harmony. Looks like he's been there for a while, so you're probably off the hook.'

'I wasn't aware that I was on the hook.'

'There you go. You were innocent and you didn't even know it.'

I thanked Weis for the tip, then got back on the road and headed for Harmony. It wasn't too hard to find the location of the discovery. I just followed a state police patrol car until I came to a cluster of vehicles by a small metal bridge off Main Stream Road. I tried to pick out someone I might know, but they were all unfamiliar faces. Instead, I settled for showing my license to the Somerset County deputy who was trying to move me on, and asked to speak to the detective in charge. After a couple of minutes, a balding man in a blue Windbreaker broke away from the group standing by the riverbank and came over to talk to me.

'Help you?' he said.

'Charlie Parker,' I said.

He nodded. One thing about gaining a reputation in Maine, for better or worse, was that most of the cops at least knew my name.

'Bert Jansen,' he said. 'You're off your turf.'

'I get around.'

I gestured toward the riverbank.

'I hear you may have found Ray Czabo.'

Jansen didn't respond immediately, then seemed to decide 'what the hell?' and echoed Ray's name.

'What's your interest in Czabo?'

'I went looking for him about a week ago. His wife said he'd moved out, but when I called by his new place there was no reply. I left my card. You'll find it underneath his door when you search his apartment.'

'Why were you looking for him to begin with?'

I decided there was no percentage in not being open with Jansen.

'I'm working for a man named Matheson. His daughter died in the Grady house. Matheson thinks someone may be developing an unhealthy interest in the house, and the local cops told me that they'd rousted Ray from the property a couple of times. I wanted to ask him what he was doing, or what he might have seen when he was there.'

Jansen took out his notebook and began writing. 'And this was when?'

'A week ago Wednesday.'

He made some more notes, then asked me if I minded hanging around for a while. I told him I had no problem with that.

'You have any idea how long he's been down there?'

'Nope. My guess would be a week or more. He's pretty bloated up.'

'Cause of death?'

'Shot in the head. Three close entry wounds, no exits. Scoop his brains out and you could use his head for a bowling ball. Probably a two-two.'

I'd never cared much for Ray Czabo, but he didn't deserve to end up dead. Three shots to the head also sounded like overkill. One shot with a .22 will leave the bullet rattling around inside, tearing up tissue until it runs out of steam. Ray must really have annoyed someone to end up with three of them in his skull.

'I guess he wasn't shot here.'

'Wouldn't think so. It's a long way to transport someone just to shoot them. Our guess is he was killed someplace else, then driven out here and buried in a shallow grave. A dog dug up his hand. It hasn't rained in a while, but there's a whole bunch of it due.'

I knew what Jansen was saying. The rain would come

and the river would rise, covering the burial site. Then, with winter settling in, it would freeze over until March, maybe even April. By the time the thaws came, there would be no evidence left that the ground had ever been disturbed.

I went back to my car, turned on the radio, and listened to NPR until the ME arrived. I watched her descend to the body and then, finally, the corpse was taken from the riverbank in a white bodybag. Jansen came over to speak to me shortly after and told me that the ME estimated that Czabo had been in the ground for up to two weeks, then let me go. I called Rachel, told her I'd be a little late, then headed for Orono.

Orono is a college town, housing part of the University of Maine. It has an intimate feel to it, and most people know one another's names, so the first guy I stopped was able to direct me to Casey Tillman's garage.

The second thing I noticed once I got there was the Lexus parked outside. The first thing I noticed was the Missing Link, who had to step aside before I could see the Lexus. Link wasn't much more than six feet tall, but he was probably the same width across. His head looked too small for the rest of his body – in fact, it looked too small, period – but I suspected that he hadn't been hired for his brain power. He had slightly Asian features, and his dark hair was tied back in a ponytail. He also seemed to have shopped in the same hoods' store as his boss, except his clothes came from the 'big man' section.

'We're closed,' he said, when I stepped from the Mustang. 'Come back later.'

'I'm here to see Casey,' I told him. 'You haven't eaten him, have you?'

Link blinked. I figured him for the kind of guy who heárd a joke at midnight, and started laughing at about 8 AM. I kept walking until I was standing in the garage's entrance.

Link lumbered after me and stopped me from going any farther by the simple measure of standing in front of me and tapping me in the chest with his index finger. It barely involved him stretching a muscle, but it nearly sent me sprawling in the gutter.

'You got a problem with your hearing?' he said.

Inside the garage's office, I could see Gunnar Tillman talking to his son. His voice was raised and he was doing a lot of finger pointing. Casey looked over his father's shoulder, saw me, and raised a hand to stop the older man's diatribe. Gunnar turned around and saw me. He didn't look happy, but I didn't think it was personal. Gunnar Tillman wasn't someone whose smiling muscles got a lot of exercise.

Casey stepped from behind his desk and walked toward me.

'What are you doing here?' he asked.

'Ray Czabo's dead,' I said.

'I know. Edna called me.'

'And you called your father.'

'I figured he should know.'

Link stood beside us, looking from me to Casey and back again. He reminded me of my dog, but without the capacity to learn. I was about to ask him to give us a little breathing space when the issue became redundant.

Gunnar Tillman pushed his way between Casey and Link. I had five or six inches on him, but it didn't make me feel any better. Gunnar pretty much sweated bad vibes.

'Who the fuck are you?' he asked.

'It's okay, Pop, he's—'

Casey's intervention was cut short by Gunnar's left hand, which slapped his son hard on the right cheek. Casey took a step backward. His eyes teared with pain and humiliation.

'I wasn't talking to you,' said Gunnar. His voice was

perfectly even, as though he had not even registered the blow he had delivered to his son.

He turned his attention back to me.

'You see what you made me do,' he said. 'He's my son, and I care about him, but you made me hit him. I don't even know you, so you better believe that I'll fuck you up good if you don't start answering my questions. Now who are you?'

'My name's Parker. I'm a private investigator.'

'So?'

'Ray Czabo's dead.'

'And?'

'Your son is seeing Czabo's wife.'

'You saying he had something to do with this?'

'I don't know. Did he?'

Gunnar reached behind his back and pulled a gun on me. The muzzle looked very big, and very black.

'You've got some fucking mouth,' he said.

Casey tried to calm his father down.

'Jesus, Pop, come on. Don't do this.'

'You got no right to say things like that, you hear me?' said Gunnar. 'Fuck.'

His son reached out and patted him on the back, gradually forcing the gun down with his right hand.

'It's okay,' he said. 'He didn't mean anything by it. Let me talk to him.'

Gunnar was slowly coming off the boil. He let out some deep breaths.

'You watch your mouth,' he told me.

He put the gun back in the waistband of his trousers and walked over to a Dodge with a yawning hood. He slammed the hood down and leaned his hands upon it, his head bowed. His son watched him until he was certain that Gunnar had regained control of his temper, then said:

'I had nothing to do with it.'

'Your old man visited Czabo. From what I hear, he threatened him. There were witnesses.'

Casey swallowed and shook his head in frustration.

'I knew Ray was following me around. I saw him take some pictures. I tried to warn him off, but he wouldn't listen. He said I was coming between him and his wife. My pop found out—'

'Found out, or was told?'

Casey reddened. He was, I realized, a weaker man than he seemed.

'I thought he could get Billy over there to talk some sense into Ray. You know, I do some things for my pop. I look after cars for him. Some of them, well, they may have ownership issues, you know what I'm saying? Ray needed to be warned off, or else things would get really bad for him.'

'Things did get really bad for him. Someone shot him in the head.'

'My pop didn't do it.'

'You're sure?'

Casey's voice lowered.

'He doesn't need that kind of heat. He's getting older now. The stuff they say about him, most of it's not true anymore. He only has a couple of guys on the payroll, and most of what they do is drive my old man to lunch. He fences some cars, distributes a little pot to the college kids, but that's about all. He's small time now, but if they caught him they'd put him away, and he doesn't want to die in jail. He didn't kill Ray Czabo. Neither did I. When the cops come calling, we'll tell them that.'

I looked over at Gunnar. He was coughing. It was suddenly clear that what I had mistaken for his efforts to control his temper were actually attempts to get his breathing back in order. He sounded sick. Billy was now beside him, holding a cup of water to the old man's lips.

'He can be a prick but he's still my father,' said Casey.

His eyes pleaded for understanding.

'And—'

Casey put a hand on my shoulder, as though to guide me away from the garage. I let him do it.

'We lost a guy, Lee Tierney,' he said.

'When?'

'Week or so back. Stabbed in the heart.'

The name sounded vaguely familiar. I recalled a story from the *Press Herald* about a stabbing in Orono. It hadn't mentioned Gunnar Tillman.

'The story I read said Tierney was mugged in the parking lot of a bar. His body was hidden under trash bags.'

'That's where they found him.'

'So where did he die?'

'Near here. My father had him moved.'

It explained why Gunnar was so jumpy.

'Any idea who might have done it?'

Casey shook his head.

'Nobody has that kind of problem with my pop. Like I told you, he's not into that stuff now.'

I didn't believe Casey, but it didn't matter.

'There was a guy,' said Casey. 'Billy said he'd seen him around. Thin, kind of greasy, long coat, looked like a bum, but a bum couldn't have taken out Lee. No way.'

I let him think that, even as I walked to my Mustang and remembered the sound that the Collector's fingers had made as they danced upon its body.

Detective Jansen called again later that day, when I was about to head over to Two Mile Lake to relieve Angel and Louis.

'You say you were over at Czabo's place?' he asked.

'That's right.'

'And you left your card?'

'I slipped it under the door. Why?'

'There was no card there when we searched the apartment. The landlord says that he hasn't been near the place, and his wife told us that she doesn't have a key. By the way, she spoke highly of you.'

'I'll bet. Do you like her for this?'

'I don't like her, period. If Czabo hadn't been hit more than once, I would have put this down as a suicide.'

'Does she have an alibi?'

'Yeah. His name's Casey Tillman. He's a mechanic. He claims they went to New Hampshire a few weeks back for a couple of days R&R. If the dates match, they may be in the clear. We're checking it. Tillman says there was no bad blood between him and Czabo. I'm inclined to believe him. The only thing suspect about him is his taste in women.'

I wondered if Jansen had made the connection between Casey Tillman and his father. I recalled my promise to Tillman not to mention it unless I had to. I decided to keep it, for the present. Neither did I mention the photographs taken by Ray Czabo that I had in my possession. I hadn't yet figured out a way to tell Jansen about them without landing me in serious trouble. Instead, I thanked him for keeping me informed. Jansen replied by letting me know that he wasn't doing it out of the goodness of his heart, and he expected me to reciprocate. I told him that sharing was at the heart of any good relationship. He said he'd rather have a relationship with Ray Czabo's old lady, then hung up.

I thought about Ray Czabo on the way to Two Mile. He was no angel, and his actions in the past had led to him being beaten up more than once, usually with some justification, but it was unlikely that his ghoulish tendencies would lead someone to kill him. I recalled the Collector, standing in the flickering light behind Denny Maguire's bar. I wondered if he kept a gun under those layers of old clothes along with a knife.

Then again, Jansen might be wrong about Ray's estranged wife, but I didn't think so. A woman who has just killed her husband, or conspired in his death, is not going to be too concerned about an old injury to him caused by someone else. When Mrs Czabo reminded me of my first encounter with her husband, the one that had left him with a broken nose, she seemed genuinely aggrieved on his behalf. She could simply have been putting on an act for my benefit, but I could see no percentage for her in that.

All I knew for sure was that Ray Czabo's death roughly coincided with the appearance of the photograph in the mailbox of the Grady house, and that someone had returned to his apartment after I'd been there, maybe to resume the search for something that had been missed the first time, or to ensure that there was no evidence left lying around. My guess was that, when the cops arrived, the apartment was neat and tidy, and the boxes that I had seen dislodged had been restored to their rightful place.

If all of those events were linked, then a possible conclusion was that one of Ray's excursions down to Two Mile had coincided with the appearance of the individual responsible for the photo in the mailbox, and that person had killed Ray in order to ensure that he didn't tell anyone of what he had seen. If that was the case, then Matheson had been right all along to worry. Pranksters don't shoot people with a .22, because it's hard to laugh with holes in the top of your head. The man – and I had no doubt that it was a man – who placed the picture of an unknown girl at the Grady house was deadly serious about what he was doing.

It was time to talk to Chief Grass again, but when I called I was told that he wasn't available. I left a message for him, but he didn't call back.

VIII

By the tenth day, the surveillance was taking its toll upon me. Unlike Angel and Louis, I could not take a break and divide the duty with someone else, and my body clock was completely confused. Even though I slept when I returned home to Rachel, or grabbed a couple of hours on the sofa bed once Angel and Louis arrived, I still found myself drifting at times. Colors appeared too bright, and sounds were either muffled or painfully clear. Sometimes I was unable to tell if I was dreaming or waking. I spoke to Matheson once or twice, and informed him that what we were doing was untenable in the long term. I agreed to complete the second week of surveillance, once I had spoken to Angel and Louis and secured their consent, but it seemed like a lost cause. I was considering taking up Clem Ruddock on his offer of some help, especially as Rachel was due any day now and I wanted to be with her. I spent most of my time worrying about her. My cell phone was always close at hand, its ringtone muted but still audible, even in sleep.

On the tenth night, I saw a figure moving among the trees beside the Grady house.

I had heard no car approach, although in my shattered state I couldn't be certain that I had not simply missed its approach. I rose and made my way through the farmhouse, stopping to retrieve my gun from the holster hanging on the back of the unmade sofa bed. It felt both strange and familiar in my hand, for it had been months since I had held it with even the vaguest intention of putting it to use. Finally, I made a call to Angel and Louis. If I was just being jumpy, the worst they could do was shout at me a little.

I opened the front door, pulling it closed silently behind me so that the wind would not catch it and alert the presence in the woods to my approach. I made my way down the slope, sticking close to the tree line, until I could smell the rotting of timbers and faint odor of smoke that hung about the place. I circled the trees, hoping to come up on the intruder from behind, but when I reached the spot where I had seen him he was gone, and there was only a stamped-out cigarette butt where I felt certain that the Collector had recently stood.

I retreated to the periphery of the forest, shielding myself behind a tree, and scanned the property. I could see no sign of movement. It didn't make me feel any less nervous. After a while, I made my way to the Grady house, keeping my back to its walls. I checked the sides, then approached the window of the old reception room at the front of the house, to the right of the door. I thought of the figure in the mirror, caught by Ray Czabo's flash bulb, but when I pressed my face to the crack in the wood I could see nothing in the darkness.

I stepped away, and aimed my flashlight at the steel door barring entry to the house. The padlock was gone. I moved closer, and tested the door by pulling it toward me. It opened with some resistance, and a lot of noise. The main door behind it was already ajar. I pushed it open a little farther and stepped back, not sure what to expect, but there was no sound from within. After a couple of seconds spent debating my choice of career, I stepped inside.

The smell of rot was stronger now, as was the chemical

stench of the wallpaper pastes. A large strip of paper had come loose from the wall of the entrance hall since I had been there last, and it hung at an angle like a bookmarked page, exposing the damp plaster beneath. I shined the flashlight on it and saw what looked like fragments of letters and drawings beneath the paper. I pulled the strip away.

The wall was covered in writing and symbols, none of them familiar to me. I thought that the language might have been Latin, but the script was so faded it was impossible to tell. I tore another strip from the wall, and more writing was revealed, this time adorned with circles and stars. There was a purpose to this, but I could not guess at what it might be. The smells of the house, seemingly intensified by my action in pulling away the paper, made me feel ill. I jammed a handkerchief to my nose and tried to breathe shallowly through my mouth as I moved toward the dining room door. I pushed at it with my foot and entered.

The connecting doors between the two rooms were open, as though in expectation of some great party that would now never take place. The mirrors stared down upon dusty floors and torn drapes. They should have reflected what I saw, but they did not. Instead, I saw in their decaying glass the gleam of lighted chandeliers, and expensive, hand-printed paper on the walls. The drapes were no longer faded and ripped, but vibrant and fresh. There were thick carpets upon the floors, and a dining table set for two people.

I felt my shoe scuff the dust upon the bare boards under my feet. There was nothing in this room but filth and dead bugs, yet in the mirror I saw the house as it might have been. I passed through the connecting doors into the reception room, and there glimpsed thick couches and matching smoking chairs, and walls lined with books, all reflected in the depths of the mirrors upon the walls.

It's his house, I thought. It's Grady's house, as he saw it in his own mind.

I felt a presence behind me, but when I turned I saw only my own reflection in the mirror in the hallway, set against the wonders of the ornate rooms at my back. But something else was there, waiting in the glass. I sensed it, even as my vision swam and a coughing racked my body as the stench of old glue and damp seemed to grow stronger.

Then I noticed for the first time that the door to the basement was no longer closed and locked. I knew there was another mirror on the door, and that if I looked into its face I would see more figments of John Grady's imagination, somehow wheedling their way into my consciousness.

'Who's there?' I called.

And a voice answered, and I thought it sounded like the voice of a little girl.

I'm here, it said. *Can you see me?*

I moved the flashlight, trying to find the source of the voice.

Here. I'm here. Behind you.

And when I spun there was a mirror, and in the mirror I saw a child, her hair matted and dirty, her red dress torn. Further back I saw another little girl, with pale cheeks and torn skin. The girl who had spoken pressed herself to the mirror as though it were clear glass, and I saw her skin flatten against it.

He's here, she said. *He never left.*

From the corner of my eye I saw a darkness pass across the mirror in the dining room. It was the figure of a man, blurred like a bad projection. It moved quickly, shifting from mirror to mirror, progressing through the rooms toward the hallway.

He's coming, said the little girl, and then she and her companions were gone.

I raised my gun. It seemed that everywhere I looked there was movement, and I thought I heard a child's voice raised in fear.

I shook my head. Now the sounds came from below me, from the basement, and I made my way toward them. In the mirror upon the door, I saw myself trapped in the Grady house that never was. The stairs to the basement descended before me. The flashlight beam illuminated strands of cobweb, the stone floor, and a single chair that stood beneath the empty light socket. It was small, too small for an adult to use, but the perfect size for a child. There were more mirrors on the walls here, but they showed no beautiful furnishings, no carpets or drapes. This was Grady's killing place, and he had no need of beauty here. I passed from mirror to mirror, my light angled away from the glass. I saw myself reflected, again and again and again.

And for a brief instant I saw another man's face, suspended behind mine, before it retreated once again into the shadows. I raised my gun, aimed it at the glass—

Then stopped. There came the sound of footsteps above me, approaching the cellar door through the main hallway. I killed the flashlight and retreated into the darkness, just as another light came from above. I heard a man's breathing, and the creaking of the banister rail as he placed his weight upon it, and then his figure came into view. He was a big man, and over his left shoulder he carried a sack. The sack was moving.

'Almost home,' he said.

The flashlight jogged in his hand as he reached the floor of the basement. Gently, he placed the sack on the ground, then unscrewed the head of the flashlight so that its bulb became a candle, and in its glow I saw his face.

'Don't move,' I said, as I emerged from the darkness by the stair.

Chief Grass didn't look as surprised as he should have done, under the circumstances. Instead, his eyes had a slightly glazed look to them. I saw the gun in his left hand, previously hidden from me by the sack. It was lodged against the head of the child inside.

'You shouldn't be here,' he said. 'He won't like it.'

'Who won't like it?' I said.

'Mr Grady. He doesn't like strangers in his home.'

'What about you? Aren't you a stranger too?'

Grass snickered. It was an unpleasant sound.

'Oh no,' he said. 'I've been coming here for a long, long time. It took a while for Mr Grady to begin to trust me, but once he did, well, everything was fine. We talk a lot. He's lonely. I brought him some company, some new blood.'

He kicked the sack, and the child within gave a muffled cry.

'What's her name?' I asked.

'Lisette,' replied Grass. 'She's very pretty, but then, you've seen her picture.'

Pretty.

I heard a distant voice echo the word, and in the mirror at Grass's back I saw John Grady reflected. His fingertips pressed against the glass, flattening as the dead child's skin had done, and he stared down at the shape of the little girl moving feebly in the sack. I saw his prominent chin, curved and jutting, his neat hair, the little stained bow tie at his neck. His lips moved constantly in a litany of desire, the words now unintelligible but their import clear.

'It's the house, Grass,' I said. 'It's making you do this. It's wrong. You know it's wrong. Put the gun down.'

Grass shook his head. 'I can't,' he said. 'Mr Grady—'

'Grady is dead,' I said.

'No, he's here.'

'Listen to me, Grass. Something in this house has affected

you. You're not thinking clearly. We need to get you out. I'm taking the girl, and then we're all going to leave.'

For the first time, Grass looked uncertain.

'He told me to bring her. He chose her. Out of all the girls I showed him, he chose this one.'

'No,' I said. 'You imagined it. You've spent too long here. Everything about this place is poisonous, and somehow it's burrowed into your mind.'

Grass's gun wavered slightly. He looked from me to the girl on the ground, then back again.

'It's infected your thoughts, Grass. You don't want to hurt this little girl. You're a cop. You have to protect her, just like you protected Denny Maguire. Let her go. You must let her go.'

But I was not sure that I believed all that I was saying, for I saw John Grady's eyes turn upon me in the mirror, and his lips formed the single word:

No.

Grass seemed to hear it, and the doubt left his eyes. He forced the gun harder against the girl's skull, then lifted the sack up, holding his prize beneath his arm as he began retreating up the stairs. I followed him all the way, reaching the top of the steps as he moved into the hallway, his back to the wall as he made for the safety of his vehicle parked outside.

Two figures blocked the doorway.

'Now where do you think you're going?' said Louis. He stood on the porch with his gun raised before him. Angel knelt below him, his own gun pointed at Grass. Seconds later, I added a third.

Grass stopped, caught between us.

'Let her go,' I said. 'It's all over.'

Grass was shaking his head, muttering something that I couldn't understand. He stared straight ahead and saw his reflection in the mirror. I couldn't see what he was staring at because the angle was wrong, but it was clear from the expression on his face that I wasn't the only one hallucinating in the Grady house.

'Chief, you rescued Denny Maguire from here,' I said. I could hear the desperation in my voice. 'Remember? You brought him out. You saved his life. You saved a child's life. You're not a killer. This is not you. It's the house. Listen to me. It's not your fault. It's something in the house.'

Slowly, Grass released his grip on the sack and let it fall to the floor, although his gun remained pointing at it. I could hear the girl crying, but I thought that I could also hear another voice. It was whispering, spilling foul words into Grass's ear.

'Don't listen to him,' I said. 'Please. Just put the gun down.'

Grass's face crumpled. He began to cry, and I was reminded of Denny Maguire weeping in his bar: two men, linked by the evil of John Grady.

'Chief,' I said.

He raised the gun and pointed it at the mirror before him.

'Put it down,' I said.

Grass was sobbing now.

'This is not a house,' he said.

He cocked the pistol – 'This is not a house,' he repeated – and turned to look at me as the gun suddenly swung toward him, the muzzle coming to rest against his temple.

'This is—'

He pulled the trigger, and the walls turned red.

IX

The figure behind the mirror stared at me as I knelt down and undid the rope that held the sack closed. The girl from the picture lay inside, her hands and feet tied and a red bandana gagging her mouth. I undid the gag first, then her hands and feet, but I did not let her look at the mirror behind me, or at the body of the man who had brought her to this place.

'I want you to go with my friends,' I said. 'They'll take care of you until I come out.'

She was crying, and she tried to hold on to me, but I forced her gently away into Angel's arms.

'It's okay,' he said, as he led her away. 'Nobody's going to hurt you now.'

I watched her until she was gone from sight. Louis remained in the doorway, waiting.

I approached the glass, my gun raised. John Grady's dead eyes widened and his lips moved faster and faster.

'Lights out,' I said, then fired.

And the mirror shattered as the process of erasing John Grady's image from the world began.

X

Two days later, I watched as a team of workmen removed every remaining mirror from the Grady house and placed them in the back of one of Matheson's trucks. Matheson himself was beside me, watching all that was being done.

One of the workmen approached us and said: 'We were pretty careful with those mirrors. They're antiques. Could be worth some money, you was to restore them some.'

'They're going to be destroyed,' I said.

The workman looked to Matheson in the hope of an alternative response.

'You heard the man,' said Matheson.

The workman shrugged, then returned to loading the mirrors.

'You think he really believed that Grady wanted him to bring a child to the house?' asked Matheson.

'Yes,' I said. 'I think he really believed it.'

'What about Ray Czabo?'

'Grass had a two-two. My guess is it will match the bullets that killed Czabo. We'll know tomorrow for sure.'

Two workmen came out, carrying one of the basement mirrors.

'You never did tell me what you saw in there,' said Matheson.

I looked at him. I recalled the face of John Grady, and the children in the dark reaches of the glass. Fumes and tiredness, I thought, just fumes and tiredness.

'I saw reflections,' I said.

He stared at me for a time, then nodded.

'Okay, then. Reflections.'

We counted the mirrors to make sure none was missing. When we were done, Matheson climbed in the cab and drove off. I followed him back to his plant. Over in a brownstone building at the back of the lot was an industrial furnace. Matheson parked the truck outside it.

'You sure about this?' asked Matheson.

'I think so,' I replied.

'I'll get some of the boys to give us a hand.'

He left me and headed for the main building. I leaned against the truck and watched the light fade. Already, it was growing dark. The wind was colder now. Soon, the snows would come.

I didn't even see the blow coming. One moment, I was looking at the sky, and the next I was lying on the ground, bright flashes exploding in my vision. I started to rise, but my balance was shot. I fell back upon the ground and tried not to retch.

The Collector stood above me. There was an old leather blackjack in his hand.

'I'm sorry,' he said.

I opened my mouth to speak, but nothing emerged. Instead, I watched in silence as he took a small, gilded mirror from the back of the truck.

I reached out a hand. I think I managed to say the word 'No.' Whatever sound I made, it caused him to look down on me.

'Burning won't be enough,' he said. 'He will still be free.'

He knelt down beside me and turned the glass toward me.

'Look,' said the Collector.

I couldn't focus. My image swam in the glass, but it did not swim alone. I saw John Grady, but not as he once was, not as he was in his pictures, or as he looked before my bullet struck the mirror in his basement. I thought I saw fear, or perhaps it was my own face that I saw. I do not know.

'He owes a soul,' said the Collector. 'He was damned, and his soul is forfeit.'

'Who are you?' I asked, but he did not reply. Later, I would find the paperwork that the Collector had completed when he bought John Grady's old books at the police sale. The name at the bottom was written in marvellously ornate script. It was quite beautiful. The man who claimed to be a nephew of one of Maine's leading book merchants had signed himself 'Mr Kushiel.' Curiously, the address he gave was that of the old state prison at Thomaston, which now no longer stands. I was tempted, for a brief moment, to look up his name, to discover its derivation, but I did not. Instead, I prayed only that I would never see him again, for any jail in which Kushiel played a role lay far deeper than the ruins of Thomaston.

But that was later. For now, I was lying bleeding on the ground, and the Collector was standing above me, the mirror tucked firmly beneath his arm. By the time Matheson returned he was long gone, and John Grady's debt was about to be paid for eternity.

XI

On 12 December, Rachel gave birth to our daughter. We named her Samantha, Sam for short. I was there when she was born. I held her in my arms, and smelled the blood upon her as the past and the present came together, interweaving, combining, binding me to what I was and to what I had become.

One child born, another saved. Perhaps Clem Ruddock was right. It is children with me, and there is a pattern to be seen, if I choose to look closely for it. There is a pattern, and I am part of it. She also has a place in it, for my new daughter will share her birthday with the anniversary of her half-sister's death, and the death of the woman who was once my wife.

There is a pattern.

I am not afraid.

I tell myself I am no longer afraid.

Mr Gray's Folly

It was, said my wife, quite the ugliest thing she had ever seen.

I had to admit that she was correct in her assessment. This was not, generally speaking, a typical occurrence in our relationship. As she approached late middle-age (with all the grace and ease, it should be added, of a funeral party stumbling in a cemetery) Eleanor had grown increasingly intolerant of views that diverged from her own. Inevitably, mine appeared to diverge more often than most, so agreement in any form was a cause for considerable, if muted, celebration.

Norton Hall was a wonderful acquisition, a late eighteenth century country residence with landscaped gardens and fifty acres of prime land. It was an architectural gem and would make us a wonderful home, since it was simultaneously small enough to be manageable yet spacious enough to permit us to avoid each other for significant portions of the day. Unfortunately, as my wife had duly noted, the folly at the end of the garden was another matter entirely. It was ugly and brutal, with unadorned rectangular pillars and a bare white cupola topped with a cross. There were no steps leading up to it and the only way of gaining access to the interior appeared to be by clambering over the base. Even the birds avoided it, preferring instead to take up positions in a nearby oak tree, where they cooed nervously amongst themselves like spinsters at a parish dance.

According to the agent, one of Norton Hall's previous owners, a Mr Gray, had built the folly as a memorial to his late wife. It struck me that he couldn't have liked his wife very much if that was what he had built in her memory. I was not overly fond of my wife much of the time, but even I didn't dislike her enough to erect a monstrosity like that in her memory. At the very least, I would have softened some of the edges and stuck a dragon on the top as a reminder of the dear departed. A little damage to the base had been caused at some point by Mr Ellis, the gentleman who had owned the house before us, but he seemed to have thought better of his original impulse and the area in question had since been repaired and repainted.

All things considered, it really was a frightful eyesore.

My first instinct was to have the blasted thing destroyed, but in the weeks that followed, I started to find the folly appealing. No, 'appealing' isn't the right word. Rather, I began to feel that it had a purpose which I had not yet surmised, and that it would be unwise to meddle until I knew more about it. How I came to feel that way, I can trace to one particular incident that occurred about five weeks after we began occupancy of Norton Hall.

I had taken a chair and placed it on the bare stone floor of the folly, as it was a beautiful summer's day and the folly offered the possibility of both shade and a pleasing aspect. I was just settling down with the paper when the strangest thing happened: the floor moved, as if, for a single moment, it had somehow become liquid instead of solid and some hidden tide had caused a wave to ripple across its surface. The sunlight grew sickly and weak, and the landscape shrouded itself in drifting shadows. I felt as if a strip of gauze from a sick man's bed had been placed across my eyes, for I could faintly smell decay in the air. I stood up suddenly, experiencing a little lightness in the head, and saw a man standing among the trees, watching me.

'Hullo there,' I said. 'Can I help you with something?'

He was tall and dressed in tweeds: a distinctly sickly-looking chap I thought, with a thin face and dark, arresting eyes. And I swear that I heard him speak, although his lips didn't move. What he said was:

'Let the folly be.'

Well, I found that a little rum, I have to admit, even in my weakened state. I'm not a man who is used to being addressed in such a way by complete strangers. Even Eleanor has the good grace to preface her orders with a 'Would you mind . . .?' followed by the occasional 'please' or 'thank you' to soften the blow.

'I say,' I replied, 'I own this land. You can't come in here telling me what I can and can't do with it. Who are you, anyway?'

But blast it all if he didn't repeat the same four words.

'Let the folly be.'

And with that, the fellow simply turned around and vanished into the trees. I was about to follow him and escort him off the property when I heard a movement on the grass behind me. I spun around, half-expecting him to have popped up there as well, but it was only Eleanor. For a moment, she was a part of the altered landscape, a wraith among wraiths, and then all gradually returned to normal and she was again my once-beloved wife.

'Who were you talking to, dear?' she asked.

'There was a chap hanging about, over there,' I replied, indicating with my chin toward the trees.

She looked in the direction of the woods, then shrugged.

'Well, there's no one there now. Are you sure that you saw someone? Perhaps the heat is bothering you, or something worse. You should see a doctor.'

And there it was. I was Edward Merriman: husband, property owner, businessman, and potential lunatic in his wife's eyes. At this rate, it wouldn't be very long before a couple of strong men were sitting on my chest until the booby carriage arrived, my wife perhaps shedding a small crocodile tear of regret as she signed the committal papers.

It struck me, not for the first time, that Eleanor appeared to have lost some weight in recent weeks, or perhaps it was simply the way the light reflecting from the folly caught her face. It lent an air of hunger to her appearance, an impression reinforced by a brightness to her eyes that I had not seen before. It made me think of a rapacious bird and for some reason the thought caused me to shiver. I followed her back to the house for tea but I couldn't eat, partly because of the way she was looking at me over the scones like an impatient vulture waiting for some poor chap to give up the ghost, but also because she talked incessantly of the folly.

'When are you going to have it demolished, Edgar?' she began. 'I want it done as soon as possible, before the bad weather sets in. Edgar! Edgar, are you listening?' And damn it if she didn't grip my arm so tightly that I dropped my cup in shock, fragments of pale china littering the stone floor like the remnants of young dreams. The cup was part of our wedding china, yet its loss did not appear to trouble my wife as once it might have. In fact, she barely seemed to notice the broken cup, or the tea slowly seeping through the cracks in the floor. Her grip remained tight, and her hands were like talons, long and thin with hard, sharp nails. Thick blue veins coursed across the backs of her hands like serpents intertwining, barely restrained by her skin. A sour scent seeped from her pores, and it was all that I could do not to wrinkle my nose in disgust.

'Eleanor,' I asked, 'are you ill? Your hands are so thin, and I do believe you've lost weight from your face.'

Reluctantly, she relinquished her grip upon my arm and turned her face away.

'Don't be silly, Edgar,' she replied. 'I'm fit as a fiddle.'

But the question seemed to make her uncomfortable,

because she immediately busied herself among the cupboards, making the kind of racket associated more with anger than with purpose. I left her to it, rubbing my arm where she had gripped it and wondering at the nature of the woman to whom I was married.

That evening, for want of something better to do, I went to the library of the house. Norton Hall had been put on the market by some sister of the late Mr Ellis, and the library and most of its furnishings were part of the sale. Mr Ellis appeared to have met a bad end: according to local gossip, his wife left him and, in a fit of depression, he shot himself in a hotel room in London. His wife did not even turn up for his service, poor beggar. Actually, there was still some speculation among our more fanciful neighbours that Mr Ellis had done away with his good lady wife, although the police were never able to pin anything on him. Whenever a particularly likely set of bones turned up on waste ground, or was found buried near a riverbank by an inquisitive dog, Mr Ellis and his missing wife tended to receive a mention in the local newspaper reports, even though twenty years had passed since his death. A more superstitious man might have baulked at buying Norton Hall under such circumstances, but I was not such a man. In any case, from what I knew of Mr Ellis he appeared to have been an intelligent man and, therefore, if he had killed his wife he was unlikely to have left her remains lying about the house where someone might trip over them and think, 'Hullo, that's not right.'

I had only visited the library once or twice – I'm not much of a man for books, truth be told – and had done little more than glance at the titles and blow dust and cobwebs from the older volumes. It was a surprise to me, then, to find a book sitting on a small table by an armchair. I thought at first that Eleanor might have left it there, but she was even less of a reader than I was. I picked it up and opened it at random, revealing a page covered in elegant, closely written script. I flicked back to the title page and found the inscription: *A Middle-Eastern Journey by J.F. Gray*. A small, tattered photograph marked the page and, as I looked at it, I couldn't help but feel a nasty chill down my spine. The man in the photograph, obviously the titular J.F. Gray, looked uncannily like the chap who had been wandering around the grounds offering unsought-for advice about the folly. But that couldn't be possible, I thought: after all, Gray had been dead for almost fifty years now and probably had other things on his mind, like choirs eternal or heat rash, depending on the life that he had led on earth. I put the thought to the back of my mind and returned my attention to the book. It was, it emerged, much more than a journal of Gray's trip to the Middle East.

It was, in effect, a confession.

It seemed that, on a trip to Syria in 1900, John Frederick Gray had acquired, through theft, the bones of a woman believed to be Lilith, the first wife of Adam. According to Gray, who knew a little of the biblical apocrypha, Lilith was reputed to be a demon, the original witch, a symbol of the male fear of untapped female power. Gray heard the tale of the bones from some chap in Damascus who sold him a part of what he claimed was Alexander the Great's armour, and who subsequently directed him to a little village to the far north of the country where the bones were reputed to be kept in a locked crypt.

The journey was long and difficult, although such challenges always seem to be grist to the mill for chaps like Gray, who appear to regard a comfortable chair and a good pipe as vices on a par with the actions of the Sodomites. But when Gray reached the village with his guides he found himself made unwelcome by the natives. According to his journal, the villagers told him that entry to the crypt was forbidden to strangers, and most especially to women. Gray was asked to leave, but he set up camp for the night some small distance from the village and mulled over what he had been told.

It was after midnight when one of the local ne'er-do-wells made his way to the encampment and told Gray that, for a not insignificant fee, he was prepared to remove the casket containing the bones from its resting place and bring it to him. He was a man of his word. Within the hour he returned, and he brought with him an ornate, and clearly very ancient, casket which he said contained the remains of Lilith. The box was about three feet long, two feet wide, and a foot high, and securely locked. The thief told Gray that the key remained always in the possession of the local imam, but the Englishman was unconcerned. The tale of Lilith was a myth, merely a creation of fearful men, but Gray believed he might be able to sell the beautiful casket as a curiosity when he returned home. He packed it away with his other acquisitions, and thought little more about it until he was back in England and reunited with his young wife, Jane, at Norton Hall.

Gray first began to notice a change in his wife's behaviour shortly after the bones arrived in their home. She grew strangely thin, almost emaciated, and began to evince an unhealthy interest in the boxed remains. Then, one evening when he had thought her to be in bed asleep, Gray found her prying at the lock with a chisel. When he tried to take the tool away from her, she slashed at him wildly before making a final strike at the lock, shattering it so that it dropped to the floor in two pieces. Before he could stop her, she had wrenched open the lid and revealed its contents: old brown bones curled in on themselves, with patches of tattered skin still adhering, and a skull almost like that of a reptile or a bird, narrow and elongated, while still retaining traces of a half-developed humanity.

And then, according to Gray, the bones moved. It was only the slightest thing at first, a rustling that might simply have been the bones settling after their sudden disturbance, but it quickly became pronounced. The fingers stretched, as if powered by unseen muscles and tendons, then the bones in the toes tapped softly against the sides of the casket. Finally, the skull swung on its exposed vertebrae and those beak-like jaws opened and closed with a faint click.

The dust in the casket began to rise and the remains were quickly surrounded by a reddish vapour. But the vapour came, not from the casket, but from Gray's own wife, emerging from her mouth in a torrent, as though her blood had somehow dried to powder and was now being wrenched from its veins. As he watched, she grew thinner and thinner, the skin on her face crumpling and tearing like paper, her eyes growing wider as the thing in the casket sucked the life from her. Through the mist, Gray caught a glimpse of the most terrifying face reconstituting itself. Round green-black eyes devoured him hungrily, the parchment-like skin turned from grey to a scaly black, and the beaked jaws opened and closed with a sound like bones snapping as it tasted the air. Gray sensed its desire, its base sexual need. It would consume him, and he would be grateful for its appetites, even as its talons ripped into him and its beak blinded him and its limbs enfolded him in a final embrace. He felt himself responding, moving ever closer to the emerging being, just as a thin membrane slipped across the creature's eyes, like the blinking of a lizard, and its spell was briefly broken.

Gray recovered himself and dived at the casket, sending the lid shooting down hard on the creature's head. He could feel the foul being hammering and thrashing from within as he took the chisel and jammed it through the loop of the lock, locking and sealing the casket. The red vapour instantly disappeared, the thing's struggles eased and, as he watched, his beloved wife crumpled to the floor and breathed her last.

There was only one page remaining in the narrative, and it detailed the origins of the folly: the digging of its deep foundations, the placing of the casket at its very bottom, and the construction of the folly itself above it in an effort to restrain Lilith forever. It was a ridiculous tale, of course. It had to be. It was a fantasy, Gray's attempt to scare the servants or to earn himself a mention in some penny dreadful.

Yet when I lay beside Eleanor that night, I did not sleep and I sensed a wakefulness to her that made me uneasy.

The days that followed did little to calm my feelings of unhappiness, or to improve relations between my wife and me. I found myself returning again and again to Gray's tale, nonsense though it had initially seemed. I dreamed of unseen things tapping at our bedroom window and when, in my dream, I approached the pane to ascertain the cause of the noise, an elongated head would emerge from the darkness, its dark, predatory eyes gleaming hungrily as it broke through the glass and tried to devour me. As I fought it, I could feel the shape of its sagging breasts against me, and its legs wrapped around me in a mockery of a lover's ardour. Then I would awake to find a small smile on Eleanor's face, as though she knew of my dream and were secretly pleased at its effect upon me.

As we grew increasingly alienated from each other, I took to spending more time in the garden, or walking along the boundaries of my land, half hoping to catch some sight of the anonymous visitor who bore such a marked resemblance to the unfortunate J.F. Gray. It was on one such occasion that I spied a figure on a bicycle making laborious progress up the hill that led to the gates of Norton Hall. Constable Morris hove into view – quite literally, for he was a large man and his considerable girth, combined with the blurring effect of the day's heat, gave him the appearance of a great, black ship appearing slowly upon the horizon. Eventually he seemed to realize the futility of his continued effort to master the hill on two wheels when gravity appeared determined to frustrate him, and he duly dismounted and walked his bicycle along the remaining stretch until he came at last to the gates.

Constable Morris was one of two policemen assigned to the little station at Ebbingdon, the town nearest to Norton Hall. He and the local sergeant, Ludlow, had responsibility for maintaining order not only in Ebbingdon but in the nearby villages of Langton, Bracefield, and Harbiston, as well as their surrounding areas, a task which they accomplished using a combination of a single dilapidated police car, a pair of bicycles, and the vigilance of the local populace. I had spoken to Ludlow only on a handful of occasions, and had found him to be a rather taciturn man, but Morris was a regular sight on the road by our property and was more inclined to spend a spare moment talking (and catching his breath) than was his superior.

'Hot day,' I remarked.

Constable Morris, red-faced from his exertions, wiped his shirtsleeve across his brow and concurred that, yes, it was indeed a devil of a day. I offered him a glass of homemade lemonade, should he choose to accompany me back to the house, and he readily agreed. We talked of local matters on the short walk to the house, and I left him by the folly while I went into the kitchen to pour the lemonade. Eleanor was nowhere to be seen, but I could hear her moving about in the attic of the house, making a dreadful racket as she tossed aside boxes and scattered crates. I chose not to disturb her with news of Morris's arrival.

Outside, the policeman was walking idly around the

folly, his hands clasped behind his back. I handed him his lemonade as I joined him, the ice cracking loudly in the glass, and watched as he took a deep draught. There were great sweat stains beneath his arms and upon his back, a deeper blue against the lighter shade of his shirt, like a relief map of the oceans.

'What do you think of it?' I asked him.

'It's good,' he replied, believing me to be referring to the lemonade. 'Just what the doctor ordered on a day like today.'

I corrected him. 'No, I meant the folly.'

Morris shifted his feet slightly and lowered his head. 'Not really for me to say, now, Mr Merriman,' he said. 'I don't claim to be an expert on such matters.'

'Expert or not, you must have an opinion on it.'

'Well, frankly sir, I don't much care for it. Never have.'

'You sound like you've been exposed to it on more than one occasion,' I said.

'It's been a while,' he said, a little warily. 'Mr Ellis . . .'

He trailed off. I waited. I was anxious to question him further, but I did not want him to think I was engaged merely in idle prying.

'I heard,' I said at last, 'that his wife disappeared, and that the poor man took his own life soon after.'

Morris took another drink of lemonade and looked at me closely. It was easy to underestimate such a man, I thought: his awkwardness, his weight, his struggles with his bicycle, all were rather comical at first appearance. But Constable Morris was a shrewd man, and his lack of progress through the ranks was due not to any deficiencies in his character or his work, but to his own desire to remain at Ebbingdon and tend to those in his care. Now it was my turn to shift beneath his gaze.

'That's the story,' said Morris. 'I was going to say that Mr Ellis didn't care much for the folly either. He wanted to demolish it, but then events took a turn for the worst and, well, you know the rest.'

But, of course, I didn't. I knew only what I had heard through local gossip, and even that was meted out to me, as a new arrival, in carefully measured amounts. I told Morris that this was the case, and he smiled.

'Gossips with discretion,' he said. 'I never heard the like.'

'I'm aware of how things stand in small villages,' I said. 'I expect that I could leave grandchildren behind me who would still be regarded with a certain amount of suspicion.'

'You have any children then, sir?'

'No,' I replied, unable to keep a twinge of regret from my voice. My wife was not particularly maternal, and nature appeared to have agreed in that assessment.

'It's an odd thing,' said Morris, giving no indication that he had noticed the alteration in my tone. 'It's been many years since children were heard in Norton Hall, not since before Mr Gray's time. Mr Ellis, he was childless too.'

It was not a topic I wished to pursue, but the mention of Ellis allowed me to steer the conversation into more interesting waters, and I jumped at the opportunity a little too eagerly.

'They say, well, they say that Mr Ellis might have killed his wife.'

I immediately felt embarrassed at speaking so bluntly, but Morris did not appear to mind. In fact, he seemed to appreciate my honesty at broaching the subject so openly.

'There was that suspicion,' he admitted. 'We questioned him, and two detectives came up from London to look into it, but it was as if she had disappeared off the face of the earth. We searched the property here, and all the fields and lands around, but we found nothing. There were rumours that she had a fancy man in Brighton, so we tracked him down and questioned him as well. He told us that he hadn't seen her in weeks, for all the trust you can put in the word of a man who would sleep with another man's wife. Eventually, we had to let the whole matter rest. There was no body, and without a body there was no crime. Then Mr Ellis shot himself, and people came to their own conclusions about what might have happened to his wife.' He drained the last of his lemonade, then handed me the empty glass. 'Thank you,' he said. 'That was very refreshing.'

I told him that he was most welcome, and watched as he prepared to mount his bicycle once again.

'Constable?'

He paused in his preparations.

'What do you think happened to Mrs Ellis?'

Morris shook his head. 'I don't know, sir, but I do know this. Susan Ellis doesn't walk this earth any more. She lies beneath it.'

And with that, he cycled away.

The following week I had business in London which could not be put off. I took the train down and spent most of a frustrating day discussing financial affairs, a frustration aggravated by a growing sense of disquiet, so that my time in London was spent with only a fraction of my attention concentrated on my finances and the remainder devoted to the nature of the evil that appeared to have tainted Norton Hall. Although not a superstitious man, I had grown increasingly uneasy about the history of our new home. The dreams had been coming to me with increasing regularity, accompanied always by the sound of talons tapping and jaws clicking and, sometimes, by the sight of Eleanor leaning over me when at last I awoke, her eyes bright and knowing, her cheekbones threatening to erupt like knife blades through the taut skin of her face. Gray's account of his travels had also unaccountably gone missing, and when I questioned Eleanor about it I sensed that she was lying to me when she denied any knowledge of its whereabouts. Both the attic and the cellar were a jumble of upturned boxes and discarded papers, the mess belying my wife's claims that she was merely 'reorganising' our surroundings.

Finally, there had been disturbing changes in the more intimate aspects of our married life. Such matters should remain between a man and his wife, but suffice it to say that our relations were of a greater frequency – and, at least on my wife's part, of a greater ferocity – than we had ever before known. It had now reached a point where I rather feared turning off the light, and I had taken to staying away from our bedroom until late into the night in the hope that Eleanor might be sleeping when at last I took my place beside her.

But Eleanor was rarely asleep, and her appetites were fearful in their insatiability.

It was dark when I got home that evening, but I could still see the marks of the vehicle tracks upon the lawn, and a gaping hole where the folly had once been. The remains of the construct itself lay in a jumble of concrete and lead on the gravel by the house, left there by the men responsible for its demolition, the paucity of its foundations now clearly revealed, for the structure itself was merely a feint, a means of covering up the pit that lay beneath. A figure stood at the lip of the hole, a lamp in her hand. As she turned to me, she smiled, a ghastly smile filled, it seemed to me, with both pity and malice.

'Eleanor!' I cried. 'No!'

But it was too late. She turned and began to descend a ladder, the light quickly disappearing from view. I dropped my briefcase and dashed across the lawn, my chest heaving and a growing panic clawing at my gut, until I reached the lip of the hole. Below me, Eleanor was scraping at the dirt with her bare hands, slowly revealing the curled, skeletal figure of a woman, the remains still covered in a tattered pink dress, and I knew instinctively that this was Mrs Ellis and that Constable Morris was right in his suspicions. She had not run away from her husband. Rather, she had been interred here by him, after she had dug her way beneath the folly and he had killed her, then himself, in a fit of horror and remorse. Mrs Ellis's skull was slightly elongated around the nose and mouth, as though some dreadful transformation had been arrested by her sudden death.

By now, Eleanor's scratching had revealed a small coffin, dark and ornamented. I started down the ladder after her as she took a crowbar and tore at the great lock which Gray had placed on the casket before he buried it. I was on the final steps of the ladder when a wrenching sound came and, with a cry of triumph, Eleanor threw open the lid. There, just as Gray had described, lay the curled-up remains topped by a strange, elongated skull. Already, the dust was rising and a thin red trail of vapour seeped from Eleanor's mouth. Her body convulsed, as if it were being shaken by unseen hands. Her eyes bulged whitely in their sockets and her cheeks appeared to collapse into her open mouth, the lineaments of her skull clearly visible beneath the skin. The crowbar fell from her fingers and I grabbed it. Pushing her away, I raised the bar above my head and stood above the casket. A grey-black face with large, dark green eyes and hollows for ears looked up at me, and its sharp beaked jaws clicked as it rose toward me. Talons gripped the sides of its prison as it struggled to rise, and its body was a mockery of all that was beautiful in a woman.

Its breath smelled of dead things.

I closed my eyes, and struck. Something screamed, and the skull broke with a hollow, wet sound like the opening of a melon. The creature fell back, hissing, and I slammed down the lid. At my feet, Eleanor lay unconscious, the final traces of the red vapour coiling slowly between her teeth. Just as Gray had done years before, I took the crowbar and used it to jam the lock. From within the box came a furious hammering, and the crowbar jangled uneasily where it rested. The thing screamed repeatedly, a long high-pitched sound like the squealing of pigs in a slaughterhouse.

I placed Eleanor over my shoulder and, with some difficulty, climbed the ladder to the ground above, the thudding noises from the casket slowly fading. I drove her to Bridesmouth, where I placed her in the care of the local hospital. She remained unconscious for three days, and remembered nothing of the folly, or Lilith, when she awoke.

While she was in the hospital, I made arrangements for us to return permanently to London, and for Norton Hall to be sealed. And then, one bright afternoon, I watched as the hole in the lawn was lined with cement strengthened with steel. More cement was poured into the hole, three containers of it until the hole was almost half full. Then the workmen began the task of building a second folly to cover the hole, larger and more ornate than its predecessor. It cost me half a year's income, but I had no doubt that it was worth it. Finally, while Eleanor continued to convalesce with her sister in Bournemouth, I watched as the last stones of the folly were set in place and the workmen set about removing their equipment from the lawn.

'I take it the missus didn't like the last folly, Mr Merriman?' said the foreman, as we watched the sun set upon the new structure.

'I'm afraid it didn't suit her disposition,' I replied.

The foreman gave me a puzzled look.

'They're funny creatures, women,' he continued at last. 'If they had their way, they'd rule the world.'

'If they had their way,' I echoed.

But they won't, I thought.

At least, not if I have anything to do with it.

The Cycle

The pain began almost as soon as she boarded the train. Usually, she planned these things so well. How could she not, after all these years? Today, though, had just been one of those bloody awful days, when nothing went according to plan. She had intended to get the five o'clock train, which would have seen her safely tucked up at home with the doors closed and a whole weekend of privacy and quiet to get over the curse. Instead, a crisis in the office meant that Dominic, her boss, had been forced to call an emergency meeting. Two days before a deadline, one of the agency's most important clients had decided that elements of the new ad campaign were 'inappropriate' and needed to be re-examined. That meant a brainstorming session which lasted until after seven, the beautiful autumn day outside slowly descending into shadows by the time she left.

She could feel it approaching, even as she left the building and headed for the station: a sense of unease, of dislocation, and a tenderness to her belly and her breasts. Her already short temper contracted even further, so that she almost bit off the head of the lazy clerk behind the ticket counter, the idiot apparently more concerned with picking his lottery numbers than ensuring that she caught her train, the closing of unseen doors already signalling its imminent departure. She was forced to sprint to make it, and that had not helped matters at all. Running, fretting and snapping at morons seemed only to exacerubate the problem.

She took a seat in the next-to-last carriage. The toilet was in the final carriage, right at the end, but the lights in the carriage were malfunctioning, flickering off and on with an angry buzzing sound, as though masses of bees were trapped within the fluorescent bulbs, so she had been forced to sit a little further forward than she would have liked. Still, perhaps it would be all right. It hadn't started yet, although it was close.

The train crawled slowly from the station. Her fellow passengers read books and newspapers, or talked nonsense loudly on their mobile phones, their lack of consideration annoying her still further but providing a momentary distraction, an outlet for her frustration. She had a phone herself, of course, but she kept it switched off on trains and buses unless it was absolutely essential to leave it active, and even then she left it on vibrate and would step out of the carriage to answer it. She was very conscious of her privacy, and it constantly amazed her that people were prepared to discuss, at high volume, the most intimate details of their lives among strangers. Her father and mother would sooner have died than engage in a conversation upon which others might eavesdrop. In fact, her parents had rarely discussed anything of consequence on the telephone. They were resolutely old-fashioned in that sense. If something was important, then it was worth discussing face-to-face. Their telephone conversations, except in exceptional cases like bereavement or illness, rarely lasted for longer than a minute or two. Their daughter had learned from them the importance of discretion in certain matters.

The raised voices were nagging at her hearing. Her senses always seemed to be more acute at this time of the month, so that even moderately loud noises became difficult to tolerate, and she was more aware than usual of distinctive smells and tastes. She wondered if others experienced it the same way she did. She could only assume that she was not unique in these sensations, although she was not the kind of person who would discuss such matters with another, even if she were not so solitary by nature.

Towns flashed by. They were making good time. She allowed herself a little sigh of relief, and breathed in deeply. As she did so, something rippled inside her. She grimaced, and shifted on her seat. Hell. The train slowed, disgorging passengers at another station. Others rarely got on to replace them at these provincial towns, and she was used to spending most of her journeys in empty carriages, especially as her destination was the last stop on the line, her house a mere stone's throw from the station. It allowed her to sleep a little later than most in the mornings, and made the trip home a little easier to bear.

She closed her eyes. Sometimes she felt lonely, living in the little village where every face was familiar to her, where every name was echoed dozens of times in the form of cousins, brothers, uncles, grandparents. Her parents had always kept themselves slightly aloof from the life of the community on the principle that good fences made good neighbours, and she was grateful to them for that. The round of meetings, charity drives, garden parties and festivals was not for her, but her desire to remain at one remove had given her a reputation around the village, particularly since she also chose to politely deflect the attentions of its menfolk. She had no intention of ever dating a man from the village, of permitting him access to the secrets of her life. She knew these men too well, and was not anxious to become one of their conquests. She had enjoyed some relationships in the city, but none that lasted. She liked men who were prepared to let her keep her distance when she chose, who wanted their own space as much as she wanted hers, but such men were harder to find than one might think. The demands that she made led her to attract those who were merely seeking casual one-night flings, or those who claimed that they appreciated her desire for independence even though, as time went on, these types inevitably grew more and more uncomfortable with it, and tried to impose their own rules. She had quickly learned that when a man said he valued a woman's independence, what it really meant was that he valued his own, and would indulge her taste for it only when it suited him to do so.

Another station passed, bringing her another mile nearer to home. The gnawing pain was stronger now, and she had a coppery taste in her mouth. She hated the cycle, the inescapable inconvenience of it. It really was a curse, but, as her mother had said to her in those first awkward months of adolescence, 'what cannot be cured must be endured'. Looking back now, she remembered the shock and amazement that she felt at the realization that her own body could do this to her, could wound her from deep within and bring her discomfort, pain and embarrassment, even as her mother had instructed her on what to do and how to prepare for it so that she was not taken by surprise. It was always easier to put up with in your own home, her mother had said, surrounded by familiar things, but you could not let it dictate how you lived your life. Yet, for the first few months, that was precisely what had happened: she was grateful and relieved once it had passed, but the relief only lasted for a week or two until it commenced, once again, its inevitable approach. It was different for the other girls: they seemed to take the changes to their bodies in their stride, and she envied them that. It was simply beyond her own capacities to do the same.

The train arrived at Shillingford, the last stop before home. Soon she would be able to lock the door and remain within the walls for the entire weekend. By Monday, it would all be over, and normal life would resume.

The door at the head of the carriage opened as the train moved off, and two young men entered. They were probably still in their late teens, although one wore a ragged line of scruffy facial hair on his upper lip, a nasty little excuse for a moustache that made him look shifty and untrustworthy. His companion, taller and bulkier, had acne pimples on his chin, bloodied where he had picked at them. They wore cheap leather jackets, and jeans that were baggy and flared.

'All right, love?' one of the boys said. She did not look at him, but she could see him reflected in the glass. It was the one with the moustache. Neither of them had taken their seats. They stood, craning their necks to catch sight of her face and body. She drew her coat a little more tightly around her.

'Aw, don't do that,' said the spotty one. 'Give us a look.'

She bit her lip. Something contracted inside her, and she jerked slightly in her seat. Her skin began to itch.

'Go on, smile,' said the one with the moustache. 'It can't be that that bad. I've got something that will make you smile.' He sniggered.

'Dyke,' said the other. He smirked at his wit.

'Nah,' said his mate. 'She's not a dyke. They're ugly. She's not that bad.' He pointed his chin at her. 'You're not a dyke, are you?'

'Get lost,' she said, despite herself. She didn't want to be drawn into an argument with them, but they had just picked the wrong evening to confront her. It was only after she had spoken that she realised how dangerous it might be to antagonise them, to draw them upon her.

'Touchy,' said Moustache to his friend. 'Must be her time of the month. They all get a bit like that.' He returned his attention to her. 'Is that it, darlin'? Time of the month? The old curse?'

His smile slowly faded, to be replaced by something infinitely more unpleasant.

'Don't bother me,' he said, so softly that she thought she might have misheard, until he repeated himself. 'Don't bother me one little bit . . .'

Suddenly, the train ground to a halt. For a moment, there was only silence, and then a voice came over the public address system.

'*We would like to apologise to all passengers for this slight delay. This is due to a temporary signal failure on the line ahead of us, which means that we have to wait for the southbound train to pass before we can continue. Again, we would like to apologise for any inconvenience caused, and assure you that we will be on our way very shortly.*'

She couldn't believe it. She pressed her face to the window and thought that she could almost see the lights of the station in the distance. She could walk to her house from here, but the old manually operated doors were long gone and she, like all the other passengers, was a prisoner of new technology. She felt nauseous, and the coppery taste in her mouth was growing more pronounced. It was now dark outside. She looked at the night sky. There were no stars visible, although a telltale edge of brightness had begun to show in the north as the clouds began to thin. This was bad, very bad. She could hear the boys whispering, and she risked a glance at them. The one with the pimples was looking over at her, and she could see the lust in his eyes.

'Unnnhhh.'

The groan of pain caused the boys to stop their conversation. She winced. The delay was just unbearable. What a bloody nuisance. She almost howled in frustration. There was no other choice: she rose, grabbed her briefcase, and headed for the last carriage. If she could get to the toilet, then she could do whatever was necessary and wait things out until the train got into the station, then slip onto the platform through the back door, avoiding the young men and the stink of their desire. She stepped into the space between the carriages, opened the door, and entered the empty compartment, the buzzing unbearably loud, the flickering of the lights paining her eyes.

Behind her, the two teenagers exchanged a look, then stood and followed her towards the carriage.

Their names were Davey and Billy. Davey was the older one, the smarter one, and he was proud of his carefully cultivated facial hair. The moustache was sometimes the difference between being served in a bar or being refused, and he was very proud of it. Billy was bigger than his friend, but dumber and more brutal. They often saw women on the trains late at night, some of them a bit the worse for wear and unlikely to put up much of a fight, but somehow the opportunity they sought had never presented itself, until now. The woman was alone, the train had stopped: even if she cried out, no one would hear her. It was perfect.

They entered the carriage. The fluorescent lights flickered and buzzed then, finally, gave up the ghost, artificial light yielding to the moon's luminescence as a great disc of white cleared the cover of the clouds and shone down upon the woods, the fields, and the silver body of the unmoving train. The toilet was ahead of them, at the far end. It wouldn't have much of a lock on it. On trains, they never did.

They were halfway down the carriage when the noise came from behind them. Something moved in the space between two seats, previously hidden from the young men by the shadows, the moonlight not yet penetrating its reaches. They turned as it unfolded itself, slowly rising up before them, taller than they were, and infinitely more powerful. There was a sharp animal smell in the carriage, and they heard a sound like a dog might make if someone threatened to remove the bone from between its paws. As Davey's eyes grew accustomed to the gloom, he saw clawed feet, longer than a human's and covered with fine dark hair that shone in the moonlight, and muscular legs that bent sharply at the knee, rising up to a flat crotch, a taut stomach, and small, pale breasts. Even as he watched, more fine hairs erupted from the pores of the skin, colonising the white spaces and turning them all to black. The tattered remains of a dress hung from the figure's arms and back, and as its fingernails curled in on themselves Davey thought he saw traces of purple varnish upon them. The hair on its upper body was thicker than that upon its legs and belly as the breasts slowly disappeared beneath it: it was denser, and tinged with white and grey, as though a great cape had been placed across its shoulders.

Then it emerged from the darkness, slowly advancing upon them, and the moonlight shone upon the woman's face. It was still changing, the features transforming before them, so that she remained clearly recognisable to Davey, like a figure glimpsed in a funhouse mirror, distorted yet familiar. Her face was lengthening, the tips of her ears extending and tufting with hair, her nose and chin elongating to form a lupine jaw, the teeth within growing sharper and shining whitely, thick strands of saliva and blood dripping from the tips. Her hands, the fingers gnarled and taloned, gripped the edges of the seat before her as her body shuddered, the change now almost complete as Davey heard four words emerge from deep in her throat, their meaning almost lost to him as the animal overcame the woman.

Almost.

'Time of the month,' she said, and Davey thought that the words were followed by something that might have been laughter before that too was transformed, becoming a growl filled with hunger and the promise of death. Her eyes turned to yellow, and the full moon was reflected in their depths. She raised her head and howled just as, too late, the boys tried to run. Davey pushed Billy out of the way, using his size to squeeze past him before Billy even realised what he was doing. A splash of warmth struck Davey's hair and back as Billy's life ended in the slashing of claws, but he kept moving, never looking behind him, his gaze focused on the rectangle of glass ahead of him, and the silver handle of the door. He was almost close enough to touch it when a great weight landed on his back, forcing him to the ground. The train jerked into motion as Davey felt hot breath upon his skin, and sharp teeth upon his neck. In his final moments, he was struck, oddly, by the realisation that he had always been afraid of women. Now, at last, he thought that he understood why.

And then Davey screamed as he took his place in the great cycle of living and dying, and the world was filled with redness.

nocturnes
A CODA

The three stories that follow were originally distributed in a companion volume to *Nocturnes* available only through John Connolly's website, and are now being presented for the first time in a mass market edition.

Contents

The Bridal Bed

Oh, such promises we make in the heat of our passion, when the breath catches in the throat and the belly trembles. Lured by the warmth of another – the scent of her, the strength of him – our tongues betray us and the words come tumbling from our mouths. The act becomes indistinguishable from the intent, and the truth is confused with lies, even to ourselves.

Do we say these things because we truly believe them, or do we believe that by saying them aloud they may become true? And, when tested, how many of us can say that we fulfilled our vows, that we did not turn away, that we did not renege on the promises we made? When our partners grow old and slow, when the light in their eyes dims and our ardour cools, how many of us are not tempted to turn away and seek our pleasures elsewhere?

Not I. I was faithful always.

I kept my vows to her, and she her vows to me, in her way.

I recall her long hair flowing, her lips pursed in amusement, and a promise unspoken in her eyes. She is beautiful, and she will always be beautiful. She will never age, never be remembered as anything other than the radiant young woman that she is now, as she stands before me and says:

'Do you love me? Will you always love me?'

'Yes,' I answer. 'Yes, and yes again.'

'Even when I am old and grey, and I have to undress in the dark so I don't frighten you?'

I laugh.

'Even then,' I reply.

She slaps me playfully, and pouts.

'That was the wrong answer, and you know it. Tell me truly: if I were to change, if I were to lose what looks I have, then would you still love me? Would you still be mine?'

I reach for her, and she struggles a little in my arms before succumbing.

'Listen to me,' I say. 'I will love you no matter what may occur, and I will always want to be with you. Would I have waited so long if I did not have such feelings for you?'

She smiles and kisses me softly on the cheek.

'Yes,' she whispers, 'you have been patient. You know I want it to be special. I want to give myself to you on our wedding night. I want to be with you then in my bridal bed.'

It was two weeks to our wedding day, and a year since we had first made our vows. Our house was built and furnished, the house in which we would raise our children and grow old together. There would be flasks of wine and her father's carriage, and feather bedding on which to lay her down. Fresh flowers would be cut, and their scent and hers would mingle in the morning light.

I walked with her to her father's house, through fields of sheep laurel and rosebay, through beardtongue and blazing star, the wind casting seeds on the air and carrying them away to fall where they would. The sun was setting, and the crows were silhouetted against the red sky like fragments of black stars drifting slowly through the firmament. Her hand was warm in mine as she slipped softly through the fields of wheat, the long stalks springing back once again behind her, covering all traces of her as though she had never been.

I left her at her father's door after one final kiss.
And we never spoke again.

Even now, I see them: a line of men moving through the fields beside me, sticks in their hands, the dogs baying by their sides. We strike firmly at the thickets and the grass, exposing dark earth and fleeing insects. There is no wind now, no breeze. The world is still, as if the life has been taken from it with her passing. We trace paths like locusts through the wheat fields, crushing the stalks beneath our feet. We search for two days without result, and on the third day we find her.

A cluster of men gathers at the entrance to a copse of ash trees, and the dogs beside them howl. I run to where they stand and, when I see her, I try to push them back, to make them turn away. I do not want them to look upon her, for she would have hated to be exposed in this way: her pale skin lacerated, her clothes bloodied, her hair tangled with leaves and twigs. Her eyes are half-open, so that she seems for a moment to be emerging drowsily from some deep, peaceful sleep, frozen for ever in the false hope of a new dawn. I strike at the man nearest me and he absorbs my blows, his strong hands closing upon me, leading me gently away. They carry her from the field in a clean white sheet and lay her down in the back of a cart, and men trail her to the village, their heads low and the dogs now silent.

We bury her in the small, raised cemetery to the north, on a patch of higher ground beneath a willow tree, and earth and rain fall together upon her casket as they cover her up. I am the last to leave her. I wait in the hope that some terrible celestial error has occurred, that the sun will shine through the clouds and warm this place, bringing her back to life; that the sound of her voice will rise from beneath the ground. I will call the others to me and we will tear the earth from above her, our bare hands clawing as we dig down. And we will lift the lid and she will be there – gasping, panicked, yet alive.

But no sound comes, and at last I turn away and follow the crowd from the churchyard.

They tracked him down within the week: a drifter, a stateless man. They hunted him for miles, through streams and forests, until at last they cornered him by an old mill. He had taken a lock of her hair and tied it with a ribbon made from the hem of her dress. There were many such ribbons in his old brown bag, encircling the hair of murdered girls. They hanged him for what he had done, and he smiled on the gallows.

But I took no satisfaction in his end, for no matter how much he suffered in his final moments it would never bring her back to me. She was gone, taken from me, and now we would never be together. For one week after she was laid to rest I did not eat, and drank only water from an old tin cup. I slept with my knees curled into my chest, in the hope that it might ease my pain, but the pain never went away. I dreamed uneasy dreams, in which the past tangled itself with a future that now would never be, and I woke to an empty bed, and the knowledge that it would always remain so.

And yet I came to love those moments when I awoke to a new day, for in that instant desire and reality were briefly one. I would hold myself still, my eyes half-open in a strange imitation of my lost bride, as if by doing so I might become one with her, that I too might be taken and join with her in another place.

On the eighth night, she called to me.

I emerged from my fitful sleep and heard the wind in the trees and the crying of an animal, except no animal had ever cried this way. It had a strange yearning to it, and a sweetness that sounded somehow familiar to me. Weakened by my lack of food, I walked unsteadily to my window and looked out upon the darkened world half-revealed. There were swaying branches and unlit windows, silent streets and the great spire of the church. Beyond lay the churchyard, the graves spread out upon their expanse of raised ground, the dead keeping watch over the living.

Something flickered among the headstones, enclosed by the branches of an old willow tree: light and more-than-light, form and less-than-form. It hung suspended above the ground and I knew that beneath it was a pile of newly turned earth, the flowers not yet entirely wilted upon it. I tried to make out features in the glow, to find some echo of her presence within it, but I was too far away. I opened the window, and the wind carried her voice to me, calling my name. A tendril extended itself from the centre of the light and seemed to beckon me towards it. I backed away, wanting to go to her but desperate also not to lose sight of that wondrous light. I felt a strange warmth on my body, as if the naked form of another were pressed hard against it. It seemed to me that I could smell her scent, and her hair brushed softly against my cheek. I wanted to go to her, and was almost at the door when my legs failed me and a terrible nausea gripped me. I collapsed even as my hand reached for the handle, my fingers scraping the metal. I cried out in desperation, and then I was falling. My head hit the floor, her voice faded, and the light of her was lost as the blackness encroached upon me.

They found me stretched by the door early the next morning. The doctor was called, a kind man who told me that despite my grief I must try to eat. He seemed surprised when I quickly agreed, and a thin soup was brought. I tried to keep down as much of it as I could, but my stomach was weak and rebelled against its first taste of food for so long. Later that day I managed a little broth and some dry bread, then walked stiffly from my bed to the jug and bowl upon my dressing table and tried to shave myself, but my hand shook so badly that I drew blood from my cheek and my eyes struggled to focus on the task in hand. I splashed water on my face to wash away the blood and soap, and when I lifted my head she was behind me. I saw her reflection in the glass as she moved about the room, folding clothes and humming softly to herself. I heard her bare feet padding across the floor, and a soft hiss as the cotton of her nightgown brushed against the foot of the bed.

When I turned to speak, the room was empty.

That night, she came to me, for I could not go to her. At first, I thought it was the moonlight glowing through my window, creating phantasms from the branches of the trees. But then came the tapping on the glass, and when I rose from my bed I could see her face beneath the veil, the whiteness of her fingers as they scraped against the glass, the pattern of the lace at the neck of the wedding dress in which she was interred, and the swell of her breasts beneath. She opened her mouth, revealing the redness within, and her tongue played across her lips. Her feet were bare and cast no shadow on the ground many feet below, and her eyes were dark and hungry.

'Do you love me?' she whispered, and the hunger in her eyes found expression in her voice. 'Will you always love me?'

'Yes,' I replied, the word catching at the desire I felt for her, and she for me. 'Yes, and yes again.'

'I wanted you to be the first,' she said. 'I wanted it to be special.' An image flashed before my eyes: her body against the green grass, her torn dress, her exposed skin.

All gone, my love, all gone.

'It will be,' I promised her. I fumbled with the latch and pushed the window open, the cool night air rushing into the room, bringing with it the smell of trees and flowers and damp, exposed earth. But even as I reached for her, she drew away from me, the light fading as she was drawn back to the place from which she had come, her hands beckoning me to follow. The shape of her disintegrated, the redness of her mouth lost in the glow, until there was just a shimmering on the hill behind the church, and then she was gone.

On what was to have been our wedding day I ate a slow breakfast, forcing myself to keep down each morsel. The doctor returned and pronounced me much improved, even in that short period. I dressed and lunched later with my family, fortifying myself with a glass of red wine. I took a walk alone that afternoon and made my preparations before returning home. After dinner, I excused myself and went to my room. There I waited, sitting silently on my bed, still clothed, until all was quiet and the rest were asleep. Then I slipped from the house and made my way through the streets to the churchyard.

The gravediggers kept their tools in a small hut by the cemetery gates, and from there I took what I needed. The place where she lay was not yet marked by a stone, but I knew where to find her, knew that she waited where the willow branches caressed the grave. Already, the light had begun to form and her voice was calling to me from above and below. I laid my coat to one side and began to dig. The ground was still soft, the earth still loose, and as I drew nearer to the coffin I heard a sound like fingers scraping on wood. I dug faster, scattering the dirt in great arcs over my shoulder, until at last I could see the name on the small metal plate and the dull gleaming of the screws holding the lid in place. By now, the sounds from within had grown more frantic and I moved quickly for fear that she might damage her hands. I placed the crowbar beneath the lid, and heaved. It moved slightly at first before it came away with a sharp crack, and she was revealed to me:

Her hands clasped across her belly, the rosary beads intertwined with her fingers.

Her eyes closed beneath her veil, her lips pale.

Her skin, once flawless, now strangely tainted.

She was still my love, as she would always be. I had promised her that I would love her, no matter what. Nature will have its way with us all, and time will wither us, but love endures.

I raised her up and clasped her to me. Some faint trace of her perfume still lingered, I thought, as I brushed a beetle from her brow. I kissed her gently, and though her lips were unmoving, yet I heard her voice murmur to me.

Do you love me? Will you always love me?

'Yes,' I said. 'Yes, and yes again.'

And she said no more as I drew her from the ground and carried her in my arms through the silent streets. Once, I stumbled and almost fell, for my body was still recovering from its privations, but I regained my balance and held her closer to me. She was cold, but it was a cold night. Soon, she would be warm again.

A lamp burned in the window of the small house as we made our way to it. Inside, cut flowers stood in vases, filling the rooms with their perfume, mingling with the scent of my bride. We stood upon the threshold, we two, gazing upon the white sheets, the plump pillows, the feather mattress that would cushion us on this, our wedding night.

Softly, I kissed her cold cheek.

'Welcome, my love,' I whispered, and I lay with her at last upon her bridal bed.

The Man from the Second Fifteen

Asquith was lost.

No, that wasn't quite true. Asquith, had there been anyone around to ask him, could probably have guessed his location to the nearest twenty miles, which meant that technically he was 'astray' rather than actually lost, but that was small consolation to him. The rain beat hard against his windscreen, and the wipers could do little more than spread the water thinly against the glass. The headlamps offered him glimpses of gorse and tall trees. Occasionally, another car would round a bend, blinding him briefly, its occupants invisible to him as they continued on their way, presumably far more certain of the direction in which their final destination lay than was their fellow traveller on these West Country roads.

Softly, Asquith damned their hides.

The reunion of the Maldon College Second Fifteen had, as usual, been a raucous affair, notable mainly for the degree of damage caused to the host premises, and the amount of money squandered on alcohol and food, although money was not a worry for the Maldon old boys. Poor people did not go to schools like Maldon. Even the gardener at Maldon was wealthier than his peers, for the institution was predicated on the belief that one got what one paid for. Unfortunately, while Maldon could afford the best of staff it was often required to take students from the shallower depths of the gene pool, since intellectual ability was a minor consideration where acceptance to Maldon was concerned. Thankfully, such failings were rarely an obstacle to its students' progress in life, academic achievement being largely subsidiary to wealth, a good name, and a suitably accommodating family business involving the transfer of other people's money from one location to another in return for a sizeable commission.

To his credit, Asquith was not such a fellow. As in most things, he occupied the middle ground: averagely intelligent, averagely handsome, averagely equipped for the sporting field. He was, in essence, the kind of chap who found his place in the Second Fifteen and kept it with little difficulty, while secretly envying the achievements and abilities of those in the First Fifteen. Still, such rejections were more than two decades in the past, and the Second Fifteen's activities were now limited to boozy weekends every couple of years. Asquith, who had always fancied himself as a hunting and fishing sort of chap, even though his job in the City gave him little time for either, had particularly enjoyed this most recent of reunions as it offered him the opportunity to ride with the local hounds, pepper grouse with buckshot, and to assist in the trapping and killing of a badger believed, probably erroneously, to be spreading some form of disease.

Now, as he drove, Asquith was considering the purchase of a large gun which would enable him to pursue his newfound enthusiasms on a more regular basis. He was already picturing a walnut stock and twin barrels when the front of his car struck an obstacle on the road, the impact shuddering sickly through the body of the vehicle. He braked hard, paused to compose himself, and killed the engine, leaving only the lights on. Reluctantly, he opened his door and exposed himself to the fury of the elements. Head low, he stepped around the car, bending down to examine his bumper and the slick tar under his wheels. There was nothing to be seen, he thought, not at first, but when he looked closer he saw what appeared to be grey animal fur trapped in the grille of his radiator. Asquith reached out to touch it and realised that it was not fur, but rough cloth. He gripped the material tightly in order to free it, but something soft beneath squished wetly against his hand and he withdrew his fingers suddenly. He raised his hand to his face and thought, with disgust, that he smelt putrefaction upon himself.

Squatting down, he used his fountain pen to free the offending matter from the metal. It fell to the ground and Asquith poked at it gingerly with the base of his pen. It looked like meat: overcooked, rotting meat. The grey cloth was inseparable from it, as though it had been pressed into the very flesh and absorbed into its decay.

Briefly, Asquith considered throwing his pen away, sorry that he had used it to free this foul object, sorrier still – now that he examined it more closely – that he had allowed his own fingers to sully themselves upon it. He stood and raised his hand to the rain, rubbing the fingers together in an attempt to free any lingering traces of matter or odour, then dried them with a rag from the glove compartment of the car.

It was only then, as the shock dissipated, that he began to make the connection between the fragment of matter and its possible source. He looked around, and thought that he heard a sound in the undergrowth. Although not, by nature, a sensitive man, Asquith was briefly troubled by the feeling that he was being watched from the bushes.

'Hello,' he called. 'Anyone there?'

This time he heard it clearly: a scurrying, the breaking of twigs, branches swishing, quickly growing fainter as whatever he had struck slunk away into the dark reaches of the forest. Asquith did not even consider following. Instead, he backed towards his car, slid into the driver's seat, and reached for the ignition key in order to be on his way.

His car keys were gone.

Asquith searched the floor, emptied the glove compartment, and tapped his pockets twice over. He stepped back into the rain and shook himself, hoping to hear the reassuring jangle of metal from somewhere on his person, but there was only silence. He retraced his footsteps, carefully examining the road around his car, but found nothing. After an increasingly agonised ten minutes, he gave up and slammed his hands against the bonnet in frustration. Lowering his forehead to his arms, he allowed the rain to beat upon his balding head, as if it were punishing him for his foolishness. He had been in this position for some time when he heard, once again, a noise from the bushes, and felt the presence among the leaves. Briefly, his anger overcame his fear and he began to shout.

'Damn you!' he shouted. 'Give me back my keys. I know you have them, and I know you're in there. Give them to me!'

There was no reply.

Asquith, remembering the old adage that one can catch more flies with honey than with vinegar, managed to soften his tone before he spoke again.

'Look,' he said, 'if I hurt you, I'm sorry. I'll happily take you to the nearest hospital, but I need my keys if I'm to do that. Otherwise, well, we'll both be stuck out here, and that can't be good for you or for me, now can it?'

He waited, but there was nothing.

Then he heard it: the soft tinkling of his keys. Whatever lay in the darkness was mocking him, taunting him. While he had been worrying about the fate of whatever he had hit, the individual in question – and Asquith didn't doubt for a moment that it was a person, because rabbits, voles and rats didn't crawl off into the bushes after being struck by a car, then make a full circle of the vehicle and steal the driver's keys in revenge – had apparently been conspiring to maroon him on a country road in the middle of a rainstorm. This was clearly a person of at least moderate intelligence, albeit one, judging by the lingering stench on Asquith's fingers, who was not in the first bloom of health.

'Blast!' said Asquith. 'Damn and blast you!'

With that, he walked back to the driver's side of the car, leaned in, and pulled the lever to pop the boot. He strode around and armed himself with his favourite nine iron from his golf bag, then advanced on the bushes.

'Now see here,' he said. 'I've apologised for what happened. I've offered to help you. I want my car keys. Hand them over.'

The keys flew from the bushes and landed on the grass verge by the side of the road. Relief flooded Asquith's features. Slowly, he moved toward them, the golf club still gripped in his right hand. He lowered himself, his eyes never leaving the tangle of wood and leaves before him, and reached for his keys.

They moved.

For a moment, Asquith couldn't believe what he had witnessed. His keys had jumped, almost as if they had a life of their own. He made a quick grab for them, but again they pulled away from him, and this time he saw the length of thin gossamer that had been wrapped around the key chain. He made one final attempt to grasp them, but they were already disappearing back into the bushes. Asquith caught a final glimpse of wet, shining metal, and then they were gone.

Unthinkingly, Asquith went after them.

Branches tore at his jacket, and he felt thorns scrape at his face, but he didn't care. He struck at the offending bushes with his golf club, beating a path through them until they cleared and he found himself in the understorey of the thick woods that bounded the road on either side. Fallen leaves mingled with dense ferns, and he stumbled as his feet struck stones hidden in the greenery. The rain was thinner here, the canopy above offering him some shelter from the worst of it. There was movement all around him as those drops that made it through struck the vegetation, causing it to tremble slightly, as though in fear of what might be about to occur. Ahead of him, Asquith saw a sapling shake as it sprang back into place, disturbed by the passage of a body of some size. Asquith wiped his face with the back of his jacket, clearing his eyes. Some of the adrenaline was seeping away now, and he felt the first real stirrings of fear. He could return to the road, he thought, perhaps lock his doors and wait for another car to come. But he had not seen another car in the last ten miles that he had travelled, and it was now well past midnight on a back road in an unfamiliar part of the country. Who knew how long he might have to wait, seated in his car, damp, the doors locked, his eyes trained on the hedges and trees by the roadside, fearing to sleep in case he awoke to hear a tapping at his window and turned to see . . .

To see what? That was the big question. Asquith thought again of the odour on his fingers after he had touched the material on his car. It might not have come directly from the body that he had struck, he supposed, but then what was an unknown individual doing crossing the road in the dead of night carrying rotting flesh? Somehow, that was almost as bad as the possibility that the individual in question might have some dreadful malady that had caused the rot Asquith had smelt. He had never heard of a case of leprosy in the West Country, but one never knew. Some of these communities were terribly isolated. Lord alone knew what they could be hiding. One sometimes read the most dreadful stories in the newspapers.

No, he had come this far, and he had his golf club. Asquith was a big man, running to seed now but with years of rugby for the Second Fifteen behind him in his youth. Some of that bulk was still visible upon his shoulders and chest. He was reasonably certain that he could still take care of himself, and his quarry was wounded. He wished that he had his long-dreamt-of shotgun with him now. A golf club was not nearly so persuasive, or reassuring.

Asquith reached the sapling and pushed it gently to one side. Beyond lay a clearing, perhaps seven or eight feet in diameter, surrounded by thick trees. Dead branches littered the ground, broken here and there by the tops of ferns. In the middle lay his keys. Asquith stepped forward: one step, then another, his eyes never leaving the circle of trees around him. The rain had eased now. Soon, it would cease altogether.

'Where are you?' he said. 'Think I'm going to fall for that again?'

He lowered his golf club, then snaked it out and placed the rubber grip firmly in the centre of his key ring. He felt the ring move as his tormentor tried to pull the keys away, then the resistance ended and they lay still.

'Not so clever now, are you?' asked Asquith.

He raised his right foot, took a third firm step, and felt the ground give way beneath him. From all around, it seemed, he heard cracking, and then he was falling into darkness, the lip of the hole receding from him as the trap opened up. He smelled damp earth, and tree roots brushed his face. His head impacted heavily on a jutting rock, and pain seared through him as he landed, dazed and bleeding, on a floor of stone and dirt. Something jabbed hard into his side, breaking the skin. He reached out to push it away, and his fingers closed around a shard of bone. It was half of a human femur. He could just about make out its shape when he raised it to the moonlight shining down from above.

And beyond the bone, there appeared a head. It leaned over the lip of the hole, silhouetted against the sky looking down upon him. Asquith felt himself weakening, and tasted blood upon his lips, yet even in his diminished state he thought that the head appeared deformed. It was grotesquely thin, and its ears were very large and pointed. They reminded him of a bat's ears. He heard a kind of chittering from above, as if the thing were congratulating itself on its work, and then it retreated and all was darkness and silence.

Asquith didn't know how long he had lain unconscious. His wristwatch had shattered when he hit the ground, but in any event he was unable to see it because the moonlight had now been blocked out, the scattering of branches and leaves above the hole having been replaced while he was out cold. He drew a breath, then almost retched as he smelled the stench from around him. He tried to stir himself, but a lancing pain shot up from the base of his foot and he knew immediately that his ankle was broken. His left hand, too, appeared to be injured, badly sprained at the very least. He raised himself up using his right hand and felt it sink into something soft. The rotting smell grew stronger.

Asquith reached into his pocket for his matches, hoping to gain some insight into his surroundings. Even with his damaged limbs, he had confidence in his own strength. When he had played for the Second Fifteen, he was noted for his ability to take the most brutal of punishment yet still dust himself off and persevere until the end. He had played games with a cracked rib, a broken nose, and a lacerated scalp that had turned his shirt from white to red. It was not all that long ago in the great scheme of things. Those triumphs were not yet ancient history.

His left hand jogged slightly on the ground as he rummaged in his jacket, sending a pain shooting up his arm. Asquith groaned, and heard a soft chittering in reply.

Immediately, he froze.

'Who's there?' he asked. His voice seemed to echo around him, and Asquith knew that the hole was much larger than it had first appeared. He sensed it stretching out to his right and left, even in the darkness.

The chittering came again, closer now. Asquith moved his fingers and felt them close around something metal: his golf club. He waited, trying to sense the position of the presence in the hole.

'Who are you?' he repeated. '*What* are you?'

The sound grew louder, and Asquith struck, lashing out from right to left with the heavy club. He felt it make contact with the thing's skull, and rough cloth brushed his hand as it fell. He raised the club again and brought it down, smashing repeatedly, feeling warm liquid splash his face in the darkness. He kept hitting it until at last it lay still, and the chittering ceased.

Asquith leaned back and breathed deeply, ignoring the smell, grateful now only that he was alive. He laid aside the club and found his matches. Gripping the box gently between his knees he removed a single match. Help would come eventually, he knew. He still had his strength. He would call, and keep calling, until someone heard him, or until he had no voice left with which to shout. He would survive. He might not have made the First Fifteen, but damned if he wasn't going to be present at the next reunion of the Second, and with quite the tale to tell.

And then the chittering came again, first from his left and then from his right, from above him and behind him, a great chorus of it rising in anger and hunger, increasing in pitch until it was joined by the sound of flapping wings and snapping teeth.

Asquith struck the match, and in its flickering light he caught glimpses of grey, leathery skin and elongated skulls, and sharp white teeth that jutted out from snoutlike jaws at obtuse angles, overlapping and exposed where they met. He saw red eyes, and sunken breasts on the females. He followed thin arms along the rims of dark wings until he reached the long, clawed fingers, their talons like yellowed half-moons curling in upon the black night of the palm.

And Asquith knew that he would not survive, and he wondered in his final moments if perhaps this situation might not have arisen had he been good enough for the First Fifteen. The match burned his fingers, yet still he held onto it until at last he could take the pain no longer, and he was plunged once again into darkness. The air around him was suddenly filled with movement, and he felt teeth upon him, and he prayed for the end to come quickly.

And his prayers were answered.

The Inn at Shillingford

There had long been an inn at Shillingford. The village lay at a crossroads: secondary roads now, but once the main arteries from north to south and east to west in this part of the country. The coming of the big 'A' roads rendered the town less important than it once was, but it was the motorways, blindly scything through the countryside, blighting and polluting, that finally sounded the death knell for Shillingford and its sole source of bed and board. The inn sat forgotten at the top of a small hill some half a mile beyond the eastern edge of the village, a relic of another age. Only a wooden sign, almost entirely devoured by damp and rot, indicated to the passing traveller that this was once a place to eat and rest briefly upon life's journey.

But had that traveller taken the time to follow the overgrown road up the hill, he might have noticed something strange about the old stone building: the faint smell of burning that still hung around it; the blackening of its walls; the scorched hole in its slate roof. Perhaps, after all, it was not the motorways that brought an end to the hospitality offered by the inn. Perhaps also, if one were to listen to local gossip, one might learn that the fire that destroyed the inn at Shillingford was not accidental, but was set deliberately, although even the most tenacious of investigators would find it difficult to obtain sufficient evidence to ascribe blame for the incident. In truth, a great many people had been present on the night that the inn burned, so that the responsibility for what occurred might justifiably be termed collective.

Note the use of that word: 'responsibility'. Not guilt. No one ever felt guilt for destroying the inn at Shillingford, and no regret showed upon their faces as the building, and its innkeeper, succumbed to the flames. The police looked into the matter, of course, aided by the local constable who helped in every way to ensure that the verdict reached on the demise of the innkeeper, Joseph Long, was one of accidental death.

And why did he have to die? That, sadly, is another story, and one that need not concern us here. Suffice it to say that a number of young women disappeared in the locality and suspicions about their disappearance centred on the innkeeper. There was never sufficient proof to charge him with anything, and no bodies were ever found. It was said, though, that many a hungry traveller had complimented Mr Long on his meat pies, remarking to him that they had a distinctive, although not unpleasant, taste. Mr Long, with a bashful smile, would claim credit for them, explaining that he cooked them himself in the kitchen. Vegetarians, it must be said, found the cuisine at the inn somewhat limited (although, as someone once blackly remarked, while there might not have been vegetables in the pies, it was quite possible that they might have contained vegetarians).

The inn at Shillingford was, in effect, a one-man operation. Joseph Long made the beds in its five small rooms, and farmed out the used linen to a woman in the village who would deliver them back, crisp and clean, three times every week. Long had once been married, although he claimed that he and his wife did not get along and that she had subsequently left him and gone to live in France. Once again, local gossip suggested that she was known to offer her favours to guests at the inn and had been punished by her husband for her infidelity, her remains disposed of in a bathtub (for a guest at the inn was once heard to remark that the bath in room three was scarred by what he felt certain were acid burns).

And so the inn was consumed, and Joseph Long died along with it. Curiously, the village itself began to die not long after, as its young people left and its old people stayed, moving from house to shop, shop to church and, finally, church to cemetery, where they made their final homes. Few lights burned in Shillingford, and those travellers who were unfortunate enough to be forced to negotiate its single cracked main street often found themselves shivering slightly at the bleakness of the place.

Then, in the final years of the last century, Shillingford became the recipient of some much-needed good fortune. An amusement park was established outside Morningdale, a town five miles to the west, with vertiginous roller coasters and nausea-inducing rides. The road between Morningdale and the motorway was upgraded, and as Shillingford was the only village on the route it also benefited from the improvements. In addition to the road, new houses came to be built, and small stores opened in the hope of gaining both local and passing trade.

And a man named Vincent Penney bought and restored the inn at Shillingford, and celebrated its grand reopening with an invitation to the villagers to come and enjoy a complimentary drink and some cocktail sausages. The villagers of Shillingford, never ones to turn down something for nothing, duly made the trek up to the inn, enjoyed Mr Penney's largesse for as long as it took them to finish the sausages, then promptly left and never returned again. Their brief visit simply confirmed them in their view that there was something wrong with the inn at Shillingford, and no amount of fancy carpeting and wood panelling would ever make it right again.

Thus it was that while Shillingford slowly prospered, Mr Penney's investment appeared destined to go unrewarded. During the summer months he made a small loss, and during the winter months he made a large loss. The five rooms above the bar were never fully occupied, and those guests who chose to spend the night complained of bad smells and problems with the plug holes, which spat filthy water when the hot taps were turned on. Two years after the grand opening, Vincent Penney decided to sell up and cut his losses, assuming he could find anyone to take the place off his hands. When no such buyer could be found, Mr Penney closed the inn and departed for Spain. He left the matter in the hands of his solicitors, who quickly relegated its sale to the lower regions of their list of priorities, from which it seemed unlikely ever to rise, especially after another fire – this time bearing the imprint of a single hand, and one possibly not unrelated to the Penney dynasty and its desire for insurance money – returned the inn to its previous blackened state.

It was shortly after eleven on a cold November night when Mr Adam Teal found himself on Shillingford's once very depressing main street, now transformed into a vaguely depressing main street by the arrival of one or two tourism-related enterprises. Beside him on the passenger seat of his car lay a very old, and very outdated, guide to this part of the countryside, left to him by his retired predecessor, Mr Ormond. Teal was that rarest of rare birds: an insurance salesman with a conscience, which meant that he was more popular with his clients than he was with his employers, a situation that had led to his transfer from London to the countryside so that he might sell less potentially ruinous insurance to the kind of people who kept their money in biscuit tins amid stale crumbs and mouse droppings.

But, as is the case with men who pride themselves on a particular virtue, Teal had a particular vice with which to balance it. He was, in that quaint phrase, a 'ladies' man', and found that his job occasionally offered him the opportunity to indulge his tastes for relatively anonymous liaisons. Teal was not married and so viewed these flirtations as mostly harmless, the scrupulous manner in which he approached his work further enabling him to convince himself that they were not the symptoms of some greater moral decay.

Nevertheless, today had been another unprofitable day in a string of unprofitable days, which hung heavily about Teal's neck like a noose. Now he was tired and hungry, and his guidebook informed him that the only lodging within thirty miles, apart from deserted amusement park hotels, was located in the small hamlet of Shillingford.

Teal followed the directions in the book, and it was not long before he came to a winding road marked by a decaying sign. It curved through thick forest until it came at last to the little inn, lights burning in its downstairs windows but not, it seemed, in any of the upstairs rooms. Teal parked his car, removed his overnight bag from the back seat, and knocked loudly on the door. After a short time, he heard the sound of a key turning in the lock, and the door opened wide to reveal the remains of a fire smouldering in a small hearth, a trio of armchairs surrounding it, and a reception desk to the right with five alcoves behind it, four of which contained a numbered key. The key to the third room was absent.

A man peered from behind the door. He was taller than Teal by about a foot, and his face was mostly obscured by a thick beard and unruly hair. He wore an overcoat over his nightshirt, and his feet were bare and encrusted with dirt.

'Come in, come in,' he said. 'You're most welcome, most

welcome indeed.' Teal entered, and the innkeeper closed the door behind him.

'You're in number two,' he said, and handed Teal a key with that number carved upon its head.

'Don't you want me to register?' asked Teal.

'No need,' said the innkeeper. 'You're the only guest, and it's late. Best that you get to your room now, and worry about such things in the morning.'

The salesman did not protest. He followed the innkeeper to the upper floor of the inn, where he was shown into a huge but only adequately furnished room, with a double bed, a battered armchair, and a wardrobe sufficient to accommodate the assorted costumes of a moderately sized theatrical troupe. An open door led into a bathroom which contained a shower stall and bath, a toilet and an enormous washbasin. To the right of the basin was a connecting door leading to the room next door.

Curious, thought Teal. He checked the door, but it was securely locked. There was no key in the keyhole.

'Sleep well, Mr Teal,' said the innkeeper from his post at the bedroom door, and so grateful was the guest for a room and a warm bed that he did not even think to ask how the innkeeper had discovered his name. Instead, he requested some food, and was promised a plate of bread and assorted cheeses, and a large pot of tea.

'We're out of pies,' explained the innkeeper. 'Can't get the ingredients.'

With that, he left to assemble his guest's modest repast.

Teal prepared himself for bed, and was already half-asleep on his feet when he heard the sound of a tray being placed on the floor outside his door, accompanied by a soft knocking. When he reached the door the innkeeper was gone, but there was food waiting, and a steaming metal pot of strong tea. He ate a little of the bread and cheese, and permitted himself a single cup of milky tea, before retiring for the night.

Less than an hour after closing his eyes, Teal awoke to noises coming from the room to his left. It sounded like furniture being moved around, and Teal was most aggrieved to have his sleep disturbed by such inconsiderate behaviour from a fellow guest. He supposed that someone had arrived shortly after him, seeking shelter for the night, but he could not imagine why the individual in question felt compelled to rearrange his room upon arrival. Wearing only pyjamas, he raised himself from his bed, opened his door, and entered the corridor. He strode to room three and rapped sharply on the door. The noises from within instantly ceased, and Teal thought he heard the sound of footsteps approaching the door at the other side. The steps sounded soft, and slightly wet, as though the individual in question had recently been bathing. The door did not open, yet Teal was aware that the new guest was listening at the other side of the wood.

'I say,' said Teal. 'I do wish you'd keep the noise down in there. I'm trying to sleep.'

There was no reply. Teal, with no further outlet for his frustrations, sighed loudly and prepared to return to his room. As he did so, his feet slid upon the floor, almost causing him to lose his balance. Supporting himself against the wall, he looked down and saw that a clear, sticky substance had adhered to the soles of his feet. It resembled wallpaper paste in its consistency, but smelled infinitely worse. Teal attempted to trace its source, and found that it appeared to be seeping from under the door of room three. Carefully, he backed away, rubbing his feet against a hall rug to clean them of the fluid. Then, puzzled and uneasy, he returned to his bedroom and locked the door. He cleaned the remainder of the substance from his feet using the shower head, then went to bed. No further sounds came from the room next door and, after a time, Teal prepared to drift off to sleep once again.

His eyes snapped open. It took him a moment or two to register the sound: it was softer than before, as though the person making it were anxious to avoid detection. He heard a clicking, then tumblers turning. Finally, there came a soft creaking. Teal looked first to his bedroom door, but it appeared firmly closed. He turned his attention instead to the bathroom. Its door, too, was closed, but from behind it Teal could clearly hear something moving across the tiled floor. A smell began troubling his nostrils, and he recognised it as the same odour that had come from the substance seeping from beneath the room next door.

Teal leaped from his bed and, finding no more suitable weapon to hand, armed himself with a brass bedside lamp, having first yanked the plug from its socket. His throat was dry, and his hands were trembling, as he approached the closed bathroom door.

'You in there,' he said, and he was pleased to note that his voice was not shaking quite as much as his hands. 'I'm armed. I suggest that you return to your own room instantly, or I shall have no choice but to summon the innkeeper or, worse, to take matters into my own hands and force you back there myself.'

Something warm and sticky touched Teal's bare feet, and he stepped back hurriedly to avoid the stream of viscous fluid that now poured slowly from the bathroom. The unseen presence struck the door, causing it to shudder, and then, as he watched, frozen despite himself, the knob slowly began to turn. Casting aside his lamp, Teal gripped the doorknob and pulled back with all his might. More clear liquid oozed from the bathroom keyhole, making his hands slippery. He felt a cry emerge from his lips, and began to shout.

'Help me,' he cried. 'Please, help me. Someone is trying to enter my room!'

There was no reply. The presence on the other side of the door yanked hard at the handle, almost wrenching it from Teal's fingers. He gripped again, as tightly as he could, and lowered himself slowly down. Carefully, so as not to get any of the sticky paste on his face, he placed his right eye as close as he could to the keyhole.

At first he could see nothing except a vague whiteness, and he thought the substance had somehow clogged the aperture entirely. Then the whiteness shifted, and Teal caught a glimpse of scorched flesh, damp with the sticky mucus, and grey-green legs, mottled with decay, and a distended stomach, swollen with gas. There was something about the shape of the body, the way that it moved . . .

It was a woman, Teal realised, or something like a woman. And suddenly the being on the other side of the door ceased its attempts to gain entry to his bedroom. There was silence for a moment, and then a blur of white as the thing moved and, for a second, Teal saw through the keyhole a single black eye, ringed with red like a fresh coal on a hot fire. The eye narrowed. Teal heard a frustrated exhalation of breath, and then the eye was gone. There came a wet sound, and then the connecting door closed and all was quiet.

Teal's breath emerged in a single sob. His hands continued to grip the doorknob, his knuckles white beneath the skin. Slowly, he loosened his hold upon it and checked through the keyhole once again. When he was certain that the bathroom was empty, he quietly opened the door, slipped the key from within, and locked it from his side. He moved away from the door, feeling the carpet squelch beneath his feet, damp with the woman's secretions.

His bedroom door was now slightly open. Teal could not recall if he had locked it when he'd returned from his trip to the other room. It could have been the case that he had simply closed it, and the latch had not caught. It had certainly been closed when the woman in the bathroom caused him to leave his bed, but perhaps his exertions had rattled the floorboards and the walls, thereby causing it to open. He went toward it, closed it properly now, and locked it securely. Here, too, the carpet was damp, although whether from Teal's earlier visit to room three or through some other agency he was unable to say. Teal felt panic rising, and fought against it. He fumbled for a light switch, but the sole illumination in the room came courtesy of the two bedside lamps, one of which now lay by the bathroom door while the other stood unlit on the other night stand. Still, Teal could see that his room appeared empty. There was only the bed, the armchair, the two night stands—

And the great wardrobe that now lay at his back.

Teal sprang away from it, retreating slowly to his bed. He reached for the lamp and pressed the switch, instantly filling the room with a soft orange glow. The illumination cast the wardrobe partly in shadow, but Teal could see that one of its three doors was ajar. No sounds came from within, but Teal was now close to the limits of his endurance, fearful that he had managed not to lock the woman out of his room, but had somehow contrived to secure her inside with him.

Teal's legs struck the edge of his bed. Unable to take his eyes from the wardrobe, he took almost a quarter of a minute to register the sensation of wetness against the back of his thighs, and heard the sound of fluid dripping from the sheets onto the floor. Behind him, something moved damply upon the mattress. Slowly, Teal turned his head, and saw the shape of a woman beneath the sheets. Her sparse grey hair was slick and thin against a yellowed skull. A patina of thick liquid lay across her body, and Teal had a sudden image of fat melting in a pan.

Slowly, the woman pushed back the sheet, inviting him to join her. Her back was to him, and he saw the open, bloodless wounds upon it, and patches of scarred, burned tissue. Her hands were less damaged, but her nails were long and curled like corkscrews. The woman began to turn her head, and Teal saw that whatever her hands had been spared was made up for by the damage to her face. He glimpsed bone, and tendons, and bare teeth exposed by the scorching of her lips. The teeth parted, and the remains of a tongue licked provocatively at them.

Teal screamed. He ran for the bedroom door and fumbled with the key in the lock. There came the sound of sheets being thrown from the bed, and damp feet falling softly upon the carpet. Teal's fingers fumbled with the key, so badly were they trembling, but at last it turned in the lock. He wrenched the door open and fled into the corridor, abandoning his case and his clothes, descending the stairs and racing past the fireplace and into the night. He thought that he heard the sound of something sliding down the stairs at his back, moving on its belly like some great white leech, but he did not look back. His car was still in the yard, but the keys were in the bedroom.

Teal kept running, and lost himself in the welcome embrace of the darkness.

A farmer found him early the next morning. Teal was lying in a ditch, sobbing. The police were called, and at last his story was dragged from him. His car was traced, parked where he had left it beside the burned out remains of the inn. His overnight bag was on the front seat, and his keys were in the ignition. The conclusion was largely obvious: Mr Teal had followed the road to the inn, found that it was no longer open for business, and had decided to sleep in the back seat of his car. That he had chosen to change first into his pyjamas was seen as a token of eccentricity, and little more.

Mr Teal left the insurance business shortly afterwards. He offered his employers two pieces of advice before he left. The first was that they should regard the town of Shillingford as largely devoid of insurance potential, and the second was that they should update the guidebooks given to their sales representatives. He also announced that he would never again sell an insurance policy, and subsequently embraced the monastic life, where he remained happily celibate for the rest of his life.

The inn at Shillingford remains closed to this day.

Or open, perhaps, depending upon one's misfortune.

Acknowledgments

This book is something of a labour of love, and a great many people have played a part in its publication, offering support, encouragement and advice over the long period of its gestation.

Nocturnes might never have appeared at all had BBC Northern Ireland not approached me, shortly after the publication of my first novel in 1999, and asked if there was anything I might be interested in writing for them. I had always been fascinated by supernatural stories, ever since I was a young reader, and I was curious about writing for radio. It seemed to me that there was something very appealing about the thought of a voice reading a ghost story aloud to a driver alone in a car, or to someone curling up in bed before turning off the light. In the end, I wrote five tales for the BBC, which were broadcast on Radio Four in 2000 and read by a very wonderful actor named Tony Doyle, now, sadly, no longer with us. As I write, a further five stories are scheduled to be broadcast in 2004. Nine of those tales are contained in this volume.

I owe an immense debt of gratitude to Lawrence Jackson, the producer of both sets of stories for the BBC. Lawrence was the first to read them, the first to offer suggestions on how they might be improved, and the first to reassure me when I felt my confidence in them flag. I will always be grateful to him for gently coaxing these stories from me. Without him, and without the willingness of the BBC to offer them a home, they would not exist in this form.

I am also indebted to Sue Fletcher, my wonderful and very faithful editor at Hodder & Stoughton. Short story collections are difficult propositions for publishing houses, but from the very beginning Sue, and all those at Hodder who are as much friends as publishers, were unstinting in their support for *Nocturnes*. To Sue, Martin Neild, Jamie Hodder-Williams, Kerry Hood, Lucy Hale, Auriol Bishop, Hannah Norman, David Brimble, Swati Gamble and everyone at Hodder in London, and to Breda Purdue, Ruth Shern, and Heidi Murphy at Hodder Headline Ireland, I extend my appreciation for all that you've done.

Finally, I will always be grateful that I have found myself in the care of my agent Darley Anderson, who must sometimes wonder at precisely what he has let himself in for by taking me on. His friendship has, quite literally, changed my life. I would be lost without him, and without his marvellous staff. To Darley, Lucie, Julia, Emma and Elizabeth: thank you.

Finally, to my family, to Jennie, and to Cameron and Alistair, thanks for putting up with me.